THESE TWO
ARE RED-H
SOME VE

Naked
AMBITION

SHOW & TELL
by
Rhonda Nelson

JUST 4 PLAY
by
Cindi Myers

Rhonda Nelson can't remember when she hasn't had her nose buried in a book and, most likely, her husband can't, either. Though she took several creative writing courses in college, she never considered a career in writing until her mother pointed out — as mothers are everlastingly wont to do — that she should give it a try. Thus, after giving up her dream of becoming an intergalactic princess or a mermaid — it was a toss-up because both are so cool — an author was born! (Thank you, Momma.)

Rhonda married her very own hero many moons ago, and she and her family make their home in a small town in northern Alabama. Between volunteering at her children's school (she's practising a new word called "no") and the typical glamorous duties of a domestic goddess (does it ever end?), she escapes into her office where it's *safe* to talk to the voices in her head, to tell their stories, and hopefully to entertain her readers. If you like a little giggle amid the sizzle, then her books just might be for you.

Cindi Myers believes in love at first sight, good chocolate, cold champagne, that people who don't like animals can't be trusted, and that God obviously has a sense of humour. She also believes in writing fun, sexy romances about people she hopes readers will fall in love with.

Blessed with an overactive imagination and a love of reading, Cindi wrote her first story at age eight about the family's Siamese cat. At age 12 she submitted her first manuscript, hand-written and illustrated with crayon drawings, to Little, Brown and Company. She received a very kind rejection letter advising her to study hard and keep working and one day she might be a real writer.

In addition to writing, Cindi enjoys reading, quilting, gardening, hiking, and downhill skiing. She lives in the Rocky Mountains of Colorado with her husband, whom she met on a blind date and agreed to marry six weeks later, and three spoiled dogs.

Cindi loves to hear from readers. Email her at Cmyers1@aol.com.

Naked
AMBITION

It's time for some very adult fun...

Rhonda Nelson &
Cindi Myers

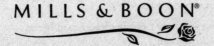

*MILLS & BOON and MILLS & BOON with the Rose Device
are registered trademarks of the publisher.*
Harlequin Mills & Boon Limited,
Eton House, 18-24 Paradise Road, Richmond, Surrey, TW9 1SR

NAKED AMBITION © by Harlequin Enterprises II B.V., 2004

The publisher acknowledges the copyright holders of the
individual works as follows:

Show & Tell © Rhonda Nelson 2003
Just 4 Play © Cynthia Myers 2003

ISBN 0 263 84501 X

024-1004

*Printed and bound in Spain
by Litografia Rosés S.A., Barcelona*

CONTENTS

Dear Reader

While cruising the internet looking for sex toys –
research for my first Blaze™ novel *Just Toying
Around*… I swear! – the same word kept popping
up. Tantra, or Tantric. Intrigued, I decided to do a
little investigating and discovered that Tantric sex,
though I'd never heard of it, had been around since
3000 BC and, despite its dusty spiritual heritage,
was swiftly gaining a new popularity. It didn't take
long to imagine a hero and heroine getting caught
up in the mystical world of *Tantra*, and thus Knox
and Savannah's story was born.

Journalist Knox Webber needs a weekend lover
with one special requirement – he can't be
attracted to her. Knox is on the scent of a great
story, but in order to prove the touted Tantric way,
which promises heightened awareness, spiritual
gratification and hour-long full-body orgasms, is
nothing but a farce, Knox needs to attend one of
the popular Tantric Sex Clinics on the West
Coast…and he needs a partner who won't distract
him from his main goal – getting the story.

Savannah Reeves – his arch-enemy – fits the bill
perfectly. But as the weekend progresses, sexual
tension between them explodes and the resulting
heat soon burns up all preconceived notions about
the ancient art of lovemaking. Chemistry or Tantra,
they wonder…and will it last once the weekend
is over?

I hope you enjoy Knox and Savannah's sexy
romantic romp.

Enjoy!

Rhonda Nelson

SHOW & TELL

by
Rhonda Nelson

Once upon a time there was a towheaded, chubby-cheeked, demonic little prankster who grew into one of the best-looking, most hardworking, kindhearted and admirable men I have ever known – my brother, Greg Moore.

Being smarter than 98 percent of the population called for a great dedication, eh, Bubba?

1

KNOX WEBBER ABSENTLY SWIRLED the liquor around his glass as he watched the naked couple displayed on his television screen gyrate in sexual ecstasy. They sat in a pool of fuzzy golden light, face to face, palm to palm, the woman's hips anchored around the man's waist. Her long blond hair shimmered over her bare shoulders. She threw her head back and her mouth formed a perfect O of orgasmic wonder. The video's hypnotic narrator droned from the hi-fi speakers placed strategically around Knox's plush glass-and-chrome apartment.

"Let the tantric energy flow. You'll feel the power wash over you, through you and around you as your male and female energies merge. This wave of utter bliss will transport you and your partner to a new plane in sexual rapture, a new plane of enlightenment and awareness, where you'll flow in harmony with your lover and the rest of the world. Synchronized, controlled breathing is essential…"

Sheesh.

Knox snorted and hit the stop button on his remote control. He'd seen enough. He'd watched the how-to video on one of the best home-theater systems money could buy—a fifty-five-inch digitally mastered screen with superior resolution, picture in picture, and quality sound—and he still thought the entire concept of tantric sex was a load of crap.

Regrettably, it was becoming an increasingly popular load of crap and it just might be the one story he'd been looking for, the one pivotal article that would give him an edge over his competitors. Knox currently enjoyed a top spot in the Chicago scene of investigative journalism, but it wasn't enough. He wanted more. He wanted a Pulitzer. A wry smile twisted his lips. Granted, this story most likely wouldn't win him the coveted award, but it could put him that much closer to his goal. The thought sent a shot of adrenaline coursing through his blood.

Call it journalistic intuition, all he knew was each time Knox caught the scent of a good story, he'd get a curious feeling in his gut, an insistent nudge behind his naval that, so far, had never steered him wrong. This sixth sense had propelled him into his current comfortable position with the *Chicago Phoenix,* had earned him a reputation for staying on the cutting edge of journalism and keeping his finger on the fickle pulse of American society.

The nudge was there now, more insistent than ever, prodding him into action. But for the first time in his life, for reasons that escaped him, he found himself resisting the urge to pick up the scent and track down the story.

Knox chalked up his misgivings to inconvenience. Naturally, in the course of his work, he'd been mightily inconvenienced and had never minded the hassle. It was all part and parcel of his chosen career path, the one he'd taken despite howling protests from his more professionally minded parents. His mother and father considered Knox's career choice beneath him and were still clinging to the hope that he'd eventually come to his senses and use his Ivy League education for a more distinguished career.

They'd have a long wait.

Knox was determined to make his mark in the competitive world of investigative journalism, no matter the inconveniences. This wasn't just a career; it was his identity, who he was. He was a show-and-tell journalist—he unearthed facts, then he showed them to the American public, told them in his own outspoken way and encouraged them to draw their own conclusions.

He'd hidden in small dark places and he'd assumed countless disguises, some of which were completely emasculating, Knox thought, shuddering as he recalled the transvestite debacle. He'd made it a point to befriend a scope of unwitting informants, from assistants to top city officials to the occasional pimp and small-time thug, and all species in between, creating a network of eyes much like the Argus of Greek mythology.

The idea of being inconvenienced didn't disturb Knox—it was the form of inconvenience he was concerned about. Knox preferred to work solo, but for this particular story, that simply wasn't an option.

He'd have to have a partner, and a female partner at that. A wry smile turned his lips. After all, he couldn't very well attend a tantric sex workshop with a man.

Knox studied the glossy tantric sex pamphlet once more. This clinic—Total Tantra Edification—in particular was his target. While some workshops were probably on the up-and-up, something about this one didn't feel quite right. Hadn't from the beginning when this idea had first taken hold. The little brochure was chock-full of glowing testimonials from happy couples who had sworn that the workshop had saved their marriages, had brought their flat-lined sex lives from the brink of death via the energized, intimate therapy. Women, in particular, seemed to be thrilled with the results, citing multiple orgasms and even female ejaculation.

And why not? Knox wondered with a crooked grin. The whole technique seemed geared toward female gratification—a new twist in and of itself. According to his research, men avoided physical ejaculation completely, thereby prolonging their erections, and instead strove for full-body inner orgasms. The blast without the shower, so to speak, Knox thought.

Expensive tantric weekend workshops were becoming almost as common on the West Coast as surfers at the beach. While they hadn't gained as much popularity on the East Coast, interest in the subject was nonetheless increasing. A popular cable music program recently polled eighteen- to twenty-four-year-olds, and when asked what sexual subject they'd most like to learn about, tantric sex topped the list.

No doubt about it, it was a timely story. The nudge tingled behind his navel once more.

In this case, it was also a load of New Age baloney taught by aging hippies in unbleached hemp togas bent on feathering their retirement nests. Knox was sure of it. He glanced at the so-called instructors featured on the inside page. Drs. Edgar and Rupali Shea smiled back at him, the picture of glowing serenity and marital bliss.

Knox didn't buy it for a moment.

Honestly? What self-respecting man would purposely deprive himself of an orgasm during sex and claim inner enlightenment was better? Knox snorted, knocked back the dregs of his Scotch. Not a real man. Not a man's man, anyway. Sex with no orgasm? It was like a hot-fudge sundae minus the hot fudge. Hell, what would be the point?

Certainly, without ejaculation a man could keep an erection longer. But as long as one didn't detonate upon entry, what difference did it make? As long as you didn't leave your partner in the lurch—unforgivably lazy in his opinion—what was the problem with racing toward release? With grabbing the brass ring?

Absolutely nothing. While the concept of tantric

sex had originated in India around 3000 B.C. and
might have been genuinely used with a noble goal in
mind, in today's time the technique had simply become a new twist on an old game designed to milk
desperate couples out of their hard-earned money.
Greedy, marketing-savvy businessmen had taken the
concept and bastardized it into a hedonistic, spiritual
fix-all.

Knox firmly intended to prove it and he couldn't
do it alone. He'd have to have a partner.

Several possible candidates came to mind, but he
systematically ruled them out. He didn't have a single female acquaintance who wouldn't expect his un-
divided attention, and this would be a business trip,
not a weekend tryst celebrated with fine food and
recreational sex. Complete focus would be mandatory in order to preserve the integrity of the story.

Knox liked sex as much as the next guy—he was
a man, after all. It was his nature. And while the
entire workshop would be centered around the technique of tantric sex, Knox knew better than to think
he'd be able to do his job with any objectivity and
be testing the theories at the same time. He'd have
to have complete focus. So he'd have to take along
a female who could appreciate the job he'd come
there to do, and he could not—*absolutely could
not*—be attracted to her.

Three beats passed before he knew the perfect
woman for the job, and when the name surfaced, he

involuntarily winced with dread—Savannah Reeves, his archenemy at the *Phoenix*.

The idea of having to share his byline with the infuriating know-it-all—honestly, the woman could strip bark off a tree with that tongue of hers—was almost enough to make Knox abandon the whole scenario, but he knew he couldn't.

He had to do this story.

This story would change his life. He could feel it. Couldn't explain it, but intuitively knew it all the same.

And if that meant spending a weekend with a woman whose seemingly sole goal in life was to annoy him, then so be it. Knox could handle it. All modesty aside, he could handle just about any woman. A quick smile, a clever compliment and—voilà!—she was his.

But not Savannah. Never Savannah.

She seemed charm-proof. Knox frowned, studied the empty cut-glass tumbler he held loosely in his hand. The one and only time he'd attempted the old routine on Savannah, she'd given him a blast of sleet with those icy blue eyes of hers and laughed in his face. His cheeks burned with remembered humiliation. He'd never repeated the mistake. It had been a lesson well learned and, while he didn't outright avoid her—he wouldn't give her the satisfaction—he'd made a conscious effort to steer clear of her path. She…unnerved him.

Nevertheless, he seriously doubted that she'd let

her personal dislike of him keep her from jumping at the chance of a great story. Since she'd joined the staff a little over a year ago, she'd made it a point to usurp prime articles from him, to try to keep one step ahead of him. He'd never had any real competition at the *Phoenix* until her arrival. Though she irritated the hell out of him with her knowing little smiles and acid comments, the rivalry nonetheless kept him sharp, kept him on his toes.

Knox thoughtfully tapped the brochure against his thigh and once more reflected on his options…and realized he really only had one—Savannah. She was the only woman who fit the bill. Though he thoroughly dreaded it, he'd have to ask her to accompany him on the trip to California, to play the part of his devoted sex partner. A bark of dry laughter erupted from his throat. Oh, she'd love that, he thought with a grim smile.

Generally speaking, Knox was attracted to just about every woman of the right age with a halfway decent rack. Shallow, yes, but, again, his nature. He couldn't help himself. He didn't always act on the attraction—in fact, he was quite selective with his lovers—but it was always there, hovering just beneath the surface.

Regardless of his hyperlibido, Knox didn't doubt for one minute that one icy look, one chilly smile from the admittedly gorgeous Savannah Reeves would wilt even his staunchest erection. Savannah was petite and curvy with short jet-black hair that always looked delightfully rumpled. Like she'd just rolled out of bed. She wore little makeup, but with a smooth, creamy complexion and that pair of ice-blue eyes heavily fringed with long curling lashes, she hardly needed the artifice. No doubt about it, she was definitely gorgeous, Knox admitted as he forced away her distracting image.

But looks weren't everything.

Regrettably, Savannah Reeves had the personality of a constipated toad and never missed her daily ration of Bitch Flakes. Knox suppressed a shudder.

He definitely wouldn't have to worry about being attracted to her. He simply wouldn't allow it. And she certainly wasn't attracted to him—she'd gone out of her way to make that abundantly clear. Also she'd likely appreciate being in on the job.

In short, she'd be his perfect partner for this assignment. And she was too glory hungry to let a little thing like personal dislike get in the way of a fantastic byline. If he really wanted to, Knox thought consideringly, he could make her wriggle like a worm on a hook.

The idea held immense appeal.

"NOT NO, BUT HELL NO," Savannah Reeves said flatly as she wound her way through the busy newsroom to her little cubicle.

Knox, damn him, dogged her every step.

"But why not? It's a plum assignment, a great

story and a wonderful opportunity. What possible reason could you have for saying no?''

Because I don't like you, Savannah thought uncharitably. She drew up short beside her desk and paused to look at him. She fought the immediate impulse to categorize his finer physical features, but, as usual, failed miserably.

Knox Webber had wavy rich brown hair cut in a negligent style that implied little maintenance but undoubtedly took several time-consuming steps to achieve. His eyes were a dark, verdant green, heavy-lidded, and twinkled with mischief and the promise of wicked pleasures. His lips, which seemed perpetually curled into an inviting come-hither grin, were surprisingly full for a man, but masculine enough to make a woman fantasize about their talent.

Even her, dammit, though she should know better.

If that weren't enough, he had the absolute best ass she'd ever seen—tight and curved just so and… Savannah resisted the urge to shiver. In addition to that amazing ass, he was tall, athletically built and carried himself with a mesmerizing long-limbed, loose-hipped gait that drew the eye and screamed confidence. He'd been born into a family of wealth and privilege and the very essence of that breeding hovered like an aura about him.

Though she knew it was unreasonable, Savannah immediately felt her defenses go up. She'd been orphaned at six when her parents had been killed in a car accident. With no other family, she'd spent her childhood in the foster-care system, passed from family to family like a yard-sale castoff. Did Knox know how lucky he'd been? Did he have any idea at all? She didn't think so. From what she'd observed, he seemed content to play the black sheep of the family—to *play* at being a journalist—until his father turned the screws and capped his sizable trust fund. And the hell of it was, Knox made it all look so damned easy. He was a talented bastard, she'd give him that. It was enough to make her retch.

"Come on, Vannah," Knox cajoled, using the nickname that never failed to set her teeth on edge. He was the only person at the *Phoenix* who dared call her that and the implied intimacy of the nickname drove her mad. "This is going to be a helluva story."

She didn't doubt that for one minute. Knox Webber didn't waste his time on anything that didn't promise a front page. And he had to be desperate to ask her for help, because she knew he'd rather slide buck naked down a razor blade into a pool of alcohol than ask her for a favor.

Still, there was no way in hell she wanted any part of a story with him, phenomenal byline or no. She didn't have to possess any psychic ability to know that the outcome could be nothing short of disastrous. An extended weekend at a sex workshop with Knox? The one and only man she didn't have a prayer of resisting? The one she continually fantasized about? A vision of her and Knox naked and sweaty loomed instantly in her mind's eye, making her tummy quiver with perpetually repressed longing.

No way.

Savannah firmed her chin and repeated her last thought for his benefit. "Forget it, Knox. Ask someone else." She gave him her back once more and slid into the chair behind her desk.

"I don't want to ask anyone else. I've asked you." Knox frowned at her and the expression was so uncharacteristic that it momentarily startled her. Savannah blinked, then gathered her wits about her.

"I can't believe you won't even consider it," the object of her irritation repeated stubbornly. "I thought you'd jump at the chance to have a go at this story."

Savannah tsked. "I warned you about that. Thinking upsets the delicate balance of your constitution. Best to avoid the process at all costs, Webber."

He muttered something that sounded suspiciously like "smart-ass," but Savannah couldn't be sure.

Still he was right. Had any other male co-worker asked her, she wouldn't have hesitated. In fact, it was almost frightening how much their minds thought alike. She'd been toying with the idea of a tantric sex article for a couple of weeks now and had been waiting for the concept to gel. She'd simply let him get the jump on her this time—a rare feat, because she'd made a game out of thwarting him.

"You don't know what it is, do you?" Wearing an infuriating little grin Savannah itched to slap off his face, Knox leaned his incredible ass against her desk.

"Know what *what* is?" Her eyes rounded. *"Sex?"* With an indelicate snort, Savannah booted up her laptop and did her best to appear unaware of him. "Granted, I might not have as much experience as you—I'm sure you'd give the hookers in the red-light district a run for their money in the experience department—but I'm not completely ignorant, for pity's sake," Savannah huffed. She cast him an annoyed glance. "I know what sex is."

Though it had been so long since she'd had any, her memory was getting a little fuzzy about the particulars. If she didn't get laid soon, she'd undoubtedly be declared a virgin again simply by default. Or out of pity. Twelve- to fourteen-hour workdays didn't leave much time for romance. Besides, after Gibson Lyles III, Savannah didn't put much stock in romance, or in men, for that matter. She sighed. Men were too much work, for too little reward.

"Not just sex," Knox said. *"Tantric sex.* Do you know what it is?"

Savannah loaded her web browser, busying herself with the task at hand. "Sure. It's a complex marriage of yoga, ritual, meditation and intercourse."

Alternately, he looked surprised then impressed. "Very good. See? You're perfect."

"Be that as it may, I'm not going. I have work to do. Go away." Savannah smoothed her hair behind her ears and continued to pretend he wasn't there.

No small feat when every single part of her tingled as a result of his nearness. Which sucked, particularly since, for the most part, she couldn't stand him. *"Go away,"* she repeated.

Knox continued to study her and another maddening twinkle lit his gaze. "I see. You're scared."

Savannah resisted the urge to grind her teeth. "Scared of what?"

"Of me, obviously." Knox picked an imaginary fleck of lint from the cuff of his expensive shirt. "Why else would you refuse such a great opportunity when it's painfully obvious that you've been considering the topic as well?" Something shifted in his gaze. "That…or you're into it."

"Ooh, you've found me out. Good job, Columbo. And don't flatter yourself. I am *not* afraid of you." Savannah chuckled. "I've got your number, Slick. Nothing about you frightens me." Savannah figured providence would promptly issue a bolt of lightning and turn her into a Roman candle for that whopper, but thankfully she remained spark free.

The silence lengthened until Knox finally blew out an impatient breath. "Won't you even consider it?"

"No."

His typically amiable expression vanished. "This is a great opportunity. Don't make me play hardball."

Exasperated, Savannah leveled a hard look at him. "Play whatever kind of ball you want, Knox. But you won't make me play with you. I'm not one of your newsroom groupies. Now get out of my cubby—you're crowding me.''

Wearing a look of supreme frustration, Knox finally stalked off, presumably to ask another female to do his bidding. Good riddance, Savannah thought, though she did hate the missed opportunity.

But even had she been inclined to accept the offer, she really wouldn't have had the time to pursue the assignment—groveling to Chapman, her diabolical boss, and covering all of the demeaning little stories he gleefully threw her way were taking up entirely too much of her time.

Savannah and Chapman were presently embroiled in the proverbial Mexican standoff, neither of them willing to budge. The problem revolved around a libel suit that had been filed against the *Chicago Phoenix* as a result of one of her stories. To Chapman's extreme irritation and despite various threats, Savannah stood by her story and refused to compromise her journalistic integrity by revealing her source. Chapman had bullied and blustered, wailed and threatened everything from being demoted to being fired, but Savannah simply would not relent. Her credibility would be ruined. To give up this source would ultimately wreck her career.

Besides, it was just wrong. She'd given her word and she wouldn't compromise her integrity simply for the sake of the paper. That's why they employed high-powered attorneys. Let them sort it out. She'd only been doing her job, and she'd done it to the absolute best of her ability. She refused to admit any wrongdoing, and she'd be damned before she'd claim any responsibility.

Savannah had been educated in the school of hard knocks, had been on her own since she'd turned eighteen and was no longer a ward of the state. She'd put herself through college by working three grueling jobs. Sure, covering the opening of a new strip mall was degrading, but if Hugh Chapman thought he could get the better of her by giving her crappy assignments, then he had another think coming. She stiffened her spine. Savannah was certain she was tough enough to take anything her mean-spirited boss could dish out.

Don't make me play hardball.

A premonition of dread surfaced as Knox's parting comment tripped unexpectedly through her mind.

She was wrong, Savannah decided. She was tough enough to take anything *but* a weekend sex workshop with Knox Webber.

2

"...SO YOU SEE, this story has incredible potential. I have it on good authority that the *Tribune* is considering the angle as well."

Predictably, Hugh Chapman, editor in chief of the *Chicago Phoenix* bristled when taunted with the prospect of their rival paper possibly getting a scoop.

"You don't say," the older man grunted thoughtfully. As tall as he was wide, with large fishlike eyes, thick lips, a bulbous nose and pasty complexion, Chapman bore an unfortunate resemblance to an obese albino guppy. But Hugh Chapman was no harmless fish. He'd been in the publishing business for years and Knox didn't think he'd ever met a man more shrewd or calculating. Vindictive even, if the rumors were true.

Playing him was risky, but Knox desperately needed to do this story and he'd already tried the ethical route. It hadn't worked, so he'd been forced to employ a different tactic. His conscience twinged, but Knox ignored it. He'd given Savannah a chance to make the trip to California of her own accord.

She'd refused. If Knox played his cards right, in just a few minutes she'd wish she hadn't.

Knox heaved a dramatic sigh. "Yeah, I'm afraid so. I'd really like to get the jump on them. Pity Savannah didn't go for the idea," Knox said regretfully. "And I can't do it without her. Oh, well. You win some, you lose some. I'm sure we'll beat them to the punch on something else." Knox smacked his hands on his thighs, seemingly resigned, and started to stand.

"Call her in here," Chapman said abruptly.

With an innocent look, Knox paused. "Sorry?"

"I said call her in here. You need her to go—I'll make her go." His beefy brow folded in consternation. "Presently, Ms. Reeves is in no position to refuse me. She's skating on thin ice as it is."

"Oh, sir, I don't know," Knox protested. "I didn't—"

"Webber, do what I told you to do," Chapman barked.

"Right, sir." Knox's step was considerably lighter as he crossed the room and pulled the glass door open. "Savannah Reeves, Mr. Chapman would like to see you."

Savannah's head appeared from behind her cubby. Knox's triumphant expression combined with the boss's summons seemed to register portents of doom because, within seconds, her pale blue eyes narrowed to angry slits and her lips flattened into a tense line.

She stood and made her way across the room. Tension vibrated off her slight form.

"I told you not to make me play hardball," Knox murmured silkily as she drew near.

"If you've done what I think you've done," she returned with a brittle smile, obviously for the benefit of onlookers, since she clearly longed to strangle him, "you will be *so* very sorry. I will permanently extinguish your 'wand of light.'"

Knox choked on a laugh as she swept past into the inner sanctum of Chapman's office. In traditional tantra, the Sanskrit word for penis was *lingam*, which translated into "wand of light." She certainly knew her stuff, Knox thought, surprised and impressed once more with her knowledge of the subject. He'd been right in forcing her hand. Annoying though she may be—the bane of his professional existence—Savannah Reeves was a crackerjack journalist. Very thorough.

"You wanted to see me, sir," Savannah said.

Knox moved to stand beside Savannah, who seemed determined to pretend he didn't exist. She kept her gaze focused on Chapman and refused to acknowledge Knox at all. His conscience issued another screech for having her called on the carpet, but he determinedly ignored the howl. If she had simply used her head and agreed, this could have all been avoided. It was her own fault.

Chapman gave her a long, unyielding stare, so hard that Knox himself was hard-pressed not to flinch. His scalp suddenly prickled with unease. What was it Chapman had said? She was on thin ice? Why? Knox wondered instantly. Why was she on thin ice?

"I understand Knox has asked you to accompany him on an extended weekend assignment and you have refused," Chapman said.

She nodded. "Yes, sir. That's correct."

Chapman steepled his fingers so that they looked like little pork sausages. "I'm not going to ask you why you refused, because that would imply that I care and I don't—that you have a choice, and you don't. You will go. Understood?"

She stiffened. "But, sir—"

Chapman's forehead formed a unibrowed scowl. "No buts." He looked meaningfully at Knox. "Surely it's not going to be necessary for me to remind you of why it would behoove you not to argue with me about this."

Though she clearly longed to do just that, Savannah's shoulders rounded with uncharacteristic defeat. She sighed. "No, sir. Of course not."

Knox frowned. What in hell was going on? How had she managed to land her name on the top of Chapman's shit-list? What had she done? he wondered again.

"That's what I thought. Knox," Chapman said, "see Rowena and have her tend to the necessary arrangements." He nodded at Savannah. "The two of you should get together and make your plans."

Knox smiled. "Right, sir. Thank you."

Savannah didn't say a word, just turned and marched rigidly out of the office. Knox had to double-time it to catch up with her. "What was that all ab—"

"That," Savannah said meaningfully, "is none of your business, but that's probably never stopped you before. Honestly, I can't believe that you did that— that you went to Chapman." She shook her head. "I knew you were a spoiled little tight-ass and a first-rate jerk, but it honestly never occurred to me that you'd sink so damned low."

Knox scowled at the tight-ass remark but refused to let her goad him, and followed her into her cubicle once more. "In case you haven't noticed," Knox pointed out sarcastically, "it's our job to make *everything* our business. That's what journalists do. Besides, I gave you the opportunity to do the right thing."

She blasted him with a frosty glare. "Wrong. You gave me the opportunity to do what *you* wanted me to do." Savannah shoved a hand through her hair impatiently, mussing it up even more. She took a deep breath, clearly trying to calm herself but failing miserably. She opened her mouth. Shut it. Opened it again. Finally she said, "Did it ever occur to you that I might have plans for this weekend? That it might not be convenient for me to jaunt off to California with you?"

Prepared to argue with whatever insult she hurled

next, that question caught him completely off guard and Knox felt his expression blank.

"I thought so." She collapsed into her chair. "You pampered prep-school boys are all the same. Contrary to popular belief, Mr. Webber, the world does not revolve around you and your every whim." She laughed, but the sound lacked humor. "We peasants have lives to."

Peasants? Knox scrubbed a hand over his face and felt a flush creep up his neck. She was right. He hadn't considered that she'd have any plans. He'd just assumed that, like him, work didn't leave time for anything else. "Look, I'm sorry for wrecking your plans. That was never my intention. I just—"

"You didn't wreck my plans, because I didn't have any," she said tartly. She turned back to her computer, doing her best to ignore him out of existence.

Knox blinked. Felt his fingers curl into his palms. "If you didn't have any plans, then what the hell is the problem?" he asked tightly.

"I *could* have had plans. It's just a lucky coincidence that I don't."

Knox blew out a breath. "Whatever. When would you like to get together and see to the details of this trip?"

She snorted. "Never."

"Vannah…" Knox warned, feeling his patience wear thin.

"Savannah," she corrected, and he could have

sworn he heard one of her teeth crack. "You can brief me on the plane. Until then, get away from me and leave me alone."

"But—"

She glanced up from her computer. "You might have won the battle, but you certainly haven't won the war. You've forced my hand, but that's all I'm going to allow. Do not speak to me again until we're on our way to California or, Chapman's edict or no, you'll be making the journey solo."

A hot oath sizzled on Knox's tongue, but he bit back the urge. He'd never met a woman who infuriated him more, and the desire to call her bluff was almost overpowering.

But he didn't.

He couldn't afford the risk. This story meant too much. He knew it and he needed to keep the bigger picture in focus.

Instead, though it galled him to no end, Knox nodded succinctly and wordlessly left her cubicle.

SAVANNAH HAD SILENTLY PRAYED that Knox would screw up and talk to her so that she could make good on her threat, but he didn't. Per her instruction, he hadn't said a single word to her until they boarded the plane. Since then he'd seemed determined to treat this assignment like any other, and even more determined to ignore the fact that she'd been an unwilling participant.

A typical man, Savannah thought. If he couldn't

buy it off, knock it down or bully it aside, then he ignored it.

They'd flown out of O'Hare at the ungodly hour of five in the morning and would arrive in sunny Sacramento, California, by nine-thirty. At the airport, they would rent a car to finish the journey. The Shea compound was located in the small community of Riverdale, about fifty miles northwest of Sacramento. Barring any unforeseen complications, they should arrive in plenty of time to get settled and attend the Welcome Brunch. Classes officially started at two.

A volcano of dread erupted in her belly at the thought, but rather than allow it to consume her, Savannah channeled her misgivings into a more productive emotion—anger.

She still saw red every time she thought about Chapman's hand in her humiliation. Quite honestly, she'd been surprised that he hadn't taken every opportunity to belittle her in front of her co-workers— to make an example of her—and could only assume he acted on the advice of the paper's attorneys. Chapman seemed the type to feed off others' misfortune, and, frankly, she'd never liked him. She wasn't the least bit surprised that Chapman had sided with Knox. Knox was the golden boy, after all.

But the *Phoenix* had an unparalleled reputation, and she would have been insane not to accept employment at one of the most prestigious papers in the States. She had her career plan, after all, and wouldn't let a little thing like despising her boss get in the way. Though she assumed he'd never give her a glowing recommendation, her writing would speak for itself.

As for Knox's role in this…she was still extremely perturbed at him for not taking no for an answer. Without a family or mentor to speak of, Savannah relied solely on gut instinct. She had to. She didn't have a choice. In the absence of one perception, others became heightened, supersensitized. Just as the blind had a keener sense of smell, she'd developed a keener sense of perception, of self-preservation. When Knox had walked up and asked her to share this story with him, her knee-jerk gut reaction had been swift and telling—she'd almost tossed her cookies.

Going on this trip with him was the height of stupidity. Savannah could be brutally honest with herself when the need arose and she knew beyond a shadow of a doubt that this attraction to Knox was a battle she could not win. If Knox so much as touched her, she'd melt, and then he'd know her mortifying secret—that she'd been lusting after him for over a year.

Savannah bit back a wail of frustration, resisted the childish urge to beat her head against the small oval window. She didn't need to be here with him— she needed to be back in Chicago. Investigating the missing maintenance hole cover Chapman would have undoubtedly assigned her next. Watering her plants. Straightening her stereo wires, her canned goods.

Anything but being here with Knox.

Though she'd been making a concerted effort to imagine him away from the seat next to hers, Savannah was still hammeringly aware of him. She could feel the heat from his body, could smell the mixture of fine cologne and his particular essence. The fine hairs on her arms continually prickled, seemed magnetically drawn to him. Savannah surreptitiously studied him, traced the angular curve of his jaw with her gaze, the smooth curve of his lips. A familiar riptide of longing washed through her and sensual fantasies rolled languidly through the private cinema of her mind. She suppressed a sigh. No doubt about it, he was a handsome devil.

And due to some hideous character flaw on her own part—or just plain ignorance, she couldn't be sure—she was in lust with him. The panting, salivating, wanna-rip-your-clothes-off-and-do-it-in-the-elevator, trisexual—meaning "try *anything*"—type. Had been from the very first moment she'd laid eyes on him the day she joined the staff at the *Phoenix*.

Of course, he'd screwed it all up by opening his mouth.

Thanks to Gibson Lyles III, Savannah recognized the cool, modulated tones of those born to wealth. There'd been other signs as well, but initially she'd been so bowled over by her physical reaction to him that she hadn't properly taken them into consideration. The wardrobe, the posture, the polish. It had all been there once she'd really looked. And one look had been all it had taken for her to delegate him to her *hell-no* list. Since then she'd looked for flaws, probably exaggerated a few, and had not permitted herself to so much as like him.

Savannah knew what happened when rich boys took poor orphans home to meet the parents. Her lips twisted into a derisive smile. The rich boy got an all-expenses-paid tour of Europe…and the poor orphan got backhanded by reality.

Thanks, but no thanks.

Frustration peaked once more. Why had he demanded that she come? Why her, dammit? There were other female journalists employed at the *Phoenix,* other women just as qualified. What had been so special about her that none of the others would do?

When Savannah contemplated what this extended weekend would entail, all the talk of sex, having to share a room with him, for pity's sake, it all but overwhelmed her. How on earth would she keep her appalling attraction for him secret during a hands-on sex workshop? What, pray tell, would prevent her from becoming a single, pulsing, throbbing nerve of need? How would she resist him?

She wouldn't, she knew. If he so much as crooked a little finger in invitation, she'd be hopelessly, utterly and completely lost.

Savannah knew a few basic truths about the art of tantric sex, knew the male and female roles. Knew

that the art of intimate massage, of prolonged foreplay and ritual were particularly stressed themes
throughout the process. But that was only the tip of
the iceberg. There were other, more intimidating—
and intimate—themes prevalent as well.

Tantrists believed that humans possessed six chakras—or sources of energy—and that during life, these
energy sources got blocked due to the traumas humans suffered. But once these chakras were unblocked, and energy was free to move as it should,
then when the male and female bodies merged, these
energies merged as well, creating a oneness with a
partner that transcended the physical and, thus,
turned sex into a spiritual experience.

But how could a person take it seriously? Take
some of the lingo for instance. His penis was a
"wand of light." The Sanskrit word for vagina was
yoni, which translated to "sacred space."

Please.

Who could say this stuff to their partner with a
straight face? Sorry. She just couldn't see herself
looking deeply into the eyes of her lover and saying,
*Welcome to my sacred space. Illuminate me, baby,
with your wand of light!*

Frankly Savannah didn't know what tact Knox
wanted to take with this story, but she thought the
whole idea was ludicrous. She liked her sex hot, frantic and sweaty and she didn't want to learn an ancient
language to do the business either. Honestly, whatever happened to the good old-fashioned quickie?

She supposed she should give the premise the benefit of the doubt—that was her job, after all—but she seriously doubted that a massage and a few chants thrown in amid the usual twenty-minute flesh session would result in a spiritual experience for her. She liked the rub, lick and tickle approach, thank you very much. But to each his own, she supposed.

Knox elbowed her. "Hey, would you like anything to drink?"

Savannah started, then turned to see that the stewardess had arrived with the refreshment cart. "Uh…sure. A soda would be nice."

"Ditto," Knox said. He upped the charm voltage with a sexy little smile. "And an extra pack of peanuts, too, if you've got any to spare."

The flight attendant blushed and obligingly handed over the requested snack. Savannah rolled her eyes. And women were accused of using feminine wiles? What about men? What about masculine wiles? Knox, for example, had just dazzled that woman with nothing more than a little eye contact and a well-turned smile.

"Want some peanuts?" Knox asked, offering the open pack to her.

"No, thank you."

Knox paused to look at her and sighed. "What have I done now?"

Savannah inserted the straw into her drink. "I don't know what you're talking about."

"Sure you do. The temperature around your seat

has dropped to an arctic level, when, just moments ago, I was enjoying the chilly-but-above-freezing climes of your sunny disposition.'' He smiled, the wretch. ''Clearly, I've offended you once again. Don't be shy. Go ahead. Tell me what odious man-thing I'm guilty of now.''

Savannah felt her lips twitch but managed to suppress a grin. ''You're breathing.''

Knox chuckled, a low rumbling sound that made his arm brush against hers and sent a shower of sensation fizzing up her arm. Savannah closed her eyes and pulled in a slow breath.

''I'm afraid I'm not going to attempt to remedy that offense,'' he told her. ''I like breathing. Breathing is best for my continued good health.''

''So is leaving me alone.''

''Come on, Savannah. How long are you going to keep this up?''

''Dunno.'' She pulled a thoughtful face. ''Depends on how long I'm going to have to work with you.''

''Can't you even admit that this is going to be one helluva story? A coup for both of us?''

He was right. She'd grown increasingly weary of covering the mundane, was ready for a real assignment. Still...

''I don't have a problem with admitting that at all. I just don't like your methods. It was high-handed and sneaky, and I don't appreciate being made a pawn in the game of your career.''

Knox shifted in his seat, then emptied the rest of

the peanuts down his throat and finished the last of his drink before he responded. "Sorry," he mumbled.

Savannah blinked and turned to face him. "Come again?"

"I said I was sorry," Knox repeated in a little bit stronger voice.

Savannah widened her eyes in mock astonishment, cupped her hand around her ear and made an exaggerated show of not hearing him correctly. "Sorry, didn't catch that? What did you say again?"

"I said I was sorry!" Knox hissed impatiently. He plowed a hand through his carefully gelled hair, clearly out of his comfort zone when issuing an apology. "I shouldn't have gone to Chapman. But you didn't leave me any choice. I have to do *this* story and I needed *you* to go with me."

"Why me?" Savannah demanded quietly, finally getting to the heart of the matter. "Why not Claire or Whitney? Why did it have to be me?"

"Because I..." Knox swallowed, strangely reluctant to finish the thought.

"Because you what?" Savannah persisted.

He finally blew out a breath. "Because I couldn't take anyone with me who might be attracted to me. Or that I might be attracted to."

Slack-jawed, for a moment Savannah was too stunned to be insulted. She managed a smirk, even as dismay mushroomed inside her belly. "That irresistible, are you?"

"No, not to you," he huffed impatiently. His cheeks reddened. "You don't have any trouble at all resisting me. Hell, you've made a point of ensuring that I know just how resistible to you I am. *You* were the only logical choice. We have to stay focused, to remain objective. If I had asked any other woman at the *Phoenix* to make this trip with me, then you know as well as I do that they would have considered it a come-on. An invitation for seduction." He smiled without humor. "Did that occur to *you?*"

Savannah had readied her mouth for a cool put-down, but found herself curiously unable to come up with one. He was right. The idea of him wanting to seduce her had never crossed her mind—she'd been too worried about how hard it would be not to seduce him.

She'd known that he'd never been romantically interested in her—she'd purposely cultivated a hate-hate relationship with him to avoid that very scenario. Savannah knew she should be pleased with how well her plan had worked, but she found herself perversely unable to work up any enthusiasm for her success. He'd chosen her because she'd led him to believe that she wasn't attracted to him and because he, by his own admission, wasn't attracted to her.

All of that effort for this…this nightmare.

Irony could be a class-A bitch, Savannah thought wearily.

"Are we going to be able to get past this and work together?" he asked.

Savannah heaved a put-upon sigh. "Yeah…so long as you don't pull a show-and-tell session with your 'wand of light.'" She inwardly harrumphed. Didn't look like that would be a problem. And she was happy about it, dammit. This was a good thing. Really. She didn't want him to be attracted to her, any more than she wanted to be attracted to him.

Knox grinned, one of those baby-the-things-I-could-do-to-you smiles that made a woman's brain completely lose reason—including hers. "Let's make a deal. I won't show you mine unless you show me yours."

Savannah smirked, even as she suppressed a shiver. "Well, that'll be simple enough—*I* don't have a 'wand of light.'" She nodded succinctly. "Deal."

A sexy chuckle rumbled from his chest. "Deal."

3

"ARE YOU READY to discuss our cover?" Knox asked, when he'd finally navigated the rental car out onto the busy freeway.

He would have liked to cover everything while in the air where she couldn't have done him any bodily injury, but after his bungled apology, she'd feigned sleep for the rest of the flight. Knox didn't feel quite as safe in the car and he grimly suspected she wasn't going to care for the cover story he'd devised for the two of them. He'd made the mistake of filling out the application and accompanying questionnaire while still angry with her. Knox winced as he recalled the uncharitable things he'd had to say about his "wife's" shortcomings in bed.

She'd undoubtedly kill him.

Savannah fished her sunglasses from her purse and slid them into place. She'd dressed for travel in a sleeveless sky-blue linen pantsuit that perfectly matched the startling shade of her eyes and showed her small, curvy form to advantage. She wore simple diamond studs in her ears and her short black locks were delightfully mussed. Her lipstick had worn off hours ago, but refreshingly unlike most females, she didn't seem to mind.

Knox was still trying to decide how much to tell her about their cover story when she said, "Sure, go ahead and fill me in."

He swallowed and strove for a nonchalant tone. "We're registered as Mr. and Mrs. Knox Weston. Your first name is Barbie. We've been having a little—"

"Barbie?"

Knox winced at her shrill exclamation. "That's right."

With a withering smirk, she crossed her arms over her chest and turned to face him. "And why is my first name Barbie?"

Knox cast about his paralyzed mind for some sort of plausible lie, but couldn't come up with anything halfway believable and settled for the truth. "Because I was pissed and knew you would hate it." He threw her a sidelong glance and was pleased that he'd been able to—it meant that he still had his eyes and she hadn't scratched them out yet. "It was a petty thrill. I regret it now, of course," he quickly imparted at her venomous look. "But what's done is done and I can't very well tell them that I've made a mistake, that I didn't know my own wife's name." He forced a chuckle. "That would look pretty odd."

Looking thoroughly put out, Savannah studied him until Knox was hard-pressed not to squirm. "A petty thrill, eh?" She humphed. "Is there anything else—

besides my name—that you might have falsely reported about me? Anything else I should know about?''

He shifted uncomfortably. ''Er—''

''Knox…'' Savannah said threateningly.

Knox considered taking the next exit. If she went ballistic and attacked him, he didn't want any innocent bystanders to be hurt. ''Well, just for the sake of our cover, you understand, they, uh…might think that you're frigid and unable to reach climax.''

Knox heard her outraged gasp and tensed, readied himself for a blow.

''Well, that can be easily explained,'' she said frostily, ''when I tell them that you're a semi-impotent premature ejaculator.''

Knox quailed and resisted the natural urge to adjust himself, to assure himself that everything was in working order. ''Well, I—I can hardly see where that will b-be necessary,'' he croaked. ''One of us had to have a problem or we wouldn't have needed the workshop in the first place.'' A good, rational argument, Knox thought, congratulating himself.

She laughed. ''Oh, I see. And *I* just had to be the one with the problem? Why couldn't *you* have been the one with the problem?''

''Because I—''

She chuckled. ''Because you're such a stud that the idea of your equipment not passing muster—even fictitiously—was too much for your poor primitive male mind to comprehend. How pathetically juvenile.'' She smiled. "Do continue. We'll be there soon and I want to make sure that I'm completely in character."

Knox frowned at the words "pathetically juvenile," but under the circumstances, he let it pass. He cleared his throat and did his best to maintain his train of thought. "We've been married for two years and have never been completely satisfied with our, er, sex life. We're looking for something more and long for a closer relationship with one another. Our marriage is on the rocks as a result of our failure to communicate in the bedroom."

She snorted. "Because I'm frigid."

"Er...right."

"And you're impotent."

"Ri— Wrong!" Sheesh. A bead of sweat broke out on his upper lip. "That's, uh, not what our profile says."

"Because you filled it out. Look, Knox, if you think for one minute that I'm taking the total blame for our sorry sex life and our failing marriage during this farce, you'd better think again. You wanted this story, so you'd better damn well be ready to play your part. If I'm frigid, then, by God, you're going to be impotent."

Knox felt his balls shrivel up with dread. He set his jaw so hard he feared it would crack. She had to be the most competitive, argumentative female he'd ever encountered. The bigger picture, he reminded himself. Think of the bigger picture. "If you insist," he said tightly.

"I do."

"Fine." He blew out a breath. "There are still a few more things we need to go over. As for our occupations, I'm a veterinarian and you're my assistant."

She quirked a brow. "That's a bit of a stretch."

Smiling, Knox shrugged. "I got carried away."

Savannah's lips curled into a genuine smile, not the cynical smirk she usually wore, and the difference between the two was simply breathtaking. It was a sweet grin, devoid of any sentiment but real humor. To Knox's disquiet, he felt a buzz of heat hum along his spine.

"Be that as it may, I hope we're not called upon to handle a pet emergency," she said wryly. "I don't know the first thing about animals."

"What? No Spot or Fluffy in your past?"

A shadow passed over her face. "No, I'm afraid not."

Knox waited a beat to see if she would elaborate, and when she didn't, he filed that information away for future consideration and moved to fill the sudden silence. "Look in the front pocket of my laptop case, would you?"

Savannah turned and hefted the case from the back floorboard. She unzipped the front pouch. "What am I looking for? Your Viagra?"

"No." He smiled. "Just something to authenticate our marriage. Our rings are in there."

A line emerged between her brows and she paused to look at him. "Rings?"

Knox reached over, pilfered through the pocket and withdrew a couple of small velvet boxes. "Yeah, rings. Married people wear them. Fourth finger, left hand, closest to the heart."

"Ooh, I'm impressed. How does an impotent bachelor like you know all that sentimental swill?"

"I'm not impotent," Knox growled. "And I know because, having been best man at three different weddings in the past year, it's my business to know."

Savannah nodded. "Hmm."

"Hmm, what?" Knox asked suspiciously, casting her a sidelong glance.

She lifted one shoulder in a negligent shrug. "I'm surprised, that's all."

"Surprised that I've been a best man?"

"No, surprised that you had three male friends. I've never seen you with anyone but the opposite sex."

Knox shivered dramatically. "Oh, that's cold."

"Well, what do you expect? Us frigid unable-to-climax types are like that."

Smothering a smile, he tossed the smallest box to her. "Just put on your ring, Barbie."

Savannah lifted the lid and calmly withdrew the plain gold band. Anxiety knotted his gut. Though it had been completely unreasonable, Knox had found himself poring over tray after tray, trying to find the perfect band for her finger. He'd finally gotten disgusted with himself—they weren't really getting married, for Pete's sake—and had selected the simple unadorned band. Savannah didn't seem the type for flash and sparkle.

She seemed curiously reluctant to put it on, but finally slipped the ring over her knuckle and fitted it into place. She turned her hand this way and that. "It's lovely. And it fits perfectly. Good job, Knox. It had never occurred to me that we'd need rings. Where did you get these?"

With an inaudible sigh, Knox opened his own box, snagged his equally simple band and easily pushed it into place. "My jeweler, of course."

She winced. "Would have been cheaper to have gone to the pawnshop."

"Call me superstitious, but I didn't want to jinx this marriage—even a fake one—with unlucky bands."

"Unlucky bands?" she repeated dubiously.

"Yes. Unlucky. Think about it—if they'd been lucky they'd still be on their owners' fingers, not in a cheap fake-velvet tray in a pawnshop." He tsked. "Bad karma."

She chuckled, gazing at him with a curious expression not easily read. "You're right. You are superstitious."

"We're here," Knox announced needlessly. He

whistled low as he wheeled the rented sedan into a parking space in front of the impressive compound— *compound* meaning *mansion*. The nudge behind his navel gave another powerful jab as Knox gazed at the cool, elegant facade of the Shea's so-called compound. When Knox thought of a compound, rows of cheap low-slung utilitarian buildings came to mind. This was easily a million-dollar spread and there was nothing low-slung or utilitarian about the impressive residence before him.

The house, a bright, almost blindingly white stucco, was a two-story Spanish dream, with a red tiled roof and a cool, inviting porch that ran the length of the house. The front doors were a work of art in and of themselves, arched double mahogany wonders with an inlaid sunburst design in heavy leaded glass. Huge urns filled with bright flowering plants were scattered about the porch, along with several plush chaise longues and comfortable chairs.

Knox would have expected a place like this to have been professionally landscaped, but there was a whimsical, unplanned feel to the various shrubs and flora, as though the gardener had simply planted at will with no particular interest in traditional landscaping. There were no borders, no pavers, and no mulch to speak of, just clumps of flowers, greenery and the occasional odd shrub and ornamental tree. Julio, his parents' gardener, who was prone to a symmetrical design, would undoubtedly have an apoplectic fit if he saw this charmingly chaotic approach to landscaping.

"Quite a layout, huh?" Savannah murmured.

Knox nodded grimly. "Quite."

Savannah unbuckled her seat belt. "Before we go in, just what exactly is your opinion of tantric sex?"

Knox surveyed his surroundings once more. "In this case, I think it's a lucrative load of crap."

"For once we're in agreement."

A miracle, Knox thought, wondering how long the phenomenon would last. "Get your purse, Barbie. It's show time."

SAVANNAH ABSENTLY FIDGETED with the ring on her finger. It wasn't uncomfortable, just unfamiliar, and it fit perfectly. She covertly peeked at it again and a peculiar ache swelled in her chest. The smooth, cool band was beautiful in its simplicity and made her wonder if she'd ever meet anyone who would long to truly place a ring on her finger and be all to her that the gesture implied.

She doubted it.

Knox had unwittingly tapped her one weakness with the ring he'd bought her as a prop—her desire to be wanted.

Other than those few woefully short years with her parents, Savannah had never been truly wanted. While she'd certainly stayed with a few good families during her stint in the foster-care system, most families had taken her in either for the compensation or to add an indentured servant to their household. Sometimes both. A live-in maid, a built-in baby-sitter. But no one had ever truly wanted her.

Savannah had made the mistake of letting that weakness impair her judgment once with Gib, but she'd never do it again. Rejection simply hurt too much and wasn't worth the risk. She'd learned to become self-reliant, to trust her instincts, and never to depend on another person for her happiness.

''Wow,'' Knox murmured as they were led down a wide hall and finally shown into their room.

Wow, indeed, Savannah thought as she gazed at the plush surroundings. The natural hardwood floors and thick white plaster walls were a continued theme throughout the house, creating a light and airy atmosphere. Heavy wooden beams decorated the high white ceilings, tying the wood and white decor together seamlessly.

A huge canopied bed draped with yards and yards of rich brocade hangings occupied a place of honor in the middle of one long wall. Coordinating pieces—a chest of drawers, dresser and a couple of nightstands—balanced the room perfectly. A dinette sat in one corner and a small arched fireplace accented with rich Mexican tile added another splash of color and warmth. Multicolored braided rugs were scattered about the room, adding more depth to the large space. Light streamed in through two enormous arched windows. It was a great room, very conducive to romance, Savannah thought.

A ribbon of unease threaded through her belly as she once again considered why she was here—and what she'd have to resist. Savannah glanced at the bed and, to her consternation, imagined Knox and her vibrating the impressive four-poster across the room, her hands shaped to Knox's perfectly formed ass as he plunged in and out of her. She imagined candlelight and rose petals and hot, frantic bodies tangled amid the scented sheets. Savannah drew in a shuddering breath as dread and need coalesced into a fireball in her belly.

Knox cased the room, checked out the closet and adjoining bath. He whistled. "Hey, come check out the tub."

Given her wayward imagination, Savannah didn't think that would be wise. Visions of Knox wet and naked and needy weren't particularly helpful to her cause.

"So," Knox said as he returned from admiring the bath. "Which side of the bed do you want?"

Savannah blinked, forced a wry smile. "I think the question is which part of the floor do you want?"

Knox glanced at the gleaming hardwood and absently scratched his temple. He wore an endearing smile. "Do I have a prayer of winning this argument?"

"No." Savannah hated to be such a prude, but having to sleep next to him would be sheer and utter torture. Simply being in the same room with him would be agonizing enough. Savannah grimly suspected that were they to share that bed, she'd inexplicably gravitate toward him. Toward his marvelous ass. Considering he didn't reciprocate this unholy attraction, she wasn't about to risk embarrassing herself and him.

He sighed. "As the lady wishes. I suppose we should head to the common room for the Welcome Brunch."

Savannah nodded. Without further comment, the two of them exited the room and, with Knox's hand at her elbow, they made their way down a long wide hall back to the foyer and then into what had been dubbed the common room. A long table piled with food sat off to the side of the enormous room and little sofas and armchairs were grouped together to encourage idle chitchat. Savannah's stomach issued a hungry growl, propelling her toward the food.

"Hungry, are you?" Knox queried.

"Ravenous."

"I offered to share my peanuts with you," he reminded teasingly.

Savannah grunted. "I wasn't about to partake of your ill-gotten gains."

Knox chuckled, a deep silky baritone that made her very insides quiver. Jeez, the man had cornered the market when it came to sex appeal. It was the same sort of intimate laugh she assumed he'd share with a lover. Something warm and quivery snaked through her at the thought.

"I simply flirted a little, Savannah. It's not like I

raped and pillaged. Honestly, have you not ever batted your lashes and tried to get out of a speeding ticket?''

''No,'' she lied as she selected a wedge of cheese and a few crackers.

He chuckled again. ''Liar.''

''That's different,'' she said simply for the sake of disagreeing with him, which she did a lot. ''And it's Barbie, you idiot. Do you want to blow our cover from the get-go?''

''Whatever.'' He paused. ''Oh, look, our host and hostess have arrived.''

Savannah turned and her gaze landed on an older couple—early to middle fifties, she guessed. Bare feet peeked from beneath the hems of their long white robes. The woman wore her completely silver hair in a long flowing style that slithered over her shoulders and stopped at the small of her back. Silver charms glittered from her wrists and a large, smooth lavender stone lay suspended between her breasts via a worn leather cord. This woman seemed to embody everything their glossy pamphlet proclaimed. Serenity, harmony and all those other adverbs that had been touted in the trendy brochure.

As for the man, a calm strength seemed to hover about him as well. He appeared relaxed yet confident, as though he was the only stud for his mare. A niggle of doubt surfaced as Savannah studied the two. Could the art of tantric sex really be all this couple claimed it was? Quite honestly, it seemed impossible to Savannah, but for the first time since she'd accepted that she'd be working on this story with Knox, Savannah wondered if she'd been too hasty in forming her opinions.

The man smiled. "Welcome. I'm Dr. Edgar Shea and this is my lovely wife and life partner, Dr. Rupali Shea. We're so glad that you're here." He paused. "Some of you are here as a result of frustration, some of you are here as a result of your partner's prodding, and some of you are here because you're simply curious." His grin made an encore appearance. "Regardless of why you are here, we're exceedingly glad and are looking forward to teaching you everything we've learned about the art of tantric lovemaking. What we will teach you, what we'll freely share and will graphically demonstrate for your benefit, will change your lives…if you are open to the possibilities."

"At the beginning of each session," Rupali began, "we like to do a little preliminary test, to see for ourselves just how much ground we need to cover, to see which couples will require one-on-one instruction." She paused and smiled to the room at large. "Now don't look frightened. It's a simple test. But first we'll introduce ourselves and share our inadequacies. No embarrassment, no boundaries," she said. "Only truth healing."

Savannah and Knox shared a look of dread. She almost felt sorry for him, but quickly squelched the sentiment. This was a hell of his own making. He could burn with humiliation for all she cared. The couples around them looked as miserable as she and Knox and that made Savannah feel marginally better. As she listened, one man admitted chronic masturbation as his problem. There were a couple of other women delegated to the frigid-and-couldn't-reach-climax list, and even more men who embarrassingly mumbled impotency as their major handicap.

Rupali beamed at them when they were finished. "Now, for the test." She paused again, garnering everyone's attention with the heavy silence. She steepled her fingers beneath her chin. "Do any of you know what the most intimate act between lovers is?" she asked. "I'm sure that all of you are thinking about intercourse, or possibly oral sex...but you'd be wrong. It's kissing. Kissing requires more intimacy than any other facet of lovemaking. And that will be your test. You will embrace your partner and kiss, and Edgar and I will observe." She beamed at them. "See, that's easy enough."

Savannah heard several audible sighs resonate around the room, but hers and Knox's weren't among them. Kissing? Kiss Knox? In front of all these people? Right now? Knox seemed to be equally astounded, as he wore a frozen smile on his face. Panic ping-ponged through her abdomen, the blood rushed to her ears and every bit of moisture evaporated from Savannah's mouth.

Knox drew her to him, anchored his powerful arms about her back and waist. Longing ignited a fire of

need in her belly. ''Quit looking like she's just issued
a death sentence,'' he hissed through a brittle smile.
''We're supposed to be married, remember?''

Savannah made the mistake of looking up into his
dark green eyes and felt need balloon below her belly
button. An involuntary shiver danced up her spine
and camped at her nape. Oh, hell. She was doomed.
''Right,'' she said breathlessly.

''It's just a kiss,'' he said unsteadily. ''We can
handle it.''

''On my count,'' Rupali trilled. ''Three, two,
one...kiss!''

With equal parts anticipation and anxiety, Savannah's eyes fluttered shut as Knox's warm lips descended to hers. The exquisite feel of his lips slanting
over hers instantly overwhelmed her and she swallowed a deep sigh of satisfaction as his taste exploded on her tongue. He tasted like soda and peanuts and the faint flavor of salt clung to his lips. *And
oh, mercy, could he kiss.* Savannah whimpered.

His kiss was firm yet soft and he suckled and fed
at her mouth until Savannah's legs would scarcely
support her. Oh, how many times had she dreamed
of this? How many times had she imagined his
mouth hungrily feeding at hers, his built-like-a-brick-
wall body wrapped around hers? With a groan of
pure delight, she pressed herself even more firmly
against him and felt her nipples tingle and pearl. A
similar experience commenced between her thighs as
her feminine muscles dewed and tightened. Their

tongues played a game of seek and retreat, and for
every parlay, Savannah grew even more agitated,
more needy. Knox tightened his hold around her, and
she felt his hand slide from the small of her back and
cup her bottom. Another blast of desire detonated,
sending a bright flash of warmth zinging through her
blood.

From the dimmest recesses of her mind, Savannah
realized that the room had grown ominously quiet.
She reluctantly dragged her lips away from Knox's
and laid her head against his rapidly rising chest.

Edgar and Rupali Shea grinned broadly at them.
Their eyes twinkled knowingly. "Clearly Knox and
Barbie have passed our little test with glowing marks
and no one-on-one instruction will be required."

A titter of amusement resonated around the room.

Savannah's cheeked blazed and it took every
ounce of willpower not to melt out of Knox's embrace. She extricated herself with as much dignity as
she could muster, considering she'd all but lashed her
legs about his waist and begged him to pump her
amid a room of confessed sexually challenged spec-
tators.

She was pathetic. Utterly and completely pathetic.
How on earth would she keep her attraction for him
secret now? How? she mentally wailed.

Deciding the best defense was a better offense,
Savannah leaned forward and whispered in his ear,
"How about a little less tongue next time, Slick? I
don't know what you were looking for back there,

but I had my tonsils removed years ago.'' She patted his arm and calmly moved to pick up her plate.

Knox's dumbfounded expression was unequivocally priceless, igniting a glow of another sort.

4

A LITTLE LESS TONGUE? Knox wondered angrily. To his near slack-jawed astonishment, he'd never enjoyed kissing another woman more. He'd been so caught up in the melding of their mouths that all he could think about was how amazingly great she tasted, how wonderful her lips felt against his, and how much he longed to have her naked and flat on her back...

It was too much to contemplate. This was Savannah.

Savannah.

Admittedly, he'd always thought her gorgeous. The first time he'd met her, he'd felt the familiar tug of attraction. But then she'd blasted him with a frigid blue stare and she'd opened her sarcastic mouth, and he'd never entertained another amorous thought about her. That's why he'd chosen her for this trip, dammit, and yet the moment his lips had met hers he'd gone into a molecular meltdown. He'd wanted to show her how hot she made him, tell her how much he wanted her and...

And seconds after that mind-blowing kiss, Savannah had calmly offered criticism and then just as calmly returned to her lunch.

Knox was unequivocally stunned.

He'd been too bowled over by the impact of that kiss to even regulate his breathing, much less pretend that he hadn't been affected…and she'd not only been unaffected, but apparently had been so unmoved by the experience that she'd been able to remain detached and offer advice.

Heat spreading up his neck, Knox loaded his own plate from the buffet and inwardly fumed. He'd always considered himself an attentive lover, had always prided himself on learning what techniques turned a woman on, what would give her pleasure. He liked a vocal partner, one who didn't expect him to be a mind reader. He liked hearing what made a woman hot and enjoyed doing it for her even more. Throughout his career in the bedroom, he'd heard countless breathy pleas—*harder, faster, there* and *there,* and *almost* and *oh, God, there! Touch, suck, lick* and *nibble,* even *spank,* he'd heard it all.

But never—*never*—had he ever had a woman criticize his kiss.

His kiss had always been above reproach, with no room for improvement. Though most men considered kissing as a simple means to an end—Knox included, most of the time—he'd nonetheless made it a point to excel at that particular form of foreplay.

Ask any man and he'd tell you that, given the choice of having his tongue in a woman's mouth, or his hand in her panties, the panties would win hands down every time. That was the ultimate goal, after all, and men were linear thinkers. Point A to point B in the most economical fashion.

Sure they might get distracted by a creamy breast and pouty nipple, might even linger around a delightful belly button for a few seconds, but settling oneself firmly between a woman's thighs was always, without question, the ultimate goal.

While kissing Savannah a few moments ago—though the kiss couldn't have lasted more than thirty seconds—Knox's thoughts had immediately leaped ahead to the grand finale. He'd already imagined plunging dick first into the tight, wet heat of her body. Had been anticipating her own phenomenally cataclysmic release as well as his.

While she'd been critiquing his kiss.

Knox had never anticipated being attracted to her and had known that she wasn't attracted to him, had chosen her for that particular reason. But having the knowledge confirmed in such a humiliating fashion wasn't an easy pill to swallow. Particularly since he'd all but devoured her and had made such a horny ass out of himself. Jesus. After that lusty display, there couldn't be one shred of doubt in her mind about how he'd reacted to her. How hot he'd been for her.

All due to a simple kiss she hadn't even enjoyed.

Simmering with indignation once more, Knox cast a sidelong glance at the object of his present irritation. Savannah's cheeks were a little pink—obviously embarrassed by his zealous response to their "test"—but aside from that, she appeared completely composed. She absently nibbled a cracker, her perceptive gaze roaming around the room people-watching, presumably looking for fodder for their story.

Which was exactly what he should be doing, Knox realized with an angry start. He mentally snorted. Undoubtedly she was already forming an angle, had already thought of an intro to their piece. Well, he'd have the most input, thank you very much. This story had been his brainchild, and if there had been any way he could have done it without her, he would have. And he wished he could have. They'd scarcely begun this damned workshop and already he'd become too distracted by the supposedly *undistracting* female he'd brought with him.

How screwed up was that?

"I hope you don't plan to pout the entire afternoon," Savannah said with a sardonic smile. "Honestly, Knox, it was only a small criticism. Surely that enormous ego of yours can take one minor unflattering assessment."

Ignoring a surge of irritation, Knox mentally counted to three, then arranged his face into its typically amiable expression. "Pout?"

Her eyes narrowed, clearly seeing through his innocent look. "Yes, pout. You've been glowering at the room at large for the past five minutes. Jeez, I didn't mean to hurt your feelings.'' She neatly bit the end off a stalk of celery. Her lips twitched. ''Frankly, I wasn't aware that you had any.''

Ah…back to familiar ground. Knox forced a smile, affected a negligent shrug, though he longed to wrap his hands around her throat and throttle her. He'd learned to appreciate her acidic sarcasm, but right now he wasn't in the proper humor to applaud her clever witticisms. He ignored her last comment and decided a change of subject was in order.

''So, what's your initial impression of the Sheas?'' Knox asked.

Savannah winced, wiped a bit of salad dressing from the corner of her luscious lips. ''They're what I expected…but then again they're not.'' She paused consideringly. ''I don't know. It'll take more than a welcome speech for me to make an accurate assessment.''

''I didn't ask for an accurate assessment. I asked for an initial impression.''

''There's a difference?''

He nodded. ''Of course.''

''What is it?''

She had to be the most infuriating female he'd ever met. ''Stop being difficult and answer the question.''

Seemingly resigned, Savannah blew out a breath. ''They were impressive, Knox,'' she admitted reluctantly. ''If I was like these people, desperately looking for a way to better my relationship with a significant other, my husband, or simply needing a little show-and-tell to jump-start my sex life, I'd like them. They seemed genuine.''

Secretly he agreed. Hokey togas aside, the Sheas seemed to share some secret something. Something the rest of the room lacked, or wasn't privy to. Still... '''Seemed' is the key word.''

''I know.'' Savannah discarded her empty plate and dusted her hands. ''So what's next on the agenda?''

Knox stacked his empty plate on top of hers. ''We pick up our registration packets.''

She nodded. ''Then let's do it. I want a chance to go over everything before our first class starts.''

Still feeling a little put out, Knox followed Savannah from the large common room and into the hall where the registration table had been set up. Several couples had been equally eager to start and Knox recognized the one in front of them with a little wince of dread—the masturbator and his wife.

Savannah's steps slowed. ''Is that who I think—''

''Yes, it is,'' Knox hissed through a false smile as the couple in question turned with bright grins to greet them.

''Hi,'' the wife enthused. ''Knox and Barbie, right? We're the Cummings. I'm Marge and this is my husband, Chuck.'' With a roll of her eyes, she jabbed her husband in the side. ''Jeez, Chuck, where are your manners? Shake Knox's hand.''

Knox felt his frozen smile falter and his gaze

dropped to Chuck's outstretched hand with a paralyzing dread.

Beside him, Savannah covered her mouth with her hand and quickly morphed a chuckle into a convincing cough. He'd kill her when this was over with, Knox decided. He'd simply wring her neck.

The silence lengthened past the comfortable and Knox was resignedly readying his hand for the shake when Marge chirped "Gotcha!" amid a stream of high-pitched staccato laughter. The laugh went on and on and had the effect of fingernails on a chalkboard.

Chuck, too, was caught up in a fit of hilarity. His beefy face turned beet-red and, wheezing laughter, he pointed at Knox. "Man, if you could have seen your face! Oh, Marge, that was priceless. Utterly priceless. The best one yet."

Marge's laughter tittered out and she wiped her streaming eyes. "It's a little joke we like to pull," she confided, as though this whole scene was perfectly normal. "Everyone knows Chuck's a chronic masturbator—hell, I had to pry his hand away from his groin during your kiss a little while ago—so no one ever wants to shake his hand. *Ever,*" she added meaningfully. "I mean, who would, knowing where it's been, right?" She and Chuck shared a secret smile. "So we like to pull a little prank with it. We've gotten a variety of reactions, but yours was by far the best we've seen in a long time. You looked like he'd whipped out his poor overworked penis and asked you to shake it.''

Marge and Chuck dissolved into fits of whooping laughter once more.

Savannah, of course, was observing the whole scenario as he would expect—tickled to death at his expense. Her pale blue eyes glittered with barely restrained laughter. Knox could tell she was on the verge of pulling a Marge and he cast her one long, pointed look to dissuade her. Hadn't she ever heard of loyalty? She was supposed to be his wife, dammit, and should be outraged on his behalf. Not quivering with amusement over his immense discomfort.

Knox decided this was the point where he was supposed to laugh and managed to push a weak little ha-ha from his throat. It was exceedingly difficult, considering he longed to plant his fist through a wall. Or possibly Chuck's face.

"FYI, he's left-handed," Marge shared with another maddening little smile. "You could have shaken it without a thing to worry about."

Knox forced his lips into a smile. Thankfully, Marge and Chuck's turn at the registration table came, sparing him a reply.

"Well," Savannah whispered through her curling lips, "that was certainly interesting."

Knox felt a muscle jump in his jaw. "You think?"

"Funny, too."

"I'm glad you were amused," Knox ground out.

"Marge was right," she went on to his supreme

annoyance. She rocked back on her heels. "The look on your face *was* priceless. I wish I'd had a camera."

Knox smirked. "You're really enjoying this, aren't you, Savannah?"

She aimed a smugly beautiful smile in his direction, clasped her hands behind her back and batted her lashes shamelessly. "Yes. Yes, I am." She sighed. "After what you pulled with Chapman, can you really blame me?"

Knox exhaled wearily. He supposed not, and reluctantly admitted as much. "Still," he told her. "Gloating does not become you. Enough already, Savannah. We've got a job to do," he reminded her pointedly, as much for his own benefit as hers. Focus, Knox told himself. The big picture. He needed to push the kiss and the masturbator encounter out of his mind and keep the ultimate goal in sight—the story.

"I know that," she snapped, clearly perturbed at the reminder. "Believe me, that's the only reason I'm here—for the story. Let's just register and go back to our room. I want to prepare for this class." She chuckled darkly. "And let's pray there aren't any more surprise tests."

Damn right, Knox thought. At the moment, he wasn't up for another failing grade from "Barbie."

As soon as they returned to their room, Savannah made a beeline for the bathroom. She needed a few moments alone—just a few precious seconds away from Knox's distracting company to regroup and pull herself together. Once behind the closed door, she blew out a pent-up breath, then ran the tap and splashed cold water on her face. It felt cool and refreshing and helped alleviate some of the tension tightening her neck and shoulders.

Her muscles had atrophied with stress after The Kiss.

Sure, she'd managed to put on a good enough show, had forced herself to appear cool and unaffected when the truth of the matter had been that Knox's kiss had all but melted her bones. When his talented mouth had touched hers...

Mercy.

Remembered heat sent a coil of longing swirling through the pit of her belly. Her nipples tightened and a familiar but woefully missed warmth weighted her core.

She'd known—hadn't she?—that he would be utterly amazing. Her every instinct had told her so, just as every instinct had warned her against him. She'd managed to undermine his self-confidence this time, managed to miraculously pull off a grand performance, but he'd undoubtedly see through her if anything like that happened between them again.

Though she hadn't yet had a chance to go through the curriculum, Savannah nonetheless knew that the kiss was just the beginning of what the workshop would entail. She and Knox would be called upon to do much more than kiss. The success of the Sheas' workshop depended upon it.

She wished that she and Knox could keep up the ruse without having to participate physically in class, and the wishing, she knew, was an act of futility. They would have to participate to some extent in class, otherwise they'd call attention to themselves, or, worse still, would lead the Sheas to believe they needed more intensive therapy.

Savannah shuddered. Neither scenario inspired confidence.

Irritation rose. Savannah ground her teeth and resisted the urge to beat her head against the door. This was precisely why she didn't want to be here, she inwardly fumed. Savannah knew her limits, knew her shortcomings and knew what sort of effect Knox Webber had on her libido. Attending a sex workshop with him was like waving a joint in front of a pot-head.

Knox would be addictive to her and the addiction could only lead to heartache—hers.

She simply wouldn't allow it.

Chapman had forced her hand by making her attend. Despite her misgivings, Savannah would do her job and write a great story—and she'd do all that the task entailed, including being an objective participant in this godforsaken workshop—she was a professional, after all. But she would not let it become personal.

She wouldn't.

Seeing as sex was about as personal as it got, Savannah wasn't exactly sure what her heartfelt affirmation meant, but it made her feel better and she'd use any means available to shore up her waning confidence.

A tentative knock sounded at the door, startling her.

"Savannah…you all right in there?"

"Y-yes, of course." Savannah flushed the commode for appearance's sake, drew in a deep bolstering breath and smoothed her hair behind her ears.

"I, uh, wouldn't bother you, but I need to change and, frankly, I've gotta go."

Frowning, Savannah opened the door. "Change?" she asked. "Change for what?"

Knox had tossed a long white garment over his shoulder. It looked suspiciously like the same sort of costume the Sheas wore.

"For class," he told her. "We have to wear a *kurta.* I'm going to feel like a complete moron," he confided with an endearing, self-conscious smile, "but they're mandatory. I laid yours on the bed."

Good grief, Savannah thought, wondering what other little surprises would be in store for this weekend. She sighed heavily and massaged the bridge of her nose. "A *what?*"

"A *kurta.* It's an Indian gown."

Savannah eyed the getup warily. She crossed her arms over her chest. "You've got to be kidding."

"Nope…and it gets worse."

The hesitation in Knox's voice alerted her more than the actual words he'd said. "Worse?"

He winced regretfully. "Yeah—no undergarments. And no shoes."

Savannah blinked, flabbergasted. She was supposed to walk around naked under a toga? "No undergarments?" she repeated blankly, certain that she'd misunderstood him.

He tunneled his fingers through his hair, mussing up the wavy brown locks. "Yeah, I'm afraid so. It's to promote chakra healing, and, of course, the symbolic message of no boundaries."

And easy access, Savannah thought, for those graphic hands-on demonstrations. Her mouth parched and dread ballooned in her chest.

"Uh, if you're finished in there..." Knox reminded her.

Belatedly Savannah realized she still stood in the threshold of the bathroom. "Oh, sure. Sorry," she mumbled, hastily moving out of his way.

"I've had a quick look through the itinerary for the weekend," Knox called through the door. "After you get dressed, you might want to flip through it."

"I plan to," Savannah murmured absently as she picked up the long, white gown. The cool, soft cotton material smelled of fresh air. It had probably been line-dried, Savannah decided, not tossed into an industrial-sized appliance. Still, knowing that she'd be walking around buck naked underneath the almost see-through fabric quickly dispelled any pleasant musings.

Oh, hell. Knox would be out of the bathroom soon, so unless she wanted to do a little striptease for him, she'd best change before he came out. Savannah hurriedly removed her shoes, pantsuit, bra and undies, then picked up the gown and pulled it over her head. The fabric settled on her shoulders lightly, whispered over her body and came to rest just above her ankles. It felt surprisingly…good. Wicked even, if she were honest. Something about the way the garment caressed her body made her feel beautiful, free and sexy. She particularly liked the way the material felt against her bare breasts and rump.

"Are you dressed yet?" Knox called.

Savannah scrambled up onto the bed, put her back against the headboard and settled a pillow over her lap. She grabbed the handbook and made herself look studious and calm. It took a tremendous amount of effort.

"Uh…yeah," she finally managed.

Knox exited the bathroom. He'd obviously brushed his hair, as the brown waves were once more smoothed back into place. His lips were curled into an almost bashful, self-deprecating grin and those incredibly lean cheeks were washed in an uncharacteristic pink. He'd folded his clothes and had tucked them up under his arm. A curious emotion swelled in Savannah's chest.

Knox gestured to the *kurta.* "I don't think that I've

ever felt more emasculated in my life. If I'd known that wearing a damned dress with no drawers on underneath would be a mandatory part of this workshop, I simply would have said to hell with the story and found something else to write about.''

Well, Savannah thought, as every drop of moisture evaporated from her mouth, he might feel emasculated, but he definitely didn't *look* emasculated.

In fact, if he looked any less emasculated, he'd be X-rated. She could clearly see through the fabric, and the impressive bulge beneath indicated that Knox Webber was, without question, the most unemasculated man she'd ever seen—and he wasn't even hard. Fascinated, she swallowed. That was just…him. Just…there. All him.

Sweet heaven.

Every cell in her body was hammeringly aware that less than five feet from where she sat stood the most incredibly sexy, most generously endowed man she'd ever seen in her life. She instantly imagined him out of the *kurta* and sprawled on the bed next to her. Her blood thickened and desire sparked other fantasies, so she took her wicked illusion to the next level and imagined herself sinking slowly onto the hot, hard length of him. Sweet mother of heaven…

Savannah bit her lip, fully engrossed in the picture her wayward imagination had conjured. Up until now she'd always been preoccupied with his ass—he had an amazing ass, after all—but Savannah grimly suspected that fixation had just been replaced with another. Honestly, how did he make all of that fit in—

"What about you? Do you feel ridiculous?" Knox asked.

Savannah blinked drunkenly and then, feeling stupid and ashamed, recovered the next instant. "Er, yes. Yes, I do."

Knox paused to look at her. A line emerged between his brows. "You're acting weird. Are you sure you're all right?"

"Yeah, I'm fine." She manufactured a smile and thumped the booklet that lay in her lap. "Just thinking about some of the names for these classes."

Seemingly satisfied, Knox smiled knowingly. "You mean like *Love His Lingam, Rejuvenate His Root?*"

Savannah laughed. "Yeah. And *Sacred Goddess Stimulation.*"

Thank God those classes would come later, Savannah thought. They got to learn all about their chakras first with *Beginning Tantra, Energetic Healing*.

"So, what do you say?" Knox asked. "Ready to go get your chakras aligned?"

Savannah heaved a put-upon sigh. "Honestly, Knox. This isn't like the front end of your car. You're not getting anything aligned. Haven't you done your homework? You're getting unblocked." Savannah slid from the bed and gathered her things.

"Getting what unblocked?"

A sly smile curled her lips. "Well, for starters, your ass."

5

FOLLOWING SAVANNAH out the door, Knox involuntarily tightened the orifice in question. *"What?"*

"For someone who was so determined to do this story—*had* to do this particular story," she emphasized sarcastically, "it would seem that you would have put a little more research into the project."

"I did my research," Knox insisted with a sardonic smile. "But I didn't come across anything that suggested tantra partners began foreplay with an enema."

Savannah chuckled darkly. "Who said anything about an enema?"

"Well, how else—" Knox drew up short as realization dawned. His ass instantly clenched in horror.

Oh, hell.

Catching his appalled expression, Savannah's pale blue eyes sparkled with amusement. That sinfully beautiful mouth of hers curved ever so slightly with mockery. "Aha. Light dawns on marble head."

Knox swallowed and continued to follow her down the hall. He'd rather be eviscerated with a rusty blade than even think about anal sex, much less discuss the loathsome subject with Savannah. He didn't need to get unblocked, thank you very much, and after a moment told her so. Forcibly.

She winced, clearly enjoying his discomfort. "Don't worry, Knox, I was kidding about the visit to the back door. But I have to say, you have one glaring characteristic of a man who needs to have his root chakra unblocked."

A muscle worked in his jaw. Knox knew better than to ask, but found himself forming the question anyway. "Really? And what characteristic would that be?"

"You're a tight-ass. I think I've pointed that out to you before."

Knox smirked. "Cute."

He held open the heavy front door and allowed her to pass. Their first class was on the south lawn in the outdoor classroom. Butterflies and bumblebees flitted from flower to flower through the Sheas' eclectic garden, Knox noticed as he and Savannah made their way across the lush lawn. Grass pushed between his toes, bringing a reluctant grin to his lips. It had been a long time since he'd been barefoot in the grass.

A peek at Savannah confirmed that she was enjoying the sensation as well. A small smiled tilted her lips and she'd turned her face toward the kiss of the sun. A light breeze ruffled her black bed-head locks and that same breeze molded the white, all-but-see-through *kurta* to her small, womanly form.

It was at this point that Knox became hopelessly distracted.

Naturally, over the course of Savannah's career at the *Phoenix,* Knox had observed her body and noted its perfection. He was a man, after all, and men—being men—tended to notice such details.

But noticing and really appreciating were two completely different things.

Knox's gaze roamed leisurely over her body and, much to his helpless chagrin, his visual perusal ignited a spark of heat in his loins.

The delicate fabric lay plastered against the unbound globes of her breasts, and the rosy hue of her nipples shadowed through the clinging material. Knox could easily discern the flat belly, the sweetly curving swell of her hips and the black triangle of curls nestled at the apex of her thighs.

She was beautiful. Utterly and completely beautiful and...

And feeling his dick begin to swell for sport, Knox mentally swore and made a determined effort to direct his lust-ridden brain toward a more productive line of thought—like his story. With that idea in mind, he studied his surroundings.

Picnic tables, some already occupied with couples, were arranged in a large circle beneath a huge whitewashed octagon canopy. Crystals of various sizes and shapes dripped like icicles from the perimeter of the canopy, sending rainbows of colorful reflected light dancing through the air. The tinkling tones of wind chimes sounded, adding another element to the mystical environment. A white silk chaise sat upon a raised dais in the center of the outdoor room. Who knew what sort of depraved acts had been committed upon that little bench, Knox thought with a grim smile.

"Where should we sit?" Savannah asked as she surveyed the circle of tables.

"Somewhere in the middle," Knox told her. "If we sit in front, we'll look eager and too easy to snag for demonstrations. If we sit in the back, they'll think we're bashful and will want to draw us in and make us participate." He guided her toward an appropriate table.

Savannah grinned. "Why do I feel like this is the voice of experience and not a fabricated load of BS?"

"Because it is. I honed the skill in grade school."

With a roll of her eyes, Savannah sat down. "Sounds like you were trying to figure out a way to do the least amount of work possible."

Knox returned her grin and attempted to sit down next to her. He wasn't used to navigating in a dress and almost toppled chin first into the picnic table when the hem of the *kurta* caught the seat. He scowled, smoothing the damned gown back into place. "That was one of the perks," he finally said. "Be sure and take good notes. I always copied someone else's."

She gave him a droll glare. "I'm sure you did."

Actually, he hadn't. He'd only been trying to needle her. What did she think? That he'd been able to sail through an Ivy League school on nothing but his parents' money and his charming personality? And she had the nerve to think him a snob?

She'd never said it, of course. Just like none of his other co-workers had ever said it. But Knox knew they were laboring under the mistaken assumption that his wealthy background had afforded him his present career and, moreover, that his being talented could have nothing to do with it.

Knox smothered a bitter laugh. Let them think what they would. Screw 'em. He didn't care. In fact, he purposely invested a great deal of time making sure that no one—least of all any of those co-workers at the paper—knew just how much he longed to be respected for his work, rather than simply tolerated with virulent envy.

Between his condescending co-workers and equally condescending parents, Knox was doubly determined to succeed.

For reasons that escaped him, Savannah's opinion, in particular, annoyed the hell out of him. But what did he expect? That after spending one day with him, she'd see him any differently than she always had? That his character would have suddenly jumped up a notch in her esteemed estimation? Not likely. And he didn't care, dammit. He *did not* care. When he made it, when he proved himself, she'd be just like everyone else—eating crow.

Curiously, the thought didn't inspire the smug sat-isfaction Knox anticipated and, instead left him feeling small and petty. He shrugged the sensation aside and focused instead on the Sheas as they finally moved onto the dais.

"Welcome to your first class," Edgar began. "The title of this lesson is *Beginning Tantra/Energetic Healing.* We have much ground to cover over the course of this weekend and everything we teach you will be built upon these basic tantric principles, so please have your pad and pencil poised and be ready to learn."

"Before we begin," Rupali said to the class at large, "there are a few things we must cover." She steepled her fingers beneath her chin, the picture of glowing serenity. "I'm sure you are all wondering why you've been asked to wear the *kurta* and remove your shoes. Let me address the *kurta* first. The *kurta* denotes purity, helps promote chakra healing and enables us all to remove psychological boundaries. At times, our clothes can be our armor against our sensual selves." Her keen gaze landed pointedly on a few people. Savannah, too, Knox noticed with mild surprise. "We'll have no armor here. Only truth and healing." She paused. "As for not wearing shoes, we need to be grounded to Mother Earth, to let her energy flow up through our feet and connect us once more with the force of all that's natural, that's pure. Curl your toes in the grass—let it massage your feet," she instructed. "Isn't it nice? Can you feel

Mother Earth's power?'' she asked, smiling. "If not,
you will by the end of this clinic, I promise you. All
of you will leave here with a new sense of energy,
of purpose, of happiness.''

"That's a mighty big promise,'' Savannah whispered from the side of her mouth.

Knox nodded. "Yeah, but it's what she didn't
promise that's wise. She didn't promise impotent
men erections, and she didn't promise you frigid-
unable-to-climax types an orgasm.''

"You're right,'' she quietly agreed. "It's inferred,
but not stated. Smart move. Very crafty.''

"Are there any questions so far?'' Rupali wanted
to know. "If not, then we'll move on to the next
item on the agenda before we officially begin class.
In order to insure that you fully understand and appreciate what sort of sexual gratification tantra can
add to your sex lives, you need to understand what
was lacking in the first place, and you need to be
able to instantly discern the vast difference between
the lovers you officially are today and the new lovers
you will become. What I'm about to ask of you will
be exceedingly difficult, but it's simply crucial to the
success of your experience—you must abstain from
physical intercourse until the end of the workshop.''

A chorus of shocked gasps and giggles echoed under the pavilion.

"It's crucial,'' she repeated firmly. "Men, through
tantra we're going to teach you the most effective
way to bring your lover pleasure. We're going to

teach you to worship your goddess. The techniques you will learn will enable you to prolong your own inner release as well as hers.''

''Likewise ladies,'' she continued, ''we will teach you the most effective way to worship your man, to massage and heal, and bring pleasure beyond anything he's ever experienced before. We want you to make love, want to encourage you to grow spiritually as well as sexually with your partners. But there are lessons to be learned first.'' She laughed. ''Lessons that will have you writhing with pleasure and begging for the most carnal form of release. But you can't have it…yet. Consummation will occur on Sunday night and not a moment before. Does everyone agree to this rule?''

After a few reluctant nods and one gentle but firm admonishment to Chuck, who'd been busy throughout her speech, Rupali finally concluded, and Edgar stood once more.

He clapped his hands together. ''Okay, let's begin,'' he said.

While Edgar began a brief summary of each of the chakras, Knox's thoughts still lingered over Rupali's revelation—no consummation until Sunday. He couldn't begin to imagine why this was relevant to him as he and Savannah weren't going to be consummating anything. Still…

Just knowing that they were going to have to participate in everything—learn all of the supposed pleasure-enhancing techniques—up until that point and then miss the grand finale was heartily depressing. Unreasonable, he knew. The whole point of bringing Savannah along was to remain asexual about the entire concept, to remain focused on the story. The nudge was still there, powerful as ever.

Jeez. He was pathetic. Obviously, he was so preoccupied with his pecker that being denied even mythological sex irritated him. Knox cast a sidelong glance at his companion and felt his lips twitch with wry humor. If she had any inkling of the direction of his thoughts right now, she'd undoubtedly pull a Lorena Bobbitt and permanently extinguish his "wand of light" like she'd so lethally threatened before.

So, he could either keep this one-sided attraction to himself—which unquestionably would be the sanest and most healthy thing he could do—or he could work on her until it was no longer one-sided.

With luck, the weekend would be over before he came to a clear decision.

"DOES ANYONE KNOW what the word *tantra* means?" Edgar asked. "It means to weave, or extend."

Right, Savannah thought. She'd known the answer, but couldn't make her sluggish brain form the required definition—she was too busy mourning the loss of the great spiritual sex she'd never intended to have in the first place.

And not just any sex.

Sex with Knox.

Savannah knew she shouldn't feel like wailing with frustration. Shouldn't feel like whimpering with regret. But she did. He'd been sitting beside her for the past hour, and her palm had literally itched to reach over to shape her hand to the oh-so-clearly defined length of him. She wanted to stroke him, to feel him grow in her hand, grow inside her. Which was ludicrous. Knox had admitted that the sole reason he'd asked her to attend this sex workshop was because she happened to be the only woman he could bring along that he *wouldn't* want to sleep with. He'd admitted that he didn't find her the least bit attractive.

And that was a good thing, dammit. She didn't want him to be attracted to her. It would be nothing short of ruinous. She'd already dated a pretty prep-school playboy and he'd given her the old heave-ho the minute his parents had squawked their disapproval. As far as the Lyleses had been concerned, Savannah had been foster-care trash, not worthy of their precious pedigreed son.

There were a gazillion reasons why she shouldn't have hot, sweaty phenomenal sex with Knox. Savannah's insides grew warm and muddled at the mere implication of the act. Still, he was like Gib, he had a love-'em-and-leave-'em reputation, he was a co-worker... The list went on and on.

Yet none of them—or the combined total—could hold a candle to the ferocity of the attraction.

Every part of him that was male drew every part

her that was female. She yearned for him. Longed to have those big beautiful hands of his shaped around her breasts. That talented mouth tasting every mole, every freckle, everywhere that was white and everywhere that was pink.

And she wanted to touch him as well, wanted to slide her fingers over each and every perfectly formed sinew. Wanted to feel that powerful body unleashed with passion and, ultimately, sated with release. She sighed.

She just wanted.

Savannah swallowed another frustrated wail. She'd kept her distance, hadn't she? She'd even made herself dislike him, all in an effort to avoid this very predicament. All of that hard work for this beautiful mess.

Even if the talk of sex finally sparked some latent interest in him, he'd never be so pathetically unprofessional as to act upon it. For reasons Savannah didn't understand, this particular story was incredibly important to him. He'd coerced her into coming, after all. He'd never jeopardize the story, regardless of how much he might like to overthrow his traditional tastes and take her for a quick tumble between the sheets.

So she needed to put the whole idea out of her mind. She'd forget that damned kiss and pray they wouldn't have to participate in that madness again. She'd ignore the enormous penis draped across his thigh beneath that *kurta* and her own beaded nipples and moist sex and…

And, Savannah realized with mounting frustration, she'd undoubtedly end up masturbating the entire weekend, just like poor oversexed Chuck.

"Hey," Knox said as he gently nudged her in the side. "I thought I told you to take notes. You stopped at the genital chakra."

That seemed appropriate, Savannah thought. "Sorry," she mumbled.

"Don't worry about it. We've got to go over all of it and work on unblocking as many chakras as we can tonight for homework. At the end of this lesson we move on to building trust between partners and the art of erotic massage." Knox waggled his brows suggestively. "They have scented massage oil in the gift shop."

Six and a half feet of gloriously oiled, aroused male loomed in her mind's eye. "Great," she managed to deadpan. "You can rub it all over yourself."

Shaking his head, Knox tsked under his breath. "Now what could we possibly learn from that? How can we do this story justice without at least trying some of the techniques?"

She couldn't fault his reasoning, though that was her first impulse. Still, if they tried one, she'd want to try them all. Which meant it would be best to forgo the whole lot. "I suppose you should have thought of that before you hauled me to a sex workshop."

"Who said anything about having sex? It's just a massage. Are you planning on giving this story anything but your best objective opinion?"

Savannah bristled. "Of course not."

"Then it's a no-brainer," he said with a negligent shrug. "Tell you what, I'll go you one better and do you first. How does that sound?"

Like torture, Savannah thought. Delicious torture, but torture all the same. "Whatever." She gestured toward the Sheas. "They're about to conclude the lesson. Shut up and pay attention."

"In a few moments we'll take a short break, and then we'll move on to part one of our erotic massage lesson," Edgar said. "Before we stop, however, let's take a moment to quietly reflect and connect with our lovers."

Oh, hell, Savannah thought with a premonition of dread. That didn't sound good.

"Everyone please stand," Rupali instructed. "For some, this is a very difficult exercise, but Edgar and I didn't promise that this weekend would be easy. The level of intimacy we want our students to achieve requires that fears and inadequacies be set aside, that the true self be revealed."

Savannah resisted the urge to squirm. It was sounding worse.

"One of the simplest ways to do that is to maintain eye contact, to search your partner's eyes and reveal past hurts, regrets, happiness and love." Rupali paused and gauged the room's reaction to her words.

"In time, you will be able to look into your partner's eyes and see your *Imago,* or mirror image, reflected back at you. While you might be uncomfortable now, the longer you practice tantra, the more you strive for a more spiritual union, you will eventually learn to prize this very special connection."

Edgar set the timer on his watch. "Men, pull your women to you, so that their heart beats against your chest. So that you can feel the steady rhythm of her life force thumping against you."

Knox, damn him, didn't appear the least bit annoyed or uncomfortable by this new test as, smiling, he did as Edgar instructed and pulled her firmly up against the hard wall of his magnificent chest.

With a decidedly sick smile, Savannah's own heart threatened to pound right through her ribcage. In addition to feeling Knox's heartbeat, she felt the telltale ridge of his "wand of light" against her belly button and, to her eternal chagrin, her "sacred space" swiftly grew warm and wet. If he'd branded her with the damned thing, she couldn't have felt it more.

"Now, women, wrap your arms about your man's waist. Wrap him in your love. Let him see it." Edgar chuckled. "It's true men are visual creatures. They have to see to believe. Make him *believe.*"

"For the next ninety seconds," Rupali said, "we're going to stand together and gaze into each other's eyes. Blink if you must, but try to maintain eye contact. Don't look away and do not speak. Say it with your eyes, use your brow chakra to learn your lover's secrets. You may begin…now.''

Feeling utterly and completely ridiculous, not to mention incredibly uncomfortable, Savannah did as Rupali said and looked up into Knox's twinkling green eyes. Commiserating laughter lurked in that verdant gaze, Savannah noticed to her marginal relief. She quelled the desire to squirm. Her breasts had already tightened into hard little buds and if she moved as she wished to, she might not be able to stop. Pathetic, but true.

Knox's eyes were heavy lidded, with long, curling lashes. The green was pure, just flecked with lighter and darker hues, but no shades of brown commonly found in a color as dark as his. Some of the humor faded from his gaze and another indiscernible emotion took its place. Something heavy and intense and altogether sexy. Savannah pulled in an unsteady breath. She thought she saw a reciprocating heat, but knew that couldn't be the case. Simply wishful thinking on her part.

Still, the longer the stare went on—Jesus, who would have thought that a minute and a half would seem like a lifetime?—the more aroused she became. Her limbs had grown heavy and she'd transferred some of the weight by leaning more closely into him. She had the almost overpowering urge to lower her gaze to his lips, then let her own mouth follow that path.

If she lived to be one hundred, she didn't think she'd ever want to kiss a man more.

The desire was completely out of the realm of her limited experience. The pressing need built and built until the longing and weight of that heady stare seemed almost unbearable. Savannah felt herself sagging closer and closer to him and, though she knew better, she simply didn't possess the strength to stop it. If this didn't end soon, she'd—

"Time's up," Edgar called, and the group underneath the pavilion heaved a collective sigh. "Now kiss your lover, then we'll adjourn for a break."

A relief of another sort gripped Savannah and she eagerly met Knox's mouth as it descended hungrily to hers. The unmistakable—enormous—length of him nudged her navel and, rather than be alarmed, which would have been the intelligent reaction, Savannah merely smiled against his mouth and thought, *Oh, thank God, I'm not the only one, after all.*

Knox Webber could claim he wasn't attracted to her, but she'd just been presented with some hard evidence that proved otherwise.

Granted, men awoke with a hard-on, and could typically get it up for just about any woman. His reaction was likely due to part of the intense lesson and all the talk of genital chakras, but for this moment—*just this one*—she would pretend otherwise. Savannah generally avoided lying to herself at all costs, but surely this one little fib couldn't hurt. Right?

It's not like she'd ever be so cork-brained as to delude herself into thinking that he felt anything but mild disdain toward her. She may have been able to turn on his "wand of light," but when it came to generating any real interest, the lights were off and no one was home.

6

KNOX STARED DOWN into Savannah's ice-blue gaze and the effect of that cool stare left him anything but chilly. The first fifteen to twenty seconds of their so-called exercise she'd been adorably shy, utterly miserable and obviously so far out of her comfort zone he'd found himself smiling to reassure her.

Knox was a man who always questioned everything—that insatiable curiosity had prompted his career choice. Savannah's reaction to this particular test raised many questions, the most pressing of which was, who or what had happened to her to make her so damned distrustful? Because something definitely had.

At some point in her life, or perhaps repeatedly, she'd been deeply hurt. Betrayed. The knowledge made his mind momentarily go black with rage and the unreasonable urge to right old wrongs for her, heal old hurts.

How could he have been so blind? He could see the truth now, hovering beneath the bravado, beneath the sarcasm, and he wondered again how he'd ever missed it in the first place. Knox mentally snorted.

Hell, he knew how. She'd never let him close enough. Never let anyone close enough, for that matter.

To be honest, Knox hadn't been thrilled with the prospect of another test, but when Edgar had instructed them to wrap their arms about their woman, Knox had grown decidedly more enthusiastic about the lesson. He'd watched her emotions flash like neon signs through her eyes and the one that finally managed to completely undo him was passion.

Those cool blue eyes had rapidly warmed until they glowed like a blue flame. A resulting heat swept him from the top of his head to the tips of his bare toes. His heart had begun to pound, sending the blood that much faster to his throbbing groin. The hairs on his arms prickled and the nudge he normally associated with work began an insistent jab.

As the seconds ticked by, Savannah gravitated closer and closer to him until he could feel her budded nipples against his chest. Could feel the rhythmic beating of her heart as the Sheas had instructed. Feeling that rapid, steady beat did have a curious effect on him, Knox conceded. He'd never thought much about his heart, other than being aware that it pumped his blood, but something about feeling hers made him want to pull an Alfalfa, cancel his membership in the He-Man-Woman-Hater's Club and beat his chest and roar. He'd made her heart pound. Him. What a turn-on.

Knowing that she was naked underneath that

gown, that nothing more than a thin wisp of cotton separated his skin from hers tortured him, made his hands itch to feel her through the fabric. Knox pulled in a shaky breath and quelled the almost overwhelming urge to back her onto the picnic table, hike up that *kurta* and bury himself into the slick velvet heat of her body. Piston in and out of her until their simultaneous cries of release rent the air and he spilled his seed deep into the tight glove of her body.

Clearly he'd lost his mind, to be having such thoughts about Savannah. They were here to do a job, nothing more, and yet he'd give everything he owned right now just to kiss her. Just to taste her. Just one small—

"Time's up," Edgar called. "Now kiss your lover and we'll adjourn for a break."

Kiss your lover…

Knox groaned with giddy relief and quickly lowered his mouth to hers. To his immense delight, Savannah met him halfway and her mouth clung to his, fed greedily until nothing existed but the feel of her against him, the exquisite taste of her on his tongue.

What the kiss lacked in finesse it more than made up for with passion. She lashed her arms about his neck and all but crawled up his body to get closer, ran her hands all over him, cupped his ass and growled her approval right into his mouth. She eagerly explored his mouth, slid her tongue around his, tasted the fleshy part of his lips. She nibbled and sucked, and it occurred to Knox that, at some point in the near future, he'd like to have her do the same thing to his rod. She wriggled and writhed, alternately sighed and purred with pleasure and each little note of praise caused *both* of his heads to swell, particularly the one below his waist. It jutted impatiently against her.

He might as well have jabbed her with a hot poker, for the way she abruptly tore her mouth from his and stepped back. With a frustrated huff, she looked up and glared at him. "Good grief, Knox," she hissed. "You're supposed to be impotent. Could you at least try to stay in character?"

Knox blinked, astounded. In character? She'd been acting? Again?

Savannah looked down at the front of his tented *kurta*. Her lips curled into that oh-so-familiar mocking smile. "Well, at least the premature ejaculator part looks real. You've got a huge wet spot on the front of your dress."

Mortified, Knox felt a blush creep up his neck. "It's not a dress," he ground out.

Luckily the rest of the class had moved toward the refreshment table, which had been set up on the lawn. Only the Sheas lagged behind. To his further humiliation, the two of them noticed the evidence of his mortification and smiled knowingly.

"I see you've made progress already," Edgar said. "Embrace your healing, Knox," Edgar encouraged with a fatherly clap on the shoulder. "There's no shame in flaunting your seed. There is power in pro-creation.''

Rupali gestured toward Savannah's pearled nip-ples. ''Likewise, Barbie,'' she said mistily. ''You should be proud of your puckered breasts. They await your lover's kiss with tight invitation. Someday the milk of life will pour from those twin orbs. Flaunt them, as Edgar said.'' She smiled serenely, cupped her own breasts reverently. ''Embrace your feminin-ity. Be proud of being a woman.''

Having blushed to the roots of her hair, Savannah managed a strained smile and nodded mutely. The Sheas threaded their fingers together and walked away, presumably to offer more little bits of tantric wisdom to other students.

Enjoying her discomfort, Knox smiled. ''I see I'm not the only one who had a hard time staying in character.''

Savannah closed her notebook and clipped her pen to the front. She gave him a blank look. ''I'm sorry, what?''

''Staying in character,'' he repeated. ''I'm not the only one who got hard.'' He stared pointedly at her breasts.

She gave him a frosty glare and her lips formed a withering smirk. ''I was cold, you moron. What's your excuse?''

His eyes narrowed. ''Your tongue was in my mouth.''

''And less of yours was in mine this time. Well

done, Knox. It's nice to know I'm not going to be choking on yours the entire weekend.''

No one could deliver a backhanded compliment quite like Savannah. Knox ignored the gibe and refused to let her change the subject. "You were not cold. You were hot, *damn hot,* and I could feel you.''

"How could you not feel me?" she asked, her voice climbing. "Edgar made us practically crawl into each other's *kurta*s. Basic physiological fact, Knox. The human body's normal temperature is ninety-eight-point-six degrees. That's hot and that's what you felt. End of story.''

The hell it was, Knox thought, but whatever. He didn't know what sort of insanity was eating at his brain to make him want to force her into admitting that something had happened between them. She was right to play it down. Keep it professional. He'd play it her way.

Or maybe not.

Knox shoved a hand through his hair and sighed heavily. "You're right. It is a little chilly out here today." Another lie. It was a pleasant seventy, at least.

Her gaze flew to his. "I'm right?" she asked, then nodded emphatically. "Right. Of course, I am.''

Knox suppressed a triumphant smile. So it was okay for her to lie about the attraction and make him feel like a class-A jackass, but apparently she didn't like wearing the shoe on the other foot.

Women, Knox thought. Had the Lord ever made a

more fickle creature? This was a prime example of why he'd never decided to keep one around on a permanent basis. They said yes when they meant no, and no when they meant yes. Who needed the grief? The confusion? Knox kept in touch with a select few women who knew him and knew the drill. Great date, great conversation, great sex. No strings. Everybody went home happy.

He would reluctantly admit that at times he longed for a deeper relationship, something more like his parents had. But so far he hadn't found anybody he'd want to spend a solid week with, much less the rest of his life. He was too preoccupied with the present to contemplate the future, at any rate.

Savannah could lie to him—and probably herself—all she wanted, but Knox knew the truth. Cold, hell. She'd been hot for him. If that kiss had been any hotter, the two of them would have surely gone up in flames. He'd never been so turned on from a mere kiss. Savannah Reeves had one talented mouth and it made Knox wonder just what other hidden abilities she possessed, and made him all the more determined to find out.

Without question, this unplanned, unwanted attraction posed many problems. For instance, how were they supposed to get through the rest of the weekend without going insane with lust? If he and Savannah detonated with heat over a couple of kisses, what would happen when they moved on to erotic massage, to *Love His Lingam,* and *Sacred*

Goddess Stimulation? What would happen on Sunday night, when the rest of the class was putting all their new know-how into practice? Furthermore, and more important, how on earth would he be able to maintain the focus needed to pull together an objective story if all he could think about was how much he wanted to plant himself between her thighs?

The two of them locked in various depraved positions flitted rapid fire through Knox's mind—his own personal little porn show where he and Savannah starred in hedonistic orgasmic splendor. He'd read the *Kama Sutra.* In his mind's eye Knox had her all but standing on her head when Savannah abruptly tapped him on the arm.

"Pay attention," she whispered. "They're about to resume the lecture."

Knox started, then moved to sit back down at their table. Savannah took her place beside him and, thankfully, began to take notes while Edgar and Rupali lectured on the importance of trust and announced that they would be doing a couple more little exercises before the lesson concluded for the day. They would have a great deal of "homework" this first night and would be provided ample time to get it all done.

In addition, all evening meals would be served in their rooms, with special instructions on how to enjoy them. Rupali and Edgar shared a secret smile that inspired equal parts curiosity and apprehension.

Great, Knox thought, as a wave of trepidation and anticipation washed over him. As if he didn't have enough to worry about.

SAVANNAH DIDN'T KNOW what was worse—attending the nerve-racking classes, or being alone with Knox. By the time they'd finished that last trust exercise, which she'd failed miserably at and which had consequently been added to their considerable homework, Savannah's raw nerves had been ready to snap. She'd tried to play off that second kiss with Knox, but it hadn't worked. Not by any stretch of the imagination.

He'd known, damn him.

She could see it in the cocky tilt of his head and the even cockier curve of his splendid lips. As if that gigantic ego of his needed another reason to swell, Savannah thought derisively. Even if he hadn't known then, he would have by the end of that lesson. Edgar and Rupali were firm believers in the oral chakra and the powers of kissing. According to Edgar and Rupali, the act taught patience to the men and promoted sexual harmony for the women. They'd had them necking at the end of each additional test, as well as the conclusion of the lecture. To her helpless joy and consternation, she and Knox had practically stayed in a perpetual lip-lock the rest of the afternoon.

If that hadn't been enough to shake her generally stalwart fortitude, there had been the *homework*.

When they'd returned to their room this afternoon,

they'd found several things awaiting them. Fresh *kur-tas*, a new booklet that gave detailed information on how to unblock each of the chakras—and there was a lot more to it than even Savannah had realized—as well as instructions which had to be followed to the letter for the rest of the evening.

They were supposed to begin their evening with a shared bath.

Knox, damn him, had raised a hopeful eyebrow at this news, but Savannah had quickly disabused him of that notion.

The shared bath had also come with a few handy tips on how to enhance intimacy, like soaping your lover's body, washing each other's hair and light genital massage, along with the stern reminder that intercourse was forbidden.

Savannah had to admit that it sounded absolutely wonderful. That huge sunken marble tub might as well have had *Do It Here* written on little sticky notes scattered all over it—on the recessed steps, the back, the front and the side. It was a veritable Garden of Eden.

Furthermore, the idea of Knox's hands, slick with soap and hot water sliding all over her body was enough to send her heart rate into warp speed. Her palms actually tingled when she thought about giving him the same treatment, smoothing her own hands over the intriguing masculine landscape of his magnificent form. Over that incredible ass she'd finally gotten her greedy little hands on this afternoon. Honestly, she'd almost climaxed from the thrill of it.

She'd said no to the bath when she'd wanted to say yes, but to do anything different would have been a complete overthrow of her principles.

One of them had to remain focused and, though he'd claimed he'd brought her here because he didn't find her attractive, apparently Knox's primitive base instincts had overridden her general lack of appeal because, since that second kiss, he'd made absolutely no attempt to hold back.

In fact, Savannah grimly suspected he was goading her on purpose, arousing her for the pure sport of it. Because he knew he could, the bastard.

She had no idea how she should combat such an attack, but had finally decided that if he didn't back off soon, she'd launch an offensive of her own. If he continued to play with her and use her own reckless desire against her, Savannah would begin a similar assault upon his weakened libido and she'd have him begging for mercy.

While she'd lacked confidence in just about every other aspect of her life, there were two areas in which she knew she excelled. She was a damn fine journalist and, when she was with someone she trusted without question, a sadly rare occurrence, she was one hell of a lover.

Savannah might not have had as many partners as Knox, but it wasn't so much the quantity as the quality, and she'd never failed to satisfy a man in the bedroom. Savannah enjoyed sex, was very uninhibited, and those qualities came through in her performance. In fact, she'd never had bad sex. If her partner didn't do it for her, she'd simply roll him over and take care of matters herself. Savannah grinned. What man didn't like that?

There was something so elemental, so raw and intense when it came to sex. Any pent-up emotion could be vented, exorcised, and the simple act made her feel more human, more connected, than any other.

And it had been too long, Savannah thought with a despondent sigh. She imagined the combined factors of sexual deprivation and Knox were the reason she was so rabidly horny now. She hadn't made love since Gib.

Initially she'd been too hurt to even consider building a relationship with another man. Then once she'd gotten past that point, her career had begun to take off and there simply hadn't been time.

Savannah didn't do casual sex. In addition to it not being safe, there was nothing casual about sharing your body with another person. At least, not for her. Her character had not been formed for that increasingly popular pastime and she'd just as soon go without.

Until now.

Now she'd become the proverbial bitch in heat. She wanted Knox—had always wanted Knox—but had managed to keep the attraction under control by avoiding him as much as possible and by generally striving to be the most unpleasant person on the face of the planet anytime he was around.

But she couldn't do that now. They were here, sharing a room, and while he might sound like Gib, and occasionally act like Gib, Savannah knew her desire to dislike Knox had been more of a defense mechanism than anything else. Just a way to prevent herself from liking him because she didn't want to make the same mistake twice.

Knox chose that particular moment to open the bathroom door. Scented steam billowed from behind him as he strolled in all his almost-naked glory to the bed to retrieve his clean *kurta*. He'd anchored a bath sheet loosely about his waist and a few small droplets of water skidded down the bumpy planes of his ridged abdomen. An inverted triangle of dark brown hair dusted his chest and arrowed into a slim line that bisected that washboard abdomen and disappeared beneath the line of his towel.

His muscular legs and arms were covered in the same smattering of hair, and had it continued around to his back like a pelt, Savannah might have stood a prayer of not melting into a puddle of panting female at the mere sight of his practically naked body.

But it didn't.

He was perfect, damn him, and she hungered for him as if she hadn't eaten in weeks and he were a decadent slab of prime rib.

She swallowed and did her best to rid her expression of any lingering lust. ''You've been in there forever. I-is there any hot water left?'' She strove for a put-out tone, but the sound was more breathless than irritated.

''Yeah,'' he said distractedly. His brow puckered and he lifted the *kurta* from the bed, tossed it aside and glanced at the floor. He bent over and checked beneath the bed skirt, and then paused, seemingly at a loss. He settled his hands at his hips, causing every well-formed muscle to ripple invitingly. Particularly his pecs. Savannah had always been a sucker for a gorgeous set of pecs.

''Have you lost something?'' Savannah asked.

''Yeah. My underwear. Have you seen them?''

He knew perfectly well that they weren't allowed to wear any underwear. He was simply trying to annoy her, to remind her that he wouldn't be wearing any. Savannah glanced to the prominent bulge beneath his towel and sighed. As if she'd need reminding.

''No, sorry. I haven't.'' She smiled sweetly. ''I seem to have lost mine as well. While you're looking for yours, why don't you be a dear and look for mine, too?''

Surprised, his patently perplexed expression vanished and he slowly looked up. A playful gleam suddenly lit his gaze. ''Sure. I'd be happy to. Er…wanna tell me what they look like?''

Uh-oh. This wasn't exactly the scenario she'd hoped for. For some reason, she'd thought he'd feign sudden inspiration and laughingly remember the no-undergarment rule. She should have known better. He rarely resisted a challenge.

Still Knox needed to know whom he was dealing with, and this seemed to be as good a way as any to teach him, Savannah decided, warming to her tact.

"They're black silk. There's not much to them, barely a scrap of fabric. You might have a hard time finding them."

Knox's eyes darkened and she watched the muscles in his throat work as he swallowed. Feeling decidedly triumphant, Savannah stood and started toward the bathroom.

"Black silk, eh?" Knox said, his voice somewhat rusty. "Are there, uh, any distinguishing features? Anything that would make them more recognizable?"

Savannah paused with her hand on the doorknob and turned around. Her amused you're-playing-with-fire gaze met his and held it. "Yeah. They're thong underwear. Black lace with little black pearls."

Silence thundered between them at this glib description, then, his eyes never leaving hers, Knox casually dropped his towel. The sheer power—utter perfection and beauty—of his nude body rooted Savannah to the floor.

Seeing an outline of his penis hadn't prepared her for the actual article. He was only semiaroused, yet huge and proud—as he most certainly had every right to be—and every cell in her body responded to the blatantly virile part of him. She couldn't have looked away if she'd wanted to.

Knox picked up the *kurta* and, with a sexy grin, said, "Pity we can't wear underwear this weekend. I'd love to get a peek at that particular pair of panties. If you find them, why don't you show them to me?" He paused and his voice lowered to a more intimate level, sending a chorus of shivers down her spine. "I'll bet you look great in them."

Savannah determinedly ignored her initial impulse, which was to walk across the room, drop to her knees and suck him dry. Another talent of hers, if she did say so herself.

However, she would not let him win this little scene.

She'd been prepared for a battle royal and the smug devil thought he'd gotten the better of her with this little display. He'd best think again. She'd seen a dick before. Granted not one as splendidly formed as his, but she was familiar enough with the male anatomy not to look like the shocked little virgin he apparently expected.

Savannah shot him a confident grin. "Not nearly as good as I look *out* of them."

With an exaggerated swing of her hips, she sauntered into the bathroom and shut the door.

Then she ran her bath, settled into the hot fragrant water, and imagined a naked Knox on the other side of the door...imagined everything she'd ever wanted to do with him and to him and everything she'd ever wanted him to do to her....

With a frustrated groan of the hopelessly, futilely aroused, she spread her thighs, parted her curls and, with a whimper of satisfaction...pulled a Chuck.

7
_____

SAVANNAH APPEARED considerably less tense after her bath, Knox noted. Her movements were languid, leisurely and there was something altogether relaxed about her. She'd towel-dried her hair and the blue-black locks curled madly around her face, sprouting up in chaotic disarray all over her head like little question marks. She looked charmingly unkempt as always. He grinned. Even wet, she looked messy. She'd removed her makeup and her pale skin glowed with health and vitality. Her cheeks held a rosy hue and that plump bottom lip looked a little swollen, as though she'd been chewing on it.

Knox felt his eyes narrow and suspiciously considered her once more.

Relaxed, rosy and a swollen bottom lip. She'd obviously had more than a bath, Knox realized, astonished. He knew perfectly well what a woman looked like after release and clearly, by the sated look of her, she'd had a damn good one. He didn't know whether to be irritated or pleased. Irritated because he would have gladly taken care of her—would have loved to have brought her to climax—or pleased because she'd been so hot for him she'd had to take care of herself.

He decided to be pleased and covertly considered her once more. It was a rare woman who felt comfortable enough with her body to tend to her own needs. In his experience, women loved to be touched but didn't necessarily enjoy touching themselves. Clearly Savannah didn't suffer from any such inhibition. A snake of heat writhed through his belly at the thought. But that's the kind of woman she was. She would never rely solely on a man to get what she wanted, Knox thought with reluctant admiration. She had to be the most self-reliant woman he'd ever known.

Once again Knox wondered about her past. Just who exactly was Savannah Reeves? What had made her so independent, so determined to be an island unto herself? What had made her into this distrustful, autonomic loner? He knew absolutely nothing about her, he realized. Where she'd grown up, whether or not she had any brothers and sisters—nothing.

What was *her* story? he wondered, and felt a familiar nudge. Knox didn't know, but he firmly intended to find out before this weekend was up. Right now, however, they had other issues to deal with.

Like dinner.

A wonderful spread complete with all the romantic trimmings had arrived just moments before she'd walked out of the bathroom and distracted him. Knox had had a moment to peruse the instructions and he strongly suspected that Savannah would not enjoy their next assignment.

Which meant he wouldn't either because he would starve.

"Did you enjoy your bath?" Knox asked lightly.

Savannah pilfered through her toiletries until she located a bottle of moisturizer, uncapped the lid and poured a little into the palm of her hand, then began to massage the cream onto her face and neck. "Immensely," she all but sighed. "That's a great tub."

"Yeah, it is," he agreed, imagining her naked in it, her little fingers nestled in her curls and her head thrown back in orgasmic wonder.

Savannah's gaze lit upon the dining cart and a smile bloomed on her slightly swollen lips. "Oh, good. The food's here. I'm *starving*."

Knox smiled knowingly. He'd just bet she was. Having a bone-melting climax typically did that to a person. Still, he had a feeling she was about to lose her appetite.

Savannah made her way across the room and inspected their meal. She took a deep breath, savoring the hickory scent of grilled steak tips with sautéed mushrooms, au gratin potatoes and steamed asparagus. "Oh, this looks heavenly," she groaned with pleasure.

Wondering how long it would take her to figure out what was wrong with the *heavenly* meal, Knox started to count. *One…*

She moved things around on the tray. "I love steak. And this looks wonderful."

Two...

"And I haven't had it in a long time. What a treat." Her brow wrinkled. "Hey, where's the—"

Three.

"—silverware?"

"There isn't any."

Her head jerked up and her delighted expression vanished. "What?"

"There isn't any," Knox repeated. He rattled the instructions for their meal in his hand meaningfully. "Here're our instructions. Would you like to read them yourself or would you rather I summarize them for you?"

Predictably, Savannah marched across and the room and snatched the sheet from his hand. "I'll read them myself, thank you."

Three beats passed before she'd gotten past the mystical mumbo jumbo and found out why they didn't have any utensils. Her outraged gasp sounded, and then she glared at Knox as though it were *his* fault. As though this were his idea. Hell, he hadn't made the rules.

"Feed each other?" she growled with a lethally icy look. "It's not enough that you've hauled me across the country to this godforsaken workshop, that I've had your tongue down my throat all blessed day, and now—*now*—if I want to have anything to eat it has to come from your fingers?" she asked incredulously. Those chilly blue eyes blasted him with another arctic look. She crossed her arms over her chest and, with a grim disbelieving look, she shook her head. "This is insane and is *so* not going to happen."

Knox shrugged. "I thought it sounded fun."

She snorted. "You would."

"And I'm hungry."

She hugged her arms closer around her middle and gazed longingly at the tray. "I was."

Knox paused, then said, "I agree that the shared bath was an unreasonable expectation, one I would have done had you been willing. But surely we could at least make an effort with this exercise." He lifted a shoulder. "Like you said, we've been kissing all day. How could me feeding you be any more personal? We've got to participate in as many of these exercises as we comfortably can to lend credibility to our story, to do our best work. What's the big deal?"

Indecision flashed in her eyes. She fidgeted and glanced back at the dining cart with another woebegone look. He knew he had her when her stomach rumbled. Knox suppressed a triumphant grin.

"Oh, all right," she finally relented. "But no funny stuff, Knox. I'm hungry. I want to eat, unblock a few chakras and go to bed."

Savannah pivoted, stalked back to the dining cart and swiftly began to move the plates and glasses onto the table. She didn't bother with the fresh-cut flowers and bent over and extinguished the candle with a determined breath.

Knox waited until she'd finished arranging things to her satisfaction and then joined her at the table. "What would you like to start with?"

"Oh, no," she said with a calculating grin. "I'll feed you a bite first, that way you'll understand exactly how I want you to feed me."

Knox knew he was going to enjoy this too much not to be at least a little accommodating. He nodded. "Fine."

Her cheeks puffed as she exhaled mightily. "So, what do you want to start with?"

"Steak."

Savannah picked up a steak tip. "Okay. Open up."

Knox did. Her fingers stopped just shy of his lips and she tossed it into his mouth so hard it bounced off the back of his throat and almost back out of his mouth. Knox managed to hang on to it and, smiling at her ingenuity, chewed the tasty morsel. This was not going as he'd planned. Next she'd be catapulting potatoes into his mouth and throwing asparagus at him like javelins.

And she looked so damned pleased with herself, Knox thought. Those clear blue orbs sparkled with unrepentant laughter.

Knox finally swallowed, cleared his throat and gave her a droll look. "I'll need to see you balance a ball on your nose before I feed you like a seal."

Tongue in cheek, her lips twitched. "I didn't mean to throw it quite s-so hard."

"Right." It was his turn. He selected a steak tip and held it up for her inspection. "Ready?"

She nodded and hesitantly opened her mouth. Knox fed her the bite without incident and was careful not to let his fingers linger. He wanted her at ease, not guarded. This, too, was another trust builder and Savannah so desperately needed to learn to trust someone.

Knox had decided that person should be him.

He didn't know when he'd come to the decision or, for that matter, even why. But he wanted to be worthy of her trust. Wanted to be the person who brought her out of her isolated existence. He supposed he'd fully realized the extent of her distrustful nature this afternoon when they'd been practicing another faith-building exercise. It should have been simple. All Savannah had to do was stand in front of him, fall backward and allow Knox to catch her.

She couldn't do it.

Just as she'd start to fall backward, she'd abruptly stop and right herself. They practiced over and over again. But for all that work, she still hadn't been able to trust him enough to catch her. As a result, they were supposed to practice that exercise tonight, too. An idea occurred to him.

"Why don't we look at that chakra homework while we're eating dinner?" he asked.

Savannah nodded. "That's a good idea. Don't touch anything. I'll get the book."

She double-timed it back and opened the volume to the appropriate page. "Give me another bite of steak, would you?" she said as she perused the page.

She absently opened her mouth for three more bites before Knox finally laughed and said, "Hey, what about me?"

Distracted, Savannah picked up a bite of steak and placed it on his tongue, then unwittingly licked her fingers.

His dick jerked beneath the *kurta*.

"Okay," she said. "We'll pass this book back and forth. I'll start with the first one, which is the perineum chakra or root chakra," she said. "Then you can take—"

"Er…why don't we skip that one?" Knox suggested. He knew all he needed to know about that particular chakra.

"Consider the story, tight-ass," she said with an infuriating little grin. "We'd hate to mislead our readers by not having all the facts."

"I'm not a tight-ass," Knox growled.

She grinned. "Hit a nerve, did I?"

"I'm driven. That doesn't make me a tight-ass— it makes me a professional."

She tsked under her breath. "A professional wouldn't balk at learning about his root chakra… unless he was a tight-ass."

Knox heaved a mighty sigh. "Fine. Gimme some potatoes, would you?"

Savannah tensed but loaded the requested side dish onto a couple of fingers and gave him a bite. Knox wrapped his lips around her fingers, sucked the potatoes off and sighed with satisfaction. "Mmm," he groaned. "Those are good. Want some?" he asked innocently.

Her shoulders rounded and she shot him a put-upon look. "Oh, hell. Why not? Yes," she sighed. "I do."

Knox curved a couple of fingers and scooped up a generous bite and ladled it into her mouth. Her eyes rounded with delighted wonder. "Oh," she said thickly. And then, "Ohh, these are great. More, more."

Laughing, Knox scooped up another helping and she wasn't so quick to avoid his fingers this time. She actually licked off a hunk of cheese that she'd missed on the first go around from his index finger. The slide of that tongue felt great and it didn't take much imagination to picture her lips wrapped around another prominent part of his anatomy. Still, she'd just begun to marginally relax, so Knox tried to appear unaffected.

He nodded to his plate. "How about letting me try that asparagus?"

"Sure." She picked up a spear and fed it to him. "What do you think? Is it good, or should we stick with the steak and potatoes?"

Swallowing, Knox nodded. "It's good, too. Hell, all of it's good." He inspected the table. "What did we get for dessert?"

Savannah peeked beneath a couple of smaller lids and her eyes all but rolled back in her head. A purr of delight emanated from her throat. "Strawberries and fresh cream. Forget the chakras. Let's eat. We can study later."

"Agreed."

Without further discussion, they promptly began to feed each other. Savannah loaded her fingers while sucking her bites from his and vice versa. Knox made sure that he got a suggestive lick in every third or fourth bite, but rather than giving him a frosty glare, Savannah eventually began to take it as a challenge. Sucking particularly hard one time, giving a clever flick of her facile tongue another. She was so damned competitive, she didn't intend for him ever to get the upper hand. Big surprise there, Knox thought. She took everything as a challenge and he seemed to be her favorite opponent.

Knox tolerated the main course with amazing restraint, but began to have a problem when they moved on to dessert. Watching Savannah's lips pucker around a strawberry, watching her lick the cream from his finger and around her mouth without having a screaming orgasm was proving to be damned difficult. To be honest, he didn't particularly like strawberries, but kept eating them anyway so that he could taste her fingers. He'd never imagined that feeding someone, or being fed, could be so damned erotic.

But it was.

And they'd get to repeat the whole process tomorrow night, and the next.

Savannah polished off the last strawberry with a deep sigh of satisfaction. Her tongue made a slow lap around her lips, making sure that she'd savored every bit of the arousing dessert. "That," she said meaningfully, "was excellent."

Without a doubt, Knox thought. He seriously doubted he'd ever eat again without thinking about this experience. Gave a whole new meaning to the term finger foods.

Savannah stood, placed her palms on the small of her back and stretched. *Newton's Third Law: For every action there is an equal and opposite reaction.* For reasons that escaped him, this was the thought that tripped through his head as Savannah's naked breasts were pushed up and against the thin fabric of her gown. He longed to taste her through the fabric, to draw the crown of that creamy breast into his mouth.

Savannah finally relaxed. "I'll wheel this dining cart out into the hall, then we'll get started on our chakra lessons."

"Fine." Knox lay down at the foot of the bed.

Her step faltered on her return trip to the table. "What are you doing?"

He gestured to the bedside lamps. "Better lighting."

"Right." She smirked.

Oh, hell. One step forward, two steps back. She didn't drop her guard for anything. "You can lean against the headboard," Knox told her. "We'll be more comfortable."

"There is that. You'll need to be comfortable when we unblock your perineum chakra."

"My perineum chakra isn't blocked," Knox said through gritted teeth.

"We'll see," she said maddeningly.

Savannah retrieved the book, then did as Knox suggested and settled herself against the headboard of the bed. The bedside light cast part of her face in shadow and the other in stark relief. The pure white gown practically glowed, giving her an almost ethereal appearance. Knox swallowed as an unfamiliar emotion clogged his throat. If he'd ever seen a more beautiful woman, he couldn't recall.

"Okay," she sighed. "Let's get down to business." She read for a moment and then her laughing gaze tangled with his. "According to this, the root chakra deals with the desire to own and possess. People who have difficulty expressing themselves, who limit spontaneity, and are inflexible are generally tense in this chakra." She gave him a pointed look. "In short, they are tight-asses. Like you." She frowned innocently. "Do you have a problem with hemorrhoids, Knox?"

His lips twisted into a sardonic smile. "Right now, you're the only pain in my ass."

She laughed—actually laughed out load, a femininely melodious sound. He'd worked with her for over a year and had never heard her more than chuckle briefly. Another breakthrough, Knox decided, irrationally pleased with himself.

"In order to unblock this chakra, you're supposed to insert your finger into your lover's *rosebud* and—"

Knox felt his butt draw up again. "*What?* What's a rosebud?"

She grinned evilly. "It's tantric slang for asshole."

"Nobody is going to insert anything into my rosebud," Knox said flatly.

"It won't bloom," Savannah warned.

"Good."

Wearing a wicked smile, she shrugged. "Okay, for the sake of our respective rosebuds, let's just assume that neither one of us is blocked in the root chakra."

Knox felt his ass relax. "That'll work for me."

Savannah read on for a moment, then looked up. "Okay, we're supposed to align our chakras, express our love—"

Knox sat up. "Align? Did you say align?"

"Yes."

He smiled triumphantly. "And isn't that what I told you we were supposed to do in the first place?"

Savannah gazed at him. "You might have," she admitted hesitantly.

He collapsed onto the bed once more. "I knew it. I knew we were supposed to align something, by God."

She heaved an exasperated sigh. "You don't align your chakras until you unblock them. We've unblocked our root chakra. Now we align, express our love, and chant *lam*."

Savannah set the book aside, moved away from the headboard and lay down in front of Knox. "We're aligned. Now chant."

Knox frowned. "You call this aligned? Shouldn't you be closer?" He gestured to the thirty-six inches that yawned between them.

"This'll do."

Knox shook his head doubtfully, snaked an arm around her waist and tugged her toward him. He fitted her snugly up next to his body and growled low in his throat. "Now *this* is aligned."

She looked up at him and twin devils danced in her eyes. She batted her lashes. "Express your love, Knox."

Knox grinned. "I love your ass."

Another laugh bubbled up, making her shake against him. She smelled like strawberries and cream and apple lotion, and she felt utterly incredible in his arms. Lust licked at his veins, stirred in his loins.

"That'll do," she finally replied. "Let's chant. *Laaaammmmmm. Laaaammmmmm.*"

Knox made a halfhearted attempt but couldn't continue. The absolute absurdity of it hit him and he'd begun to laugh and couldn't stop. "Can you believe that right now, while we're lying here, people in this house are having their r-rosebuds digitally probed and are chanting this stuff?"

Savannah giggled. "And Chuck's probably whacking off."

Knox guffawed until his sides hurt, then rolled over onto his back and smoothed his hair off his forehead. He blew out a breath. "Because they think that this is going to cure them, that this tantric stuff is going to fix whatever is wrong with their lives."

Savannah's chuckled tittered out. "It's kind of sad, huh?"

"Yeah," Knox admitted solemnly. "It really is."

"If it doesn't work, we'll report it," she said at last. "That's what we do."

"I know."

"I'm looking forward to writing this story," she admitted, much to his surprise.

"*We're* writing," Knox felt compelled to point out. "*We're* writing this story."

"About that…" She winced. "Just exactly how are we supposed to do this story? I've always worked alone—I've never collaborated on an article before."

"Neither have I," Knox confessed. "I suppose we should just toss out ideas until the right one fits and go from there."

"What if we don't agree? What if you don't like my ideas and I don't like yours? Then what?"

He shot her a look. "Sounds like you've already made up your mind to hate my ideas."

She grinned. "Well, of course."

Another laugh rumbled from his chest. "Don't hold back, Savannah. Tell me how you really feel." Knox sighed. "I don't know. Let's just cross that bridge when we come to it. We're still a long way from putting pen to paper."

Savannah's breath left her in a small whoosh and she pulled away from him and sat up. "I don't know about you, but I'm tired and don't feel like having anything else unblocked and aligned tonight."

"Nah, me neither."

Knox sat up as well. He snagged a pillow from the bed and found a spare blanket in the chest of drawers. Sleeping on the floor didn't appeal to him whatsoever, but he'd made a great deal of progress with Savannah tonight and he didn't want to jeopardize it by begging for a spot in the bed. He fixed his pallet on top of the floor pillows and gingerly lowered himself onto the lumpy makeshift bed.

"G'night, Knox," Savannah murmured.

He smiled and glanced up at her. "Night." *See, he mentally telegraphed to her, see how damned sweet I can be?* She turned off the light, plunging the room into darkness.

He heard Savannah settle in and sigh with satisfaction. Knox twisted and turned, fluffed and flattened pillows. Hell, he'd be better off sleeping in the damned bathtub, he decided, after several failed attempts to get comfortable. He groaned miserably and rolled over again, this time cracking his elbow painfully against the wall.

Savannah heaved a beleaguered breath. "Oh, for pity's sake, Knox, just get in the bed."

He stilled. "Really?"

"Yes," she huffed. "I suppose if I can kiss you all day and eat from your fingers, I can stand to have you sleep beside me. Just stay on your side and keep your hands to yourself."

Knox happily hoisted himself from the lumpy pillows, trotted over to the bed and slid under the covers. He thought he heard Savannah whimper when his weight shifted the mattress.

"Are you all right?" he asked.

He felt her move onto her back. "I'm fine." She paused. "Look, Knox, I'm used to sleeping alone, so I generally hog the whole bed. If I roll onto you, or crowd you, just shove me back onto my own side."

"Sure," he said, mildly perplexed. Was she a thrasher or something? he wondered. "I'm used to sleeping alone, too. You do the same for me."

"I will." Something ominous lurked in her tone.

Knox smiled. "G'night, Vannah."

She rolled onto her side once more, giving him her back. "It's *Savannah*," she growled. "Now shut up so that I can get come sleep."

There's my girl, Knox thought with a sleepy smile. His bitch was back. Funny, but she didn't sound so tough anymore. Knox heard the fear and vulnerability behind the surly attitude. What would it take, he wondered, to make her lose that edge? To strip away the destructive defenses and build her back up with a more productive emotion?

Knox didn't know, but he was grimly determined to find out.

8

SAVANNAH AWOKE early in the exact position she'd feared she would—draped all over Knox.

Presently her cheek lay cuddled up to his sinewy shoulder, her arm was anchored around his lean waist and she'd slung a thigh over his delectable rear. Jeez, even in her sleep she couldn't resist him. Savannah knew that she should carefully extricate herself from him before he woke up and found her melted all over him, but she couldn't summon the necessary actions to move away just yet.

He felt...nice.

His big, warm body threw off a heat like a blast furnace, chasing away the early morning chill. She breathed in a hint of woodsy aftershave and male, and the particular essence that was simply Knox, and felt a twine of heat curl though her belly, lick her nipples and settle in her sex.

Savannah was accustomed to waking up hungry, but the appetite that plagued her this morning wouldn't be satisfied with a mere muffin and a cup of coffee. She wanted an order of Knox with hot, sweaty sex on the side.

On the side of the bed.

On the side of the tub.

Her side.

His side.

Inside or outside.

Any side.

She honestly didn't care. Savannah bit back a groan of frustration. She was starving here, starving for him and the hunger had all but gotten the best of her.

Savannah had set out on this confounded assignment against her will, wholly determined to resist Knox. She'd known that the story had immense potential, and she hadn't underestimated her attraction, but she had underestimated Knox.

He wasn't the shallow, thoughtless, lazy playboy she'd forced herself to believe he was.

Some innate sense of self-preservation had kicked in when she'd first met him, because her subconscious had recognized him as a potential threat to her heart. Savannah had looked at him and unfairly projected each and every one of Gib's character flaws upon Knox.

While the character flaws had been false, one glaring fact still remained—Knox still posed a threat to her heart. If she let down her guard one whit, Savannah knew Knox would burrow beneath her defenses, fasten himself onto that traitorous organ and, short of a transplant, she'd never get rid of him.

He wouldn't have a problem getting rid of her,

though, Savannah thought with a bitter smile. No one ever did. That's why, regardless of how charming and witty, how adorable and sweet—how sexy—he turned out to be, she had to keep things in perspective. Keep her defenses in place.

They'd spent scarcely twenty-four hours together and, nerve-racking kisses and chronic masturbators aside, Savannah had had more fun in this single day with Knox than she'd had in years. He'd made her laugh, a rare feat. Sad, Savannah realized, but true. Given the opportunity, she wondered, what other rare feats could Knox facilitate? What other hidden talents did he have?

He stirred beside her and Savannah tensed and held her breath, silently praying that he wouldn't wake up and find her all but planting a flag in his groin. He didn't. But to Savannah's immense pleasure and frustration, he wrapped his hand around hers and, murmuring nonsensical sounds, tugged her even closer than she'd been before. Her breasts were now completely flattened against his muscular back and, of course, reacted accordingly. They grew heavy with want and her nipples hardened into tight, sensitive peaks. Her clit throbbed a steady mantra of *I'm ready!* One clever touch, Savannah knew, and she'd shatter.

Knox, damn him, was asleep, completely oblivious to her torture and exempt from his own.

Well, Savannah thought, she could either lie there and simmer in her sexually frustrated misery, or she could get up and try to put a more productive spin on the morning. Breakfast would be served in the common room at eight, and another lecture—more erotic massage—would begin promptly at nine. This lecture in particular was supposed to be one of those graphic, hands-on demonstrations the Sheas' brochures had promised and would segue into tomorrow's *Love His Lingam* and *Sacred Goddess Stimulation*. Savannah both dreaded and looked forward to those lessons. She'd be less than honest if she didn't admit to at least some morbid fascination.

Besides, she liked to excel at everything and if she gleaned even the slightest knowledge on how to please a future lover—or please herself—then she'd leave this damned workshop better than she arrived.

A careful look at the bedside clock told her that she and Knox needed to get the lead out. They'd only unblocked one chakra and had totally skipped her building-trust homework. Humiliation burned Savannah's cheeks. Naturally she knew that she had certain trust issues—she'd never been in a relationship in her life that hadn't ended in some form of disappointment. But she hadn't realized the true extent of her distrust until yesterday. She'd been the only person in the entire class who'd flunked the ''blind trust'' test. The symbolism hadn't been lost on her or, more embarrassingly, him.

All she'd had to do was stand with her back to Knox, fall backward and let him catch her. Most couples had nailed it on the first try. She and Knox had attempted the exercise until the end of class and she still hadn't gotten it. Edgar and Rupali had shared an enigmatic look, then instructed her and Knox to work on the exercise for homework.

Quite frankly, Savannah didn't give a rip what the Sheas or any of these other people here thought about her. Beyond this weekend she'd never see them again. But that wasn't the case with Knox. She'd see him on a day-to-day basis and, during that idiotic test, she'd had the uneasy privilege of watching his emotions leap from teasing mockery to pity and, finally, to curiosity.

It wouldn't be enough that he knew she had trust issues—he was a journalist and would have to know *why.* If she wouldn't tell him when he covertly interviewed her—and she had no doubt whatsoever that he would—he'd dig around until he raked up every bit of her unfortunate past. She inwardly shuddered with dread.

She'd become a *story,* Savannah realized, an exposé, and Knox, despite his laid-back attitude, was nothing short of a bloodhound when he caught the scent of a story. He'd use his particular brand of talent to unearth every unpleasant aspect of her past and he'd pull one of his legendary show-and-tell tactics on her. While she'd love to play a little show-and-tell with him, she didn't want it to have anything to do with her private life.

Despite her present predicament with Chapman, Savannah had a good reputation at the *Phoenix.*

She'd worked hard to garner the respect of her peers, and if Knox used his trademark talent on her, she'd have to watch that respect become tempered with pity.

She would not be anyone's object of pity.

Savannah was wondering what tack she should take when Knox abruptly stirred once more. He stretched beside her, yawned, and she knew the exact instant when he awakened and the full realization of their position registered, because he grew completely still. Then he abruptly relaxed and she didn't have to see his face to know that he undoubtedly wore a cat-in-the-cream expression.

Feigning sleep, Savannah moaned softly and nonchalantly rolled away from him and onto her side. There, she thought. She'd escaped. She'd saved face and would—

To Savannah's slack-jawed astonishment, using the exact same tactic she'd just employed, Knox promptly spooned her. The force of his heat engulfed her as he bellied up to her back. He twined an arm around her middle and unerringly settled his palm upon her breast. Savannah hadn't recovered from that brazen move before he pushed his thigh between her legs and sighed with audible satisfaction right into her ear. The combined masculine weight, heat and scent of him caused a tornado of sensation to erupt below her navel.

She couldn't believe his gall. At least she'd molested him while she'd been asleep and unaware of her transgressions. Knox, the sneaky lout, was in full possession of his senses and had used the lucky opportunity to take advantage of the situation. Still, her conscience needled, she hadn't abruptly drawn away from him when she'd woken up. She'd lain there and savored the feel of him against her, just as she was doing now.

Which was madness, she thought with a spurt of self-loathing. Why didn't she just forgo all of the niceties and hand him her heart to break?

Savannah drove her elbow into his unsuspecting stomach. "Get...off...me."

Knox's breath left him in a quick, surprised whoosh and he promptly released her throbbing breast and rolled away. "Wh-what?" he asked with enough sleepy perplexity to look genuine. But she knew better.

Savannah glared at him. "I thought I told you to stay on your side of the bed."

Knox sat up in bed and rubbed a hand over the back of his neck. His mink-brown hair was mussed and the flush of sleep still clung to his cheeks. Those heavy-lidded eyes were weighted even more with the dregs of slumber. He looked almost boyish, yet the term didn't quite fit, because there was absolutely nothing boyish about the way her body reacted to his.

"Huh?" he managed.

Savannah blew out a breath. "I thought I told you to stay on your side of the bed," she repeated.

"Didn't I?" he asked foggily.

He knew damn well he hadn't, the wretch. "No," she said tightly. "You did not."

He frowned. "Oh, sorry. Hope I didn't crowd you."

"I woke up with your hand wrapped around my breast."

A smile quivered on his lips. Knox threw the covers off and planted his feet on the floor, but didn't readily stand. He leveled a droll look at her. "Funny. I woke up with your hand inches above my dick and your thigh on my ass, but you don't hear me complaining."

Savannah flushed. She could win this argument, but not without admitting fault on her own part, so she didn't bother. "Just get ready," she huffed. "We've got less than an hour before breakfast."

THEY WERE TEN MINUTES LATE for breakfast. Knox had been wrong. Savannah did take great pains with her hair—it just didn't do any good.

She'd spent the better part of thirty minutes this morning trying to force the unruly locks into some semblance of a true style and when she'd finally exited the bathroom, she'd looked exactly as she had when she'd gone in. "I don't know why I bother," she said when she walked out.

Knox had bitten his tongue to keep from saying, "Me, neither."

He kept his mouth shut, of course. He'd already

pissed her off this morning with the sleepy-hand-upon-her-breast bit and didn't dare risk her further displeasure by agreeing with her dead-on assessment about her hair. Besides, her hair had character. Knox thought it was adorable.

Having her draped all over him this morning had been a pleasant surprise. She'd smelled curiously like apples, a scent he'd associated with her before, and the feminine weight of her body nuzzled against his had been incredible. He'd felt the press of those delectable nipples against his back and that sweet hand snugged against his abdomen. If she hadn't moved when she did, his randy pecker would have nudged under her palm like an eager puppy begging for a stroke.

He'd known he shouldn't have rolled over with her, but for some perverse reason, he hadn't been able to help himself. His palms literally itched to touch her.

The one woman he'd imagined he wouldn't be hot for had unaccountably turned into the one woman he simply had to have.

Knox had never in his life longed to root himself between a woman's thighs more. He wanted her legs hooked over his shoulders, her arms lashed around his waist and her tongue in his mouth, and not necessarily in that order.

A moment after they entered, the Sheas moved to stand side by side in front of the room and garnered everyone's attention. "Greetings and good morning to you,'' Rupali said. Knox noticed that when Rupali moved forward to speak, Edgar instinctively moved slightly back and behind her. Support, Knox realized with a jolt of surprise and admiration. ''We hope that you all passed a pleasant night and adhered to the rules set out for this retreat.'' She paused. ''Did everyone adhere to the rules?''

A chorus of assents passed through the room, though Knox spotted at least two guilty faces. One was Chuck's, of course.

''What about homework?'' Edgar asked. This time, it was Rupali that moved behind him. So the respect and support was reciprocated, not just one-sided.

Despite all of the questions and doubts surrounding this workshop and tantric sex in general, Knox had to admit that their relationship seemed genuine. They obviously cared very deeply for each other.

What would it be like to be on the receiving end of such unwavering love and support? Knox wondered as a curious void suddenly shifted in his chest. What would it be like to have someone who believed in you so much that they instinctively knew to get behind you when you needed it, or perhaps even when you didn't? He'd had that sort of support from his family until he'd majored in journalism, but after that he'd lost their encouragement. It had hurt, but the desire to succeed had been a balm to his disappointment.

''Let's have a status report on our chakras,'' Edgar

said. "We'll start and go around the room. Tell what sort of breakthroughs you experienced, as well as how many chakras you believe you unblocked. Who would like to go first?"

Several hands shot into the air at this question. Needless to say, his and Savannah's weren't among them. Chuck and Marge began and proudly reported that they'd unblocked their perineum, genital and belly chakras. Several other couples continued in this vein sharing their experiences, reporting multiple chakra breakthroughs. Knox began to get a little nervous. He hadn't realized just how little he and Savannah had gotten done last night. They'd have to take their break this afternoon and play some catch-up; otherwise they were going to be lagging behind the rest of the class. That was simply unacceptable. Knox didn't lag behind anyone.

Apparently, the realization had hit Savannah as well. Her lips had flattened into an adorably mulish expression. Knox felt his lips twitch. He knew that look—heaven knows he'd seen it often enough—and it meant watch your back.

"Is there anyone who hasn't reported?" Rupali asked.

"Knox and Barbie haven't," Marge replied helpfully. Knox gritted his teeth and smiled at her.

"Well, Knox and Barbie," Rupali said. "How did it go?"

Knox looked to Savannah, hoping in her ire, she'd step up and answer the question. For all appearances she smiled encouragingly, but Knox saw the evil humor dancing in that ice-blue gaze. Her look clearly said, "You made your bed, now lie in it."

"We, uh, worked on the trust exercise so much that we only got the r-root chakra unblocked," Knox reported. From the corner of his eye, he saw Savannah's eyes narrow fractionally. Obviously, she didn't appreciate taking the blame for their poor performance.

"Don't be so modest, baby," Savannah said sweetly. "Tell the rest."

The rest? Knox wondered as his breakfast curdled in his stomach. His smile froze. "That's private, pumpkin," he all but growled through gritted teeth. He had absolutely no idea what she was talking about, but instinctively knew she intended to humiliate him. Royally.

"Nothing is private here, Knox," Rupali reminded with a smile. "Truth and healing, remember? You obviously have something to be proud of. Barbie is proud. Please share," she encouraged gently.

"I—"

"Oh, very well," Savannah said, with a humbly mysterious look about the room. "I'll tell them." She paused dramatically. "After we unblocked Knox's root chakra—which took a great deal of time because of his tight-ass tendencies—he got an *erection!*"

This theatrical announcement was met with a mass

of delighted oohs and aahs and a spattering of applause.

Savannah clasped her hands together excitedly and looked meaningfully around at everyone. "It lasted for almost *two whole minutes!*"

She was evil, Knox thought as he felt his face flame with embarrassment. Evil. And he would make her pay. With a grand show of delighted support, Savannah grabbed hold of his arm and pressed close to him. "I'm so very proud of you, baby."

Edgar and Rupali beamed at him. "That's indeed something to be proud of, Knox. Congratulations on your erection."

Knox had been congratulated for many things over the years, but he could truthfully say that having a man congratulate him on an erection was a wholly new experience. A couple of the truly impotent men glared enviously at him.

"Er, thank you," he muttered self-consciously.

Beside him, Savannah sighed with sublime satisfaction, the faux picture of wifely adoration.

Rupali threaded her fingers through her husband's. "This is precisely why we have opened our home and hearts, why we decided to start this clinic. So that impotent men like Knox can come and reclaim their masculinity. With harmony and truth healing and the art of tantric ritual, perhaps he will be able to surpass even this breakthrough and lead his lover to climax." She gave Savannah an enigmatic look. "I don't think your problem lies in the lower chakras, Barbie. You will learn what I mean, and I would appreciate your telling me when it happens."

Looking somewhat startled, Savannah merely nodded. Now what did Rupali mean by that? Knox wondered. After a moment, he leaned over and asked Savannah.

She shook her head, clearly bewildered. "I have no idea."

"Well, tell me when it happens. I want to know, too."

"Oh, hell, Knox, you know as well as I do that nothing is going to happen."

"Now how would I know that?" he replied sardonically. "Just think about me and my whopping two-minute erection."

She had the nerve to laugh. "Save your indignation. After this morning, you deserved it."

"I wasn't the only one copping a feel," Knox replied, somewhat miffed. "And I wasn't the one who was so horny I had to masturbate during my bath to get some relief."

Her head jerked around and her stunned gaze found his.

"Yeah, that's right," he said with a crafty grin. "I know."

He had to give her credit—she recovered well. She blew out a disbelieving breath. "Don't be ridiculous. Honestly, Knox, the size of your ego never ceases to amaze me. I—"

"It wasn't the size of my ego that sent you into

the bathroom and had you slipping your finger into—"

"Shut up," she said, squeezing her eyes tightly closed.

Knox tapped his finger thoughtfully against the chin. "Come to think of it, I think that was a violation of the rules. Perhaps I should report *your* climax—seeing as you're frigid and that would be a breakthrough," Knox threatened. "Then the whole room could applaud you and celebrate your orgasm."

"I'm sorry," she hissed.

"What?"

"I'm sorry, dammit."

He eyed her, his gaze lingering on her guarded expression. "Just what exactly is the problem?" Knox wanted to know, serious now. "What have I done—besides making you do this story—that has you alternately assaulting my character and my ego?" *Why don't you like me?* he demanded silently. *Why can't I charm you? For the love of God, why do I even care?*

She swallowed. "Nothing. It's my problem, not yours."

Oh, no. That was the closest thing to a personal admission she'd ever made and he had no intention of letting her get away with not finishing the thought. *"What is it?"* he pressed.

"We don't have time to go into this right now," Savannah hedged. She tucked her hair behind her ears. "Trust me, it's nothing. You're right. I've been unfair."

"If it was nothing, you wouldn't want to go for my throat every time the opportunity presented itself. Spill it, Savannah. I've got a right to know."

"Y-you remind me of someone, that's all."

"I remind you of someone," Knox repeated. "Who?"

Seemingly embarrassed, she huffed a breath and refused to look at him.

"A guy?" Knox guessed, annoyed beyond reason.

"Yes," she finally relented. "A guy. Are you happy now?"

No, he wasn't. He was anything but happy. "If I remind you of a guy and it's not a good thing, then one could logically deduce that this particular guy was a bastard who broke your heart. Am I right?"

"He did not break my heart," Savannah insisted icily. "I hadn't given him my heart to break."

No, only her trust, Knox realized, which any moron should have realized was almost as precious as her heart. "Do I look like him?"

"No."

"Do I act like him?"

Her shoulders slumped with an invisible weight. "I'd made myself believe that you did. But you don't."

Knox scowled, hopelessly confused. "If you no longer believe I act like him, then what's the problem?"

She emitted a low, frustrated growl. "Being here with you, this whole workshop…" She gestured wildly. "How am I supposed to stay out of the bathroom," she said meaningfully, "and not do what I—"

"Masturbate?"

"—did, when I'm here with *you* and we're surrounded by sex, sex and more sex?" Her voice climbed. "How am I supposed to think about anything else with all this talk of orgasms and erections and—"

Understanding suddenly dawned and Knox felt a self-satisfied grin spread across his lips. "You want me."

She shot him a dark look. "I didn't say that."

Something warm and tingly moved through his rapidly swelling chest. *"You want me."*

She paused. "Don't look so proud of yourself. I'd want just about anybody under the circumstances."

"Yeah…but you're not here with *anybody*. You're here with *me*."

"Brilliant deduction, Einstein."

"Would it make you feel any better if you knew I was having the same problem?"

She snorted. "Don't lie. You've already told me that the reason you brought me here was because you *weren't* attracted to me."

"Things have changed."

"Yes, I'm sure they have. You're a man and you've decided to make do with whomever is available. Which happens to be me. Meanwhile, neither one of us has any business being attracted to the other because we're here to do a job. And we can't truly do that job correctly unless we have sex, so it really is a screwed-up conundrum, isn't it, Knox?''

Another thought surfaced and suddenly everything became clear. ''Ahh,'' Knox said with a knowing twinkle. ''You wanted me *before* we left Chicago. That's why you didn't want to come. That's why you were so determined not to attend this workshop with me.''

''Keep this up, you cocksure moron. You're quickly losing your appeal.''

Savannah promptly stood and followed the rest of the group to the classroom, leaving Knox to glow with her revelation.

Savannah Reeves wanted him…and apparently always had. What to do with this new information? Knox wondered. Just exactly what the hell was he supposed to do? She'd told him for a reason—she hadn't just dropped this little bomb without some inkling of the consequences.

Did she expect him to be a hero and abstain, or was she simply putting the ball into his court? Did she want him to take the sexual lead, so that any blame could be laid squarely on him when this weekend was over?

Knox didn't know, but he knew he'd better figure it out. Otherwise, he feared he might single-handedly be responsible for Savannah never trusting a man again.

9

SAVANNAH COULDN'T BEGIN to imagine what had possessed her to all but admit that she'd been lusting after him for a year, but once the burn of humiliation cooled, she knew she'd undoubtedly feel better. It would be a relief not to have to pretend that she didn't want him. Since he'd deduced what had occurred during her bath last night, Savannah thought with a rueful grin, she hadn't been doing such a great job of pretending otherwise anyway.

He'd seen right through her.

The only reason she'd been able to hide the truth as long as she had was because she'd made a point of avoiding him.

But she couldn't avoid him here.

He was everywhere.

In her mind, in her mouth, beneath her hands, in her room, even in her bed.

Everywhere.

She couldn't escape him and was rapidly losing her resolve to try. The attraction had simply become bigger than she could handle, more than she could conceivably take on. She'd been doomed from the

moment Chapman, the vengeful bastard, had forced
her to come on this ill-conceived trip. No, Savannah
thought with a dry chuckle, she'd been doomed from
the moment she'd met Knox. It had all been simply
a matter of time before she'd fall victim to his lethal
appeal and her equally lethal attraction.

Knox sat down on the padded mat next to her. The
hairs on her arms prickled at his nearness, seemingly
drawn like a lodestone to him. For reasons she didn't
dare dwell on, all of the chairs had been removed
from the room and had been ominously replaced with
big cushy mats.

"Have they started yet?" Knox whispered low.

God, she even loved the sound of his voice. It was
deep and smooth and moved over her like an old
blues tune. Could she get any more pathetic? "Not
yet," Savannah finally managed.

Confusion cluttered his brow. "What are the mats
for?"

"Dunno." *And don't care to speculate,* Savannah
thought.

Knox glanced idly around the room. "Well, at
least we know they aren't going to ask us to do it
yet. That doesn't happen until tomorrow."

Tomorrow. The word hung between them and conjured a combined sense of anticipation and doom.
Savannah didn't dare let herself think about what
would happen tomorrow afternoon after they'd com-
pleted their so-called tantric-lovemaking training,
and were sent to their room armed with that knowl-

edge and a long night ahead of them. She supposed they should work on the story that they'd come here to get, but without actually having tried tantric sex to see if it truly worked, she didn't know how exactly they were supposed to do that.

When they'd first arrived, doing a fair article without participating in tantric sex seemed plausible. Now it didn't, and she could no longer tell if that idea was a product of journalistic integrity or sheer unadulterated lust. Probably a combination of both, Savannah decided.

With a sexy curl of his lips, Knox shifted on his mat and leaned closer to her. "I know this is going to sound strange," he confided, "but I'm starting to like this *kurta*. It's extremely comfortable. Feels good. I like being…unrestricted."

Savannah felt her lips twitch and tried not to think of which part of him was so friggin' unrestricted. Clearly he'd decided to torture her with his new information. His effort was redundant—she couldn't possibly want him any more. "It's a progressive-thinking man who can admit that he likes wearing a dress."

"It's not a dress," Knox corrected amiably. "It's a *kurta*, and if they have them in the gift shop, you can bet your sweet ass I'm buying one and taking it home."

Savannah chuckled drolly. "If you wear it anywhere but at home, I would strongly advise you to put on some underwear." She looked pointedly—

longingly—at his crotch. "Your entire package is plainly visible through the fabric."

"So is yours," he murmured suggestively. "Tell me, is that little star-shaped thingy on your right butt cheek a mole or a birthmark?"

He'd studied her ass that closely, eh? Swallowing her surprise, Savannah said, "It's a birthmark."

He nodded thoughtfully. "I thought as much."

Before Savannah could ponder that enigmatic comment any longer, the Sheas stood before the class and called order to the room.

"This morning we're going to teach some of the finer points of erotic massage," Edgar said. "Now, so that you understand the difference, erotic massage and genital massage aren't the same thing. We will cover those genital areas that bring such pleasure tomorrow, in *Love His Lingam* and *Sacred Goddess Stimulation.* I'm sure you are all looking forward to that," Edgar said with a small smile.

"What we're going to show you today, however," he continued, "will be how to heighten full-body awareness to bring ultimate pleasure. There are other areas of our bodies that enjoy touch. Our faces, for instance. Which is where we'll begin. We'll take our time about this, so that both partners can enjoy the exercise. To get the full enjoyment of this lesson, the receiver should be nude; however, we will leave that option up to each of you." He smiled encouragingly. "Men, you shall be givers first."

Nude? Savannah thought frantically as the couples

around them swiftly began to disrobe, including the Sheas. Savannah watched in fascinated horror as Edgar and Rupali casually slipped out of their *kurtas*.

"Givers sit crossed-legged and cradle your receiver's head in your lap," Edgar said.

Knox shrugged loosely, heaved a resigned breath and moved to draw his *kurta* over his head. He wore the slightest, sexiest grin, and those slumberous dark green eyes glinted with wicked humor and hidden sin.

"What the hell are you doing?" Savannah hissed, her heart beating wildly in her chest. "You don't have to get undressed. Clothing is optional."

"And I'm opting to come out of it." His lips tipped into a slow, unrepentant grin. "When I'm the receiver, I don't want anything between your hands and my skin."

His words sent gooseflesh skittering across her own skin. Nevertheless, unreasonable though it may be, she only wanted him naked with her. Not with a roomful of observers. A wee bit possessive, but she couldn't help herself. Her eyes narrowed. If even one of these sexually repressed sluts so much as looked at him, she'd break their fingers.

"Then you can be nude in our bedroom," she said icily. "But not here."

He paused, something shifted in his gaze and he smiled knowingly. "Ah, so you want me nude all to yourself?"

Did he have to be so arrogantly perceptive? Savannah thought with a stab of irritation. Was she that transparent? "What I want is for you to leave your clothes on," she told him, struggling to keep her patience.

"Knox? Barbie? Is there a problem?" Rupali asked.

To Savannah's continued mortification, the whole nude room turned to stare at them. "Uh, no. We're fine, thanks."

"There is no shame in flaunting our nude bodies," Rupali said with that misty tone. "We were created to delight in their perfect design. The human form is art in motion. You will find no judging eyes here." With a melancholy smile, she gestured to herself. "My own body is growing old and wrinkled. My breasts aren't as firm as they used to be, nor my stomach as flat." She straightened. "But I am proud, because this is the body I live in, and I am beautiful to myself."

Savannah envied the woman's confidence. In an age where the words *thin* and *youthful* defined beauty, Rupali could look at herself and feel imperfect but proud. How often had Savannah looked into the mirror and thought, *If only my breasts were larger? If only my thighs were thinner?*

Be that as it may, she was still just modest enough not to want to get naked in front of a roomful of strangers. Savannah summoned a wobbly smile. "I-I'd prefer to stay dressed."

Rupali nodded. "As you wish."

Everyone settled into the required position at Edgar's instruction. "Let's begin with a scalp massage," Edgar told them. "Be sure and ask your receiver what feels good to her. What she likes. Learn what makes your lover feel good and commit it to memory. Trust me," Edgar laughed. "You will reap the benefits of your effort tenfold."

Knox slid his fingers into her hair and began to knead her scalp with strong little circling movements. Savannah couldn't help herself, the audible moan of pleasure slipped past her smiling lips before she could stem it.

"Like that, do you?" Knox asked. She'd closed her eyes, but could hear the humor in his voice.

"Indeed, I do," she sighed softly.

Savannah had always enjoyed having her hair washed at her hairdresser's, had always found it relaxing, but she couldn't begin to compare that crude rubdown to the sensation of having Knox's warm, blunt-tipped fingers manipulating her tense scalp. The light scratch of fingernails, the strong press of his fingertips swirling over her head, lulled her. He caressed every inch from her hairline at her forehead, to the very nape of her neck, where tension had the tendency to gather. She hadn't anticipated this to be such an erotic experience, but a warm sluggish heat had begun to wind through her seemingly boneless body, proving her wrong.

"Let's move on, class," Edgar said, to Savannah's supreme disappointment. "Givers, move your attention to your receiver's face. So much emotion, so much feeling is transmitted through the muscles of our face. Consider the smile and the frown. These muscles, too, need attention. Caress your lover's face, and, remember, be sure to ask her what she likes,'' Edgar reminded. ''Watch for what makes her feel good.''

Savannah smothered a sigh of satisfaction when she felt Knox's big warm hands cradle her face, felt them slide over her cheeks as he mapped the contours of her face. He smoothed his fingers over her closed lids, slid a thumb over the curve of her eyebrow, down her nose. *Heavenly,* she thought as another smile inched across her lips.

Knox brushed the back of his hand down the slope of her cheek. That move was more tender, more reverent, and somehow more personal than the others. Savannah longed to open her eyes, to look into his, and see if she could discover any inkling of his present thoughts, but the idea was no sooner born than abandoned, because Knox suddenly slid his thumb over her bottom lip.

Savannah had the almost irresistible urge to arch her neck, open her mouth and suck that thumb. She so desperately wanted to taste him that any part would do, and this particular part was most readily available. She settled for licking her lips after his finger had moved on, searching for even the smallest lingering hint of him.

To her immense gratification, she heard the breath

stutter out of Knox's lungs, felt a slight tension creep into his touch. He shaped her face once more with his hands, slid them down her arched throat and back up and around again. His touch grew slower yet more deliberately sensual. Savannah struggled to keep her breathing at a normal respiration, but it was getting considerably more difficult with each passing second.

Desire weighted her limbs and something hot and needy unfurled low in her belly, arrowed toward her wet and pulsing sex. She pressed her legs together and bit back the urge to roll over, scale his magnificent body and impale herself on the hard throbbing length of him.

If he could turn her into a quivering lump of lust with a scalp and face massage, just exactly how would she manage to control herself when he moved on to other erogenous zones? She wouldn't be able to bear it, Savannah decided. She simply—

"Before we continue," Edgar said, interrupting Savannah's turbulent thoughts, "let's change positions. Both the men and women need to find out how it feels to touch and be touched."

"Couples tend to get carried away as this lesson progresses," Rupali chimed in with a dry chuckle. "Please go ahead and change positions."

A reprieve, Savannah thought, profoundly relieved. As she sat up, she glanced at Knox and her gaze tangled with his. His eyes were dark and slumberous and a knowing, self-satisfied twinkle danced in those wickedly arousing orbs. The wretch knew exactly what he'd been doing to her, knew that he'd lit a fire in her loins that only a blast from his particular *hose* would put out.

Savannah narrowed her eyes into a look that promised retribution and more. Nobody set her on fire, then failed to get burned.

He would pay. With pleasure.

KNOX HAD SEEN that look in Savannah's eye before and knew it boded ill, undoubtedly for him. A flush of arousal tinged her creamy skin and her eyes were as hot as a blue flame. He'd known what he'd been doing to her during that massage, known that he'd lit her up.

Who would have ever thought that something as simple as a scalp and face massage could ignite such a blazing fuse of sexual energy? He'd listened to her little purrs of pleasure, felt her alternately go limp with relaxation and then vibrate with tension.

It had been the most singularly erotic sensation Knox had ever had.

Knox had been sexually active since his early teens. His sexual experiences had run the gamut of the highly romantic, to the down and dirty, and all species in between. He'd been drizzled in chocolate and licked clean, had eaten grapes from the pale pink folds of a woman's sex, had done it in a cab, in an elevator, and once in the bathroom of his dentist's office.

Yet, for all of his vast experience, nothing had

prepared him for the complete and total, all-consuming need he felt for Savannah. With each touch he'd become more aroused, more hungry for her. Feeling the delicate planes of her face beneath his hands, the soft swell of those lush lips, the sweet curve and soft skin of her cheek beneath his knuckles...

Something had happened to him in that instant, something so terrifying that Knox didn't dare name it, much less contemplate it. He'd looked at that beautiful, serene face of hers, that mess of bed-head curls, and a curious emotion had swelled in his chest, pushed into his throat and had forced him to swallow. His hands had actually trembled.

The picture she'd made in that instant was indelibly imprinted in his mind. No matter how much she blared and blustered, no matter how much blue sleet she slung in his direction, Knox would always remember the way she'd looked right then. She didn't know it yet, but she'd never be able to freeze him out again.

"Okay," Rupali said. "Let's begin."

Savannah leaned over him and smiled. "Let me know if I hurt you."

Oh, hell.

She slid her small fingers into his hair and rolled his scalp in little circles, front to back and side to side, alternating pressure with light touches and firmer kneads until Knox heard a long, decidedly happy growl of approval and realized it had come from the back of his own throat. She skimmed her fingers over the sensitive skin behind his ears, tunneled them into the thick hair at his nape. She scratched and massaged, kneaded and rubbed. Unexpected pleasure eddied through him and, though he imagined Edgar and Rupali would think that he'd totally missed the point of this exercise, it didn't take long for Knox to decide that those talented little fingers could be put to better use south of his navel.

He was a man, after all. He wouldn't be satisfied until her hand was wrapped around his throbbing rod, pumping him until he exploded with the force of his climax.

Still, Knox thought, as Savannah's fingertips slid through his hair once more, this was nice. Perhaps Edgar was onto something with all this erotic massage stuff. Every muscle was languid and relaxed, save for his dick—hell, he could do a no-hands pushup, he was so friggin' hard right now.

"Are you planning on hosting a party down there?" Savannah leaned down and asked him.

Knox slowly opened his eyes. "What?"

She was smiling one of those secret little smiles that made Knox feel as if he'd been caught with his fly down. "Are you planning on having a party down there?" She glanced pointedly at his groin. "You've erected quite a tent."

"Not a party," Knox told her silkily. "An intimate dinner for one. You hungry?"

Her eyes narrowed and then she licked her lips suggestively. *"Starving."*

If he hadn't been exercising tremendous control, Savannah would have turned him into the premature ejaculator she'd claimed he was with that little dramatic display.

"Givers," Rupali said, "move on to your receiver's face. Remember to note what pleases your lover."

"Would you like to know what pleases your lover, Savannah?" Knox murmured. "Would you like me to tell you?"

She swallowed and he felt her fingers tremble against his cheek. "I don't have a lover."

"That can be easily remedied."

She laughed softly, swept her fingers over his brow, down his cheek and along his jaw. "You wouldn't say these things if there was any blood left in your head."

Knox laughed. "If I'm not mistaken, *all* of it's in my head."

"Not the one that is responsible for logical thinking." She pressed a couple of fingers against his lips. "Shut up, Knox. People are starting to stare."

"Let 'em. I'm like Rupali. I'm proud. Besides, I've got something to prove." He grinned. "I'm going to break my two-minute erection record."

She tsked regretfully and massaged his temples. "Sorry, can't let that happen. Someone must protect our cover."

"Baby, you can't stop me."

"Wanna bet?"

Knox stilled and looked up at her. Clearly she hadn't gotten it yet, and wasn't going to until he spelled it out for her. "Savannah, my head is in your lap, inches away from the part of you that I want more than my next breath, and your hands might be on my face—which feels lovely, by the way—but in my mind, your hands are wrapped—along with your lips—around my rod and I'm seconds away from coming harder than I ever have in my life." He paused and let that sink in, watching her expression waver between determination and desire. His gaze held hers. "There is absolutely nothing you can say that's going to make me lose this erection."

A long, pregnant pause followed his blunt soliloquy. She blinked drunkenly for a second, then recovered and said four words that were guaranteed to make any hetero male lose even his most valiant erection.

"Chuck's whacking off again."

"Aw, Savannah," Knox woefully lamented. With a wince of regret, he squeezed his eyes shut but couldn't force the image away. The ick factor of Chuck and his happy hand swiftly deflated Knox's prized hard-on.

"And the big top comes down," Savannah whispered dramatically.

Knox opened his eyes and glared at her with amused accusation. "You are evil."

She smiled with faux modesty. "I try."

Knox felt a silent laugh rumble deep in his chest. "I'm sure you do."

A comfortable silence ensued, broken only by the soft sighs of pleasure that ebbed through the room. Savannah continued her sweet assault upon his face, gently massaging him. He'd let his lids flutter closed, but could feel the kiss of her gaze examining his every feature, measuring the muscle and bone against her hands. He heard a poignant, almost resigned sigh slip past her lips and wondered just what heavy realization she had come to. What he'd give to have even a glimpse into those thoughts.

Just as Knox was truly beginning to relax, Rupali interrupted the sensual play with more instructions. The givers and receivers were once again directed to change positions.

"We will massage backs and bellies, rumps and thighs, calves, insteps and even the smallest toe," Rupali told them. "No part of our bodies—aside from our genitals—shall be overlooked."

"You will know your lover's body better than your own by the end of this day," Edgar chimed in. "You will know what he or she likes, and you will discover neglected areas of your own body that bring pleasure when touched. Think of your lover's body like a musical instrument. Her sighs, her moans of pleasure, are your music, her quivers your applause."

"Women, the same holds true for you," Rupali shared. "Every indrawn breath, every expression of pleasure, every guttural growl from your man is his own primal music. While learning how to play your man, and while you, in turn, are played, your inner harmony begins to take form. The voice of your one-being will become clearer.'' She paused. ''Seek that place, class. *Kundalini*,'' she emphasized. ''Combined life force and sexual energy. Once you have experienced it, nothing else will ever suffice.''

Knox whistled low, and he and Savannah shared a look. Her beauty, the absolute perfection of her face, struck him once more and the desire to reach out to slide his fingertips over those smooth features almost overpowered him.

Once you have experienced it, nothing else will ever suffice.

Knox grimly suspected those words held a double meaning for him. After Savannah…no one else would ever do.

10

THOUGH IT TOOK a monumental amount of restraint, Savannah limited her bath to just that—a bath. She and Knox had managed to make it from class back to their room after the all-day erotic massage session and, though her limbs had quaked and were limp as noodles, and her loins had been locked in a pit of permanently aroused despair, she'd managed to survive without begging him to plunge into her and put her out of her sexually frustrated misery.

Her only consolation was that Knox had been mired in that pit as well and, quite honestly, had not fared as well as she. Savannah's lips quivered. Her nipples didn't quite cause the stir his prominent erection did. When Knox was aroused, everyone knew it, could hardly fail to notice. She hated to dwell on it so, but Savannah couldn't seem to conquer her fascination with his enormous…article.

Neither could anyone else, for that matter, a fact that both annoyed and delighted her. For all intents and purposes of this workshop, that colossal penis was *hers* and hers alone. Both men and women alike gazed at them with envy, the men at Knox because they longed to be equally blessed, and the women, like her, were most likely astounded at the sheer size of him. Savannah enjoyed the being envied part—it was their greedy gazes lingering on her borrowed penis that pissed her off.

She'd heard a couple of the women talking about the phenomenon on the way out. ''Pity he can't keep it up longer than two minutes though,'' one had said regretfully and to Knox's extreme embarrassment. During that session, his problem had seemed genuine to all. Every time that sucker had stood at attention longer that it should, Savannah had whispered the magic words, and *poof!* it would disappear. The magic words being, ''Chuck's whacking off again.'' Cruel, she knew, but not any more cruel than what she'd suffered.

If she possessed even a shred of sanity by the time this workshop was over, Savannah would consider herself extremely lucky.

The evening ahead would undoubtedly be as trying as this day had been. As soon as she'd mentioned taking a bath, Knox had proclaimed it an excellent idea, and had once again tried to come out of that damned *kurta.* Truthfully, Savannah would have liked nothing better than to have taken him up on the idea, would have liked nothing better than to have had his hot, hard wet body wrapped around and pulsing inside hers. The tub had been designed for sin and so had his body and she wanted it more desperately with each passing second.

Quite honestly, Savannah didn't have a clue what they were supposed to do now. She'd laid all her cards on the table, and she supposed Knox had, too. He'd admitted that he wanted her now, and it was the *now* that kept messing with her head, the *now* that she was having trouble getting past.

A part of her wanted to say, *Consequences be damned, you've wanted him forever, here's your opportunity, just go for it already!*

But another part hated knowing that he *hadn't* wanted her to begin with, that it had taken a sex workshop for him to consider her attractive, and she seriously suspected her newfound appeal had more to do with convenience than actual interest. If she gave in to her baser needs and rode him until his eyes rolled back in his head as she so very much wanted to do, would she regret it later? Or would she regret it more if she didn't?

Savannah didn't know and, luckily, wouldn't have to decide until tomorrow…provided she didn't expire from longing first.

Knox rapped on the bathroom door, startling her. "The food's here. Come feed me."

A wry grin curled her lips as she opened the bathroom door. "I should let you starve," she told him.

"Why?"

"Just for the hell of it."

He shivered dramatically. "Chilly, chilly." That verdant green gaze was shrewd and glinted with humor. "You must not have had as much fun in the tub this evening. Don't worry, I can cure what ails you.'' His voice was low, practically a purr, and it sent a flurry of sensation buzzing through her.

She'd just bet he could, Savannah thought with a mental ooh-la-la. Did she have a prayer of resisting him? she wondered with furious despair.

After everything else they'd been through over the past twenty-four hours, feeding each other seemed downright tame. They spoke little during the meal, just systematically fed each other the tender strips of Hawaiian chicken, green beans, and macaroni and cheese, the latter being particular messy and involving a lot of cleanup.

Which meant a great deal of licking and sucking, and tongue in general.

Presently, a couple of Savannah's fingers were knuckle deep in Knox's hot mouth, and he'd decided to make a grand spectacle of getting her clean. He slid his tongue along her finger and alternately nibbled and sucked. Soft then hard, slow and steady, and, all the while, his heavy-lidded gaze held her enthralled.

Initially Savannah had managed a mocking smile, but she gloomily suspected it had lost its irreverent edge and had been replaced by a stupidly besotted grin. Her pulse tripped wildly in her veins and the desire that had never fully receded came swirling through like a riptide, washing away reason and rationale and anything that closely resembled common sense.

Knox finally commenced his cleaning and released her tingling fingers. "Savannah…can I ask you something?"

She blinked, still wandering in a sensual fog. "Sure."

"Where are you from?" he asked lightly. "Where did you grow up?"

The fog abruptly fled. Savannah suppressed a sigh and took a couple of seconds to shore up her defenses and decide how she should respond. She'd known that he'd ask—she'd watched the very questions form in his mind. Perhaps if she told him enough to satisfy his curiosity, he'd leave well enough alone. One could hope, at any rate.

Savannah pushed her plate away. "I grew up in lots of different places."

"Military?"

She blew out a breath. "No…foster care. My parents died when I was six."

Knox winced. "Oh. Sorry." He looked away. "Damn, I—"

Savannah hated this part. It was the same scenario every time. As soon as she told someone about her parents, they always apologized and then lapsed into an uncomfortable silence. She'd secretly hoped Knox would be different, but—

"That sucks, Savannah," Knox finally said. He plowed a hand through his hair, clearly out of his comfort zone, and his concerned gaze found hers. "I know that sounds so lame, but damn…that just really sucks.''

No points for eloquence, Savannah thought as her heart unexpectedly swelled with some unnamed emotion, but he definitely scored a few points for the blunt, wholly accurate summation. ''Thank you. You're absolutely right.'' She smiled, blew out a stuttering breath. ''It did suck.''

He arched a brow, leaned down and casually rested his elbows on his knees and let his hands dangle between his spread thighs. ''No family you could have gone to live with?''

''No,'' Savannah replied with a shake of her head, shoving the old familiar hurt back into the dark corner of her heart where she kept it. ''There was no one. We were a family of three and they died…and then there was me.''

''No brothers or sisters?''

''Nope.'' Time for her part of the interview to be over, Savannah decided, drawing in a shaky breath. She smacked her thighs. ''No more questions, Knox…unless you want to answer a few of mine.''

He smiled and lifted one heavily muscled shoulder in an offhanded shrug. ''Go ahead. Shoot. My life is an open book.''

We'd just see about that, wouldn't we? Savannah thought. ''Why do you work so hard at looking like you don't work hard?''

His affable mask slipped for half a second, and if

she hadn't been watching closely, she would have missed it altogether. "What?"

Savannah leveled him with a serious look. "I've watched you. I used to think that everything just came so easily to you…but I was wrong. You work very hard at your job, yet you make it a point to look like you don't." She paused. "Why is that, Knox?"

He looked away. "I don't know what you're talking about."

"The hell you don't. Be honest."

Knox swallowed. "Do you want the truth?"

"No," she deadpanned. "Tell me a lie. Of course, I want the truth!"

He smiled at that, then looked away once more. "It's simple, really. Everyone expects me to fail, and I don't want anyone to know just how much I want to succeed." He laughed self-consciously. "There you have it. My big dark secret."

He was right. It was simple, and yet more meaning and explanation lurked in that one telling sentence than she could have hoped for. Another thought surfaced.

"What do you mean *everyone?*" she asked.

Another dry humorless laugh rumbled from his chest. "Just what I said—everyone. Parents, coworkers, they all expect it." He passed a hand wearily over his face. "My parents keep waiting for me to come and work with my father, and so does everyone at the *Phoenix*. No one realizes that I'm not going anywhere, that I've chosen my career." His determined, intent gaze tangled with hers. "I'm a journalist. This is who I am, what I do. Does that make sense?"

Regret twisted her insides. Suddenly lots of things were beginning to make sense, Savannah thought, including the fact that she'd been no better than anyone else, if not worse. She'd taken one look at Knox, panicked, and had not gone to the trouble to look beyond her first impression, beneath the surface of his irreverent attitude. She'd formed the one uncharitable opinion and held fast to it, because she'd been too terrified to face the alternative.

Savannah swallowed. "It, uh, makes perfect sense. And Knox, for what it's worth, I think you're one helluva journalist."

His guarded expression brightened and dimmed all in the same instant. He looked away. "You're just saying that."

Savannah grinned at him. "Have you ever known me just to toss out a compliment?"

Those sexy lips tipped into an endearing smile. "No."

"Then the proper response is thank you."

He nodded. "Thank you."

The mood had become altogether too serious, Savannah decided. "We should get started on those chakras," she told him.

Knox winced, rubbed the back of his neck. "You're right. Do you mind if I grab a quick shower first?"

Savannah shook her head. "I need to organize my notes. We have a story to write, after all."

And she had some thinking to do…and a decision to make.

"I SWEAR I'LL CATCH YOU."

"I know that," Savannah said, exasperated.

"Then what's the problem?"

She speared her fingers through her hair and glared at him despairingly. "I can't let myself fall. I—I just can't do it. It's not a question of you being able to catch me—it's the whole idea of letting you. Don't you get it?"

Regrettably, he did, Knox thought. They'd been at this blind-trust test for the better part of thirty minutes and she still hadn't been able to let him catch her. Her reticence made perfect sense, now that she'd shared a little of her history.

Though Savannah had been very glib about the loss of her parents and her childhood, Knox had nonetheless glimpsed the little girl who'd felt abandoned beneath the woman who had learned to cope. Hell, no wonder she had trust issues. She'd had to learn to trust herself and no one else. She was completely alone. That wholly depressing thought had fully hit him while he'd been in the shower.

Savannah Reeves didn't have anyone.

Not a single living soul in this world to share her life with. Granted, his parents hadn't always supported him the way he would have liked…but at least they were there. Had provided the necessities and more to see him raised.

Savannah had gone through the foster-care system and apparently had come through the experience without so much as a mentor. If there had been any-body—anybody at all who'd made a difference in her life—she would have shared that. What she'd said had revealed a lot, but what she hadn't said revealed more.

In all truth, Knox could have waited to take his shower in the morning, but after listening to her re-signedly tell him about her parents, Knox had sud-denly been filled with self-loathing and disgust. He'd turned into the whiny little rich boy he'd always sworn he'd never become. So what if his parents didn't like his job? They'd get over it. So what if his co-workers at the *Phoenix* didn't respect him? He'd do his job to the best of his ability, and he'd *make* them, by God. He wouldn't leave them a choice.

When compared with the trials of Savannah's life, Knox's little letdowns had seemed petty, selfish and small. *He'd* felt small, and Knox had decided that the only way he could redeem himself was to become someone she respected…and someone she trusted.

Thus, he'd come out of his shower prepared to conquer her trust issues. Knox frowned. So far, it wasn't working.

"Okay," Knox finally said. "Let's try something different. Face me and fall forward."

Savannah heaved an impatient sigh. "This is pointless. I'm not—"

"Do it."

"Oh, all right." She moved to stand in front of him.

"Now look at me and fall."

She chewed anxiously on her bottom lip, fastened her worried gaze onto his and fell…right into his outstretched arms.

Knox grinned, unaccountably pleased. His mood lightened considerably. "Now that's more like it."

She smiled hesitantly. "It is, isn't it? Thanks, Knox. That was a good idea."

His chest swelled, amazed that he'd been able to impress her. "Okay, now let's try this. Stand with your side to me and fall."

She did, from both sides, and both times fell right into his arms.

"And now for the final test," Knox teased. "Let's try the blind-trust test again."

Savannah's hopeful smile warmed him from the inside out. She swallowed and nervously gave him her back. For half a second, Knox thought she would go for it, would take the proverbial plunge, but just short of letting gravity have its way, Savannah drew up short with a frustrated wail of misery.

"Why?" she railed with a whimper. "Why can't I do this?" Defeat rounded her shoulders and the breath left her lungs in a long, dejected whoosh.

Knox, too, felt the drag of disappointment.

"You'll get it," he encouraged. "You've definitely made some improvement."

"I know, and thank you." She shot him a sheepish look. "I don't mean to sound ungrateful. I just— I just *hate* to fail."

Knox summoned a droll smile. "I don't think anyone particularly cares for it."

Some of the tension left her petite frame and her lips twitched adorably. "I suppose not."

"Why don't we move on to the chakras? We're behind, you know." Knox strolled across the room and sprawled across the foot of the bed as he'd done the night before. He heaved a disgusted breath. "Marge and Chuck are beating us."

Savannah cast him a sidelong glance. "Humph. Mostly Chuck just beats himself."

Knox felt his eyes widen and a shocked laugh burst from his throat. He looked over at Savannah, pushing down his smile. "So, what's the next chakra we're supposed to unblock?" Knox asked innocently. He knew, of course. He simply enjoyed messing with her.

Her gaze twinkled with perceptive humor. "It's the genital chakra, which you well know," she added pointedly. She settled herself against the headboard, placed the book in her lap and opened it to the appropriate page. He watched her lips form the words as she read silently. After a moment, she looked up. "Well, now this is interesting. According to the book, this chakra can be one of the most difficult to deal with.''

"That being the case, should I get naked?''

"I think not.''

"Damn,'' Knox said with chagrin. "Funny, but I distinctly remember you saying that I could be naked in our room.''

Though she refused to look at him, Knox discerned a slight quiver at the corners of her lips. "I lied. Now shut up and listen.'' She paused and read some more. "I—I don't think either one of us is blocked in this chakra.''

That figured. This was the only one he'd looked forward to working on. Knox scowled. "Are you sure? I'm feeling a little blocked. I think that you should unblock me. Does it say how you're supposed to do that?''

Savannah poked her tongue in her cheek. "Yes, as a matter of fact, it does.''

Anticipation rose. Knox turned over onto his back and laced his hands behind his head. "Then do it.''

"Are you sure?'' she asked gravely.

Oh, was he ever. "Yes, I'm sure.''

"Well, if you're sure.'' Knox felt the bed shift as she moved into a better position. "You'll need to roll over.''

Something in her too innocent tones alerted Knox to the fact that all was not as it seemed. Obviously he wasn't going to get the hand job he'd been dreaming of. With a premonition of dread, he opened his closed eyes and glanced at her. Just as he suspected, mischief danced in that cool blue gaze. "Roll over?" he asked slowly. He dreaded asking, but knew he must. "Why?" he asked ominously.

"Because, according to my handy booklet, I'm supposed to unblock your root chakra while I'm unblocking your genital chakra." She smiled. "So why don't you—just try to relax and I'll—"

Realization dawned, and the semiarousal he'd enjoyed instantly vanished. His ass shrank in horrified revulsion. Knox slung an arm over his eyes. "Forget it," he growled.

"—make this as painless as possible." She paused. "What?" she asked innocently.

"Forget it."

"Are you sure? I'd be happy—"

"Savannah…" Knox warned. What was with the preoccupation with a person's ass? Knox wondered.

She laughed, not the least bit repentant. "I tried to tell you that we weren't blocked. Let's just chant the couples blessing and move on."

"What's that?" Knox asked, still perturbed.

Savannah aligned her body with his and Knox felt marginally better. She pillowed her head on the crook of her arm and held the book aloft with her other hand. Amusement glittered in her eyes and her lips were twitching with barely suppressed humor. "Okay, I'm supposed to say, 'I love you at your lingam and bless your wand of light.'" She promptly dissolved into a fit of giggles.

Knox laughed as well. "And what am I supposed to say?"

"You're supposed to say, 'I love you at your yoni and bless your sacred space.'"

How could people say this stuff with a straight face? Knox wondered. "Consider yourself loved and blessed," he said dryly. "Let's move on. What's next?"

Savannah sat up and wiped her eyes. "The belly chakra."

"Does my ass have anything to do with this one?" Knox asked suspiciously.

"Er...I don't think so."

He nodded. "Then continue."

"Okay, now this one is actually pretty interesting," Savannah said. "Our bellies are the feeling centers. Our emotions are energy in motion and tend to grow out of our bellies and take whatever path is appropriate for their expression."

Knox nodded thoughtfully. That did make a sort of strange sense. He considered his nudge. It definitely came from his belly. "That one seems almost plausible," Knox admitted.

Savannah's brow furrowed thoughtfully. "It does, doesn't it? Just think of butterflies in your belly, and nausea, and that sinking sensation when something isn't quite right. Gut reaction, gut feelings." She hummed under her breath, read a little more. "I can actually relate to this one. We're supposed to chant *ram* now."

"Ram," Knox deadpanned. "I'm unblocked, what about you?"

"Ram, it's a miracle, so am I."

Knox grinned. "Amazing, isn't it?"

She grinned adorably. "Without a doubt."

"What's next?"

Savannah flipped the page. Her eyes widened. "Ooh, the heart chakra. The center of love, courage and intimacy." Her brow wrinkled in perplexity. "A broken heart is most often the cause of a block in this chakra. We're supposed to share our hurts with each other to promote healing. It also says that a woman generally has to feel love in this chakra before she can experience sexual intimacy and that, likewise, a man must have sexual intimacy with a woman first in order to build trust." She snorted. "Hell, no wonder we're all screwed up. Men and women are completely opposite."

A bark of dry laughter bubbled up Knox's throat. "Was there ever a doubt?"

Savannah thwacked him with the book. "Pay attention. You're supposed to be telling me about all of your old heartaches."

"Sorry, I can't."

"Why not?"

"Because I don't have any."

Savannah raised a skeptical brow. "You've got to be kidding. You've never had your heart broken?"

"No," he sighed, "can't say that I have."

She paused. Swallowed. "Well, I don't know

whether to congratulate you, or offer my sympathies.''

The confident smile Knox had been wearing slipped a fraction. ''What do you mean *offer your sympathies?*''

The twinkling humor had died from her eyes and had been replaced with something mortifyingly like pity. ''Well…that's just sad, Knox.''

Knox blinked, astounded. ''You think it's sad that I've never had my heart broken?'' Was she cracked or what? he wondered, feeling a curious tension build in his chest.

Savannah sighed, seemingly at a loss to explain herself. Finally she said, ''Not that you haven't had your heart broken, but that you've never been close enough to another person for it to have happened. Everybody needs their heart broken at least once.''

He scowled. ''I think I'll pass.''

That soft sympathetic gaze moved over him. ''You don't get it. It's what you're missing up until you get your heart broken that makes it all worthwhile.''

''Is that the voice of experience talking?'' Knox asked, mildly annoyed.

He didn't know why her words bothered him so much, but they did. His skin suddenly felt too tight and his palms had begun to sweat. What? Did she think him incapable of love? Did she think him too shallow for such a deep emotion? If he ever found the right person, he could love her, dammit. He was capable of loving someone. He'd simply not found anyone he wanted to invest that much emotion in, that's all. But it didn't mean he couldn't do it.

Savannah's gaze grew shuttered and she tucked her hair behind her ear, an endearingly nervous gesture. "Yes, it's the voice of experience. I've…almost had my heart broken."

"Almost?" Knox questioned skeptically.

"I'm still in denial."

"Oh. Well, I still wouldn't think it would be a pleasant ordeal," Knox replied drolly.

She smirked. "No, it wasn't."

"You should probably share this with me," Knox told her magnanimously, "seeing as we're supposed to heal old hurts to unblock this chakra."

She pinned him with a shrewd glare. "You have absolutely no interest in unblocking my heart chakra, you great fraud—you're simply curious."

Smiling, he shrugged. "There is that."

Savannah picked at a loose thread on her *kurta,* but finally relented with a sigh. "There was someone once," she admitted. "His, uh, parents didn't approve of me, though, so he broke up with me and went to Europe."

Knox abruptly sat up. *"What?"*

She laughed without humor. "It's true, I swear."

"What kind of a pansy-ass were you dating?" Knox asked incredulously.

She lifted her shoulders in a halfhearted shrug. "A spineless one with no class, as it turned out."

That summed it up nicely, Knox thought. What

sort of ignorant prick let his parents pick his girl-friend? he wondered angrily, much less ditched Savannah for Europe? Hell, no wonder she didn't trust anybody. No wonder she couldn't pass that blind-trust test. When had anyone ever given her a reason to trust them? When had anyone been worthy of it?

"I've had enough heart chakra healing," Savannah told him. "Let's move on. We're almost finished."

It took a considerable amount of effort, but Knox finally forced his violent thoughts away and managed to concentrate on the task at hand. "Sure. What's next?"

"The throat chakra, the source of authentic expression." She chewed the corner of her lip and read some more. "Okay, we're supposed to hear and heed our inner voices, express our most dangerous emotions, even rage. But we have to learn to do this in gentle tones with our lovers and save our loud voices for when we're alone."

Knox nodded. "That's simple enough. We're not supposed to scream at one another."

"Right. We're supposed to tell our truths and sing our true songs, sanctify sex and choose words that glorify our sexual organs, such as *sacred space, wand of light,* etc...."

"Got it. What else?"

Her brow furrowed. "This is another one that sort of makes sense. Communication flows through this chakra. Think of some of the things that happen physically to you when you get upset.''

"Like what?'' Knox asked, not following.

"A lump in your throat, for instance. Or being too overcome to speak.''

He nodded. "Makes sense. Anything else?''

Savannah glanced at the book. "Uh…we're supposed to place our hand over each other's throats and tell each other to sing our true songs, then chant *ham.*''

Knox leaned forward and placed his hand over Savannah's slim throat. He grinned. "Sing your true song, baby. *Ham.*''

Savannah reciprocated the gesture. "Ditto.''

"How many more of these chakras do we have?'' Knox asked as he rolled back onto his side.

"Just two.''

"Okay.''

"Why? Do you want to quit for tonight?''

"No. We're going to need lots of time tomorrow night to work on *Love His Lingam* and *Sacred Goddess Stimulation.*'' And he couldn't wait.

Savannah pulled in a slow breath. "Right,'' she all but croaked. "Okay, the next one is the brow chakra, logic and intuition, the tird eye and all that. Think of people with psychic ability, or with a keen mind. Dreams and such. All of those things are a product of the brow chakra.''

Another one that was almost plausible, Knox thought, as possible angles for their story spun through his mind. His grandmother had been physic, so he knew such powers existed. "Are you blocked in that chakra?"

"No," Savannah said. "Are you?"

"No."

Another smile quivered on her lips. "Then we're supposed to join brows, stare at each other until our eyes seem to merge and say, "'I r-rejoice in how you comprehend and intuit.' Then we chant *ooo*."

Smiling, Knox rubbed the back of his neck. "You've got to be kidding."

"Nope," she said, tongue in cheek.

"Okay." Knox rolled himself into the center of the bed, then sat up on his knees. Savannah set the book aside and, mischief lighting her eyes, assumed the position as well. Gazes locked in mutual amusement, they leaned forward and their brows met.

"I feel utterly ridiculous," Savannah said, her sweet breath fanning against his lips. "What about you?"

"Most definitely."

The words were no sooner out of his mouth than an altogether different sensation took hold. Several sensations, in fact. The simultaneous registration of her sweet scent, the press of her body and the proximity of her lips hit him all at once. His heart thundered in his chest, pumping his blood that much faster to his groin. Fire licked through his veins, and he burned with the need to possess her, to lay her down, spread her thighs and bury himself so deeply into her that there would be no beginning and no end, just *them*.

Savannah's eyes darkened with desire, the heat burning away any vestiges of lingering humor. He could feel the quickened puff of her breath against his lips, heard her swallow.

Knox's blood roared in his ears, drowning out any would-be protests. He'd kissed her repeatedly since the beginning of this damned workshop, but it had always been at Edgar or Rupali's prompting. He hadn't taken the plunge and made the conscious decision to kiss her, taste her of his own accord. But he was making that decision now—he couldn't help himself—and he wanted her to know the difference and, more important, to feel it.

Knox gently cupped her face, held her gaze until his lips brushed lightly over hers. He hovered on a precipice, he knew, yet he didn't possess the power to keep from plunging headlong over it. Then his eyelids fluttered closed under the exquisite weight of some unnamed emotion…and he sighed…and eagerly embraced the fall.

11

SAVANNAH HAD KNOWN the moment that her brow touched his that she'd made a tactical error—she'd touched him. She knew, didn't she, that she couldn't touch Knox without melting like a Popsicle on the Fourth of July? She knew, and yet it hadn't made one iota of difference because she simply could not resist him. She had been inexplicably drawn to him from the moment she'd first seen him, had been lusting after him in secret torment every day since.

Just seconds ago, she'd watched the humor fade from his gaze, chased away by the power of a darker, more primal emotion. His entire body had grown taut, and then, as though he'd made some momentous decision, she'd discerned a shift in his posture. Then those amazing hands she'd imagined roaming all over her body in all sorts of wicked acts of depravity had cupped her face in a gesture so truly sweet she'd almost wept with the tenderness of it.

In the half second before his lips touched hers, Savannah realized the import of that soft touch, and her heart, along with the rest of her wayward body, had all but melted.

Knox Webber wanted her. *At long last.*

With a sigh of utter satisfaction, Savannah eagerly met his mouth, threaded her fingers through his hair and kissed him the way she'd always dreamed of kissing him. She poured every single ounce of belated desire into the melding of their mouths and was rewarded when Knox responded with a hungry growl of pleasure. The masculine sound reverberated in her own mouth, making her smile against his lips. His tongue slid over hers, plundered and plumbed, a game of seek and retreat that soon had Savannah's insides hot, muddled and quivering with want.

Knox molded her to him, slid those talented hands down her back and over her rump, and back up again. His hands burned a heated trail of sensation everywhere they touched and she longed to have them plumping her swollen breasts, sliding over her belly and lower, then lower still until his fingers worked their magic on the part of her that needed release most of all.

As though he'd read her mind, Knox smoothed his hand up her rib cage and cupped one pouting breast. She sagged under the torment of the sensation and, with a groan of satisfaction, Knox followed her down upon the bed. His warmth wrapped around her and the long, hot length of him nudged her hip.

She sucked in a harsh breath between their joined mouths and then sent her hands on their own little exploration of his body. The smooth, hard muscles of his shoulders, down the slim indention of his spine and back over the tautened sinews of his magnificently formed back.

Having mapped that terrain, she moved onto the sleek slope of his chest, the bumpy ridges of his abdomen, and over one impossibly lean hip. He was magnificent, the most perfectly put-together man she'd ever laid her greedy little hands upon. She claimed each perfection as her own. *Mine,* Savannah thought as she grasped his shoulders once more. *Mine,* she thought again as she slid her hand down his side. *Mine, mine, mine,* with each new part.

All mine.

Savannah winced as the *kurta* bunched annoyingly beneath her hungry hands. Knox had thrown one heavily muscled thigh across her leg and Savannah had the hem in her hand and had begun to swiftly tug it up his body before the significance of what she was doing surfaced in her lust-ridden brain.

Swallowing a cry of regret, she tore her mouth from his and pried his hand off her breast. "We can't...do this," she breathed brokenly.

Knox's lips curled in invitation and he nuzzled the side of her neck. "Oh, but we can," he told her. He tugged at the neckline of her *kurta,* attempted to bare her breast. "Come on, I'll show you mine if you show me yours."

Savannah dragged his head away from her neck and ignored the fizzle of warmth his wicked lips had created. Ignored his invitation to play a sexy game of show-and-tell. "Knox," she said desperately. "*Think*. We can't—"

"Thinking is overrated. In fact, you've told me repeatedly that I should try not to think. Remember? Something about it upsetting the delicate balance of my constitution." He bent his head and sucked her aching nipple into his mouth through the soft cotton fabric. The shock of pure sensation arched her off the bed and rent a silent gasp from her throat.

Sweet heaven.

Though it nearly killed her, Savannah wrenched his head from her breast. "Stop. We have to talk. We can't—"

"Talk?" Knox tsked and thumbed her nipple distractingly. "You know we can't talk for more than two minutes without arguing. This is a much more agreeable way to pass the time and you know it." He slid his fingers up her thigh and brushed her feminine curls.

Savannah bit her bottom lip and whimpered, resisted the urge to press herself against those teasing fingers. Knox took her hesitation as permission, and gently stroked her through the fabric.

She squirmed with need and her clit throbbed and her womb grew even heavier with want, but Savannah managed to stay his hand with a will born of stubborn desperation. "*Listen,* please," she insisted breathlessly. "We can't do this *now*."

She watched Knox's sinfully sculpted lips ready a protest, but the *now* registered a second before he could push the sound from his lips. He arched a sulky brow. "What do you mean *now?*"

"The rule," Savannah reminded impatiently. "No sex until tomorrow night."

For better or for worse, she'd just told Knox Webber that she'd sleep with him tomorrow night, Savannah realized. She refused to consider anything beyond Sunday, anything that might remotely resemble second thoughts or regrets. She'd wanted Knox…forever. There was simply no other way for this weekend to end. She'd known the outcome, had known this would happen, the moment Chapman had commanded that she come to this workshop.

And, though it sounded like a lame excuse, at least they would know for sure if there was any real merit to the tantric way. They would be able to lend true credibility to their story.

That should please Knox, anyway, Savannah thought with a prick of regret. After all, that's what had brought them here.

"Are you saying what I think that you're saying?" Knox asked carefully. Desire tempered with caution glinted in that sexy green gaze.

Savannah swallowed tightly. "Yes, I am." She managed a shaky grin. "It's inevitable, right? And then there's the story to consider."

A shadow shifted over his face and he grew unnaturally still. "The story?"

"Right." Savannah shrugged out from under him and stood. "I mean, how can we really tell our readers if there is any truth to the whole concept of tantric sex if we don't try it?"

Knox stared at her for several seconds with a curiously unreadable look, then he abruptly smiled, but it lacked his typical humor. "You're right. We need to do it, we need to sacrifice ourselves, for the sake of the integrity of our story."

There was subtle sarcastic tone to Knox's voice that needled Savannah. Honestly, she didn't think it would be that big a damned sacrifice. Clearly she'd said something that had pissed him off, but she didn't have a clue what that something could be. *Sacrifice?* she wondered again, even more perturbed. If she hadn't stopped him just a few minutes ago, they'd undoubtedly be enjoying the aftermath of an earth-shattering orgasm, and yet now—because he'd have to wait until tomorrow—he was sacrificing himself? Well, to hell with him, Savannah thought.

"I'm going for a walk," she said tightly, and headed for the door. She was embarrassingly close to tears.

"Savannah, wait," Knox said. He muttered a hot oath and pushed a hand through his hair. "I'm bungling this."

She paused and turned around. "Bungling what?"

His tortured gaze met hers and held it. "If we make love here tomorrow night, it's not going to have anything to do with a damned story," he said heatedly. "At least, not for me. I want you, dammit—I want you more than anything—but it doesn't have anything to do with getting a story. And I certainly don't expect you, nor want you, to sleep with me for the sake of one. Do you understand?''

Something light and warm moved into her chest and swelled. She blinked, swallowed. "I think I'm getting it."

"Good."

"I'm still going for a walk."

He nodded.

Savannah opened the door, then paused. "Just so you know," she said haltingly, "it wouldn't have been about the story for me, either." Her wobbly smile made an encore appearance. "It was only a face-saver, you know, in case you regretted things later."

His steady green gaze rooted her to the floor with its intensity. "I won't regret it."

"Neither will I," Savannah murmured, and prayed fervently that statement proved to be true.

"DON'T WE NEED TO GET that last chakra out of the way before we go to breakfast?" Knox asked. He didn't want anything besides *Love His Lingam* and *Sacred Goddess Stimulation* between him and Savannah after they wound up classes today.

"Yes, we do," she called from the bathroom. "Just let me finish my hair and we'll go over it."

Her hair, Knox thought with part chuckle, part snort. Well, he had several minutes then and he would use them to think about everything that had happened between him and Savannah last night. She'd cut her walk short—after catching Chuck and his hand making love on the front porch—and when she'd returned, they'd lain in the dark and talked and laughed until the wee hours of the morning.

They'd talked about everything from favorite soft drinks, to work, and a multitude of subjects in between. Had even managed to agree—after *much* discussion—on what angle to use for this story. Knox had picked up on a great deal of hostility between her and Chapman, but when he'd asked, naturally she'd clammed up and quickly changed the subject. Knox didn't know what had happened to create such animosity, but as soon as he returned to Chicago, he was determined to find out. If not from Savannah, then from a different source.

Journalists didn't come any finer, more professional, than Savannah Reeves. If there was a problem, undoubtedly it was on Chapman's end, not hers. And if that were the case, and Chapman had been treating her unfairly, he would soon be held accountable. Knox's hands involuntarily balled into fists. Boss or no, Chapman would pay.

Savannah finally emerged from the bathroom wrapped in a towel Knox mentally willed to fall off but, to his regret, didn't. Other than a hint of makeup and the fresh look of her, Knox could discern no significant difference. Her hair still looked as if it had been hit with a weed-whacker, then combed with a garden rake. He grinned. Adorably messy, as always.

Catching his smile, Savannah's steps faltered as she went to put her things into her overnight bag. "What are you smiling about?" she asked cautiously.

Knox rested his chin on his thumb and index finger. "Your hair," he replied honestly.

She rolled her eyes. "This is as good as it gets. If you're ashamed to be seen with me, I suggest you get over it."

"Who said anything about being ashamed? I like it."

She shot him a look. "Right."

"I do," Knox insisted. "It looks all messy, like you just rolled out of bed."

She heaved a resigned sigh. "Wow, Romeo. Is that supposed to be a compliment? Gonna write me an Ode to Bed Head?"

"Of course it's a compliment. Your normally quick wit seems a little sluggish this morning. Didn't you hear the part about the bed?"

"Yes, and I fail to see the relevance."

"Of course, you don't. You're not a man."

Savannah's lips curled. "Another brilliant observation. The power of your deductive reasoning astounds me."

"Aw, hell. Think for a minute, Savannah. If I look at you and think that you just look like you rolled out of bed, then what other things am I likely to think about?"

"Bad breath, drool, pillow creases—"

Knox chuckled. "You're thinking like a woman. Think—"

Her eyes widened in mock astonishment. "Imagine that."

"Come on. Think like a man," Knox told her.

Savannah shrugged. "I don't know. I—"

"Then I'll tell you. I'm thinking about what you were wearing in that bed. Do you sleep in the nude, in a T-shirt or a silk teddy? What have you been doing in that bed? Better yet, what could you do with me—or—to me in that bed? What would I do to you if I had you in bed? What would—"

"I've got it," Savannah interrupted, her face flushed. "You look at my hair and think about sex."

"Right."

"Knox, when do you look at a woman and *not* think about sex?"

"I've just paid you a compliment, right?"

"I suppose."

"Then the proper response is thank you," he said, reminding her of the proper compliment etiquette she'd been so quick to share with him.

A slow grin trembled into place. "Thank you."

"You're welcome." He smiled contentedly. "Now what about that crown chakra?"

Savannah pulled her *kurta* on over her head, tugged it into place and then shimmied out of the towel. What a dirty trick, Knox thought. He'd been nice enough to drop his towel for her and she couldn't show a little consideration and reciprocate the gesture? "I'll get the book," she said drolly. "You just sit there."

Knox frowned innocently. "What? What did I do now?"

"Couldn't you have gotten this book and gone over it yourself while I was getting ready?"

"No."

She looked taken aback at his simple, honest reply. "Why the hell not?"

"Because I've been thinking about having sex with you."

A shocked laugh burst from her throat and she flushed to the roots of her hair. She swallowed and seemed incapable of forming a reply. Speechless *and* blushing, Knox thought. Damn, he was good.

"The crown chakra," Knox prodded.

"Right." The tip of her tongue peeked from between her lips as she turned to the end of the booklet. "Okay," she began. "The crown chakra is the center of spiritual connectivity. Now that all of our chakras have been unblocked, we're supposed to imagine white light and lotus blossoms flowing from the tops of our heads." Savannah's twinkling gaze met his astounded one.

"*What?*"

"Lotus blossoms and light flowing from our heads." She twinkled her fingers above her head. "We're supposed to merge and inhale one another and feel in unity with the universe. We chant *mmm.*"

"Should we merge now or later?"

Her lips twitched. "Later. Come on, we're going to be late for breakfast."

Knox heaved an exaggerated sigh and reluctantly stood. "I'd rather inhale and merge with you."

"Later," she laughed.

He would take that as a promise.

"WELCOME TO THE long-awaited *Sacred Goddess Stimulation* class," Rupali said with a secret smile. "I know you have all looked forward to this, but, before we begin, I would like to take a moment to caution you about what you are about to see and hear in this particular class." She paused. "This is a very dramatic lesson, very graphic. There is simply no way to adequately show you how to perform these services for your lover without demonstrating them. You are welcome to practice on your lover during class, but your time would be best spent observing and learning from Edgar and me. If you are in any way going to be uncomfortable with what I have just explained, then you shouldn't be here."

Well, that ruled her out, Savannah thought. That huge map of a vagina sitting on the easel next to Rupali had, quite frankly, shocked the crap out of her. "Knox, I—"

"No."

Well, all righty then. Savannah settled back into her seat, and did her dead-level best to ignore the huge vaginal chart.

"Is there anyone who would like to leave this class?" Rupali asked.

Several headshakes and soft-spoken no's filtered through the room, assuring Savannah that they were all a bunch of perverts, herself included. She didn't know exactly what all *Secret Goddess Stimulation* entailed, but she strongly suspected that it would have been something better learned in the privacy of their room with a handy how-to video.

"Okay, then. Let's begin." Rupali looked to her husband and he stepped forward.

"Men, this class is about learning how to properly please your woman, what makes her feel good, what will bring her pleasure." His gaze lingered on the class at large for a moment, then he continued. "First, we're going to cover the basic anatomy of the female sex."

To Savannah's growing discomfort, Edgar pointed out all of the necessary female parts, lingering particularly on the clitoris, which he described as the pearl of sensation.

Edgar held up a glass jar—his *yoni* puppet—and demonstrated the proper way to find a woman's G-spot. He curled his ring finger and wiggled it back and forth. "Can everyone see? It's not the depth, the length, or the size which stimulates this concentration of sensitive cells, it's the positioning. Once you get it right, you'll be able to bring her to climax—possibly even ejaculation—every time you make love." He smiled. "And, yes, I said ejaculation. Though it's

known to be a rare occurrence in traditional intercourse, women can and do typically ejaculate during
tantric sex. Ah, I see a few skeptical faces in the
crowd. In just a few moments I will provide the proof
of that statement.''

Rupali laughed. ''I think it is *I* who will be the
one providing the proof, darling.''

Savannah had to confess a degree of morbid fascination. She'd read about female ejaculation before,
but had never imagined she'd get to witness the phenomenon.

''Jesus,'' Knox breathed next to her.

''What's the matter?''

''I don't know if I can watch this,'' he said.

''What?'' She swiveled to look at him. ''I thought
this was the class that you'd been waiting for?''

A muscle worked in his tense jaw. ''Yeah, but I
was wrong. I don't want to look at this woman's
yoni—I want to look at yours. This is too weird, too
cracked. It's like watching my parents.''

''Well, it's too late now,'' Savannah hissed.
''We're stuck here. Just avert your eyes.''

''Can't,'' Knox said. ''It's like looking at a high-
way accident. You dread it, but you can't look
away.''

''Well, try. It'll be over soon.''

Knox startled her by sliding his hand in hers, sending a flush of delight and warmth straight to her rapidly beating heart.

It wasn't over soon—it lasted forever. Rupali and

Edgar were seasoned tantrics and believed in letting
the class get their money's worth because, much to
Knox and Savannah's horror, Edgar showed how to
pleasure Rupali repeatedly. With his hand, his penis
and a few battery-operated gadgets that Savannah
had never seen. Several members of the class had
decided to test their newfound knowledge during the
session as well. So, not only did they get to see Rupali and Edgar's ''sacred spaces'' and ''wands of
light,'' they got to see several others, too.

In addition to those orgylike images, Rupali and
Edgar made good on their promise—Rupali ejacu-
lated. Knox had become increasingly miserable
throughout the lesson, but seemed particularly dis-
turbed by watching Rupali's *amrita*—or ''sweet nec-
tar''—arc through the air like a clear rainbow.

Soon after Edgar and Rupali announced a brief
intermission for refreshments between classes. *Love
His Lingam* would start momentarily.

''I want to go to the room,'' Knox whispered
tightly.

''You don't want to participate in *Love His Lingam?*''

''No.''

''Knox, I hesitate to bring this up, but you're the
one who planned this trip and you're the one who
wanted to do this story. I'm not remotely interested
in going in here and learning how to blow you or
give you a hand job—I can do that without any instruction and guarantee that you won't have any

complaints. But if we're going to do this story the way we should, then you know we need to just suck it up and go.''

Knox grinned. "Suck it up, eh?''

She jabbed him. "You know what I mean,'' she said impatiently.

"Oh, all right,'' Knox finally relented. "But I am not going to like it,'' he growled.

"I didn't say you had to like it, I just said you had to suck it up.''

"Only if you will, baby,'' Knox muttered. "Only if you will.''

Savannah conjured a sexy grin, leaned forward and, to Knox's complete astonishment, stroked him through the *kurta* the way she'd been wanting to for the past forty-eight hours. "You can bet your sweet ass.''

12

BY THE TIME Rupali had finished *Loving Edgar's Lingam,* Knox was in a shell-shocked, near-catatonic state. Sure he'd gleaned a few little tidbits of knowledge about his equipment that he hadn't known, such as where his supposed G-spot was located. That, Knox remembered with ballooning horror, explained the acute fascination with the *rosebud*.

His G-spot would remain a virgin, thank you very much.

Edgar had also lectured on attaining the inner orgasm, and had preached against the "squirt," which was reputed to waste a man's sexual energy and rob a woman of her potential multiple orgasms.

In order to avoid the outer orgasm, men were encouraged to practice deep, controlled breathing and to tighten their pubococcygeal and anal sphincter muscles—Knox inwardly shuddered—and to draw the force of their inner ejaculation up through their unblocked chakras, then out of their crown chakra.

Kind of like a volcanic orgasm, Knox had decided after watching Edgar shimmy and shake and look all but ready to blow. Knox winced. Quite frankly, the process looked—and sounded—painful. It had also been very noisy.

Honestly, he hadn't heard so much groaning, moaning and grunting since he'd visited the pig barn at the county fair as a child. Apparently, though, noisy sex promoted tantric energy and so the class was encouraged to sing with their true voices and get as loud as they wished tonight.

Tonight.

Undoubtedly the whole damn villa would come crumbling down around them, brought on by the racket and vibrations of noisy sex.

Edgar and Rupali stood arm and arm in front of the class their cheeks flushed from an exertion Knox would just as soon forget. "This concludes our teachings," Edgar said, smiling. "We hope that what you have learned will promote sexual health and healing, and will deepen your sexual and spiritual connection with your lover."

"Tonight, you will go to your rooms and put all of the lessons we have taught you into practice," Rupali interjected airily. "Open yourselves up and connect with each other as you never have before. Embrace your lover, let your true songs be sung, and seek the harmony of the *kundalini*." She smiled. "There are no additional instructions for tonight. Build upon the intimacies of the shared bath and dinner. Enhance them to fit your purposes, your pleasures. Go…and enjoy. We will meet in the common room and share our experiences and bid our farewells in the morning.'' The class began to disperse eagerly.

Savannah turned to Knox and a tentative, endearing smile curved her lips. ''Well,'' she said nervously.

Anticipation and some other curious emotion not readily identified mushroomed inside him. With effort, he swallowed and threaded his fingers through hers and tugged her toward their room. He grinned. ''Come on, Barbie.''

The walk back to their room seemed to take forever and in those few interminable minutes, a fist of anxiety tightened in Knox's chest, momentarily dousing the perpetual fire he'd carried in his loins.

He'd made love to women countless times, had committed carnal acts so depraved and hedonistic they would make even the unflappable Dr. Ruth blush. Knox was no stranger to sex and was confident in his ability to pleasure a woman.

But Savannah Reeves wasn't just any woman and the importance of that fact had hit him just seconds ago when she'd turned to him with eyes that were equally lit with desire and trepidation. Knox inexplicably knew that this woman—this time with this woman—was going to be different...and it scared the living hell out of him.

He could feel the tension vibrating off her slim frame as well, and wondered if she had suddenly had second thoughts. Knox opened the door and let her pass. Her anxious expression made him feel like a class-A bastard. He'd pushed her into this, he knew. He hadn't left well enough alone and now—

Savannah whirled around as soon as the door closed behind them, grabbed on to the front of his *kurta* and launched herself at his mouth.

Knox staggered back against the wall as the force of her desire blindsided him. Savannah's tongue plunged hungrily in and out of his mouth, suckled him, and burned through any doubts as to why she'd been anxious.

She wanted him.

She was here in his arms, feeding at his mouth, her hands roaming greedily over him, as though she couldn't—wouldn't—ever get enough of him.

Knox sucked in a harsh breath and a strange quiver rippled through his belly. The nudge commenced with an insistent jab. Lust detonated low in his loins, made him want to roar with desire, haul her to the bed and plow into that hot, wet valley between her thighs.

With a growl of pleasure, Knox molded her slim, supple body more closely to his, felt her squirm against him in an unspoken plea for release. Her pebbled breasts raked across his chest, igniting a trail of indescribably perfect sensation.

Savannah drew back. Blue flames danced in her somnolent gaze. ''Do you know how I got through that last class?'' she asked huskily.

Knox shook his head.

''I kept thinking about getting to do all those

things to you. My hands on your body, you in my mouth…'' She pulled in a breath. ''I have a very keen imagination and for the past several hours, I've been imagining this night,'' she said, her foggy tones almost hypnotic. ''Imagining everything that I want to do to you—and with you—and everything I want you to do to me.'' She cocked her head invitingly toward the bathroom. ''Now I want to show you. Whaddya say we start with a bath?''

Savannah stepped back and, in a gesture so inherently sexy it stole his breath, she pulled the *kurta* up over her head and let it drop to the floor. Then, with a saucy wink, she turned and walked to the bathroom.

She'd undoubtedly be the death of him, Knox thought, if indeed a man could expire from sexual stimulation. But, oh, what a way to go…

SAVANNAH POURED a bottle of scented oil that had magically appeared in their bathroom today into the steaming tub and felt a feline smile of satisfaction curl her lips. She'd been waiting for this day forever, had been waiting for this time with him forever, and now—at long last—she would have him.

Repeatedly, she hoped.

Something, warm, hot and languid snaked through her body at the thought, sending a pulse of sensation straight to her quivering womb. Her breasts grew heavy and her nipples tightened and tingled hungrily in anticipation of Knox's hot mouth.

The object of her lusty thoughts chose that moment to stroll naked into the bathroom. Savannah let her gaze roam over his magnificent body slowly, committing to memory each perfect inch of his impressive form. His eyes were dark and slumberous, and burned with a heat she recognized because it sizzled in her as well.

Her gaze skimmed the broad, muscled shoulders, washboard abdomen, lean waist and then settled drunkenly on his fully erect—*enormous*—penis, the one she simply couldn't wait to take into her mouth and, later, feel throbbing deeply inside her. His thighs were powerfully muscled, yet lean and athletic. And, oh, that ass… There was absolutely nothing about him physically that could be improved upon. Even his feet were perfect.

Savannah pulled in a shuddering breath as every cell in her body became hammeringly aware of him, clamoring for him and the cataclysmic release she knew she would find in his arms.

While she'd been openly appraising him, she in turn had been undergoing a similarly intense study. Knox's hot gaze had raked down her body in a leisurely fashion that felt more like a caress than a mere look, and the heat that presently funneled in her womb as a result of that narrow scrutiny was rapidly whipping her insides into a froth of insatiable need.

His lips quirked into a slow sexy grin. ''You've told me what you've been thinking about today. Why don't you get in that tub and I'll *show* you what I've been thinking about.''

Oh, sweet heaven. Savannah's bones all but melted. She stepped into the warm, scented water and sank down until only the tips of her breasts peeked above the foggy surface.

Knox slid in behind her so that she sat in the open vee of his thighs. Savannah's eyes fluttered shut and a sound of pure contentment puffed past her smiling lips as he snaked an arm around her waist and tugged her back against him. His warmth engulfed her, the hot, hard length of him pressed against the small of her back. Knox reached around her, filled his cupped hands with water and then palmed her breasts, kneaded them, rolled her beaded nipples between his thumb and forefinger. Savannah gasped, curled her toes and pressed her back more firmly against him.

He nuzzled her neck. ''This was one of the things I've been thinking about,'' Knox murmured huskily. ''Feeling your plump breasts in my hands, thumbing your pouty nipples. Do you have any idea how perfect you are? How absolutely beautiful?'' His hands mimicked his words and played languidly at her sensitized breasts, forcing another gasp of pleasure from her lips.

Savannah didn't bother to answer, but raised an arm, cupped the back of his head and turned to find his lips. She kissed him long and hard, soft and deep, slow yet purposefully, and all the while, Knox continued a magnificent assault on her aching breasts.

Then he moved lower, over her trembling belly, until finally he parted her curls and swept a finger over her throbbing, woefully neglected clit. Savannah jerked as sensation bolted through her, and she whimpered against his plundering mouth.

Knox drew back and slid his fingers into the hot, wet folds of her sex. "I've been wanting to do that as well," he said, rhythmically stroking her. "Feel the slick heat of your body, swallow your gasps, taste your groans."

Savannah's feminine muscles clenched beneath the exquisite pressure of his fingers. A long, slow drag, a swirl over her nub, and back again, over and over with his tender, mind-numbing assault. Her breath came in rapid, helpless puffs. Savannah felt her womb quicken, recognized the sharp tug of the beginning of a climax. She bit her bottom lip, a pathetic attempt to stem the steady flow of longing hurtling through her. He rocked gently behind her, mimicking the steady thought-shattering pressure. It built and built, like the tightening of a screw until something inside her finally—blessedly—snapped. Her body bowed from the shock, the explosion of sensation, and wept with the pulsing torrent and sweet rain of release.

Knox continued to gently rub her, light delicate strokes that made the orgasm seem to go on forever, more than she could bear.

She twisted away from those wicked fingers and turned around, straddled him and kissed him deeply

once more. She sucked his tongue, nipped at his lips.
The feel of his wet, hard body, slickened with the
vaguest hint of oil, felt excessively hedonistic beneath her questing palms. Savannah pulled in a shaky
breath as she felt the incredibly long length of him
slide along her nether lips. She pressed her aching
breasts to his chest and quivered with delight as his
masculine hair abraded her sensitive nipples. She slid
her hands down the smooth planes of his chest, ran
her nails over the hardened nubs of his nipples and
was rewarded when Knox hissed with pleasure.

"Damn," he groaned.

Savannah smiled evilly. "Oh, no baby, that's not
a damn. *This* merits a damn." She reached down
between their practically joined bodies and took him
in her hand.

Knox drew in a sharp breath and jerked against
her palm. "Y-you're right," he stuttered. "That is
most definitely a damn."

Savannah ran her hand up and down the length of
him, palmed the sensitive head of his penis and mar-
veled once again over the sheer size of him. He was
extraordinarily large, marvelously huge…and for the
time being, all hers. Every splendid inch of him.

She worked the length of him, up and down, long
steady strokes, feathery touches, but soon touching
him simply wasn't enough.

She wanted to taste him.

She gestured toward the steps and gently moved
his body in that direction, and eventually managed

to put him exactly where she wanted him—in her mouth.

Knox's swiftly indrawn breath was music to her ears. Sing your true songs, indeed, Savannah thought with a smile as she licked the swollen head of his penis. She alternated nibbles and sucks down the sides of him, ran her lips up and down his long length, and cuddled his testicles. Emboldened, she touched her tongue to those, too, and pulled one into her mouth and rolled it around her tongue.

Knox jerked and hissed another tortured breath. "Damn."

Savannah paused her ministrations. "Yeah, that should qualify as a damn." She smiled against him. "And so should this."

With that enigmatic comment, Savannah wrapped her lips around him, took him fully into her mouth and sucked hard. She curled her tongue around him, licked and suckled, over and over, and dragged him deeper and deeper into her mouth. She worked his base, gently massaged his testicles, and slid him in and out of her mouth. Knox's breath grew ragged and his thighs tensed, heralding the arrival of his impending climax.

When the first taste of his salty essence hit her tongue, Savannah drew back, took him in her hand and pumped him hard. She felt the rush of his orgasm shoot through the length of him like a bullet down the barrel of a gun, then felt him jerk and shudder as the hot blast burst from his loins. She milked him, drawing every last ounce of pleasure from him that she could.

Knox halted her ministrations with the touch of his trembling hand. "Enough," he growled. He stood and drew her up with him. "Let's go to bed."

She'd thought he'd never ask, Savannah thought. Knox snagged a towel from the bar and gently swabbed down her body, then hastily ran it over himself as well. Within seconds, they were rolling around the bed, a tangle of desperate arms and legs. The first orgasm had merely taken the edge off, but hadn't begun to dull the attraction. She still wanted him more than she wanted her next breath. Still couldn't wait to feel him plunging into her, couldn't wait to have his hot hands anchored at her waist while she sank down upon him.

Breathing hard, Knox pinned her down and his gaze tangled with hers. "You've tasted me—now I want you to lie still and take it while I taste you."

What? Savannah thought. Did he expect her to argue? She giggled. "Go ahead," she told him. "Eat me."

His eyes widened, then narrowed and his slow, sexy grin melted into one of the most sensual smiles she'd ever seen. "Oh, you are evil."

Savannah raked her nails over his chest. "Yeah…but you like it."

Those dark green eyes twinkled. "Yeah, I do." He bent down and drew her budded nipple into his mouth, pulling the air from her lungs in the process. "And I like this, too."

"Mmm," Savannah sighed. "So do I."

Knox thumbed one tingling nipple while he tortured the other with his mouth. He swiveled his tongue around the sensitive peak, then sucked it deeply into his mouth. Savannah pressed her legs together as the one sensation sparked another deep in her womb. Her clit pulsed and her feminine muscles contracted, begging—crying—for release. Seemingly reading her mind, Knox slid his hand down her shuddering belly and slipped his fingers into her drenched curls.

Savannah whimpered and pressed herself shamelessly against him, willing him to put her out of her sexually frustrated misery. She was on fire, burning up from the inside out, and the only antidote to this mad fever was a shot of him planted deep inside of her.

Knox kissed his way down her belly, swirled his tongue around and inside her navel, and then continued a determined path down to her sex. He knelt between her legs, parted her nether lips, then fastened his mouth onto the small hardened nub of desire hidden in those quivering folds and sucked hard. He worked his tongue up and down her valley, thrust it inside her, then suckled her again. Savannah bowed off the sheet, bucking beneath the most intimate kiss. Lust licked at her veins, and a deep tremble shook her seemingly boneless body.

He slid a finger deep inside her and hooked it around, savoring the moment that she practically arched off the bed. A groan tore from her throat and her eyes all but rolled back into her head.

The ultrasensitive patch of cells could only be her G-spot. Up until this very minute, Savannah hadn't known that she had one.

"Did you…learn that…this weekend?" Savannah asked brokenly as her hands fisted in the sheets.

Knox massaged the tender spot, while lapping at her clit with his wicked tongue. "I improved my technique, yes."

If he improved it any more, she'd undoubtedly burst into flames, shatter and fly into a million little pieces. The thought had no sooner flitted through her mind than the climax caught her completely unaware and broke over her like a high tide, sweeping her under, drowning her in the undertow of sparkling release.

She'd barely caught her breath before Knox snagged a condom from the nightstand, ripped into the package with his teeth, withdrew the thin contraceptive and then swiftly rolled it into place. Seconds later, he'd positioned himself between her thighs and then, with a primal groan of satisfaction, plunged into her.

The room shrank, swelled and then righted itself in the same instant. It was all Savannah could do to keep from passing out, he filled her so very completely. She stilled, waiting for her almost virgin-again body to accommodate his massive size.

"Are you all right?" Knox asked. Concern lined his brow.

Savannah resumed breathing and then tentatively rocked her hips against him, drawing him deeper into her body. "Yes, I am. I just—"

"I just nearly killed you because I plowed into you like a battering ram." He winced. "I'm sorry, I—"

"Knox," Savannah interrupted, "no one appreciates the fact that you have learned to apologize more than me...but we really need to work on your timing."

His face blanked. "My timing?"

"Yes, timing. For instance, now—while you're inside me, where I have wanted you to be for oh-so-long—is not the time to be apologizing. Now you need to be fu—"

The rest of her sentence died a quick death as Knox drew back and plunged into her once more. Savannah hiked her legs up and anchored them around Knox's waist, parlayed his every thrust. She rocked against him, clamped her feminine muscles around the hot, slippery length of him and shuddered with satisfaction as the friction between their joined bodies created a delicious draw and drag as he pumped frantically in and out of her.

Knox bent down and latched his mouth onto one of her nipples, sending another bolt of pleasure down into her quivering loins. Savannah ran her hands down his back, reveling in the taut muscles rippling beneath her palms, the slim hollow of his spine, and then she grabbed his magnificent ass and, with a tormented cry, urged him on. Knox understood her unspoken plea and upped the tempo, pumped harder and faster, pistoned in and out of her.

Harder, faster, and harder still.

She caught another bright flash of release and felt her body freeze with anticipation. Her heart threatened to beat right out of her chest and her breathing came in short, little jagged puffs. The tension escalated, steadily climbing like a Roman candle shot into the sky, then having gone as high as it could, exploded into a billion multicolored stars. Slowly, she drifted back to earth, spent but sated…and thoroughly pleasured.

With a guttural cry of satisfaction, Knox plunged into her one final time, his body bowed with the redeeming rapture of release. He shuddered violently, then his breath left him in one long whoosh and he sagged against her.

Knox rolled them quickly onto his side and fitted her more closely to him. He pressed a lingering kiss in her hair between rapid breaths. "Savannah, that was—I've never—"

Savannah felt a slow smile move across her lips and something warm and tingly bubbled through her chest. "A wordsmith, and yet you're speechless," Savannah teased.

"That," he said meaningfully, "was indescribable."

Savannah heaved a contented sigh. "It really was, wasn't it?"

Knox absently drew circles on her arm. "It was," he agreed.

She'd known it would be, Savannah thought. She'd never doubted it. She'd wanted Knox Webber since the very first moment she'd seen him. She'd yearned for him in secret silence and had nearly gone crazy as a result of the one-sided attraction. Her breathing had barely returned to normal and yet just feeling him next to her did something to her insides. She should be exhausted, she shouldn't be thinking about the delicious weight of his body pressed against hers, or the long, semiaroused length of him nuzzled against her hip.

Yet she was.

Were he to roll over and kiss her right now, she'd eagerly spread her legs and beg him to fill her up once again. The moment Knox had entered her, it was as though a wellspring of repressed emotion had been plumbed. Colors seemed brighter, scents stronger, her entire world had come into sharper focus. In that instant, Rupali's sage words had come back to her. *I don't think your problem lies in the lower chakras...*

And the older woman had been right. Knox had touched her heart. He'd fixed something this weekend that had been broken inside her. If nothing ever came of their time together, then at least she would have that.

Savannah had never felt anything like this before, had never had a lump in her throat after hours of mind-boggling, body-drenching, sweaty, wonderful sex.

But she did right now, and Savannah grimly suspected that were she to truly consider its origin, she would weep with regret.

So she wouldn't.

She'd simply tell herself that the reason she was so utterly moved by their lovemaking was the result of years of pent-up emotion and stress. She'd tell herself that the feelings that were currently taking root in her foolish heart were a product of a weekend of tremendous sexual stimulation, even possibly the result of the tantric rituals. She would tell herself these things…and pray that by the end of this weekend she'd believe them.

The alternative was unacceptable—she wouldn't permit herself to fall in love with Knox Webber…if it wasn't already too late.

13

_____

WHEN KNOX AWOKE on Monday morning, the first few tendrils of pink were spreading across the horizon, chasing away the early gray of dawn. Savannah was spooned with her back to his belly and he'd cupped her breast and slung a thigh over her inert form sometime during the night.

Feeling her next to him, having that delectable body snuggled up against his, engendered a host of sensations, of feelings. Before he'd so much as opened his eyes a smile had unaccountably curled his lips and a light, warm emotion had filled his chest, then inexplicably crowded into his heart.

Knox knew his heart had absolutely no business getting involved in what had happened between him and Savannah—it was supposed to have been sex and nothing more—but he gloomily suspected this feeling currently lurking in his chest was more than he'd bargained for, and definitely more than she had.

Knox had thought that the nudge of the story had brought him here, but he knew better now. The insistent nudge that had propelled him to this place didn't have anything to do with a story…and never had, Knox realized belatedly.

It had been Savannah.

When he'd failed to act on his own, his nudge had taken over and done the business for him, had made sure that he'd found her.

Knox recognized a good thing when he had it, and Savannah Reeves was a good thing. She was bright and witty and charming, and sexy as hell, and just being with her made him feel like a better man, made him *want* to be a better man. Knox didn't have a clue what the future might bring, but the idea of a future without her in it held absolutely no appeal.

He supposed he was in love with her, and he waited for the mental admission to jump-start a wave of panic, for the fist of anxiety to punch him in the gut, at the very least prod his insides with a finger of dread.

It didn't.

Instead, his chest swelled with the sweet, foreign emotion, forcing a contented grunt from his lips. He didn't have any idea how Savannah felt about him and wouldn't allow himself to think about it. If she hadn't fallen in love with him, he'd make her. It was as simple as that.

Given her history, Knox knew he'd have his work cut out for him—she'd have to trust him before she'd love him, he knew—but he hadn't gotten this far in life without patience and tenacity. He had the attraction working in his favor and would just build on that until she was ready for more. As far as a plan went, it might not be the best one, but it was the only one he had at present.

Failure was not an option. Come hell or high water, he'd make Savannah Reeves his.

A glimpse of white at the window snagged his attention. Rupali and Edgar were just scant feet outside their bedroom window. Edgar drew up short and parked a wheelbarrow filled with various shrubs and flowering plants. They were landscaping? Knox wondered. At this hour of the morning? The thought drew a reluctant smile. They were truly a bizarre pair, but this life they'd chosen seemed to fit them.

In fact, tantric sex seemed to fit them, too.

Knox was certain now that the Sheas believed and put into practice everything they taught. They weren't the crooks he'd originally thought them to be. True, some of the practices and beliefs were out of the realm of his comprehension, his scope of understanding, and he seriously doubted he'd ever become a true tantrist, but he no longer believed that it lay out of the realm of possibility—just his.

Knox watched as the Sheas joined hands, lifted their faces to the sky and chanted. An early morning breeze lifted Rupali's long white hair, billowed their *kurtas* out around them. After a moment, they stepped back and Knox watched Rupali draw something from her pocket—multicolored rocks, they seemed to be—and then toss them into the air. To Knox's astonishment, Edgar began to unload the wheelbarrow and place the plants and shrubs where the rocks had fallen.

That explained the whimsical feel to the landscaping he'd noticed when they'd first gotten here, Knox thought with soft, disbelieving amusement.

Savannah stirred beside him and he bent his head and pressed a kiss to her achingly smooth cheek. A lump of emotion formed in his throat, and for one terrifying instant, Knox's considerable confidence wavered and he wondered if he'd really be able to make her love him. Could he really do it?

A sleepy smile curled her lips and she stretched languidly beside him. "Good morning," she murmured groggily.

Knox's gaze caressed her face, lingered over each and every line and curve. "So far," he said. "I'm here with you."

Savannah sighed with sleepy pleasure and rolled to burrow into his chest. She nuzzled his neck and snaked an arm around his waist. The hard-on he'd awoken with promptly jerked for sport. But that was hardly surprising, was it? He was a man and, were that not enough explanation, he was a man in bed with a naked woman.

"What time is it?" she asked.

"It's early. Pushing six, I'd say."

She smoothed her hand up his side, sending a wave of gooseflesh skittering across his skin. Smiling, Knox sucked in a trembling breath.

"Good," she murmured. "We've got time."

"Time for what?"

"Here, I'll show you."

Savannah rolled him onto his back and straddled him. Her wet sex rode the ridge of his erection and Knox watched her eyes flutter shut and her lips slip into one of the most sensual smiles he'd ever seen. With a growl of satisfaction, he anchored his hands on the sweet swell of her hips and rocked her against him.

The picture she made in that moment was utterly incredible. Those jet-black bed-head curls sprouted in sexy disarray all over her head and the rosy tint of sleep clung to her creamy cheeks. Her eyes were lit with the blue flame of desire, still slumberous and heavy lidded, weighted with the vestiges of sleep. Pale pink nipples crowned the full globes of her breasts, and her belly was gently rounded and completely feminine. The thatch of silky curls at the apex of her thighs rocked against him and...

And the rest of that thought fragmented as Savannah took him in her hand, swiftly sheathed him with a condom, then slowly sank down onto him. Her wet, tight heat gloved him so thoroughly that it ripped the very breath from his lungs.

Savannah's eyes fluttered shut. She smiled with sublime satisfaction and bit her bottom lip. A purr emanated from her throat as she buried his dick as far into her heat as she possibly could.

She flexed her naughty muscles around him. "Do you have any idea how long I've been wanting to do

this? How many times I've done it in my dreams?''
she asked. She lifted her hips and settled onto him
once more.

"N-no," Knox breathed raggedly. "Tell me."

Savannah winced with pleasure, slid up and down
in a long, sinuous motion. He felt the greedy clench
and release of her body as she moved above him, felt
the exquisite friction of their joined parts.

"More times...than I...can conceivably count...
this weekend.'' Her breath came in startled little
puffs as she upped the tempo, rode him harder.

"I would have g-gladly accommodated you,"
Knox replied, thrusting into her, matching his rhythm
to hers. Savannah's skin glistened, had flushed into
a becoming rosy hue. She arched her neck and little
nonsensical sounds—the sound of great sex—bubbled up from her throat.

The fire in his loins rapidly became an inferno that
engulfed every inch of him. He felt her tense, watched
her mouth open in a silent gasp. She pumped harder
and harder on top of him, rode him frantically, clearly
racing for the brass ring of release. Knox leaned up,
latched his mouth around one nipple and sucked hard,
flattening the crown of her breast deep into his mouth.
He reached down between their joined bodies and
massaged the nub hidden in the wet folds of her sex.

Savannah cried out, bit her lip and whimpered.

He felt her muscles contract, felt her entire body
still in awe of the explosion of the coming climax.

The gentle pulsing and rush of heat was all it took to send Knox past the point of endurance and he joined her there in the brilliant flash of release.

Savannah sagged against his chest, not pulling away, but keeping him inside her. Something about the gesture made him want to roar his approval, made him feel more elementally manly. Instead, he trailed his trembling fingers down her spine, then slid his hands back up and hugged her close.

Savannah leaned up and glanced at the top of his head. Her brow creased with perplexity.

Knox frowned. "What? Is something wrong with my hair, because if it is," he said, imitating her, "this is as good as it gets and—"

He felt her laugh against him. "No, it's not your hair. I was just looking for some lotus blossoms. I know this is going to come as a shock…but I can't find any."

Knox chuckled. "Come as a shock, eh? I didn't feel any lotus blossoms fly out of my skull, but I sure thought my head was going to blow off during that last go-around." He lowered his voice. "That was awesome."

She flushed adorably. "Thank you. I try."

"Ah, so I'm not the only one who has learned how to take a compliment."

Her twinkling gaze met his and she winced with regret. "I hate to, but we've got to get up."

"I know," Knox said reluctantly.

"Everyone will be giving their progress reports

this morning. It'll be interesting to see what everyone will have to say.''

He'd thought about that as well. He arched a brow and lazily swirled circles on her back. "Given any thought as to what you're going to say?" he asked innocently.

Savannah gently raised herself off him and rolled back onto her side of the bed. He immediately missed her warmth. "Yes, as a matter of fact I have."

Knox waited. "Well?" he finally prompted.

She swiveled her head to look at him. "I'm going to say that my 'sacred space' has never been so magnificently illuminated, and that you have the biggest 'wand of light' I've ever seen."

His "wand of light" stirred at the compliment. "High praise, indeed."

"What about you? Surely you're going to correct my frigid-unable-to-climax legacy."

Knox grinned. "You can bet your sweet ass, baby. I'm going to report a multiple orgasm breakthrough and sing the praises of your 'sacred space.'''

She nodded, seemingly pleased. "Ugh," she groaned. "We've got to get up. They'll be starting soon, and we really need to hear everyone's input for the story." She paused. "When are we going to work on this story, by the way?"

"I thought we could work on it on the way back. Is that all right with you?"

Savannah inclined her head. "Sure, that'll be fine. Think we'll have time to finish it?"

"Yeah. I could be wrong, but I think this is going to be one of those stories that tells itself. If not, we can always finish it at my place…or yours."

She stilled and something in her gaze brightened and dimmed all in the same instant. What? Knox thought. Did she think that this had simply been a weekend fling? If so, he needed to swiftly disabuse her of that notion. She also needed to understand that he wasn't the bastard who'd broken her heart—he was someone she could trust.

"I'd, uh, planned on you spending quite a bit of time from here on out at my place, and hoped that I'd be invited to yours," Knox said, laying it all out on the line. He didn't want to frighten her, nor did he intend to mislead her.

It was a short story. He wanted her. The end.

When she didn't readily reply, Knox felt the first prickle of unease move through his belly. Savannah just stood there, looking at him with an unreadable expression that made his insides knot with anxiety. "Have I read too much into this?" he asked.

"No," she replied hesitantly, and his tension lessened slightly. "I, uh…" She shrugged helplessly. "To be honest, I hadn't let myself think beyond this weekend. I didn't want to get my ho— I just thought it would be best to hedge my bets."

"And now?" he prodded.

"And now my thoughts are along the same lines as yours."

"So we'll be spending a lot of time together,

then?'' he queried lightly, just to be sure they were on the same page.

He caught the feline smile that curved her lips a fraction of a second before she turned and headed toward the bathroom. ''You can bet your sweet ass,'' she said, giving him a wonderful view of hers.

SAVANNAH DIDN'T KNOW what to make of Knox's morning-after behavior. Frankly, she'd expected him to be charming but withdrawn. She'd expected him to try and put a more professional spin on their relationship, to try to regain some lost ground. In short, she'd expected him to act like a typical man…but as she'd learned over the course of this weekend, Knox Webber wasn't a typical man.

He'd done the one and only thing Savannah *hadn't* expected—he'd expressed a wish to see her again and, though she was trying very hard not to let her heart get carried away, if she'd understood him correctly—and she thought she had—he wanted to see her *a lot.*

Considering she'd fallen head over heels in love with him this weekend, Savannah decided that was very promising.

There had been several times over the course of last night and this morning when she'd caught Knox giving her poignantly tender looks, but Savannah had convinced herself they'd been wishful thinking, the product of her imagination…anything but what they were. She'd been so careful of getting her hopes up that she'd ignored every sign of some deeper emotion—and there had been plenty, now that she thought about it. Belated delight bloomed in her chest.

She'd have to be careful, of course. Tread carefully—she'd been burned too many times not to be a little reticent. But the idea that she might have found someone who genuinely wanted her—after almost a lifetime of being alone—was so achingly sweet.

The back of her throat burned with emotion and her insides quivered with hesitant joy. She'd longed to be wanted, to be part of a family for what seemed like forever. Someone to spend Thanksgiving and Christmas with, to help celebrate her birthday. Little things that other people simply took for granted were things that Savannah had, for the most part, never had.

Savannah didn't know anything about the Webber family other than that they were wealthy and that they didn't approve of Knox's career. Did that mean they wouldn't approve of her either? Savannah wondered, remembering Gib's family with a shudder. More important, would it matter to Knox if they didn't? Savannah paused consideringly, mulling the question over. She honestly didn't think so. If he'd gone ahead and chosen to be a journalist despite their protests, then surely he'd use the same headstrong logic when choosing a wife.

Wife?

Jeez, where had that thought come from? Savannah shot a surreptitious glance at Knox to make sure that the absurd thought hadn't somehow been transmitted from her brow chakra to his via mental telepathy. Presently, Knox was working the room, subtly interrogating couples about their tantric experience. She should be doing the same thing, Savannah thought with a stab of self-disgust, instead of mooning over her new boyfriend.

Still her shoulders drooped with relief and her heart inexplicably swelled when his gaze caught hers. Those dark green orbs shone with humor and a hint of kindled lust, but thankfully no panic or fear, which she definitely would have detected should he have been privy to her *wife* thought.

So much for treading carefully, Savannah thought with a rueful smile. She absently twisted the thin gold band on her finger, and a prick of regret pierced her heart. She knew it was foolish, but she didn't want to give it back. She wanted to keep it and wear it and be everything to Knox that the token implied.

Knox sidled up next to her and nuzzled her ear. ''Is it getting on your nerves?''

Savannah started guiltily. ''What?''

''The ring. Is it getting on your nerves?''

She swallowed and forced a smile. ''No, not at all. I was just admiring it. Don't let me forget to give it back to you. Maybe you can take them back and your jeweler will give you a refund.''

''And risk bad karma?'' Knox asked playfully. He

shook his head. "I think I'll keep them. You never know when you might need a set of bands."

With that enigmatic comment, Knox steered her toward the front of the room where the Sheas waited to bid their farewells. "Good morning, class." Edgar beamed. "Rupali and I have had the opportunity to speak with several of you this morning and, by all accounts, last night was a resounding success."

Rupali smiled serenely. "We are so very thrilled for each and every one of you. Our time together has come to an end, but please continue to use what you have learned here in your daily lives. Take the love and harmony you've found in our house home to yours. Remember truth and healing, sing your true songs, speak with your true voices and draw from the energy of Mother Earth. Cleanse your chakras, forbid blocks and continue to grow in spiritual and sexual health. Women, honor your man, never cease longing to please him. He will return your effort with pleasure tenfold."

"Likewise, men, honor your woman. Respect her, be worthy of her love, and strive to continually bring her more pleasure. For to do these things for another is to do them for yourself."

Edgar and Rupali joined hands. "We bid you well," they said in unison.

Knox threaded Savannah's fingers through hers and squeezed. "Well, that's that then. You ready?"

Savannah nodded. She supposed so. They'd donned their regular clothes this morning for the journey home, and already the bra and undies seemed to chafe her skin. She never thought she'd say it but, like Knox, she'd grown rather fond of the free feeling of the *kurta*.

Knox had gone out this morning and loaded the car, so everything had been packed. There was absolutely no reason to linger, and yet, for some reason, Savannah found herself curiously reluctant to leave.

"Barbie," Rupali called. "May I have a word before you go, please?"

Savannah nodded. Knox gave her a perplexed look, but left at her prodding when she promised to meet him at the car.

Savannah cleared her throat. "You wanted to speak with me?" she asked nervously. Something about this woman's perceptive gaze unnerved her.

Rupali laid a soft, bejeweled hand on her arm. "Did you experience any breakthroughs this weekend? Did your world shift and come back into brighter focus?"

Unbidden tears stung her eyes. A short laugh erupted from her throat and she nodded. "Yes," Savannah choked out. "It did."

Rupali nodded in understanding. "Good. I'd hoped you would. My third eye is my strongest chakra, and I had a feeling about you," she told her. "I know that you'll have cause to doubt, but you'll be all right now, you know."

"Thank you," Savannah said, inexplicably reassured by this woman's calm assessment.

To her surprise, Rupali leaned forward and hugged her in a motherly fashion, a gesture Savannah hadn't had in such a long, long time. She blinked back tears once more. "Go, child," Rupali told her. "He's waiting."

Savannah withdrew from Rupali's embrace and hurried out to the car. Knox took one look at her and his jaw went hard. "What happened?" he demanded. "What's wrong?"

"Nothing," Savannah said shakily, wiping the moisture from beneath her eyes. "Just women stuff. It's nothing. Really."

Knox didn't look convinced. "You're sure you're all right? You're sure there's nothing wrong?"

His concern touched her deeply, made her want to vault across the seat, plant herself in his lap, and rain kisses all over his outraged face. A champion, what a novel experience. Savannah's heart galloped in her chest and joy fizzed through her, until finally it bubbled right out of her mouth in a stream of delighted laughter.

Knox looked at her askance. Worry replaced the outrage. "Are you sure you're all right?"

"Yes," Savannah said emphatically. For the first time in her life *everything* felt all right.

14

ON ANY GIVEN DAY, Knox typically enjoyed walking into the offices of the *Chicago Phoenix*. His world. He loved the hustle and bustle, the murmur of conversation and the ceaseless ring of the telephones. This was the chaotic world of the newsroom, where breaking news mingled with the mundane, juicy gossip and the occasional super-hot exposé.

Their tantric sex piece wouldn't be considered any of those things, Knox knew, and yet it had turned out to be a great story that both he and Savannah were very proud of. The article had come together so seamlessly that it had, as predicted, practically written itself. He and Savannah had simply framed it up with words, ones that he hoped would do justice to their experience with the ancient technique. The piece had been informative, skeptical in a humorous way, yet left plenty of room for possibility. Ultimately it had let readers draw their own conclusions.

Knox had always worked alone, had always considered writing a solitary business. But, to his delight, he and Savannah had worked extremely well together. Their styles complemented each other and they intuitively played to each other's weaknesses. In short, they were great together. They wrote like they made love—splendidly.

Knox had left Savannah at her apartment eight hours ago and, during that time, he hadn't stopped thinking about her.

He simply couldn't.

She consumed his every waking thought and had even invaded his dreams. And he wanted to know her every thought, her every dream, her every secret. He wanted to learn all of her little idiosyncrasies, to wake up with her in the morning and go to bed with her each night. He wanted to shower her with the affection she'd missed as a child, to make up for every heartache she'd ever experienced. He wanted her to trust him…and he wanted to be her hero.

Basically, he just *wanted* her.

Knox felt the perpetual smile he'd worn since yesterday morning when his whole world had changed. To his surprise, he found himself whistling as he strolled into work this morning.

It had been late when they'd arrived back in Chicago, so after dropping Savannah off at her apartment, Knox had brought the piece down here to leave for Chapman to proofread. His boss usually arrived a good hour before the rest of the staff, and Knox knew that Chapman would be eager to read the article. Knox was equally eager to hear what Chapman thought of it.

A look through the glass confirmed his boss was

in. Knox rapped on the door and Chapman beckoned him inside.

"It's brilliant," Chapman said. "It's damn brilliant. I read it first thing this morning."

Knox slowly released the pent-up breath he'd been holding. "Thank you, sir. We're proud of it."

"And I have a surprise for you—it'll run with your byline only."

Something cold slithered through him. Knox blinked, certain he'd misunderstood. "Come again?"

"You're not sharing your byline. I never intended for you to. Ms. Reeves needed to be taught a lesson, Webber, and this is the way I've planned to do it."

Fury whipped through Knox. "Look, I don't know what's going on—"

"And you don't need to, as it doesn't concern you."

"Doesn't concern me?" Knox repeated hotly. "Like hell. I just spent the entire weekend working with her. *We*—not I—just wrote a great piece." Knox glared at him. "She did the work, she deserves the credit."

Chapman smiled infuriatingly. "Be that as it may, she's not going to get it."

Knox fisted his hands at his sides and silently willed himself to calm down. Beating the hell out of his boss, which was exceedingly tempting at the moment, wouldn't benefit anyone.

He'd heard stories about Chapman's legendary ruthlessness—hell, everyone in this city had—but had always thought they'd been exaggerated. While he'd never considered Chapman a friend, he'd none-theless always respected the man and his opinion. Clearly, that was at an end, Knox thought, swallowing his bitter disappointment.

"I don't appreciate being dragged into this," Knox said, his jaw set so hard he feared it would crack. "Furthermore, I don't care for your methods."

"You don't have to." Chapman narrowed his eyes. "Have you forgotten who is the boss here, Webber, whose name is on that door? If so, let me refresh your memory—it's mine. I do things my way, and people who don't realize that—or choose to ignore it—pay accordingly or end up unemployed. Have I made myself clear?"

Knox smirked as a red rage settled over his brain. "Perfectly."

With that, Knox pivoted and stormed from Chapman's office. He knew any argument was pointless. Several co-workers called out greetings, but Knox wasn't in any frame of mind to play the amiable rich boy today. He needed to intercept Savannah before she came in this morning and prepare her for Chapman's little bomb.

More important, he needed to make sure she understood that he hadn't played any part in it.

Anxiety roiled in his gut and his heart stumbled in his chest as the implications of what had just transpired in Chapman's office fully surfaced in Knox's furious mind.

He could lose her because of this.

He could lose her.

He'd forced her hand, had gone to Chapman and had made her go on that assignment when she'd expressly and repeatedly insisted that she didn't want to go. She'd undoubtedly believe that he'd been in on it, that he and Chapman had plotted out her punishment together. Hell, even he had to admit that he looked guilty. What was it he'd told her? *Don't make me play hardball.* Knox snorted and shook his head. What a pompous idiot he'd been.

It wouldn't matter that they'd made love all weekend, that they'd shared the most mind-blowing, soul-shattering sex, that he'd all but told her he'd fallen head over hills in love with her. Granted, he hadn't said those words per se, but surely she'd understood the implication. He hadn't been able to keep his hands off her, for pity's sake.

But none of it would matter, Knox needlessly reminded himself. She didn't trust him with her heart yet and if she talked with Chapman before Knox had a chance to talk to her, he most likely would never get the opportunity.

Nausea curdled in his stomach.

Just what in the hell had she supposedly done that would make Chapman sink to such measures of retribution? Knox wondered angrily. What unforgivable offense had she committed? Knox hadn't heard the first rumor, so whatever it was had been kept quiet.

Secrets didn't typically last in a newsroom, but obviously this one had.

Knox breathed relief when the elevator doors finally opened, hurried inside and impatiently stabbed the button for the lobby. In the end it didn't matter what she had or hadn't done.

The only thing that mattered was making sure that she understood that *he* hadn't had anything to do with this mess—that he hadn't betrayed her, and he would do whatever was necessary to make her believe it.

His insides twisted with dread and he broke out in a cold sweat. He wouldn't lose her, dammit. Knox slammed his fist into the elevator wall.

He couldn't.

SAVANNAH ROCKED back on her heels and waited patiently for the elevator to deliver her to the eleventh floor, home of the *Chicago Phoenix.* She'd awoken this morning with a lighthearted smile and the irrepressible urge to get to work. Savannah knew her anxiousness had less to do with the desire to do her job and more to do with the desire to see—and do, she thought wickedly—Knox.

It had been late by the time they'd gotten back to Chicago and, though he'd all but turned her into a quivering puddle of need with that marathon goodnight kiss, Savannah hadn't asked Knox to spend the night. He'd been very proud of their piece—as had she—and Knox had wanted to swing by the *Phoenix* and leave the article on Chapman's desk so that he could read it first thing this morning.

Though she didn't particularly care for their boss, it was obvious that Knox valued the older man's opinion. Savannah supposed that in absence of his father's approval, Knox had attached special meaning to Chapman's. She had the old bastard's number, though, and knew Knox's trust had been misplaced. She dreaded when Knox would reach that conclusion as well. She'd swallowed more than her share of disappointment and knew that it left a bitter aftertaste.

As for her, Savannah had wanted to get here early this morning to hear Chapman's opinion of the story as well. She hoped that, having gone on this little trip at his bidding to serve penance for her so-called offenses, he would back off now and let her return to her job.

Savannah chuckled. Her punishment had backfired.

Big time.

Chapman had sent her on this trip with the notion of knuckling her under, of humbling her. Little did he know that she and Knox had found something indescribably perfect together, that they'd spent the weekend in hedonistic splendor, and that he'd unwittingly forced her to admit what her heart had known all along—Knox Webber was The One.

Rather than continuing to nurse her animosity toward Chapman, it occurred to Savannah that she should thank him instead.

Doing the tantric piece with Knox had been utterly wonderful. They'd worked amazingly well together and the story had only served to whet her appetite for more. She was tired of covering the mundane, had grown weary of the half-assed assignments Chapman had foisted upon her since she'd pissed him off. With luck, when she walked into the office this morning, things would have finally changed for the better.

Savannah had no more than set foot out of the elevator when Chapman summoned her into his inner sanctum. Suppressing a secret smile, she squared her shoulders and strolled in.

"Good morning, sir," Savannah said.

"Good morning," he returned, his smile a wee bit too smug for Savannah's liking. A finger of trepidation slid down her spine. "I've had a chance to read the article you and Webber did." He inclined his head. "Great stuff."

Savannah's tension eased marginally and she smiled. "I'm glad you like it, sir. Knox and I are very proud of it."

He winced regretfully. "I've only got one minor revision, though."

"Certainly. What's that?"

"The byline," Chapman said, his fat lips curling into a malevolent smile. "I'm eliminating a name from it—yours."

For all intents and purposes, the ground shifted beneath Savannah's feet. Her ears rung, and nausea pushed into her throat. She blinked, astonished. "I'm sorry?"

"I'm sure you are."

"What?"

"I never intended to let you take credit for this story. You need to learn some respect, Ms. Reeves. You also need to learn to heed my wishes. From this day forward, you will do that. Do you understand?" he asked in softly ominous tones. "I am the boss here and you will answer my questions when I ask them, regardless of your so-called journalistic integrity...or else. Let this be a lesson to you, my dear. Don't screw with me. You'll lose."

"But I did the work," Savannah said angrily.

He leaned back in his seat and stacked his hands behind his head. "But you won't get credit for it, or any other article until you learn some respect."

The implication of everything she'd just heard hit Savannah like an unexpected blow to the belly. She swallowed her disappointment, her anger—ate it until she thought for sure she would vomit.

A horrible suspicion rose. "But Knox—"

"—has done and will always do exactly what I tell him to," Chapman said meaningfully. His eyes glittered with evil humor. "He's a model staffer."

Savannah crossed her arms over her chest and snorted with bitter regret. Her world dimmed back into its usual muted focus and the light heart she'd enjoyed only moments ago instantly turned to lead.

"I see," she finally managed. She had to push the words from her seared throat.

"Good," Chapman said. "I thought that you would when you'd been shown the bigger picture."

Without further comment, Savannah turned and walked out of Chapman's office, through the busy newsroom, and eventually out of the building. She got into her car and, amazingly dry-eyed, drove across town to her small efficiency apartment.

For those long interminable minutes, she was utterly and completely numb. It had been like Chapman's words had cut off the circulation to her feelings, had prevented her from experiencing even the least amount of emotion.

But the second Savannah entered her apartment, that tourniquet was released and the pain ripped through her, wrenching an anguished, silent sob from her throat. It drove her to the floor, the weight of the torment so unbelievably unbearable.

Savannah knew this woeful routine, had been a player in this all too familiar scene. But she didn't understand now any more than she ever had, just exactly what she'd done to deserve this kind of heartache. What made her so unworthy of even a sliver of happiness? A lump formed in her tight throat. Hot tears slipped down her cheeks and splashed onto her shaking hands. She bit her lip to stem the flow, but it didn't work. The pain was an emotion that had to come out, and this was the body's natural way to cleanse itself of hurts.

He'd known, damn him. He'd had to have known, and Chapman, the vengeful jerk, had all but told her so.

Knox has done and will always do exactly what I tell him…

And obviously he had, Savannah thought miserably as another dagger of regret twisted in her chest. Knox had forced her to take that trip, hadn't he? Had gone to Chapman when she refused. Savannah didn't think that Knox had known why she was going to be punished—he'd seemed genuinely curious about that—but she didn't doubt for a minute that he'd known what was going to happen. He'd known that Chapman never planned to let her have that byline. Had known that all of her effort had been for naught.

And if that weren't a bad enough betrayal, he'd let her go and make a fool out of herself by admitting her damned attraction. Had let her give him her body—and her heart, though he didn't know it. Humiliation burned her cheeks and her heart drooped pitifully in her chest.

Savannah had fancifully imagined spending the rest of her life with him, had imagined them working together, celebrating accomplishments, holidays, all of life's major events. She'd imagined waking up with him and going to bed with him. Had imagined a happily-ever-after.

She pulled in a shaky breath as another tear

scalded her cheek. Clearly it had all been just that—
a figment of her lonely imagination.

The whole weekend had been about the story, after
all.

KNOX HAD SPENT the entire day and the majority of
the night trying to make Savannah listen to him. But
she wouldn't. He'd repeatedly knocked on her door.
He'd alternately called her cell and her home phone
number, had even filled her answering machine tape
with the whole sordid explanation. But none of it had
done one whit of good, and as the day had pro-
gressed, he'd become increasingly panicked and
afraid that nothing ever would.

The one and only time she'd answered the phone,
it had not been with a customary hello, but a couple
of succinct words that, frankly, he couldn't believe
she'd said. He'd been so shocked she'd hung up on
him before he'd had the time to frame a reply.

Knox was at a loss. He simply didn't know what
else to do. He'd tried reasoning with Chapman once
more, but to no avail. Chapman held fast to his position and wouldn't relent. The story would run with
Knox's byline only, and Knox knew if that happened, he and Savannah would never be able to patch
things up. Frankly, even without that in the scenario,
he wasn't so confident that he could bridge the chasm
between them.

Though he knew that he shouldn't be, a part of
him was angry with her for thinking so little of him.
How could she possibly believe that he'd known

about this? After what they'd shared, what they'd done together, how could she continue to doubt him?

True, evidence certainly existed to the contrary, but he'd honestly thought that after he'd explained everything, his word would have been enough to exonerate him. Knox blew out a frustrated breath. It probably would have been with anyone *but* Savannah. She'd been hurt, disappointed too many times. She didn't trust anyone. He wondered—even if by some miracle they got past this—would she ever fully trust him? Or would she continue to paint him with the same brush of uncertainty she used on everyone else?

To his surprise, Knox found himself back at the office. Aside from the typesetters, only a few die-hard employees were there at this hour. Knox stilled as the beginnings of an idea stirred.

Only the typesetters...

When Knox had decided to pursue a career in journalism, he'd made a point of knowing the business from the ground up. He'd had a passion for the process and had wanted to experience it all—from the stories and articles that went into the papers, to layout and design, and finally...typesetting.

The idea gelled, sending a course of adrenaline rushing through his blood.

A slow smile curled his lips. Savannah Reeves would have her byline...and Knox would have her.

SAVANNAH'S HEAD FELT like it had been stuffed with cotton. Her eyes were swollen and her nose would undoubtedly require a skin graft to remove the red. But she was alive and healthy and, if for no other reason than her heart continued to beat, she'd live.

She'd heard of people dying due to grief or a broken heart, but Savannah told herself that she'd been made of sterner stuff, and surely she'd sustained more than this. If it felt like she hadn't, or if she sometimes wandered into a room and forgot what she'd been doing, then she simply told herself that it would pass.

Eventually.

But she would get over it.

Knox had called repeatedly, had knocked on her door, had left so many messages on her machine that after the fifth one, she'd hit the erase button. For one anguished second, she'd almost let herself believe him—he'd sounded so desperately sincere—but then reason had returned and she'd clung to her anger. He and Chapman had made a fool of her once—she'd be damned before she'd let them do it again.

Savannah had called in sick to work—something she'd never done before—and had decided to take this day and pull herself back together. She couldn't afford to quit, as she wasn't independently wealthy like Knox, so faxing her resignation wasn't a viable option—attractive, yes, but simply not prudent. She would, however, take a few minutes to update her résumé and put out a few feelers. As soon as she landed another job, she'd tell them both to kiss off.

A reluctant grin curved Savannah's lips. She'd said worse to Knox last night.

The one and only time she'd finally given in to her frustration, she'd answered the phone and growled a couple of choice words she'd never said before right into his ear. She'd taken advantage of his stunned silence to hang up on him. Savannah had finally grown weary of hearing the phone ring and the answering machine messages, so she'd unplugged them. A brief reprieve, she knew, as she'd have to go back to work tomorrow and deal with the whole sordid business, but for the time being she simply wanted to be left alone.

Her heart squeezed painfully in her chest as she shuffled to the door to get her paper. Might as well take a look at the damned thing, Savannah thought. It had certainly cost her enough.

Coffee in hand, she trudged back to her sofa, sat down and, with trembling fingers, finally unfurled the paper. She found the article on page three under the heading Tantric Sex—Old New Fad Or Stranger Than Fiction? Not a bad title, Savannah thought and was in the middle of a shrug when the byline snagged her attention.

By Savannah Reeves and Knox Webber.

Savannah blinked, astounded. Her heart began to race. But how had that happened? What had changed Chapman's mind? It had been thoroughly set, Savannah knew. In one of the many messages left on her machine, Knox had promised to find a way to fix this, but she hadn't believed him. Had he done this? she wondered, hope sprouting in her traitorous breast. Had Knox somehow managed to change Chapman's mind?

Well, there was only one way to find out. Savannah tossed the paper aside, scrambled from the couch and plugged her phone back in. She hit speed-dial and Chapman answered on the first ring.

"Make it quick," her boss said by way of greeting.

"Sir, this is Savannah Re—"

"I know exactly who this is," he snapped. "What do you want?"

Savannah gritted her teeth and resisted the infantile urge to smash the receiver against the wall. "I wanted to thank you for going ahead and giving me my byline. I really—"

"Don't thank me, Ms. Reeves. I had no intention of giving you that byline. You can thank Webber. He came down here last night and distracted a typesetter and added your name to the article," Chapman said stiffly. "He's been terminated."

Savannah gasped. *"You fired him?"*

"Speedily," Chapman said. "One more misstep and you'll be down at the unemployment office applying for benefits right along with him." The dial tone rang in her ear.

Savannah sank onto the edge of her sofa and let the weight of that conversation sink in before trying to stand again. Knox had distracted a typesetter?

He'd added her name? He'd gotten fired because of it? Savannah massaged her throbbing temples. It was simply too much to take in.

What on earth had possessed him to do such a reckless thing? True, Knox had always been Chapman's golden boy but, regardless of that status, Knox had surely realized Chapman would never tolerate such an overt act of defiance from one of his employees, golden boy or no. Knox had to have known that particular act of insubordination would put him out of a job. He'd had to know...and yet he'd done it.

For her? she wondered hesitantly.

Savannah stilled. She'd assumed many things on Knox's behalf over the past twenty-four hours. Sitting here and making assumptions based on word-of-mouth testimony didn't make good journalistic sense.

She'd need to go to the source.

KNOX HAD BEGUN his morning by getting fired and things had steadily proceeded to worsen from there. his mother had made her weekly you-should-come-to-work-for-your-father spiel and when she'd asked him about things at the paper, he'd made the monumental mistake of telling her he'd been fired. Since then his father had called, his sister, and his brother. Undoubtedly, his entire family—all of which was employed by Webber Investments—would be lobbying for him to join the family business.

It wasn't going to happen. Knox was a writer.

He'd find another job in his field. He would not go to work for his father.

Besides, he'd known last night when he'd made the decision to add her name to the byline that he'd lose his job. Knox grunted. Hell, it had been a no-brainer. But when it had come right down to it, making sure that Savannah knew that he was in this for the long haul, that he hadn't betrayed her and that he was worthy of her trust had been more important.

If this sacrifice wasn't enough, then he'd just think of something else until he finally convinced her that she could depend on him. Where others had failed, he would not. It was as simple as that.

Provided he could ever get her to speak to him again, Knox thought. He'd tried to call her again last night, and then again this morning, to tell her to be sure and get her paper, but apparently she'd unplugged her phone and answering machine because her line had simply rung and rung. Patience and persistence, the bigger picture, Knox told himself as he heaved a hearty sigh and dialed her number once again.

He muttered a curse and disconnected when his doorbell rang. His mother, no doubt, Knox thought with a spurt of irritation as he strode angrily to the door. He didn't have time for this, dammit. He needed to get in touch with Savannah. Needed to try—

Knox drew up short as he swung open his door and found the author of his present heartache standing on his threshold. His greedy gaze roamed over her. Her hair looked as if it had never seen a brush and her pale blue eyes were puffy and swollen. Her nose was red and a mangled tissue poked from the pocket of her wrinkled denim shirt. She looked like hell, but a hell he'd gladly embrace.

Hope bloomed in his chest. "Savannah?"

"I needed to talk to you, and calling seemed too impersonal. Mind if I come in?"

Still stunned, Knox belatedly opened the door. "Uh, sure."

Knox guided her into his living room and gestured for her to sit down.

She gazed around his spacious apartment with an appraising eye. "Nice place."

Knox rubbed the back of his neck. "Thanks."

"I heard a rumor today and I wondered if you could confirm it."

"I'll try. What was it?"

"That you went down to the paper last night, distracted a typesetter and added my name to our story, and that you got fired because of it. Is that true?"

Knox blew out a breath. "Yeah, that about sums it up."

Savannah sprang from the couch and glared at him accusingly. "You idiot! What did you do that for? Didn't you know you'd get fired? Have you lost your mind?" she ranted, that blue gaze flashing fire.

Frankly, this was not how Knox had imagined this scene playing out. He was supposed to be a hero, dammit, not an idiot. She was supposed to be grateful, fall into his arms and profess her undying love.

"No, I haven't lost my mind," he said tightly. "I've lost something a great deal more important than that."

She frowned, looking thoroughly irritated. "What exactly is that?"

"My heart."

She stilled, and her frantic gaze finally rested to meet his. "Y-your heart?"

"That's right. You're here for the facts, aren't you? Well, the fact is this—I fell in love with you this weekend. I didn't know anything about Chapman's plans, and didn't know any other way to convince you of it." Knox shrugged. "So I added your byline…and the rest is history."

"But what about your job?" she asked breathlessly. "You loved your job."

Jeez, he'd just told her that he loved her, and she was still harping about the damned job. When was she going to get it?

"Savannah, I don't give a damn about the job if it means that I'm going to lose you. Your trust means more." Knox stood and traced a heart on her cheek. His gaze searched her tormented one. "*You* mean more. I can get another job, baby. But *you're* irreplaceable."

Knox watched her gaze soften and a smile tremble across her lips. He breathed an inaudible sigh of relief. "So are you," she said. Savannah pulled her cell phone from the pocket of her jeans and punched in a number. "Chapman, Savannah Reeves here. I quit." Then she casually ended the call and, with a cry of delight, launched herself into his arms.

"I'm s-so sorry," she cried brokenly. "I should have known better—I should have listened to you. But I was so afraid of getting hurt, I—I just couldn't." She drew back and looked up at him. Blue mist shimmered in her eyes. "Thank you so much for doing this for me. I just— I don't—"

The feeling of immense dread he'd been carrying around for the past day promptly fled and his chest swelled with sweet, giddy emotion. "I know," Knox said, and cut off her inarticulate attempts to describe the indescribable.

"I, uh, love you, too, you know," Savannah said shyly.

"Yeah, I know." He cupped her cheek in his hand. "But will you ever trust me?"

Something shifted in her gaze and Savannah stepped out of his arms and turned around. Knox panicked. He'd pushed her too far again. He'd asked for too much. Dammit.

"Savannah—"

She fell backward and right into his suddenly outstretched arms. The blind-trust test. She'd done it! She'd let him catch her…which meant she trusted him. Knox felt a wobbly smile overtake him.

Savannah's laughing gaze met his. "Ask me that again."

"W-will you ever trust me?"

She arched up and kissed him hungrily. She might as well have hot-wired his groin, for the effect Knox felt. "Baby, you can bet your sweet ass."

Dear Reader

Some characters are so much fun you never want to leave them. In this story, my first Blaze™ novel, I'm delighted to revisit Jill Sheldon, whom I introduced in a previous Sensual Romance™ title, *It's a Guy Thing!*

As soon as brash, fun-loving Jill stepped onto the pages of *It's a Guy Thing!*, I knew she was the perfect heroine for Blaze. And I think she's found the perfect hero in Mitch Landry, a man of hidden passions who can capture Jill's heart.

I had a lot of fun writing this story; I hope it's fun for you too. I love to hear from readers. You can email me at CindiMyers1@aol.com, or write to me care of Harlequin Books, 225 Duncan Mill Road, Don Mills, Ontario M3B 3K9, Canada.

Happy reading,

Cindi Myers

JUST 4 PLAY

by
Cindi Myers

To my wonderful editor, Wanda Ottewell.
Thanks for all your support and encouragement.
And special thanks to Terri Clark, the title goddess.

1

JILL SHELDON BELIEVED in Happy perfume, Miracle Bras and in not letting a day go by without having fun. So when she'd seen the Help Wanted sign in the window of Just 4 Play, she'd known that was the job for her. What could be more fun than working in a toy shop?

Okay, so Just 4 Play sold sex toys and lingerie. People needed more fun in their sex lives too, didn't they? In the six months since she'd joined the staff at Just 4 Play, Jill had had plenty of good times, on the job, and off. After all, life was too short not to have fun.

"Should the musical condoms go with the other condoms or in the novelty section?" she asked as she and her co-worker, Sid Crawford, unpacked the latest shipment of merchandise one Wednesday afternoon.

Sid frowned, his eyebrow ring shifting toward his nose. "With the novelties, I think. And rearrange the display so it looks really full. This might be the last shipment we get for a while."

"Why is that?" She squeezed a condom package and grinned as a tinny rendition of "Bolero" filled the air.

"It'll take a while to get all the accounts shifted over to the new owner's name."

She set the condoms next to a box of edible underwear. Maybe she'd shelve them with the massage oil and bill the set as a total sensual experience. "I'm going to miss old Grif." She sighed, and paused for a moment in

memory of the late Griffeth Landry, former proprietor
of Just 4 Play. He'd died suddenly last month when he
was struck by lightning while playing golf. All his gold
fillings had melted, welding his mouth shut, a final irony
for a man who had a mouth every bit as big as his heart.

"Yeah, Grif was cool." Sid nodded, his pink Mohawk
swaying with the movement.

"So what's his nephew like?" Jill asked.

Sid shrugged. "Don't know. Haven't met him."

"Oh come on. You must know something. What's his
name?"

"His name's Mitchell Landry, but that's all I know."

She set aside a bottle of bubble bath and came over
to lean on a tower of boxes next to Sid. "Where's he
from? Does he live here in Boulder?"

"Don't know."

"What does he do for a living?"

"I have no idea."

"How old is he?"

Sid held his hands up in front of his face to ward off
this barrage of questions. "I swear, I don't know anything about him. Honest." He slit open another carton.
"You sure are nosy."

"I like to know things. Haven't you ever heard knowledge is power?"

"Right. When have you ever been powerless?"

She crossed her arms over her chest. "Never. And I
don't intend to be. Ever."

"Guess you're going to have to stay in the dark until
Mr. Mitchell Landry decides to grace us with his presence."

"He can't be too old if he's Grif's nephew." She
smiled. "Maybe he's young and good-looking. Maybe I

could even help him try out some of the merchandise."
She held up a pair of fur-lined handcuffs.

Sid shook his head. "You're incorrigible."

"I just know how to have fun."

"Yeah, but you gotta be serious sometimes."

This from a man with pink hair, who owned more jewelry than she did. "Life's too short to be serious," she said. She slit open another carton and pulled out a sequined bra top. Rhinestones and faux pearls winked in the fluorescent light. Her eyes widened. "Get a load of this!"

"What's it supposed to be? Some kind of costume?" Just 4 Play specialized in elaborate costumes for those patrons who enjoyed acting out their romantic fantasies.

"I think it's a harem girl." She reached into the carton and fished out a pair of filmy harem pants. "Isn't it gorgeous?"

Sid shrugged and went back to unloading boxes. "Bet it's not as popular as the French maid or Nurse Betty."

"I don't know, Sid. It's pretty sexy, if you ask me." She turned the bra top this way and that, watching the gems sparkle. "I think I'll put it on the mannequin in the front window."

"That's a good idea. That black leather is going to dry out in the sun."

She scooped up the harem pants and started toward the back of the store. "Hey, where are you going?" Sid called. "We still have another pallet of boxes to unload."

"I want to try this on. Model it for a while."

"Just make sure the customers know you don't come with the merchandise."

She grinned over her shoulder at him. "Depends on the customer."

"Girl, you're all talk and you know it."

She stepped into the dressing room and drew the curtain. So maybe she wasn't as wild as she made out to be sometimes. Half the fun was pretending. Just 4 Play was all about fun and fantasy, so what harm was there in flirting with the customers a little? She liked to think they left the store a little happier than when they'd come in and if sexy clothes and double entendres did the trick, why not?

The bra top fit snugly, accentuating her cleavage. The filmy harem pants, which she put on over a pair of pink satin panties, hung low about her waist, the shimmery gauze billowing around her legs, fastening at her ankles. She smiled at her reflection in the dressing room mirror. Not bad. This was going to be a top seller.

Now if the right man would buy it *and* the pirate costume…

She laughed. Grif and Sid had teased her about the Errol Flynn getup she'd convinced them to order. "What woman wouldn't want to be swept away by a swashbuckling pirate?" she'd argued. Apparently not enough, since the costume had been gathering dust on the costume rack for six months. Still, one day, she would find a man to wear that outfit for her.

The problem with most of the men she met was that they were too serious. She'd start out thinking they were going to have a little fun and the next thing she knew, they'd be looking deeply into her eyes and talking about marriage and kids and all kinds of complicated things like that. Whatever happened to all those commitment-phobic men she'd read about? Why did she always end up with the other kind?

She shook her head and stepped out of the dressing

room. "So what do you think?" she called to Sid. She raised her arms and twirled around.

He turned and surveyed her critically. "Rebecca of Sunnybrook Farm goes to Arabia," he said.

"Aww, come on. Don't I look a little bit exotic?"

Sid shook his head. "Sorry, sweetheart, but those big blue eyes and upturned nose, not to mention the blond curls and freckles, make you look like you just stepped off the bus from the Iowa cornfields. You'd be better off with the schoolgirl costume."

She did her best to glare at him. "It's just because I'm short. It's hard to look seductive when you're only five-two."

"Hey, don't knock it. A lot of guys go for the wholesome look."

"Wholesome is for milk." She was about to stick her tongue out at him when the bells on the front door jangled and a customer walked in.

People had a lot of different attitudes when they came into Just 4 Play for the first time. Many were nervous, jingling change, giggling, even blushing. Some knew what they wanted and headed straight for it, not bothering to look at any of the other merchandise. A few apparently thought they were entering some kind of hobby shop and, realizing their mistake, quickly retreated. Couples came in holding hands, talking quietly as they studied the displays, using the shopping trip as a prelude to a more intimate encounter.

But the man in the business suit who walked in now had an attitude Jill hadn't encountered in a customer before. From the top of his well-cut brown hair to the toes of his spit-shined wing tips, this guy was completely serious. His expression was one you'd expect to see on a banker who had just turned down your loan, and his shoulders—nice and broad, she noted—were squared like a gladiator about to do battle.

Talk about uptight, Jill thought as she glided toward him. She smiled to herself. Nothing like a challenge to get her afternoon off to a good start. By the time she was finished with Mr. Stuffed Shirt, he'd be smiling and ready to have a little fun. Judging by his sour expression, the guy hadn't had nearly enough Vitamin F in his life lately.

"Welcome to Just 4 Play," she said, coming up to him and purposely standing too close. "Are you a virgin?"

His eyes—a gorgeous chocolate-brown—widened. "I beg your pardon?"

She moved a little closer, her arm brushing up against his. She breathed in his spicy cologne. Aramis. A scent she'd always found particularly sexy. "Is this your first time to visit the store?"

"Yes." He took a step away from her and glanced around. He frowned as his gaze rested on a life-size blow-up doll wearing a red satin bikini. "I see everything I've heard about this place is true."

"Oh." She took his arm and gently tugged him farther into the shop. "Good things, I hope. Are you looking for anything in particular? Something for you and your wife?"

"I'm not married."

She smiled. So he wasn't married. How nice.

He was still looking around the room, frowning, as if he didn't approve. Well, they got people like that, too. But Jill figured since he'd walked through the door, he had to be a little bit interested. The trick was to play to that interest, until you found out what the customer really wanted. "Something for you and your girlfriend, then."

That actually got a jolt out of him. He moved out of her grasp. "I don't think my girlfriend would be interested in anything you have here."

"She might surprise you." They had stopped in the section of the store devoted to lingerie and costumes. "We have some very nice lingerie. Nightgowns and teddies. Our garter belts are very popular as well." She held up a lacy black number. "Picture her in this, with some silk stockings and stiletto heels."

A faint flush of red showed on his tanned cheeks. "That's not why I came in here."

Jill grinned and laid the garter belt aside. Who was it who said still waters run deep? She bet Mr. Starched Shorts here would be a real tiger if he let himself go a little. "Maybe you'd prefer something more sensual." She took his hand and led him toward a display of massage oils—a good place to start for novices. As they passed the front window, sunlight caught the rhinestones on her bra top, scattering reflections.

"What is that you're wearing?" her customer demanded.

She paused and held up her hands, giving a little belly-dancer shimmy. "This is part of our fantasy costume collection. Would you like to see others?"

The man's gaze swept over her, more intimate than a caress. She fought the urge to cross her arms over her breasts, shielding herself from his intense gaze. He definitely needed to learn to lighten up. "People actually wear those things somewhere besides Halloween parties?"

The amusement in his voice relaxed her. "Of course. Couples enjoy acting out their romantic fantasies. For

instance, the man might dress as a cowboy, complete
with leather chaps. Or our construction worker tool belt
is very popular.'' Her grin widened. Her customer would
look *very* nice in that particular costume. ''Or a woman
might dress as a French maid, or a nurse.'' She leaned
closer, lowering her voice to a sexy purr. ''What's your
fantasy, sir? I'm sure we've got something to help you
fulfill it.''

His eyes locked to hers, warning her she'd asked the
wrong question. Or the right one. The raw emotion she
glimpsed before the polished facade moved into place
once more hinted at a man with unplumbed depths. A
man who kept his feelings in chains, waiting for the
woman with the right key to free them....

She looked away, her cheeks warm, like a child who'd
seen something she wasn't supposed to see.

He stepped back. ''I'm not interested in fantasy at the
moment, I—''

''We also have some wonderful instructional books
on sensual massage.'' Telling herself she was silly to let
a stranger make her lose her cool, she took his hand
again and tugged him toward an old-fashioned wardrobe
filled with brightly colored bottles and jars. ''And we
have these flavored massage oils. They're very popular
with both men and women.'' She unscrewed the cap on
a tester bottle of cinnamon massage oil. She felt him
watching her, and shivers of awareness danced across
her bare skin.

''Did you know they've actually done surveys showing that one of the most arousing scents for men is the
smell of baking cinnamon rolls?'' She dabbed a bit of
the oil on the inside of her wrist and held it out to him.
''Doesn't that smell wonderful?''

His fingers around her wrist were strong and warm.

Long, sensitive fingers, the kind that could bring a lot of pleasure to a woman, if he knew how to use them. And something told her this man knew how to use all his assets. He brought her wrist to his nose and inhaled deeply, eyes closing for a second. His lips were so close to her skin she could feel the heat of his breath and her knees began to turn to jelly. She wanted to pull away from his grasp, but couldn't find the strength. What was going on here?

He opened his eyes and his gaze locked with hers once more, intense and searching. Serious, as if her flirting act hadn't fazed him one bit. He looked right past her frivolous costume and teasing manner, to a part of herself she never let anyone see.

She jerked away from him, startled. Now where had that come from? What was he doing looking at her that way—and why? "Um…maybe you'd better tell me why you came in here and I'll see if someone can help you," she said, avoiding his gaze. And the someone wouldn't be her. She replaced the bottle of oil and rubbed her bare shoulders, trying to banish chill bumps. She was used to being the one in control and she didn't like it that a stranger could take over a situation so quickly.

"I'm looking for the manager," he said, his voice portraying no hint that anything out of the ordinary had passed between them.

"Sure. That's Sid. He's in back unloading new stock." She straightened, forcing confidence back into her voice. "Tell me your name and I'll go get him."

"It's Landry. Mitchell Landry. I'm the new owner of this place."

2

MITCH'S JAW TIGHTENED as a rosy glow warmed the salesclerk's cheeks. She had the most exquisite skin… much of which was displayed to advantage in that harem girl getup. And those eyes—violet-blue and wide as a child's as she stared at him now. He almost smiled. It had been a while since he'd struck awe in a woman.

"I…I'll get Sid," she stammered, and hurried away with a rustle of silk and satin. He watched her go, intrigued. He hadn't expected such a combination of class and sass in a place like this.

But then again, when he'd learned Uncle Grif had left him a sex toy shop, he'd halfway expected to discover a dimly lit building on the "wrong" side of town, where people in black leather skulked among racks of dirty movies.

Instead he'd found this perfectly respectable-looking building in the heart of Boulder's business district. Well, respectable as long as you didn't notice that the antique armoire held an assortment of whips, handcuffs and other bondage gear, or that the walnut secretary showcased a collection of vibrators in crayon colors.

And what was with the costumes? He studied a mannequin who wore a lacy apron that barely covered her breasts, a black lace garter belt, black thong underwear, fishnet hose and spike heels. He wondered what Lana would think if he suggested she wear something like that.

He shook his head. Who was he kidding? Lana Montgomery didn't even like to leave the lights on when they were in bed. She definitely wouldn't approve of her boyfriend owning a shop like Just 4 Play. Her father and the other members of the bank board weren't exactly thrilled when they heard about it, though he'd managed to placate them with his talk of plans for the future of the building.

"Mr. Landry?"

Mitch turned and stared at the man moving toward him. This *person* had a four-inch tall pink Mohawk rising above his shaved head like a rooster's comb. The hair and the two-inch heels on his motorcycle boots made him tower a good eight inches over Mitch's own six feet. The man was dressed in black leather pants and vest, with an alarming array of silver rings and diamond studs glittering from both ears, his nose, eyebrow and lips. Mitch wasn't surprised when he opened his mouth to reveal a silver barbell piercing his tongue. "Hi, I'm Sid Crawford, the manager of Just 4 Play. Man, it's good to finally meet you."

Sid had a firm handshake and a smile that transformed his rough features from menacing to charming. Mitch almost laughed. Apparently nothing was as it seemed at Just 4 Play. "Nice to meet you, Mr. Crawford."

"Call me Sid. We aren't into formal around here."

Mitch glanced at the snake tattoo winding its way up Sid's left bicep. "No, I can see this isn't a very formal kind of place."

"So I guess you've had a chance to look around." Sid rubbed his hands together. "What else would you like to know?"

"I'll want to look at the books, of course."

"Sure. They're right back here." He followed Sid to the checkout counter in the center of the store. The manager pulled out a thick sheaf of computer printouts. "Business is real good. You don't have anything to worry about there."

Mitch's eyes widened when he read the final figure on the computer report. "This is the income for one month?" he asked.

"Oh, no, man. That's for one week."

Mitch blinked. He'd had no idea… "Who buys all this stuff?" he asked.

Sid tugged on his left earring. "Lots of people. We get a lot of married couples in here. You know, looking to spice things up. College students experimenting. Single women. Lots of single women." He grinned. "You attached?"

"Uh, not exactly." He'd been dating Lana Montgomery for several months now, but he wouldn't say they were exactly attached, though maybe in the future….

"It's a great place to meet chicks," Sid continued. "We get all kinds of people really—gays, straights, people into S&M or fetishes. You name it, we've got something to make them happy."

The rustle of silk distracted him and out of the corner of his eye, he watched the blond salesclerk sashay past. She certainly was an attractive little thing.

"So, dude, I'm sorry about your loss."

"Loss?" Mitch glanced at the books again. Was there a loss on here somewhere?

"Yeah, Grif was an awesome guy. We're really going to miss him."

"Oh, Grif. Yes, he was…awesome. Thank you." Actually, in the family, his father's brother had been known mostly for his young girlfriends, eccentric habits and outrageous taste in clothing. He and Grif had never been particularly close, though they'd stayed in touch. The last time they'd seen each other, Grif had accused his nephew of being "a regular stick in the mud." Was willing him Just 4 Play Grif's idea of a joke?

"I'd better give you this, too." Sid rummaged in the drawer under the cash register and fished out a key.

Mitch accepted the key. "What's it for?"

"It's the key to Grif's office." Sid nodded toward a door at the back of the room. "I think most of the stuff in there is personal. Grif had a sort of apartment fixed up. He liked to stay over sometimes, rather than driving back to his place in Denver. But there might be some business stuff in there, too."

Mitch pocketed the key. "Thanks. I'll take a look at it later."

The blonde moved past again, carrying a cardboard box. Mitch couldn't help watching her walk across the room. She had the most distracting sway in her hips....

"And you met Jill already." Sid nodded toward the blonde. She'd stopped before an armoire and was busy unpacking bottles from the carton and lining them up on the shelves. She ignored them, but the tension in her shoulders told Mitch she was listening to every word that was said.

"Yes, I've met Jill," he said. "She was giving me a *personal* tour of the store."

A pyramid of plastic bottles fell with a crash and Jill knelt to gather them up. "Let me help you." In three strides, Mitch was beside her, helping her gather up the bottles. He read the label on one. "Kama Sutra Sensation. Have you tried this one?"

The go-to-hell look she gave him might have

wounded a lesser man. "Why didn't you tell me you were the owner instead of letting me go on like that?" she asked.

"You didn't exactly give me a chance." All the bottles reclaimed, he offered his hand.

She hesitated before taking it and allowing him to pull her to her feet. "I must say, I was impressed with your sales technique," he said. "You shouldn't have any trouble finding another job."

"Another job!" She shoved the bottles onto the shelf and faced him, hands on her hips. "You're going to fire me just because I didn't know you were the new boss?"

"Not fire you. But you'll need to find another job when I close the place down."

"What do you mean, close?" Sid hurried over to them.

Mitch looked around at the costumed mannequins, the cabinets full of condoms and oils and lingerie and fetish toys, finally letting his gaze come to rest on Jill's pixie face, all flashing eyes and pouting mouth. "Uncle Grif might have gotten a kick out of this place, but now that he's left it to me, I intend to close it and use the space to open a restaurant." He nodded toward the reshelved massage oil. "I think most people are more interested in Kung Pao than Kama Sutra, don't you?"

"You'd better take a look at those books again," Sid said. "This place makes way more money than any restaurant would."

"Oh, I don't think this has anything to do with the money, Sid." Jill crossed her arms over her chest and glared at him.

"No, it isn't about the money." Mitch looked her in the eye, resisting the temptation to let his gaze drop lower, to her very enticing cleavage. "It's a personal decision."

Sid frowned. "Come again?"

"Mr. Landry doesn't think we're respectable," Jill said. "He's embarrassed."

"Ohhhh." Sid nodded and clapped him on the back. "Go take a look at those books again, dude. You'll get over your embarrassment, I guarantee."

Mitch shoved his hands into his pockets. "I have a younger sister, and business associates. I'll admit I don't care to have them know I own a business that sells ten kinds of dildos and fur-lined handcuffs."

"Twenty," Jill said.

He blinked. "Twenty what?"

"We have twenty kinds of dildos." She took a step toward him, backing him up against the armoire. "And we have hundreds of satisfied customers. Just 4 Play provides a needed service in the community."

"By selling musical condoms and Ben Wa beads?"

"No, by selling fantasy. And fun." She leaned closer, until the tips of her breasts almost brushed against him. "Something you apparently haven't had enough of in your life."

"Life is about more than fun." He forced himself to ignore the enticing aroma of jasmine that surrounded her. "I have work to do. Responsibilities." He straightened. "And a reputation to protect, whether you agree with that or not."

She stepped back, a scornful expression on her face that might have been more effective if it hadn't made him think of the *I Dream of Jeannie* reruns he'd seen on *Nick at Night*.

"Just 4 Play has a reputation too," she said. "And it's not as bad as you seem to think. You haven't even been here an hour and already you're making judgments. You ought to at least give us a chance to show you what this place, and our customers, are really like.''

He shook his head. ''I'm sorry, I can't do that. The architects are all ready to draw up the plans and I've started the paperwork for the construction loan and building permits.''

Sid's shoulders slumped. ''So when do we shut the doors?''

''You have a month.'' He waved his hand at the shelves of bottles, boxes and gadgets, avoiding Jill's angry face. ''You'd better start marking things down.'' He checked his watch. In thirty minutes, he had to meet Lana at the bank. ''Now if you'll excuse me, I have to go.''

Jill caught up with him at the door. ''Isn't there anything we can do to change your mind?'' she asked.

He shook his head. ''Not a thing. I'm the kind of man who, when I make up my mind to do something, it stays made up.'' He hadn't put himself and his sister through school and started his own real estate business by being wishy-washy.

''You say that as if it's a virtue.''

Her words caught him off guard. He studied the toes of his shoes for a moment, then looked up at her. ''I guess if you think life is all about fun, it isn't,'' he said. He nodded goodbye and opened the door.

He thought he'd gotten the last word, but right before the door shut, her voice drifted to him. ''If you don't have fun, you don't have a life, Mr. Landry. Too bad no one ever taught you that.''

JILL SLAMMED THE DOOR SHUT on Mitch Landry, then turned and punched Blow-Up Betty right in the stomach. ''I can't believe he would do this to us!''

Betty swung back and forth on her stand until Sid moved over to steady her. "Careful with the merchandise, sister."

She brushed by Sid and began to pace. "I mean, how can he waltz in here, take one look around and decide to shut us down?"

"He's the owner. He can do anything he wants." Sid walked over to the cash register and slumped onto the stool behind the counter. "I guess we'd better start looking for other jobs."

"I don't want another job." Jill didn't stamp her foot, but she wanted to. This was one of those times when an all-out temper tantrum would have felt good. "I want to keep this one. There must be something we can do."

"You heard the man. He's got the architects working already. In another few months people will be ordering up fried rice where the costume rack is now." He picked up the paper and opened it to the classified ads. "There must be something in here I could do."

Jill hurried over to him and grabbed his arm. "Sid, you don't want to get another job."

His eyebrow ring rose. "I don't?"

"No. If you get another job, they'll make you change your hair. Or get rid of your jewelry." She leaned closer, her voice almost a whisper. "They'll make you wear a suit. And a tie."

Sid put a hand to his throat. "A tie?" He shook his head. "There must be something I can do where I don't have to wear a tie."

"Not and still have the title of manager. Even the manager of McDonald's wears a tie. Plus, anyplace else you go to work, you're liable to have to be there at eight o'clock, or even earlier."

"Eight in the morning?" Just 4 Play opened at

11:00 a.m. and closed at 10:00 p.m. For a night owl like Sid, 8:00 a.m. might as well be the middle of the night. He laid aside the paper and gave her a stricken look. "What can we do?"

"We have to change his mind."

"How? We only have a month." He looked around the store. "By then we might be sold out of everything."

"We'll simply have to show him how important this place is—that we provide a much-needed service for people."

Sid frowned. "How can you do that? I mean, let's face it, we're not exactly the food bank. Plenty of people get along fine without candy pants and nipple rings."

"Only because they don't know what they're missing." Inspiration sent tingles up her spine. She grinned. "I've got it!"

Sid leaned away from her. "Got what?"

"I know how we can convince Mitch Landry not to close the store."

"How?"

She plucked a jar of body chocolate from a display on the counter and began rolling it back and forth in her palms. "I think a little seduction is in order." She looked at Sid. "I'll make sure our Mr. Landry gets acquainted with the delights of some of our merchandise."

A pleasant warmth curled up from her stomach as the idea took hold. Really, it was a brilliant plan. Mitch Landry wasn't a bad person, merely uninformed. He had a great body and definite masculine appeal. It might even be fun to strip away some of his stuffy attitude and inhibitions, not to mention that suit and starched shirt.

Sid looked skeptical. "You think that would really make any difference?"

She set the jar of chocolate on the counter. "Sure it

would. Once he's having so much fun with the stuff we sell, it would be hypocritical to close us down."

"You think he'd care about that?"

"You heard the man. It's not about money for him, it's about reputation. Responsibilities. He's got integrity up to his eyeballs." She gave a mock salute. "No, I just have to find a way to get him to loosen up." Half the fun would be knowing where to start.

Sid shook his head. "I don't know, Jill. I don't think it's a good idea for you to get personally involved."

"Oh come on, I'm a big girl. It's not as if I plan to get serious with the guy. We'll just have a little fun."

"He might not feel the same way. He struck me as the type who takes everything seriously."

She shrugged off the truth of Sid's words. Seducing Mitch Landry would be a dangerous game, but nobody had ever mistaken her for a coward. "I'll be doing him a favor by showing him how to lighten up."

"And if it doesn't work?"

She leaned on the counter, chin in her hands, and smiled to herself. "Then I'll have a hell of a lot of fun trying, won't I?"

3

MITCH WAS FIVE MINUTES LATE to meet Lana, but he wasn't worried, because she was guaranteed to be ten minutes late. It was one of the things that annoyed him about her. That and her tendency to be arrogant, but he supposed that came from always being at the top of the social heap.

Still, in any relationship, you had to overlook certain things. Lana had other qualities he admired: she was attractive, well-dressed, intelligent and elegant. And she had the kind of connections he needed to establish himself as a businessman in this town. Not that he'd ever date a woman solely for her social status, but it was an added plus when you were trying to get ahead.

She breezed through the double doors of the bank lobby right on schedule, at ten after. Mitch rose from his chair and went to meet her, leaning down to kiss her cheek. "Careful," she cautioned, pushing him back. "I just had my hair done."

Why that should make any difference, he wasn't sure. It wasn't as if he was going to run his fingers all through her hair in the course of a hello kiss. Not that he could anyway, she kept it so firmly pinned in place.

"Lana, darling, you look lovely as ever." Morton Montgomery emerged from his office to greet them. He patted his daughter's shoulder and shook Mitch's hand.

"I've got all the paperwork ready for you. Why don't you come right in and we'll go over it all."

Mitch followed Lana and her father into an office whose predominant theme was dead animals. Mounts of bighorn sheep, deer, elk, moose and even a mountain lion occupied most of the wall space. Mitch took a chair with his back to the lion and smothered an expression of distaste.

"So have you had a chance to check out the property yet?" Mort asked as he settled into a full-grained leather executive chair.

"I was over there this afternoon. I must say, it's not at all what I thought it would be."

Mort pursed his lips and nodded. "Still, not the sort of place you'd want your name associated with."

"What sort of place is it?" Lana looked at him, a pleasant expression on her perfectly made-up face.

Mort cleared his throat. Mitch resented the warning. He'd already agreed Lana didn't need to know the nature of the business he'd inherited. "Nothing special." He waved away the question. "A restaurant will do much better in that location, I'm convinced." His throat tightened only a little at the lie. He *had* been convinced a restaurant was a better financial venture until he'd seen the books at Just 4 Play. So convinced he'd sold most of his other real estate around town in order to put everything into this new enterprise. But who would have thought there could be so much money in sex?

"We've already had an appraisal done." Mort handed across a folder. "And here's the preliminary paperwork for the construction loan. You'll have no problem qualifying for the funds you need. All we're waiting on now are the architectural plans and the permits from the city."

"I should have everything ready in thirty days." He closed the folder and returned it to the banker.

"Excellent. I think this is going to be an excellent investment, Mitch. Something we can all be proud of." Mort grinned. "So do you two have plans for the evening?"

"We have reservations at the Boulderado." Lana picked up her purse and stood. "We need to leave now, or we'll be late."

On the way to the restaurant, Mitch only half listened to Lana's account of an annoying client who'd visited her CPA firm that day. He was replaying the conversation in Mort's office. Why did it bother him that Mort had said the restaurant was something they could "all" be proud of? Wasn't Mitch the one who was doing all the work? Wasn't he the one who'd earned the right to be proud—or not? Or did Mort think a simple business loan gave him control over the project—and over Mitch?

The maître d' at the Boulderado welcomed them with a smile and escorted them to their favorite table in the atrium. "Should I have the wine steward bring your usual?" he asked.

"Yes, James, that will be fine," Lana said as she settled into her chair.

James started to leave, but Mitch stopped him. "Wait. Instead of the merlot, let's have a chianti."

James and Lana both stared at him. "But we always have the merlot," Lana said.

He nodded and spread his napkin across his lap. "Tonight, I'd like something different."

"Yes, sir." James hurried away.

Lana regarded him with a half smile on her lips. "Feeling feisty tonight, are we?"

"Something wrong with that?" He kept his voice

light, but there was no mistaking the challenge in the words.

"No. It's just not like you to be so...different."

The truth of her words wounded him. Maybe Uncle Grif had been right. Maybe he was a stick in the mud. Well, that didn't mean he had to stay that way. People changed. He could change without sacrificing his integrity in the process.

He started by ordering broiled trout for dinner instead of his usual prime rib. Lana compressed her lips into a thin line, but said nothing. Mitch sipped the excellent wine and regarded her over the rim of the glass. Her dark hair was drawn back from her face and gathered in a low knot, the kind ballerinas wore. He supposed people would say she had a classical beauty—fine features, with deep-set green eyes and a Roman nose.

"Is something wrong?" She looked puzzled.

He shook his head and picked up his fork. "No, nothing's wrong."

"Then why were you staring at me?"

He forced a pleasant smile to his lips. "Maybe I simply enjoy looking at you."

She dismissed the compliment with a frown and began cutting up her prime rib with the precision of a surgeon. "I saw Jerry Brenham at lunch today. He says the Canterbury Apartments are going on the market next week. If you call him now, you could make a bid before anyone else."

"Actually, I'm thinking of getting out of the rental market altogether."

She raised one perfectly groomed eyebrow in question. "But why? The Boulder rental market is one of the most profitable in the country."

"Yes, but I'm tired of being a landlord." At least with

his own restaurant, he wouldn't have tenants calling him up in the middle of the night to complain about a lack of hot water or the noisy neighbors.

"You should hire a management company. Then you wouldn't have to deal with tenants."

"I like being personally involved in a business. That's why I decided to open a restaurant."

She dabbed the corner of her mouth with her napkin, careful not to smear her lipstick. "I can't imagine why. Half the fun of having money is being able to delegate the work to someone else." She stabbed at a piece of beef. "Then you can go out and make *more* money."

It always came back to money with Lana, didn't it? he thought. They'd met at an investment seminar. He'd been attracted to her from the first because she was so different from him. She had a grace and ease in social situations he wanted to emulate, and a cool reserve he felt could help him keep a tighter reign on his own sometimes tumultuous passions.

The fact that she was the kind of woman who would have never looked at him twice when he was a struggling scholarship student in college made the challenge of winning her that much more exciting. And now here they were, if not engaged, then certainly "in a relationship." But a relationship based on what—business?

They had dinner every Wednesday at the Boulderado, and attended the theater or a concert every Friday. He usually stayed at her condo two nights a week. She never stayed at his place; she said she couldn't be comfortable there.

Why hadn't he realized before how boring and predictable his life had become? He looked at his plate. Right down to the same New York cheesecake every Wednesday night for dessert.

"Mitch, why are you so quiet? Haven't you been paying attention to a word I've said?" Did he imagine a note of annoyance in her voice?

He pushed his plate away. "I don't want to talk about business tonight."

She frowned. "Then what do you want to talk about?"

He leaned back in his chair and studied her across the table. "Why don't we talk about us?"

Her eyes widened and she looked away. She balanced her knife and fork precisely in the center of her plate and folded her napkin neatly beside it. "I'm listening."

And what did he have to say? How could he describe this restlessness he felt? "Lana, do you ever think about doing things differently?" he asked.

"Doing what things differently?" She sipped her coffee.

Decaf, extra cream, no sugar, Mitch thought.

"Anything. Everything." He leaned toward her and lowered his voice. "For instance, sex."

Her eyes widened and her cheeks flushed. "What are you talking about?"

"I mean—do you ever think about…experimenting. Dressing up in sexy clothes or using some massage oil or…something."

By this time her cheeks were the color of ripe apples and her lips had almost disappeared as she compressed her mouth into a thin line. "Really, Mitch. Why would you want to do any of that?"

"I don't know…because it might be fun. Because maybe we've both been a little too…repressed."

She stared at him. "What's gotten into you?"

"Nothing's gotten into me. I just think my life has

grown a little…boring. I don't see what's wrong with
wanting to try something different.''

"I'm sorry if you think I'm…repressed.'' She jerked
her napkin from her lap and deposited it on the table.

"Lana, I didn't mean you—''

"I think I'd better leave now.'' She stood and
clutched her purse to her chest.

"Lana, I—'' The apology froze on his lips. He
couldn't say he was sorry, because he wasn't. What was
wrong with a couple talking about these things?

"Don't bother to get up. I'll call a taxi.'' She gave
him a last wounded look and hurried past him.

He told himself he should go after her. That's probably what she wanted. But why should he pursue her?
If Lana wasn't even willing to listen to his point of view,
what did that say about their relationship? He'd thought
the safe, orderly routine they'd fallen into was what he
wanted, but he realized that wasn't enough anymore.

So no, he wouldn't go after her. Actually it was a nice
change sitting here alone, sipping his wine and thinking.

Mostly he thought of Jill. How different she was from
Lana. Or from any other woman he knew. She was frank
without being crass, funny without being phony. She
looked like the girl next door and dressed like an erotic
temptress. He'd only met her this afternoon but he already felt like she knew more about him than most people. She'd picked up right away on the reason he wanted
to close Just 4 Play, and hadn't been the least bit impressed with his position or power. She hadn't cared if
he owned a whole city block of businesses or if he was
a scholarship student at the university.

He smiled, remembering the way she'd asked
"What's your fantasy?''

But his smile faded as her other words came back to

him. Was she right? Was he too uptight? Had he for-gotten how to have fun?

She couldn't know how little room in his life there'd been for fun. From the time he was seventeen, he'd been looking after his mother and little sister, Meg. He'd worked and gone to school, and been there for every band concert and school program of Meg's. Now that Meg was a premed student, she didn't need him so much—except to pay the bills. And that meant he had to devote himself to business. To meeting the right peo-ple, making the right investments. He'd worked hard to develop a certain reputation. For Meg's sake, as well as his own, he couldn't let something like owning a sex toy shop cast a shadow over everything he'd worked for. People judged you more harshly when they knew you came from nothing. If too many people thought that way, you could end up with nothing again.

He'd have time for fun later. Right now he had to take care of his responsibilities.

Which brought him back to Jill. She was one of his responsibilities now too. And Sid. He would let them know he'd treat them fairly. He'd give them a generous severance package and help them find other jobs. Maybe he'd even offer Jill a job in his new restaurant. It would be nice having her around. Maybe one day, she'd even come to think of him as a friend.

JILL WAS SURPRISED TO FIND Mitch hard at work in Grif's office when she arrived at Just 4 Play the next morning. At least, from the looks of the papers spread out on the desk in front of him, he'd been working; when she knocked on the door frame and stepped through the open door, he was staring into space.

When she came into the room, he glanced at her, then straightened. "Good morning, Jill."

"Good morning. I see you're here early."

"I've been here since nine. That's not exactly early."

"It is around here. We do most of our business in the evening, though the lunch hour is good, too. People like to pop in and pick up a few things."

"That gives a whole new slant on the idea of a quickie."

The remark startled a laugh out of her. Yesterday, Mitch hadn't struck her as a man with much of a sense of humor. Which just went to show, first impressions aren't always accurate. "Finding anything interesting?" She nodded at the paperwork on his desk.

He glanced down at the folder in front of him, then closed it. "Tell me, what did you think of Grif?" he asked.

"Grif?" The question surprised her. Why was he interested in her opinion of his uncle? "I liked him," she said. "He was a fun guy."

"That's it? A fun guy?"

"Yeah. I mean, he knew how to enjoy life." *Unlike some uptight people I could name.* She leaned against the desk. "I'll bet he was your favorite uncle, huh?"

Was the hurt that flashed across his face grief, or something else? He pushed the file away. "Did you need something?"

So much for getting to know each other better. Good thing she wasn't the type to give up easily. She flashed him her most dazzling smile. "I've been thinking about what you said yesterday." She moved around to sit on the edge of the desk. Her skirt rose up on her thigh, not an indecent amount, but enough that she was sure he noticed. She'd purposely dressed more conservatively today, in a simple skirt and sleeveless knit top. Sometimes what a man couldn't see was more enticing than what was right out in the open.

His color heightened as he glanced at her, then he jerked his gaze away. "What in particular were you thinking about?"

"What you said about most people being more interested in Kung Pao than the Kama Sutra."

"Oh?"

With one syllable, he lobbed the conversation back to her. But that one word told her a lot. He was interested all right, but determined not to show it. "I think, in general, people do tend to think about food more than sex, but maybe that's because we eat three times a day. I mean, food is always there, practically right in front of us."

"But most people don't have sex three times a day."

She smiled. "No, I think it's safe to say most people don't have sex nearly that often."

He nodded, still somber as a judge, though she thought she caught a hint of amusement in his voice. "If they did, it would severely interfere with work."

"In that case, it would probably be outlawed altogether. We mustn't let anything get in the way of the economy."

He laughed, and she counted that a minor victory. "So what are you trying to say?"

She picked up a pencil and smoothed her fingers along its length. "That sex is more special than food. That we shouldn't take it for granted. And if dressing up or playing with toys or using other things makes sex special for people, then that's a good thing, don't you think?"

He sat back, leaning away from her, his pose casual, but the tension in his shoulders letting her know he was aware of her in the way a man is aware of an attractive woman. "What's wrong with the old-fashioned way? A man and a woman, no props?"

She looked directly at him for the first time since she'd come into the office, her expression serious, chasing the mirth from his eyes. She wet her lips, her voice low, seductive. "With the right man and woman, that can be wonderful."

He held her gaze, not flinching. "Then they don't really need places like this."

"No." She leaned closer. The spicy scent of Aramis sent a warm tickle through her midsection. "Do you like cake?"

He blinked. "Cake? I guess so. It depends on the cake."

"Chocolate cake. Devil's food. With so much chocolate, it's almost black. Sinful." She wet her lips. "With chocolate buttercream icing an inch thick."

He swallowed. "And your point is?"

"Just 4 Play is like the icing on that cake. The cake is good without the icing, but it's so much better with it." She dropped her gaze to his lips. All this talk of sweet indulgences made her wonder what it would be like to kiss him.

Apparently she wouldn't find out today. "That doesn't mean I have to be the one to sell the cake." He sat forward again, his voice firm, the spell between them broken. "Or the icing. Or sex toys and lingerie."

She frowned. "You'd rather sell Chinese food. Something people can get at half a dozen other places in town."

"But not this Chinese food. I have a five-star chef who's going to create a special menu. We're not talking your average dollar-a-scoop buffet."

She crossed her arms over her chest and swung one leg impatiently against the desk. "It's still something ordinary. Expected." Why did it disappoint her so much that he'd settle for something anyone could do?

"Men have built fortunes providing people with ordinary services," he said.

She leaned forward, pinning him to the chair with her gaze. "But it's the risk-takers who've really made a difference in this world. Besides, you'd have more of a chance of making a fortune sticking with Just 4 Play. But of course, that wouldn't be respectable."

He frowned. "You say that like it's a bad word."

"Only if you're willing to settle for the ordinary, instead of the extraordinary."

"So you're saying Just 4 Play is extraordinary?"

"It could be. How are you going to know if you don't stick around and find out?"

"I guess I'll take that chance."

She slid off the desk and looked down at him. "I think you've forgotten what it means to really take chances," she said. "If you ever knew."

She turned and left, but not before glimpsing the hurt that flashed through his eyes at her parting words. Good. She'd made at least one point. And planted the seeds for further victories. She would convince Mitch Landry to see things her way. And maybe she'd show him what he'd been missing living his safe, conventional life.

4

MITCH PACED IN FRONT of his desk, debating whether to go after Jill, to tell her exactly what he thought of her unsolicited opinions and her attempts to change his mind. This was his business and he could do anything he damn well pleased with it. Why should he care what a salesgirl he'd known less than two days thought of him? He had half a mind to—

"Shit!" Pain shot through his leg as he banged against the corner of the daybed that sat against the back wall of the office/apartment. He frowned at the offending piece of furniture. The bed was covered in a fleece throw decorated with rows of bright yellow smiley faces. Another example of Uncle Grif's appalling tastes.

He sank down onto the bed, head in his hands. No, in this case, he *was* the one who'd behaved appallingly. He'd dismissed Grif as a crass playboy who'd devoted his life to golf, women and the sex toy business.

Going through this office this morning, Mitch had discovered another man entirely. He found a whole file drawer devoted to the various charities Grif supported— a mentoring program for adolescent boys, a shelter for abused women, a spay and neuter clinic for indigent pet owners. The thickest file in the drawer sent a pain through his chest.

He looked up, at the folder still sitting on the corner of the desk. From here he could read the hand-lettered label on the tab: Mary Landry Mental Health Education Foundation.

Loud, tasteless, fun-loving Uncle Grif had funded a program to educate the public about mental illness and the mentally ill. He had named it after his sister-in-law, Mitch's mother, who had spent her last years in and out of institutions, struggling for a normalcy she could never quite attain.

Mitch felt ambushed by grief for a man he'd never really known. A man he'd never have the chance to thank.

Had Uncle Grif left him these things to show how wrong Mitch had been in his judgment? Or as a way of saying he understood?

He stood and opened another folder on the desk. This one held tax forms. Despite his happy-go-lucky reputation, Grif had been a sound businessman. Just 4 Play was on solid financial footing and had increased profits every year in the three years since it had opened.

But money didn't equal respect. In yet another folder, he'd found paperwork showing the Chamber of Commerce had turned down Grif's application for membership, with a curt letter stating Just 4 Play did not enhance the family-oriented reputation they wanted to project.

He pushed aside the stack of files and stretched. A glance at his watch showed it was after noon. A good time to go out for a bite to eat. As Jill had pointed out, he had to eat three times a day, though sorry to say, he wasn't having sex three times a day. Not even three times a week. And from the way Lana had acted last night, he'd be lucky if she ever had sex with him again.

Then again, would that be such a loss?

With this disturbing thought, he emerged into the main part of the store. As Jill had said, lunchtime business was brisk, with people lined up two deep at the register and more browsing in various parts of the store. He spotted Jill in a back corner, rearranging items on a pegboard.

She glanced toward him, then quickly looked away. The deliberate snub annoyed him. Just because they disagreed on how he should run *his* business didn't mean they couldn't be civil. As her boss, it was up to him to set an example. He decided to ask her if she wanted him to bring anything back for her lunch.

She was standing on tiptoe to hang something on one of the pegs when he reached her corner. "Hello, Jill."

"Hello, Mitch." She reached into another carton, not looking at him.

"What do you have there?" He nodded to what looked like a ball of fake fur in her hand.

"Fur-lined handcuffs." She held up what he could see now was two circlets of black fur joined by a silver chain.

"Okay. But why fur?"

"It's more comfortable. See?"

Before he could react, she snapped one cuff around a pole on the display and another around his right wrist.

"Hey!" He struggled against the restraint. "What do you think you're doing?"

"Just showing you how comfortable they are." Her innocent smile failed to mask the evil gleam in her eye.

He refused to give her the satisfaction of thinking she'd bested him. He studied his cuffed wrist. The fur against his skin was cool and silky. "People actually think this is sexy?"

"It's not the cuffs themselves that are so sexy. It's the element of danger." She moved closer, her voice softer, confiding. "Of risk. Of having to trust your partner completely."

She was so close now he could see each individual eyelash, and the smattering of freckles beneath the powder on her nose. He held his breath, half-afraid she'd hear the hammering of his heart and know how she'd affected him.

"Here. You look uncomfortable." She grasped the knot of his tie and tugged it loose, then began to loosen the buttons of his shirt. She moved slowly, focused on the task, her fingers lightly grazing his skin as she parted the starched cotton.

He grabbed her wrist with his free hand. "What are you doing?" His gaze met hers, the blue depths of her eyes pulling him in even as his mind warned him to keep his distance. "Get me out of here before someone comes along and sees us." His voice was tight and husky, the voice of a stranger.

"Oh, no one's paying any attention to us." Her lips curved in a slow smile. "I thought you wanted to understand the appeal."

She stepped back, just out of his reach, and picked up a small whip, with a fringed leather tassel at the tip. "The cuffs are like this cat-o'-nine-tails. It's not really designed to harm." She flicked it across his chest, the tassel barely brushing against him. "You can use it to tickle. Or perhaps more firmly." She wielded the whip with more force this time, though still barely grazing him. "The idea is to heighten sensation."

All thought of his surroundings faded as he watched her. His skin felt feverish, his nerves raw, tingling with awareness of her—of the smooth skin of her arms brushing him as she reached for something on a shelf, of the curve of her breast outlined by the clinging knit of her sleeveless top, of the bottomless blue of her eyes as she watched him.

He reminded himself she was doing this on purpose. She was deliberately trying to make him feel vulnerable. Trying to prove some point. He wouldn't be swayed so easily. He forced a lightness into his voice that he didn't feel. "Do you always break in new bosses this way?"

"I thought you wanted to understand." She trailed the whip across his throat, tickling, teasing, stealing breath and coherent thought. "To see what it is that attracts people to these things."

"Are you into this kind of thing? Bondage?" Heat pooled in his groin and desire lent an edginess to his voice.

She stroked the handle of the whip down her throat, a half smile on her full lips. He bit back a groan, determined to maintain control. "Maybe." She leaned closer, engulfing him in the scent of jasmine. "That's what it's all about, isn't it? The experience?"

He reminded himself that they were not alone. At any moment now, someone might come down the aisle and wonder what was going on. It was important to keep his cool. Retain his dignity. And to not let Jill know she was getting to him. "I think you've made your point," he said, his voice perfectly even, emotionless.

"No. I've only just begun." She smiled, a secret, seductive look.

"I can see this is getting out of hand." He struggled once more to free his wrist from the cuff. But underneath the fur was solid steel. He was held fast.

"It's about so much more than sight. That's why sometimes people use blindfolds. To heighten the other senses." She took a black satin blindfold from the shelf and brushed it down his cheek. He glared at her, warning her she was taking this too far.

Still smiling, she laid aside the blindfold and reached for a small red bottle. "The sense of smell is important." She opened a bottle and held it under his nose. A spicy fragrance replaced the aroma of jasmine.

"Or taste." She touched her finger to his lips and he tasted cinnamon.

"And hearing." She swished the whip past his ear. He flinched, even as heat coursed through him.

"Touch." She trailed the whip down the center of his chest, the fringes dragging across his chest hair, tugging gently.

He fought to control his breathing, even as his body strained toward her. He couldn't remember wanting a woman more—needing her with an urgency that defied logic. If he wasn't held fast by the cuffs, he might have pulled her down right there in the aisle. He tried to read the expression in her eyes. Is that what she wanted, too, or was she only teasing him? Getting back at him for wanting to close the store?

"What about you?" he demanded. "What do you want?"

She blinked, and stepped back. "Wh…what do you mean?"

"Is sex the main goal for you? The sensual experience? Or do you want something more?"

She turned away, and replaced the whip on its hook. "I don't see why that should matter to you."

Her defensive tone told him more than the words themselves. "It does matter, doesn't it?" he said softly. "There has to be a connection with that other person. If you don't have that, everything else is just…make-believe."

"Whoever said there was anything wrong with make-believe?" With one quick movement, she released him. She snatched up the cuffs and replaced them on the peg-board. "Not every encounter is life changing," she said.

He rubbed his wrists and watched her as she busied herself moving things about on the display. Her head was bent, the hair parted on either side of her neck to reveal a triangle of white flesh. He fought the urge to kiss her there. "I think we're all looking for the life-changing encounters," he said. "Even those of us who don't want to admit it."

With difficulty, he turned and walked away, shaken by what had just happened, but determined not to show it. What did it mean that a woman he scarcely knew could touch him so? Was it the novelty of the experience, the charged atmosphere of this place? Or something more? Something that threatened to unman him, to destroy the control he'd worked so long to perfect?

"I SAW WHAT YOU DID." Sid's disapproving tone stopped Jill as she walked past the front counter after the noon rush had subsided.

"What are you talking about?" She pretended ignorance.

"I saw you and Mitch back there." He nodded at the security mirror angled toward the corner.

She flushed. She'd forgotten about that mirror. "He wanted to know what the handcuffs were for, so I showed him." She trailed her hand along the edge of the counter, avoiding Sid's eyes.

"You did a lot more than that."

And might have done more if they'd been alone. "So?"

"So, haven't you ever heard of sexual harassment? He could sue you!"

She laughed. "And tell a whole courtroom that I tied him up and teased him with a whip? I don't think so." She smiled, remembering the raw desire in his eyes. "Besides, I think he liked it."

"Liked it or not, you could end up in big trouble playing games like that."

"Oh, Sid, you worry too much. It was all in fun."

"It looked deadly serious from here. In fact, I'd say you're lucky looks *can't* kill, or you'd be laid out in the back room right now."

"I'm still standing, aren't I?" She leaned back against the counter, edgy with frustrated desire. The problem with a slow seduction was that Mitch wasn't the only one left aroused and unsatisfied. "Besides, what have I got to lose? If I can convince Mitch to keep this place open, you and I get to keep our jobs. If I don't, well then I'm out the door anyway, so I might as well try."

"But seducing the boss—it's a crazy idea!"

She laughed. "Unconventional maybe. Smart even. But not crazy."

"It *is* crazy. And it won't work. You heard him yesterday—his mind is made up."

"People can change their minds. Even men."

"Not men like him."

"I guess you're an expert on change, Mr. How-Many-Girlfriends-Is-It-This-Week?"

He stuck out his lower lip. "I have every intention of being faithful, as soon as I find the right woman."

"So you're saying the right woman will convince you to change your tomcat ways?"

He nodded. "When I've found the right woman, I won't need anyone else."

She laughed. "That's what I love about you, you're such a romantic."

His expression relaxed. "Speak for yourself, Miss I-Want-To-Be-Swept-Away-By-A-Knight-In-Shining-Armor."

"That's a pirate. I want to be swept away by a pirate."

"Whatever. I don't think Mitch Landry has ever been within sight of a sailing ship."

"Don't be so sure. My point is, if the right woman can make you mend your ways, then the right woman can make Mitch Landry change his mind about closing Just 4 Play."

"And you think you're the right woman?"

"Let's just say I'm a woman who always gets her man."

"Hmm. Well, if I were a betting man, I'd put my money on the man getting you. I think you're in over your head this time, Jilly girl."

She shook her head and walked away, ignoring the doubts nudging at her. For a moment with Mitch, she'd almost forgotten the rules of the game. Rules she'd established. Fun was the object. A mutually satisfying, sensual experience. A good time had by all. No need for messy complications.

Mitch's talk of "connections" and "life-changing experiences" had shaken her. Sure, those things were for some people, but not for her. What did Mitch know? Maybe he thought he'd seen some secret longing in her eyes, but he was wrong. She was attracted to his body. To his mind, even. But that was as far it went. Anything else was just his imagination.

5

MITCH SAT IN HIS CAR, trying to calm nerves that felt as if they'd been filed with sandpaper, trying to make sense of what had just happened. He couldn't remember ever feeling so vulnerable and out of control, so exposed while fully clothed, or so incredibly aroused.

It was more than being caught off guard and tied up. More than the props Jill had used in her little "product demonstration," more even than the admitted excitement of knowing that at any moment, they might be discovered.

No, something about Jill herself made his temperature rise and his mind lose track of where he was and what he was supposed to be doing. Something in the contrast between her innocent looks and her seductive words fired every synapse and sent common sense running for cover. The way she made him feel was based on instinct, not reason. The thought that anyone could reduce him to that sent a new tremor through him.

"Damn it, this is crazy!" He hit the steering wheel hard with the heel of his hand. He wasn't some pimply teenager ruled by hormones. He was a businessman—and he had no business getting involved with a woman he scarcely knew. A woman who had the power to distract him so much.

Thwarted desire replaced by a more garden-variety frustration filled him as he started the car and pulled out into traffic. He'd intended to head over to Qdoba for lunch, but he found himself driving up University Hill, toward the only apartment building he still owned, where his sister, Meg, lived with another premed student.

Meg answered the door dressed in scrubs, holding a can of soup in one hand. "Hey, Mitch!" She stood on tiptoe to hug him, then stepped back and held up the can. "You're just in time for lunch."

"How about I take you out instead?"

She tossed the can over her shoulder. It landed on the sofa and bounced twice before coming to rest against a pillow. "Let me put my shoes on and you've got a date."

Fifteen minutes later, they sipped iced tea on the patio at Qdoba. "So what's up?" Meg asked, reaching for a tortilla chip.

"Nothing's up." He rearranged the salt and pepper shakers. "I remembered you don't have classes Tuesday and Thursday mornings and I thought I'd stop by and see how you're doing."

She shook her head. "Since when do you leave work in the middle of the day to socialize? Especially with your sister?"

He pushed the salt and pepper aside and contemplated his hands, palms down in front of him on the table. They were plain, unremarkable hands, no rings, nails clean and neatly filed. No scars or calluses. Hands with no character at all.

"Earth to Mitch." Meg snapped her fingers under his nose. "C'mon, what's up? You look like you lost your best friend."

He sighed and looked up at her. Strands of her dark curly hair fluttered in the breeze from the ceiling fan overhead. She wasn't wearing any makeup and she looked about sixteen. He couldn't imagine her ever delivering a baby or performing surgery on anyone.

She looked like their mother—a small, helpless woman. Except Meg wasn't helpless. She pointed a tortilla chip at him. "You might as well tell me, 'cause you know I'm going to worm it out of you, or else I'll nose around behind your back until I find out everything. You can't keep secrets from me, big brother."

"Did you know Uncle Grif funded a foundation to educate the public about mental illness? And he named it after Mother."

"I think I remember hearing something like that. Why?"

He sat back, shoulders slumped. "I just found out. I never knew that about him. Why would he do something like that?"

"I think he had a soft spot for Mama. And I know she was fond of him. She always looked forward to his visits when she was in the hospital."

"I always thought he was just a loudmouthed playboy who spent all his money on gin, girls and golf."

She tilted her head to one side, her expression sympathetic. "And now you're beating yourself up because you were wrong." She reached out and touched his arm. "Hey it's okay. Even *you* are allowed to screw up sometimes. It proves you're human, like the rest of us."

"Great bedside manner, Doc. I feel all better now."

"You'll get over it. Grif must not have held it against you, since he left you his business."

A business Mitch hadn't even known existed until the will had been read. Maybe this was Grif's way of having the last word.

Their lunch arrived and conversation stalled as they focused on their burritos. Mitch had found that even big problems looked smaller when considered in the aftermath of any meal that included plenty of hot sauce and melted cheese.

"So how did you find out about the mental health foundation?" Meg asked just as he'd taken a bite of burrito.

He swallowed and reached for his tea. "I was going through his files at…at the business he left me."

"Oh, yes. The mysterious business." She speared a forkful of beans. "Just what *is* this business, anyway?"

"Nothing important." He ignored the scowl she sent his way and poured hot sauce onto his plate. "I'm going to close it and open a restaurant on the site."

Meg shrugged. "Sounds like a lot of work to me, but you're the big businessman."

He looked away, pretending great interest in his meal. He hoped he wasn't making a mistake with this restaurant. He'd had the idea for over a year now, ever since he first met Chef Ping. When he found out Uncle Grif had left him a prime piece of downtown real estate, it had seemed like a sign he should go ahead with the project. Now he wondered…

"How's Lana?"

"Lana?" He looked up, startled. "Uh…she's okay. Why do you ask?"

"No reason. I just haven't heard you say much about her lately. I wondered if you were still seeing each other."

"We're still seeing each other." More or less.

"I've heard more enthusiasm for the daily special at the student union. Has some of the bloom worn off the romance?"

"Why would you say that?" He stabbed at a piece of tortilla. "Just because I'm not raving about her every minute doesn't mean I don't want to continue dating her. A relationship doesn't have to have fireworks all the time.'' He scowled at her. ''There's more to life than sex, you know.''

''Whoa, whoa, slow down there.'' She put up her hands. ''Who said anything about sex?''

He opened his mouth to protest, but she shook her head. ''No, if you and Lana are having problems in the bedroom, I don't want to know.'' She dunked a chip in hot sauce. ''But you might want to think about seeing other people for a while. I mean, I'll admit I'm prejudiced, but I think you've got a lot to offer a woman, and I'm not sure Lana really appreciates you.''

He was trying to come up with a suitable retort when his phone rang. Still frowning at his sister, he jerked the phone from his pocket and flipped it open. ''Hello?''

''Hi, uh, Mitch? This is Sid.'' The manager's voice sounded strained. ''Uh, sorry to bother you, but you need to get back to the store, right away.''

''What is it? Is something wrong?'' Mitch's stomach clenched. Had they been robbed? Was some fundamentalist group staging a protest?

''I'm not sure. Uh…there's this woman here. And uh…she keeps asking for you.'' He lowered his voice. ''She's kind of upset.''

''Oh, hell.''

''What is it?'' Meg leaned toward him, her eyes questioning. ''Is everything all right?''

He covered the phone with his hand. ''It's the manager at Uncle Grif's store. There's a woman there demanding to see me.'' He put the phone to his ear again. ''What does she want?''

''I don't know. Uh…she says her name is Lana. Lana Montgomery.''

MEG HAD HEARD OF PEOPLE turning green, but she'd never actually seen it before—until now. Actually, Mitch's face went through an alarming array of colors, from ashy-white to fiery-red, before settling on this green-tinted phase. He snapped the phone shut and shoved up from the table so hard his chair almost fell over behind him. He grabbed the chair, saving it from crashing to the floor and signaled the waiter for their check. "I have to go," he croaked.

Meg tossed aside her napkin and stood also. "I'll go with you."

He shook his head. "No. You stay here and finish eating." He tossed a twenty on the table and headed toward the door.

She followed. He stopped at the exit and glared at her. "Meg, you can't come with me."

She ignored him and headed for his car. He hurried after her. "What do you think you're doing?"

The minute he unlocked the car, she opened the door and slid into the passenger seat. "Something's going on and I intend to find out what it is," she said.

He fit the key into the ignition and scowled at her. "Get out of this car."

She fastened her seat belt and returned the scowl. "Make me."

He growled and started the car. "All right. But you're staying in the car."

She turned to look out of the window so he wouldn't see her smile. Men were so predictable. Even her brother.

Mitch negotiated Boulder traffic with reckless speed, and screeched to a halt in a No Parking zone in front of a pink brick building. Meg looked up at the marquee over the building's door. Just 4 Play. Her smile broadened. She'd heard of this place. In fact, one of her girl-friends had recommended it. When Mitch jumped out of the car and went inside, she laughed out loud. So this was his secret inheritance. Oh, that was rich. Her straight-arrow brother had been saddled with a sex shop. This she had to see.

When she walked through the door, Mitch was leaning over the counter, deep in conversation with a petite blonde. The blonde pointed toward the back and he took off.

Meg walked over to the counter and picked up a pe-nis-shaped key chain. Now there was a conversation starter. "May I help you?" the blonde asked.

She laid aside the key chain. "I'm Meg Landry. Mitch's sister. We were having lunch when you called."

"Oh, I didn't call. The manager, Sid, did." She held out her hand. "I'm Jill Sheldon."

They shook hands. Meg looked around, at the candy-colored condoms, the blowup dolls, massage oils, how-to books and what looked like a belly dancer costume. Her grin widened. *Oh brother, what are you into now?* She turned to Jill. "So what's going on? Why did Mitch rush over here in the middle of lunch?"

Jill made a face. "A woman came in here this after-noon, took one look around and started hollering for Mitch."

"A woman? Who?"

"One of those society types. You know, fancy suit, fancy hair, fancy attitude." Jill's expression said Miss Fancy had left her singularly unimpressed. "She said her name was Lana Montgomery."

Meg shaped her mouth into a perfect O. "I take it Mitch hadn't gotten around to telling her about this place."

Jill leaned across the counter, ready to dish dirt. "Who is she?"

"Mitch's girlfriend. Or maybe ex-girlfriend now." She picked up a jar of body paint and studied the list of suggested uses. "Something tells me Lana's not the type to approve of a place like this."

Jill straightened. "I suppose she thinks there's something wrong with healthy sexuality. With helping people to improve their relationships and learn about their bodies—"

"Hey, I didn't say I didn't approve." Meg set aside the body paint. "To tell the truth, Lana's always struck me as somebody laced up a little too tight."

Jill glanced toward the closed office door. "Like Mitch."

"Well, yeah, big brother can be a little…intense. But he's really a great guy."

Jill raised one eyebrow. "You wouldn't be a little biased, would you?"

She grinned. "Not at all." She nodded toward the office. "So what happened before I got here?"

"Sid took this Lana chick back to the office. I think he was going to fix her some tea. If we're lucky, he slipped a tranquilizer into it."

"That would probably help." She walked over to a vibrator display and picked up a bright green model. No sense letting this shopping opportunity go to waste. "I've been thinking about getting one of these. What would you recommend?"

"We have some really nice models." Jill emerged from behind the counter and joined her at the display. "We have every color, size and shape you can think of." She began opening drawers and taking out boxes. "Somewhere in here is your perfect BOB."

Meg picked up a bright purple model. "Bob?"

"Your battery operated boyfriend." She glanced toward the office door. "Let me tell you, sometimes they're a lot less trouble than the real thing."

MITCH DIDN'T HAVE TIME to worry about Meg right now. He had to deal with Lana. What the hell was she doing here? How had she found out about the place? And what was he supposed to do with her now?

He paused outside the office door and forced himself to take deep, calming breaths. She was probably upset; fine, he had seen her upset before and he could deal with that. The main thing was to remain calm. After all, he'd done nothing to be ashamed of.

He grasped the doorknob firmly and shoved open the door, a placating speech already forming in his mind. But the scene before him froze him in his tracks.

Lana and Sid sat side by side in front of the desk. Sid's head was leaned toward Lana, an earnest expression on his face as he listened to her pour out some tale of woe, his pink Mohawk almost touching her perfectly coifed hair. The teacup looked like something from a child's toy tea set in his large hand.

"Thank you for being so understanding, Sid," Lana was saying.

Mitch made a strangled noise in his throat and they both looked up. Lana tensed and her expression grew stormy. "Mitch, how could you!"

He walked into the room and leaned against the desk, his pose deliberately casual. "How could I what?"

Two lines made a deep V between her brows and her mouth puckered in an expression of distaste. "How could you run a...a...smut shop?"

"We prefer to think of ourselves as purveyors of accessories to enhance people's pleasure and well-being.'' Sid's tongue-stud clacked against his teeth, giving him a slight lisp.

Lana stared at him, her mouth going slack. A rosy flush crept up her neck. ''Um, yes.''

She turned back to Mitch. ''Why didn't you tell me?''

''Because I knew you'd react like this. Besides, I intend to close the place down and open a restaurant.''

Sid looked pained. ''I told her.'' He rescued her teacup from her hand. ''Let me get you some more tea.''

''I don't want more tea.'' She clenched her fists in her lap. ''I want an explanation.''

Why hadn't he noticed before how shrewish she could be? He frowned. ''I don't see that it's any of your business, Lana.''

''How can you say that? Don't you realize I have a reputation in town? What will people think when they find out the man I'm dating owns a place like this?''

The man I'm dating. Was that all he was to her? Someone to escort her to dinner or to the theater, nothing more? ''Maybe they'd think you were lucky,'' he said, only half-joking.

Sid brought more tea. ''Lots of respectable people shop here,'' he said. His expression was grave as he bent over Lana. ''The mayor's wife has even been here before.''

Lana's eyes widened as she accepted the teacup. A trembling attempt at a smile even rose to her lips. ''You've been so kind,'' she said, her voice breathy.

Sid ducked his head, looking humble—or as humble as a six-foot-plus tattooed and pierced man in leather can look. ''My pleasure, ma'am.''

Lana turned back to Mitch, her smile vanished. ''This

is why you've been talking about…about sex and experimenting and being bored."

He shoved his hands into his pants pockets. It was either that or give in to the temptation to shake some sense into her. "I was only suggesting we had gotten into a rut."

"Well…fine. If that's what you want then…fine." She set down her cup so hard tea sloshed onto the desk. "You can find someone else to play your…your sex games." She grabbed up her purse and stormed out.

"Lana, wait…"

"I'll just make sure she's okay." Sid took off after her.

Mitch crossed his arms and stared at the vacant doorway. He should have been the one to go after Lana, but he couldn't bring himself to move a muscle. Whatever they'd had between them was over now. The only emotion he could muster was relief.

He sighed and straightened. That took care of Lana— now what to do about Meg? He had little hope she'd actually stayed in the car. Even as a toddler, she'd never minded very well.

He spotted her with Jill on the other side of the store and made his way over to them. "What are you doing in here?" he asked.

She held up a large purple vibrator. "I had some shopping to do." She pressed a button and the purple plastic penis waggled like a hula dancer. "Isn't it cute?"

6

ALL THE BLOOD RUSHED to Mitch's face. He grabbed the absurd toy and switched it off. "I told you to stay in the car."

She raised one eyebrow. "Since when have I ever done what you tell me?" She grinned. "Nice place you have here, bro."

His face felt hot. He was embarrassed—and embarrassed that he was embarrassed. Yes, Meg was a grown woman, but he couldn't stop thinking of her as his little sister.

She picked up a pink vibrator. "I think I like this one."

"The koi," Jill said. "A good choice. The fish's little fins provide excellent clitoral stimulation."

He wanted to put his hands over his ears. He didn't want to hear this. He turned away. He didn't want to see it, either. Behind him, Meg and Jill laughed, apparently in on some hilarious joke.

The bells on the front door jangled and Sid came back in. "I managed to get her calmed down a little, I think. At least enough to drive home without having an accident."

"What was her problem?" Jill asked.

"She doesn't approve." Mitch walked over to the counter and pretended an interest in a magazine lying there. *Piercing Times*. Who knew there were so many different places one could puncture the body?

"In my experience, when someone has such a negative reaction to something, it's because they're really more attracted to it than they think they should be." Jill laid the pink vibrator on the counter and leaned toward him. The scent of jasmine teased him and a sudden memory of her, whip in hand, flashed across his mind.

He shifted his stance, turning slightly away from her. "I don't think that's Lana's problem."

"Don't be too sure." Meg joined them at the counter. "Maybe there's really a wild woman inside that repressed, proper shell."

He shook his head. "No." If anyone was in a position to know that, he was. Lana didn't even like to make any noise when she climaxed.

"What are you going to do now?" Meg asked.

He shoved aside the magazine. "Nothing."

"Nothing?" Jill tilted her head to one side and studied him.

"If she's that upset about me owning this place, then it's probably best we don't see each other anymore."

"So you're going to let her go, just like that?" Jill shook her head. "One little disagreement and you're through?"

Why was she taking Lana's side? "You don't know anything about it," he snapped. "And it's none of your business anyway."

"I think it's more than 'one little disagreement.'" Meg joined them at the front counter. "I think things haven't been right between them for a while now—if they ever were."

He glared at her. "Stay out of this."

She shrugged. "I'm just saying you're better off without her. I never thought she was your type."

"Oh?" Jill turned to Meg. "What sort of woman do you think *is* Mitch's type?"

"Well now, let's see." She furrowed her brow. "Someone a little more laid-back. Someone who can help him loosen up. Take his mind off business." She grinned at him. "Someone who can help him have a little fun."

There was that word again—as if life was always one laugh after another. "Stop talking about me as if I'm not even here," he demanded.

Jill gave him a long look, her gaze starting somewhere around his knees and traveling upward, as if she was measuring him for an outfit—or picturing him without one. He felt warm and resisted the urge to fidget. Instead he looked straight into her eyes, intending to stare her down.

Her lips curved in a slow smile. "Yes, I'd say someone needs to help Mitch loosen up a little." She leaned closer, until her breath tickled his ear. "Wouldn't you know it? That happens to be my specialty," she whispered.

MITCH APPARENTLY HAD MASTERED the art of looking cool and collected on the outside, but Jill knew she was getting to him. His eyes darkened, his breathing came faster and a pulse throbbed at his temple, inches from her lips. He might pretend to be unmoved, but Mitch Landry kept a lot of passion reigned in beneath his businesslike facade. Meg was right. Miss Fancy-Pants Lana Montgomery was too much of a cold fish for him. A man like Mitch needed a woman who wasn't afraid to get a fire going.

She breathed in deeply, and felt her own pulse quicken as the scent of Aramis swept over her. Oh, yes. Now that Mitch was certifiably free from entanglements with any other woman, she was going to have a wickedly wonderful time showing him the delights of a walk on the wilder side of life.

"Don't you have work to do?" His eyes narrowed.

She stepped back, but slowly, reluctantly, telling him with her body and her eyes that things would be so much better if only he'd allow her to move closer. "Why yes." She turned and picked up the koi vibrator. "I need to ring this up. Let's see now, what is our family discount?"

He glared at his sister. "You're not really going to buy that."

She grinned. "Why not?"

"Because." His face burned. "Don't you have to be twenty-one to buy something like this?"

"Eighteen." Sid, who had been standing by the front window, looking out, spoke up. "Twenty-one is for alcohol." He turned to face them.

"Besides, I *am* twenty-one." Meg laid a credit card on the counter. "I know it's hard for you, bro, but I'm all grown up now."

His shoulders slumped and he smiled weakly. "When did that happen?"

Meg laughed. "Not only that, I'm a medical student." She picked up the vibrator and pointed it at him. "What I don't already know about anatomy and sexuality, I fully intend to learn."

Mitch wrapped his arm around her shoulder and pulled her close. "Be careful where you point that thing, it might be loaded."

Jill laughed. Just when she'd begun to think she had

Mitch all figured out, he surprised her with a remark like that. She always did like a man who could surprise her.

Sid joined them at the counter. "Maybe somebody should call Lana later. Make sure she got home all right."

"That's thoughtful of you, Sid, but I can promise you Lana isn't home weeping into her pillow." Mitch shook his head.

"Then where is she?" Jill asked.

"My guess is she's over at Guarantee National Bank, complaining to Daddy about what a creep I am."

"You don't think he'll withdraw your building loan, do you?" Meg asked.

"That would be one way of keeping this place open," Jill said to Sid.

Mitch frowned, letting her know he'd heard this remark. "He couldn't stop the loan even if he wanted to. The board's already approved it. But I think Mort Montgomery is a better businessman than that. He won't let Lana tell him what to do."

"So you're still planning on turning this into a restaurant?" Jill sagged onto the stool behind the counter.

"What made you think I'd changed my mind?"

"I was hoping since you didn't have Miss High Society to impress anymore, you'd ditch the crazy scheme to turn this into the Kung Pao Palace or whatever."

"Then I guess that shows you don't know me very well." He leaned on the counter, his face very close to hers. "I don't let a woman tell me what to do, either."

"Not ever?" She laid her hand over his. "Sometimes it can be a lot of fun."

He pulled away and straightened. "I'm not here to have fun. I'm here to run a business."

She shook her head. "The two don't have to be mutually exclusive, you know."

"Contrary to what you believe and what my sister says, I do know how to have fun. But I think there's a time and a place for everything."

"All right, then tell me—what do you like to do for fun?"

He blinked. "Why should I tell you?"

"Why not tell her?" Meg challenged. "Or can't you think of anything?"

"I do plenty of things for fun. I go to the gym. I go out to dinner…"

"Working out at the gym is just another kind of work," Jill said. "And everybody has to eat. Just because you do it in a restaurant doesn't make it fun."

"I can't help it if your idea of fun and mine aren't the same."

"Face it, Mitch, you've forgotten how to have fun." Meg turned to Jill. "He's been so busy looking after me and working to support us, he hasn't developed any hobbies. He doesn't play sports. I can't even remember the last time he took a vacation."

"Everybody works hard when they're starting out. I'll have plenty of time for fun later."

"How many headstones do you think that's carved on?" Jill asked. *"He said he'd have time for fun later?"*

"All right then, if you're such an expert, what do *you* like to do for fun?"

"The better question is—what don't I like to do? I like to hike or ride my bike. In the winter I ski or ice-skate. I like going to the movies or just going over to Pearl Street Mall and watching the tourists." She ticked off these activities on her fingers. "I like kayaking and swimming and dancing—I love to dance. And then of course, there's my all-time favorite fun-time activity.''

"What's that?"

She grinned. "Sex!"

"You would name that one."

"Oh, don't be such a prude. Or don't you think sex is fun?"

He reddened slightly beneath his tan. "Sex can be fun." His eyes met hers, their intensity making her heart race. "It can also be very serious. When two people love each other, it can be serious as hell."

She slid off the bench and backed away, wanting to look away from him, but unable to. "Who said anything about love?"

"Don't you believe in love?" His voice held the same mocking tone she'd used with him.

She glanced at Meg, who was examining a packet of condoms on a display against the far wall as if she'd never seen anything like them before. Sid was standing by the front window, staring out at the street.

Mitch moved closer, trapping her between him and the counter. "It's not a difficult question, Jill." His voice was low, vibrating through her, raising prickles of awareness on her skin. "Do you believe in love...or don't you?"

"I...I believe in love." She dug her nails into the edge of the counter and willed her voice not to shake. "But I don't believe it's as common as people want to believe. You can have great sex with someone and not necessarily be in love."

He smiled, a slow, seductive salute that sent heat washing over her. "Good sex maybe. But great sex...for that I think you really do need love."

Who said women were the sentimental romantics of

the world? Between Mitch and Sid, she was surrounded by men who didn't have a clue. Love was fine for songs and romance novels, but the real thing came along less than once in a lifetime. Some people never experienced it. And that was okay. You could have a lot of fun and good times without complicating things with talk of love. "You talk like an expert on the subject," she said. "And yet you let Lana walk out the door with hardly a protest."

He glanced toward the door, then his gaze fixed on her once more. "Meg's right—Lana and I weren't in love. I knew it, but sometimes it's easier to stay in a familiar situation than to try and get out there and find a new one."

Jill shook her head. "You don't need love, mister. You need someone to shake loose the cobwebs. Someone to inject a big dose of Vitamin F into your life."

"And you're that someone?"

"I'm exactly the person for the job." She leaned closer, until they were almost touching. "In fact, I have a proposition for you."

He raised one eyebrow. "What kind of proposition?"

"You've got what, about four weeks until work is supposed to start on the restaurant?"

"That's right."

She wet her lips. "Then give me that time to prove to you that this store provides an important service for people."

"And how would you do that?" His voice was low, husky.

"By teaching you more about the merchandise here. Providing a few hands-on demonstrations, shall we say." She smiled. "By teaching you how to have fun with sex."

Then she did something she'd been wanting to do ever since he'd first walked in that front door. She pulled him to her and kissed him the way a man ought to be kissed—by a woman who knew what she was doing.

7

AHA. THIS WAS DEFINITELY the way to shut Mitch up.
He thought he knew so much, with all his talk of love
and being serious. She'd show him how to live in the
moment, to let go of reason and surrender to the physical
side of things.

At first he stiffened up on her, so that it felt like kissing a mannequin. But as she molded her body to his and
traced the tip of her tongue along the contours of his
lips, he began to loosen up. Like a plastic store dummy
coming to life, he warmed to her touch. His arms encir-
cled her and pulled her more tightly against him. His
mouth opened to accept her exploring tongue.

And then his own tongue invaded her mouth, thrusting
and withdrawing slowly, teasing along the edge of her
lips before advancing once more. He tasted sweet and
salty, better than a top-shelf margarita, and packing more
of a punch. Any hesitancy had left him. He kissed her
now with a forcefulness that made her light-headed and
breathless.

All right, so she'd made her point. She'd shown him
he was attracted to her physically, whether he wanted to
admit it or not. That was enough lessons for one day.
She tried to pull away, but he crushed her to him, sliding
his hand down to cup her bottom while he suckled at
the corner of her mouth. She felt his erection against her
stomach, hot and heavy.

She choked back a moan and clung to him to keep from sliding to the floor. The rest of the world was out there somewhere far away, but all her senses focused on this moment with this man. She felt the scrape of his beard against her cheek as he turned his head to fully capture her mouth once more, heard the pounding of her pulse in her ears and the rush of breath in her lungs as she panted. Every breath filled her head with the intoxicating scent of his cologne, and the more subtle musk of sex and desire. She felt as if she were melting from the inside out, common sense and control burned away by the heat of passion. Another moan escaped her and the last vestige of sensibility surfaced to mock her. What was she doing swooning over this guy like some star-struck sorority sister? She was supposed to be the one in charge here, remember?

She tried once more to pull away, but his arms tightened until she could scarcely breathe. "Oh, no, you started this," he murmured, his breath tickling her ear.

The jangling of the string of bells on the door saved her from having to come up with a coherent reply. Arms that had held her fast now pushed her away. She staggered back and grabbed on to the edge of the counter for support.

The world came back into focus. Meg watched her from the other side of the counter, deep dimples on either side of her mouth as her eyes danced with laughter. Sid was near the door, talking to the customer, a biker in leather and chains. Or maybe he was a stockbroker? You never knew these days.

Mitch was standing not two feet away, studying her, eyes narrowed, arms crossed, a chill fast descending between them.

She looked away and brushed imaginary dust from the countertop. ''It's time for my lunch break,'' she said.

''And I have a shift at the hospital this afternoon.'' Meg stepped forward and held out her hand. ''It was nice meeting you, Jill.''

They shook hands. ''Same here,'' Jill said. ''Maybe I'll see you again some time.''

Meg smiled at Mitch. ''Oh, I think I'll be seeing you again very soon.''

When Mitch and his sister were gone, Jill gave up on her jelly legs and sank down onto the stool behind the counter. So what had just happened here? Besides a mind-blowing kissing session. Whatever else she had against him, she had to admit that Mitch Landry was one hell of a kisser. Which begged the question—if he was that good at the preliminary moves, what was he like in the bedroom itself?

The thought sent a new wave of dizziness over her and a bolt of heat straight to her groin. She shifted on the hard stool and took a shaky breath. So they'd set off some physical sparks. This was a good thing. She could use that attraction to make him see how wrong he was to close Just 4 Play. It was nothing she hadn't anticipated.

Liar! her conscience shouted.

Okay, maybe she had felt a bit overwhelmed there for a minute. She was a little out of practice. And Mitch had surprised her. Who would have thought Mr. Serious Business had the makings of a sex god?

Never mind. He only *thought* he was in charge. In no time at all, she'd make him see how wrong he was.

SOMEHOW MITCH SUMMONED the strength to stroll out of Just 4 Play as if he didn't have a care in the world, while every cell in his body was screaming at him to get back in there and finish what he'd started with Jill.

And what exactly had he started? He'd recognized her kiss as the power play she'd intended, and the knowledge had annoyed him at first. Then he felt her soft curves pressed against him and reasoned there was nothing wrong with trying to beat her at her own game.

But somewhere between trying to show her who was boss and proving he was man enough to take what she had to dish out, he forgot his objective and starting enjoying the game a little too much. She moaned and he grew hard. He pulled her closer, craving the softness of her breasts against him, the firmness of her ass beneath his hand. He wanted to bury himself in her, to hear her cry out in passion.

He wanted her to want him, not because he was someone she could conquer or control, but because she needed him with a fierceness that went beyond simple lust or physical desire.

"I thought Jill was very nice."

Meg's words pulled him back from such dangerous daydreams. He glanced at his sister, who was looking at him with that irritatingly superior expression of a woman who thinks she knows what a man is feeling. He focused his gaze on the road in front of him, though he was scarcely aware of the traffic. "There's nothing nice about her," he snapped. "She's like a piranha. Or one of those black widow spiders. The kind of woman who uses men for what she wants."

"You talk like that's a bad thing." Meg laughed. "Honestly, bro, if you could see yourself right now. You look like a general getting ready for battle."

He tightened his grip on the steering wheel. "Maybe because I feel that way."

She leaned across the seat and lightly touched his arm. "Hey, lighten up. It looked to me like you enjoyed that kiss."

Enjoy didn't do justice to how he felt about that kiss. Excited maybe. Aroused. Turned on to the power of ten. And underneath it all, like the extra bite of hot peppers on an entree, he felt the sting of fear. Jill wasn't like any other woman he'd met. She made him think things…feel things. She had the power to make him lose control. That alone was enough to send him running for cover.

"I meant what I said back there." Meg pulled him out of the fog once more.

"About what?"

"About you. You *don't* have enough fun. Even a lowly premed student knows that's a ticket to an early grave." Her voice softened. "I worry about you, Mitch."

"I'm fine." He forced himself to relax his shoulders and gave her what he hoped was a reassuring look.

"You're really okay with Lana leaving?"

He almost laughed. What did it say about him that he'd already forgotten about his girlfriend of the past year? "I guess I've seen it coming," he said. "It's kind of a relief, though I suppose admitting that makes me a jerk."

"An honest jerk, though." She laughed again. Meg was like that, seeing the humor in any situation. He smiled. He was lucky to have her around to keep him from taking life too seriously. "I was just teasing," she said. "You could never be a real jerk."

"Maybe you're prejudiced," he said. "Maybe I have hidden depths of jerkiness you'll never know."

He pulled into the lot of her apartment. As she climbed out of the car, she stopped and looked back at him. "I like Jill," she said. "I really do think she's a nice person."

He frowned. "I don't know about that."

"I think you know more than you're letting on." She gave a little wave. "Take it easy, bro." She slammed the door shut, then blew him a kiss, her lips forming the words "I love you."

"I love you, too, sis," he whispered.

He turned the car around and headed back toward the store, thinking about love, and how little he really knew about the subject. He'd loved his father, but it wasn't something they'd ever talked about. And then his father was gone.

He had probably loved his mother once, when he was younger. Before she got sick and became a stranger to him. Then he'd settled for loving a memory of her. The emotion he felt for the real woman he was responsible for was closer to pity, mingled with resentment.

Meg was the only person he could say he truly loved now, with the no-strings-attached, no-holds-barred emotion he sensed love ought to be.

As for romantic love, he could only think of it in the abstract. He had meant what he said to Jill, about needing love for sex to be really powerful. Not that he had firsthand experience, but he believed it. Good sex involved the body, but to his way of thinking, great sex needed an emotional component. Something that had been missing from his life so far. Jill could talk about fun and good times, but he was ready for something more. Something she obviously couldn't give him.

So where did that leave him—besides frustrated and still wanting her? Should he take her advice and concentrate on having fun, damn the consequences? Maybe so. If he and Jill couldn't be lovers in every sense of the word, there was no doubting they could set off fireworks in the bedroom. One kiss had left him hornier than any seventeen-year-old.

Why not take her up on her offer to "demonstrate" the merchandise in Just 4 Play? He had no intention of changing his mind about closing the store, but that didn't mean he couldn't enjoy himself for the next few weeks. And he had no doubt he *would* enjoy himself with Jill.

Maybe she had the right approach after all—go for physical pleasure, no strings attached. Consider it an experiment. One he'd be a fool not to make.

THE NEXT MORNING, Jill smoothed the leather miniskirt over her hips and smiled at her reflection in the mirror. Decked out in dog collar, metal-studded black bustier, miniskirt, black silk stockings and stiletto ankle boots, she was every man's fantasy. She picked up the cat-o'-nine-tails and flicked it at the mirror. Or every man's nightmare, depending on his point of view.

She turned away from the mirror and added a studded bracelet to each wrist. This dominatrix getup was one of their hottest sellers and she could see why. There was nothing sexier than a heady dose of power. All the leather and chains didn't hurt either.

She peered out the door of the ladies' dressing room. Good. Mitch was at the front counter with Sid, looking over an inventory list or something. She opened the door a little wider and sauntered toward the two men, hips thrust forward, swaying provocatively.

She pretended to ignore them as she strolled past, though she had to bite the inside of her cheek to keep from smiling when all conversation stopped. She walked over to the paper goods department and began straight-

ening the greeting cards, humming to herself as she
worked.

She hummed louder as she heard Mitch approach. He
stopped three feet away, as if not wanting to get too
close. Even so, her nipples rose to attention at the first
whiff of Aramis.

"No time to go home and change after last night's
costume party?"

She slowly turned to face him, eyes wide and innocent. "I'm sorry, Mitch, I was thinking of something
else. Did you say something?"

He assumed his typical frown, but not before his gaze
darted to her not insignificant cleavage framed by the
leather bustier. "What are you supposed to be, a biker
chick?"

She unclipped the cat-o'-nine-tails from her belt and
struck a pose, hip cocked. "The Deluxe Dominatrix is
one of our bestselling fantasy costumes."

"I hardly think it's appropriate for a place of business."

She laughed. Mitch was always at his stuffiest when
he was nervous. "I'd say it's very appropriate for this
particular place of business." She opened her arms wide
and slowly turned in a circle, making sure he got an
eyeful. "Apparently many men find a powerful woman
to be a big turn-on." She flicked her whip at him. "Do
you feel that way, Mitch?"

"I think you ought to be selling the merchandise, not
wearing it."

She wagged the whip at him. "Customers can't appreciate the full effect of a costume unless they see it
on," she said. "So you see, I'm doing my part to unload
all our inventory before the chopstick dealers and soy
sauce sellers move in." She leaned closer. "Besides, I

wanted to get you in the mood for your first lesson to-night.''

He took a step back. "What are you talking about?''

"I'm going to teach you how to have fun with sex, remember?''

"I don't recall agreeing to your proposition.''

She trailed the whip down his arm. "Not with words, maybe, but your kiss told me you were definitely interested.''

His eyes darkened, and a faint flush rose up his neck. "Let me make sure I understand this. You're promising four weeks of wild sex, with no strings attached?''

"Just give me a chance to show you how good a walk on the wild side can be.''

He took another step back, out of reach of the whip. "Feel free to do your damnedest then. But for now, I suggest you put that costume on a mannequin.''

She pretended to consider this "suggestion.'' "Well, I suppose I could do that.'' She grinned. "But then I'd have to walk around naked, since all my clothes are at home.''

Jaw clenched, a pulse throbbed at his temple. Without another word, he turned and stalked to the front door.

"Where are you going?'' she asked.

"To my other office. My *real* office. To get some work done.'' He left, the door bells jangling wildly behind him.

Jill looked at Sid and shrugged. "What's his problem?''

Sid shook his head. "Not a good day to mess with him, Jilly. I asked him if we could reorder some of our bestsellers, things the customers have been asking for, and he almost bit my head off.''

"He *has* been a grouch this morning." A romp under the covers was obviously just what he needed.

"Maybe he's upset about Lana," Sid said. "From what she told me, they'd been dating quite a while before she came in here that day. He could be having second thoughts."

"Oh, I'm sure that's not it. He made it pretty clear things were over between them." Her stomach tightened. But were they, really? Did Mitch still have feelings for Lana? Was he in love with her? She flicked the whip at the condom display. "If he misses Lana, then he ought to go after her and tell her, instead of moping around here and making us miserable, too."

Sid sighed. "I guess love is one of the most complicated things there is."

"So are calculus and foreign politics, which is why I don't get involved in any of them."

Sid straightened and closed the ledger. "You don't fool me, Jilly. I know you're a romantic at heart. One day you'll meet a man who'll prove it to you."

"I don't need a man to prove anything to me." She trailed the fringes of the whip along the edge of a display case. "Except that he knows when not to take things too seriously." Anyone could see Mr. Serious Businessman Mitch wasn't the man for her. Not on any long-term basis. As long as she kept that in mind, everything would be fine. Wouldn't it?

8

MITCH SPENT AN UNPRODUCTIVE afternoon at his downtown office, trying to focus on quarterly reports and rental agreements, the words a black-and-white blur on the page before him. The image of Jill in the dangerously distracting leather outfit was imprinted on his retina, the feel of her body against his tattooed on his skin.

When the point on his mechanical pencil broke for the third time in an hour, he shoved his paperwork aside and leaned back in his chair. So he'd let a sexy woman get under his skin. So what? He'd play her little games, have a little fun, and get her out of his system. Then he could get back to focusing on what was really important right now: securing his future. A future that did not include being the owner of a sex toy store.

In the meantime, he and Jill had a date, didn't they? He checked his watch. He had time to grab a bite to eat, shower and change before Jill got off work. Maybe put clean sheets on the bed. The thought made him harder than he already was. Yeah, definitely clean sheets. He didn't want Jill to think he was a slob.

When he walked in the door of Just 4 Play a few hours later, a young woman with vibrant red hair was behind the counter, adding up a stack of checks. "Who are you?" Mitch asked.

She grinned, revealing the silver tracks of braces.

"I'm Tami. You must be Mitch. Sid told me you might drop by."

He nodded. He vaguely remembered the name from the payroll reports Sid had given him. "Good to meet you, Tami." Great, one more person he was putting out of work.

"I'm just closing up," she said. "You want to take the deposit?"

"No. That's all right. Just do…whatever you normally do." And what was that? He'd have to find out. Except, why bother if the business wasn't going to be open much longer? He walked past her, into his office.

He smelled Jill before he saw her, the exotic aroma of her perfume sending a rush of heat through him. He switched on the light and she was there, perched on the edge of his desk, her long legs encased in black stockings, the tabs of a garter belt peeking beneath the hem of the short leather skirt. She twirled a pair of handcuffs from one finger. Not the fur-lined kind the store sold, but a real pair. "It's about time you got here. I was ready to call your cell phone."

"You didn't think I'd forgotten, did you?" He moved past her to collect the stack of mail from the desktop, studiously avoiding looking at her silk-encased thighs.

"No, you wouldn't forget. But I wouldn't put it past you to chicken out."

His laugh was a harsh explosion of breath. "Do you think I'm afraid of you?"

She put her hand flat against his chest and slid her palm up to cradle his neck. "No. But you might be afraid of yourself. People who keep such tight control of their emotions often are." Her voice was low, her breath warm against his cheek.

He concentrated on keeping his voice even, his tone

light. "Let me guess—you majored in psychology in college."

"Let's just say I know a lot about men." She grasped the knot of his tie and tugged to loosen it. "Are you ready for your first lesson?"

He was ready all right. He'd been ready since yesterday, when she'd made her ridiculous proposition and given him that mind-erasing kiss. He'd been on fire for her ever since, but was determined not to show it. He put his hand over hers. "Let's go back to my place."

"Oh, no. If I'm going to teach you about the shop, we should stay here." She tugged at his tie once more.

"All right." He reached around and took the handcuffs from her. "But we won't use these."

She lowered her lashes, studying him through their lacy length. A half smile formed at her lips. "You're right. Handcuffs are a little too advanced for now. We'll start with something simple."

She slid off the desk and took his hand. "First, let's take a little tour." She led him back out into the store, which was deserted now, the doors locked and lights dimmed.

Old-fashioned Tiffany-style lamps made pools of light on the antique wardrobes and bookcases that housed store displays. The genteel furnishings made the racks of bondage straps and battery-operated vibrators that much more sensual, like Victorian postcards of naked women.

The only woman he wanted to see naked was the one who held his hand. He studied the way her bottom moved beneath the caressing leather of the skirt, and thought of cupping her in his hand, feeling the warmth and smoothness of her skin.

She paused in front of a tall bookcase filled with

various bottles and jars and pulled him close to her, so that their thighs touched. Her perfume mingled with the spice and floral scents surrounding the display. "Good sex is a feast for the senses," she said, her voice hushed. "Men respond most strongly to the visual, so we have a number of items to enhance that visual experience. Costumes." She indicated her leather outfit. "Videos." She nodded to the wall of tapes in the back corner. "Props." A wave of her hand took in a pegboard of body jewelry.

He slipped his hand from her grasp and caressed her back. "I'm beginning to understand the appeal of the costumes." He tried to pull her to him, but she resisted, and continued her lecture.

"As I was saying the other day, sex also involves the other senses. Smell. Taste. Touch."

Was this to be a continuation of the little demonstration she'd given when she'd handcuffed him to the bondage display? His heart pounded in anticipation. She collected several items from the display, standing on tiptoe to reach the top shelf. "Take off your clothes."

She was taking this dominatrix gig too far, giving him orders. He put his hands behind his back. "No."

She frowned. "Mitch, if you're not going to cooperate—"

"I want you to undress me."

Her eyes widened, the pupils expanding, and she opened her mouth and let out a long breath. *"Ohhhh."* Smiling, she set aside her jars and bottles and reached once more for his tie.

He forced himself to stand still, to let her touch him without giving in to the urge to touch her in return. Instead he openly watched her, studying the curve of her jaw as she bent forward to loosen his tie, admiring the swell of her breasts above the leather corset, the slenderness of her fingers as she undid the buttons of his shirt.

Her fingernails grazed his skin and he sucked in his breath, and felt his stomach tighten as she brushed her hand across his pebbled nipples. She caressed his stomach, trailing her fingers along the dark V of hair disappearing into his waistband. His erection strained against his fly, demanding release. Instead she cupped him through the cloth and smiled up at him. "I can tell we're both going to enjoy this."

He wanted to tell her to hurry, but made himself wait. Her turn would come soon enough. She undid his belt, then slid down his zipper with agonizing slowness, her head bent over him, as if she needed to see what she was doing. When he sprang free at last she blew her hot breath across him and he jerked in her hand.

She laughed and helped him out of his shoes and socks and pants, then she reached for the fastening of her corset.

His hand stayed her. "Now it's my turn."

She pulled away. "No, I'll do it."

"But I insist." He took her wrists and pulled her hands away. She resisted a little, but finally relented. He fought a smile. She didn't like not being in charge, even in this small thing.

He made himself linger, though his first instinct was to rip away these barriers that kept him from seeing her fully. He started with the dog collar and studded wrist cuffs, then moved in and down, stripping her of the corset and skirt. When she was down to only the garter belt, stockings and ankle boots, he was tempted to stop, but continued, unfastening the garters and peeling the translucent silk from her thighs.

His efforts revealed a single butterfly tattooed at her hip, its wings an iridescent green and blue. He smoothed his hand over it. "If you hadn't noticed, I don't need any costumes or props to get turned on visually." Jill was enough all by herself. Not just her gorgeous body, but all of her, mind and spirit. She had an innate sensuality he hadn't encountered in a woman before.

She eyed his erection. "I noticed." She reached behind her for one of the jars. "But maybe some of our products would arouse you even more." She unscrewed the lid from the jar and scooped up a fingerful of some bright blue paste.

"What is that?" he asked.

"Body paint." She demonstrated by drawing a blue line from his navel down to his shaft. Two more strokes made this an arrow pointing downward. Gathering more paint, she continued the line down the length of his shaft, then circled the head. She considered her artwork. "I've always wondered what blue balls looked like. Now I'll know." She returned to her painting, caressing, stroking, all in the name of art.

She looked up at him and smiled. "Now you try."

He took the proffered jar and dipped in a finger. It was smooth and cool, and slightly slippery. Remembering pictures he'd seen in *National Geographic* as a kid, of some tribal brides, he began decorating her breasts with concentric circles of blue.

Her skin was hot, and satin smooth. By the time he reached her nipples, they were straining toward him. He caressed them with his thumb, eliciting a moan from her that sent a jolt of fierce desire through him. He shoved aside the jar of paint and pulled her to him, his head bent to suckle her.

The paint tasted of chocolate and mint, setting up a

tingling sensation in his mouth as he licked and sucked. She writhed and moaned, the force of her response arousing him all the more. He transferred his attention to her other breast, shifting her so that her legs straddled his thigh.

He pulled back enough to look at her. Her nipples were swollen and wet from his mouth, made all the more erotic by the circles of blue paint that focused his gaze on those tantalizing tips. She looked at him through half-closed eyes, hazy with desire. "Maybe we'd better go into the office," he said.

She took his hand and led him back through the store. Once again, he watched the seductive sway of her hips, his fingers itching to touch her. In the office, she stopped by the daybed, and he tried to guide her down onto it, but she pushed him back. "I still have a few more things to show you."

"I have everything I want to see right here." He bent his head to her breast once more, but she slipped away from him and out into the showroom once more.

He started to follow her, then changed his mind and lay back on the bed, hands behind his head, waiting to see what she would surprise him with next. Why had he been so resistant to this plan in the first place? A fling like this was just what he needed before he settled into the hard work of running his own restaurant. And Jill was the perfect woman to share it with.

She returned, her breasts swaying gently as she walked toward him, mesmerizing. She knelt on the bed beside him and uncapped a small black bottle. "I thought now would be a good time to explore the other senses. Smell." She wafted the bottle under his nose and he inhaled sweet strawberries. "Taste." She dotted the oil on his lips. It tasted like warm jam. "And touch."

She dribbled oil across his chest and spread it out with
her fingers. "Have you ever had a massage?" she asked.

"Once or twice at the gym—"

She straddled him, her knees on either side of his
torso, the wet heat of her desire against his stomach. He
swallowed hard. "I've never had a massage like this."

She smiled, and began kneading him with her hands,
her fingers stroking along his ribs, tracing languid circles
around his nipples. She bent and blew across his chest,
and heat blossomed along the path of her breath. The
sensation of heat, then cold, dry, then moist, sent wave
after wave of desire reverberating through him. He
arched against her, impatient with need.

But she wouldn't be rushed. She teased him, licking
at his nipples, then drawing away. She wriggled against
him, holding him captive between her thighs. He could
have thrown her off of him with one move, but forced
himself to wait, willing to let her have her way with
him. You couldn't call something torture when it felt so
good.

He cupped her breast in one hand and flicked his
thumb across her nipple, eliciting a moan. "You're very
sensitive," he said.

She nodded and caught her lip between her teeth as
he pinched her lightly. He put his arm around her and
drew her down, until he could take her in his mouth once
more. His other hand slipped between them to find her
moist clit, and began to rub gently back and forth.

"No. Not yet—" But her words died as he suckled
harder, and she leaned into him, urging him for more.
He transferred his attention to her other breast, and
plunged two fingers into her, the feel of her taking his
breath away.

She rocked over him now, head back, little moans

escaping from her parted lips. He stroked her back with his free hand, caressing her, silently urging her on. "Yes, baby," he whispered, his own desire building to the point of pain. "Let me feel you come."

The force of her climax shook them both, her body tensing around him with a power that took his breath. His heart hammered in his chest as he pulled her down against him, and he grabbed at her in desperation when she pulled away.

"It's okay. I only had to get this." She opened her palm to reveal a selection of condoms. "Do you prefer ribbed or unribbed, lubricated, flavored or plain?"

She might have been asking if he wanted cream or sugar with his coffee. He laughed and selected a condom from the pile. "I assume we sell these?"

"Of course." She knelt beside him and deftly rolled the condom over him. Her touch sent a tremor through him and he gripped the sides of the daybed to steady himself. He moved over to let her lie beside him, but she moved back. "I thought I'd be on top."

Why did that not surprise him? He grinned. "I've got a better idea. Sit down facing me." He sat up and scooted back to make room. When she was sitting, one foot on either side of the narrow daybed, he slid forward again, until he was at the point of entering her. "How's this?"

Her eyes widened as he nudged at her opening. Then she grinned and draped her legs over his. "I see there are a few things I don't have to teach you," she said.

They moved together then, face-to-face, chest to breast, stomach to stomach, thigh to thigh. He felt her tighten around him as they rocked together, coaxing him into long, smooth strokes that sent his arousal spiraling upward. He put his arms around her, holding her as he withdrew and returned, unwilling yet to surrender to the storm of sensation overtaking him. He wanted to look into her eyes a moment longer, to watch her face transformed by her need for him, to feel this closeness to her.

A low moan escaped her and she tightened around him. She cried out when he thrust against her, but not in any kind of pain. Then his own release quaked through him, leaving him breathless, sightless, deaf to any sound but the staccato drumbeat of their hearts.

He didn't know how much time passed before he opened his eyes to look at her. Her face was flushed, her hair mussed, her eyes heavy-lidded and her lips curved in a smile of satisfaction. He smoothed her hair back from her face, wondering how it was possible to feel so close to someone he scarcely knew. The thought both thrilled and frightened him. "So what happens next?" he asked.

She gently withdrew from him, to the end of the bed, avoiding his gaze. Her sudden shyness puzzled him. Hadn't she felt the connection between them? Surely sex wasn't always like this for her.

"No need to rush things," she said. "We have four weeks." She wrapped a sheet around her and stood. "I'll let you know when we can get together again." With all the dignity of a princess, she swept past him, out into the showroom where they'd left their clothes.

JILL'S HAND SHOOK as she gathered her scattered clothing from the floor. She told herself it was just the aftermath of physical release, but she knew that wasn't the only reason she felt so weak and jittery. Sex with Mitch had been incredible...awesome...fabulous. But it had also been...different. More...real, if that was any way to describe an almost out-of-body experience.

Maybe it had to do with the way Mitch always took everything so seriously. Even when she'd been trying to get him to play with the body paints, he'd drawn a very deliberate design, refusing to give in to nonsense.

And when he made love to her, it was with the same dedication and purpose. As if it mattered for more than just that moment.

She was going to have her hands full, keeping things on an even keel with him. After all, the whole point of this was to convince him to keep the store open. She wanted the next few weeks to be fun. Adventurous. Even educational. But *not* serious.

He emerged from the office and came over to her, but made no move to put on his own clothes. She watched him out of the corner of her eye, admiring his flat stomach and muscular chest. He was gorgeous. Everything she could want in a sexual partner. Her gaze shifted to his face, to the frown always lurking at the corners of his mouth. *Damn it, Mitch, why don't you smile?* she wanted to shout.

"So you're saying you intend to call the shots here," he said.

So *that* was what was bugging him. She might have known. She looked up from fastening the garter belt. "Of course. This was my idea, so I get to set the rules."

He leaned back against an antique table, arms across his chest. "Is that how it always is with you and men—you make the rules?"

She did up the leather corset. "Do you find that threatening?"

"Not threatening. But it does tell me something interesting about you."

She froze in the act of reaching for her skirt and turned to him. "What's that?"

"It tells me the only one really afraid here is you. As long as you're always in charge, always calling the shots, then you don't take a chance of getting too carried away."

Now who was playing amateur psychologist? Of all the ridiculous notions.... She shook her head and picked up the skirt. "You don't know anything."

"Don't I?" He opened his hand to reveal the hand-cuffs she'd been playing with in the office. "Where did these come from? We don't sell them in the store."

"They're Grif's. They were in his desk."

"Grif's?" He stared down at the cuffs. They glinted silver in the lamplight. "Did you and he—?"

"No!" She jerked up the zipper to her skirt. How could he think she and his uncle—? "No," she said again, her face hot with embarrassment. "He was a re-serve deputy at one time and they were part of his gear."

Mitch's shoulder's slumped. She hoped he was ashamed of himself. "No matter what you think of me, I don't go to bed with just anybody," she said stiffly.

"Hey, it's none of my business." He glanced at her. "But I'm curious. Have you ever let someone use hand-cuffs on you? Would you let someone tie you up and have their way with you?"

She tried to look unmoved, but a blush betrayed her. "That's none of your business, either."

A faint smile tugged at his mouth. "I didn't think so. You'd tie someone else up, but you'd never surrender that kind of control yourself."

"You don't know what you're talking about." She half turned away from him.

He tossed the cuffs onto the shelf in front of her. They landed with a clang and slid into a bottle of Kama Sutra oil. "I'm beginning to think I know you pretty well, Jill.

You like to have fun, but you don't want any consequences. I'm not so sure that's possible.''

"Does that mean you don't want to continue with our
little project?'' Disappointment tasted bitter in the back
of her throat.

He shook his head. "No, I'm interested in continuing.
But don't be surprised if it doesn't turn out the way you
think it will. I told you before that I'm not the type of
man who changes his mind.''

"And I told you I'm not the kind of woman who gives
up.''

He smiled then, surprising her with a grin. "Then we
make an interesting pair, don't we?''

Interesting wasn't a word she'd have used. Aggravating. Impossible. Exciting. Maddening. No, interesting
didn't begin to describe the emotions Mitch Landry
made her feel. Emotions she had to admit she wasn't
sure how to handle.

9

Jill made a point of ignoring Mitch when he came in the next morning. It never hurt to make a man wonder what you were up to—especially a man like Mitch, who had the ridiculous idea he knew her so well.

She kept busy helping one of the part-time employees, Mike, rearrange the dwindling merchandise. They were already out of some of the customer favorites, but Mitch refused to let them order anything more. Fortunately Sid had discovered some extra stock in boxes in the back of the storeroom. By spreading out the remaining merchandise and adding a few new items, the store still looked presentable.

After his shift, Mike went home, leaving Jill alone until Sid started his shift at four. About two-thirty, a timid-looking man came in and stood just inside the doorway, looking ready to bolt.

Jill assumed her most inviting smile and sashayed toward the new customer, a stocky, middle-aged man with the apprehensive look of a rabbit who'd just wandered into a wolf's lair. "May I help you, sir?" she asked.

He looked around the store, eyes wide, then turned back to Jill. "Do you have anything in here to help the most unromantic man you ever met?"

She blinked. What was with all this talk of romance all of a sudden? "Um, what exactly did you have in mind?" she asked.

He directed his answer to the floor. "My twentieth wedding anniversary was yesterday and I totally blew it. My wife says she's going to take the kids and move in with her sister if I don't make an effort to be more romantic."

"So you came here?" She wasn't sure if that was a good sign or not.

"I saw the sign that said you sold lingerie." His gaze searched the room once more and came to rest on a display of nipple rings. "Maybe I made a mistake."

He started backing toward the door, but Jill reached out and caught him. "No, we do sell lingerie. And candles and massage oil and lots of romantic things like that." She thought the guy was sweet, wanting so much to please his wife. The least she could do was help him. "Why don't you start by telling me what happened yesterday?"

He flushed. "Like I said, it was our anniversary, and I blew it."

"You mean you forgot?"

He shook his head. "Worse. I gave her a set of tires as a gift."

She stifled a laugh. "A set of tires!"

He winced. "She needed new tires. I was worried about the old ones. These were very nice." He bowed his head. "I thought she'd realize I wanted to keep her safe."

Oh, how sweet! It was all she could do not to say it. Still, she could see the wife's side. "New tires were a very practical gift. But women deal with practical things all day, from what to do about the kids' schedules to how to handle a boss's request to what to fix for dinner. So when it comes to special occasions, they want not-so-practical things. Things to remind them that they're more to you than a wife and mother. That they're special.''

He looked confused. "But what?" He nodded to the mannequin in the window, which today displayed the ever-popular French maid's costume. "Peggy would never wear something like that." His face reddened.

She smiled and patted his arm. "I understand. You want something…softer to show your wife how you feel. Come right over here." She led him to a rack filled with lacy gowns in ice-cream colors. "This is our honeymoon collection." She held up a sky-blue gown of diaphanous silk, with a matching peignoir. Lace inserts at strategic locations kept the gown from being totally revealing, while still allowing for a very sexy outfit. "I think any woman would love something like this."

"What about this?" He held up a red satin and wired bustier, with cutouts for the breasts and matching crotch-less panties.

Jill managed to keep a straight face. "That is very sexy," she said. "But is that something your wife would normally wear?"

His face fell. "No. But then, she usually wears my old football jersey and a pair of wool socks to bed."

"Then I don't think it's a good idea to start with this." She took the red satin set from him. "Maybe you could work up to it, though."

He brightened. "Maybe so."

She selected two more gown and peignoir sets, black satin boxers and a matching robe and laid them across her arm, then led him to the massage oil cabinet. "The thing to remember about women is that, while men are aroused by what they see, women respond better to the other senses—what they feel and smell and hear. So things like satin gowns appeal to them." She indicated the lingerie on her arm. "And sensuous smells like our massage oils." She uncapped a tester bottle and held it under his nose. "Sandalwood and sage," she said. "Very erotic."

"Umm, what do I do with it?" He held the bottle as if it contained volatile chemicals.

She smiled. "What I suggest is that you light some candles in the bathroom and bedroom." She pulled down a selection of lavender, vanilla and ylang-ylang scented candles. "Then run a bubble bath for your wife." She chose a sage and rosemary bubble bath. "I'm assuming you've already sent your children to stay with relatives or friends."

He nodded. "Then what?"

"You pour some wine and invite your wife to take a bubble bath. Leave the lingerie for her to put on when she's through. Tell her you'll be waiting when she's done. While she's bathing, you slip into something sexy." She held up the boxers and robe. "And you fold back the covers and warm the massage oil in a bowl of water. When she comes out of the bath, you lead her over to the bed and tell her you're going to give her the most wonderful massage she's ever had."

"But I don't know anything about giving massages." He looked doubtful.

"You can learn." She handed him *Massage for Lovers: An Illustrated Guide.* He flipped through the pages, pausing to look closer at one. "They do *that?*"

She looked over his shoulder. "That's one of the more advanced moves. I suggest you start off with her feet."

"Her feet?"

"Sure." She set aside the lingerie and poured a small amount of oil into her hands. Then she took his hand. "Pretend this is your wife's foot. You'd smooth your hands across the soles of her feet, then across the tops. Use your thumbs in a circular motion to rub along the arches. Massage the heel. Between the toes. Across the instep. Not too hard, mind you."

"That feels good." His eyes had a glazed look.

She released him and stepped back. "Everything's in the book. It's much easier than you think."

"And this massage will make her forgive me?"

"Not just the massage, but the whole experience. The fact that you took the time and trouble to put together an evening that focuses on her and how much she means to you. First you pamper her—with the wine and bubble bath, the candles, the lingerie and the massage. Then you make love to her like you're newlyweds all over again."

His face reddened. "I'm forty-five years old, not twenty."

"Sex is in the mind as much as it is physical," she assured him. "Focus on giving your wife as much pleasure as you can and I promise you, you can't go wrong."

He cleared his throat and looked around. "Do you think I need any, uh, accessories?"

"Why don't you stick to the basics at first. Then you can bring your wife with you one day and see if there's anything that interests both of you."

He looked at her again. "Do you think I could ever convince her to dress up in one of those costumes?"

She hid her smile behind her hand. "Um, maybe. Now which one of these gowns do you think your wife would like best?"

He chose the sky-blue number, as well as the black boxers and robe for himself, along with the candles, bubble bath, massage oil and book. At the last minute he added another book. *Pleasuring a Woman.* "I think I might need to brush up on a few things," he said.

She smiled and added the book to his purchases. "I don't think you have anything to worry about." She handed him his receipt to sign. "And I think your wife is a very lucky woman."

He signed the slip and returned the store copy to her. "I guess I think I'm a lucky man to have her."

She sighed and looked after him as he left the store. What would it be like to have someone who cared that much about you after twenty years? She'd never dated a single man more than nine months. Had never seen the point, really. Life was too short not to do everything you could, and be with everyone you could. You never knew when your time would be up. If you married young and made a mistake, you might live whatever time you had left full of regrets.

But she was older now. Maybe she ought to think about finding someone for the long haul. If she could only find someone who didn't believe commitment was a synonym for settling down. She didn't ever intend to settle when every day offered so many things to enjoy if you'd only look for them.

MITCH FOUND THE HANDCUFFS hanging from his office doorknob when he left work that afternoon and slipped them into his jacket pocket. Jill was busy with a customer on the other side of the store and didn't glance up when he walked past. She had gone to great lengths to avoid him all day. He hadn't pushed her, though part of him had wanted nothing more than to drag her back into the office and try for a recreation of what they'd experienced last night.

He told himself maybe they'd both benefit from a little cooling off. They'd have time enough in the next few weeks to continue their little experiment.

He reached in his pocket for his car keys and found the handcuffs again. Shaking his head, he unlocked his car door and tossed the cuffs on the passenger seat. Wait until he told Meg about this one. Well, he wouldn't tell her everything. Just enough to surprise her.

He'd asked Meg to come with him this afternoon to run an errand. "What kind of errand?" she'd asked when he'd telephoned.

"A shopping errand." He didn't care to elaborate further until they were in person. He wasn't all that comfortable with what he was going to do, but he felt he had a responsibility to see it through. He hoped having Meg along would make it easier.

Fortunately, she hadn't asked any more questions. "I'll go shopping anytime," she said. "Especially if we get to spend your money."

She was waiting for him out in front of her building. "Sharon's trying to sleep," she said as she opened the car door. "She was at the E.R. late last night." Sharon was Meg's roommate. She worked nights as an aide at Boulder County Hospital.

Meg started to sit, then jumped up again and pulled out the handcuffs. "What in the world—?" She laughed. "I have a feeling the story behind these might be very interesting."

"They belonged to Uncle Grif." He waited for her to fasten her seat belt, then pulled out of the parking lot. "Did you know he used to be a reserve officer with the Jefferson County Sheriff's Department?"

"Really?" She looked at the cuffs. "And that's why he had these things?"

"I'm not saying that's the only reason he had them, but certainly one reason. He had a gun, too."

"*Ooooh*. And what did you do with it?"

"It's locked in the safe. I have to check into the legalities of keeping it or disposing of it."

"I guess it's yours now, along with these." She hooked one end of the cuffs over the rearview mirror. They dangled there, glinting in the sunlight.

"Take those off of there!"

She grinned and shook her head. "Oh, no. I think they're very appropriate for the man who owns Just 4 Play. Think of it as an advertisement."

He frowned at the cuffs, but let the subject drop. He had more important things to discuss. "I need you to help me pick out a grave marker for Grif."

"A grave marker? Is this your so-called shopping errand?"

"I want your opinion. He was your uncle, too."

"How about a concrete golf bag and a martini glass?"

"Even two weeks ago, I would have agreed, but now I'm not so sure. There was a lot more to Grif than I thought."

"He was Dad's big brother. It stands to reason they'd be something alike."

"Yeah, but even when Dad was alive, I don't remember Grif coming around much. When he did visit, he never stayed long."

"I guess he was too busy, or… I don't know."

"Or what?"

She shrugged. "Maybe he wasn't comfortable with the whole family scene. You know, before Mom got sick, she and Dad were happy together, and they had the two of us. We were your stereotypical middle-class American family and there was Grif, a bachelor with no kids. Maybe he felt left out."

"Maybe."

"What do you think?" She angled toward him. "You

have friends who are married with kids. Do you feel like a fifth wheel around them?"

He tried to remember the last time he'd visited with any of his married friends. It had been a while. "Once friends marry and have families, they have a whole different frame of reference than you do. You don't have that much in common anymore. So maybe that was what kept Uncle Grif from coming around as much, though you'd think family would be different."

She sat back in the seat and stared out the window. "Do you think about getting married one day and having children of your own?" she asked.

"Sure." The question sent an odd tremor through his chest. "One day."

She looked back at him. "I hope soon."

He forced a laugh. "It's not like I'm that old."

"No, but I'll be going away to medical school in another year and I hate to think about leaving you here, alone. I'd feel better if you had someone special to be with."

"I'm a big boy, sis. I think I can take care of myself."

The news didn't seem to cheer her. "How's Jill?"

He didn't miss the significance of the change in subject. "Jill is fine. She's my employee. She's not 'someone special.'" He managed to keep a straight face as he told the lie. Jill was certainly more than just an employee now. As for being special...

"I don't know. I thought she was pretty special. You acted...different when you were with her."

He tightened his grip on the steering wheel. "You're imagining things. I don't act any different with Jill than I do with any other woman." Unless you count alternating between having a hard-on that wouldn't quit and wanting to break dishes out of sheer frustration whenever she was around.

Meg reached over and patted his shoulder. "You're not a very good liar, bro, but I forgive you. I'm glad to see you a little more relaxed. Whether it's Jill or the store that's done it, I'm happy."

This was her idea of relaxed? This constant feeling of being on edge? "What makes you think I'm so relaxed?"

"Not relaxed exactly, but more, I don't know, going with the flow." She reached up and thumped the handcuffs, making them jangle and dance. "For instance, a month ago you wouldn't have let these hang up here for even a minute. You were way more concerned with your image then. Maybe it was hanging around with Lana."

"Maybe it was because at the time I thought I had an innocent little sister who shouldn't be exposed to such things."

She threw her head back and laughed. "And now I've destroyed your illusions by buying a vibrator. Which works very well, by the way."

He could only take one hand off the steering wheel to cover one ear. "I don't want to hear about it."

Still giggling, she shook her head. "You are so easy to get a rise out of. It's almost not fair."

"Then don't say things to provoke me."

"I said it was *almost* not fair. It's too much fun to stop."

He pulled into the parking lot of Rocky Mountain Mortuary and Monuments. "Try to control yourself while we're in here. This is a solemn occasion."

For the next hour, they looked at marble monuments, granite memorials and simple brass plaques. Mitch rejected out of hand the alabaster angels and a heart-

shaped stone designed for a couple, but that left plenty
of choices.

"What do you think?" he asked Meg.

"The brass plaques are the least expensive."

"Many people prefer the plaques for ease of maintenance," the solemn saleswoman said. "We can also include a stainless-lined vase for flowers."

Mitch shook his head. "The plaques seem a little conservative for Grif." He glanced at the saleswoman. "My
uncle was a pretty flamboyant character."

"The rose granite is a very popular choice." She led
them to a red stone obelisk.

"It's pink," Meg said. Her eyes met Mitch's and they
shook their heads.

"White marble is a classical choice." They followed
her to a square marker in gleaming white.

"It's beautiful," Meg breathed.

Mitch ran his hand along the smooth marble. It was
cold. Refrigerator cold.

Cold as the grave.

He shivered. "It's still too plain." He looked at the
saleswoman again, not sure how to make her understand
what he was looking for, when he wasn't sure himself.
"Grif was the type of man who liked to stand out."

She smiled and nodded. "I think I know just the
thing." She led them toward the front of the showroom,
past carved cherubs and pillars, to a glossy black stone.
Mitch studied his reflection in the mirror-smooth surface.
Did he really look so stern and solemn? "This is our
Legacy model," the saleswoman said. "One of our more
expensive offerings. Some people don't like it because
they think it's too solemn. Others feel it conveys a certain dignity."

Dignity. Something he'd never associated with Uncle

Grif while the man was alive. But now, from the distance of death, he saw another side to his father's flamboyant older brother. He saw a man who had lived life on his own terms, and gone about quietly doing good, not expecting praise or accolades. That in itself was a rare kind of dignity. "I'll take it." He opened his wallet and took out a sheet of paper on which he'd scribbled a list of Grif's accomplishments. "And here's what I want on it."

He paid a deposit, not even wincing as he wrote out the check. As they walked back to the car, Meg reached over and took his hand. "I think Uncle Grif would approve," she said.

"I hope so." He slid into the car and stared up at the handcuffs hanging from the mirror and almost laughed. What a perfect symbol of the complicated man his uncle had been. And what a perfect way to symbolize his own tangled-up life. He felt caught by his uncle's legacy and his own dreams, and by one sexy, seductive saleswoman who promised heaven and in the meantime made his life hell.

SID PAUSED ON THE FRONT steps of the townhouse and nervously wiped his hands on his pants. He'd dressed conservatively, in a pair of khaki Dockers and a navy polo shirt, but the effect was offset by his pink Mohawk and the various hoops, silver balls and chains hanging about his body. He'd tried taking a few of them out, but decided the empty holes looked worse than all the jewelry. Besides, she'd seen him before and hadn't freaked out or anything.

Of course, you could say she'd been distracted by other matters at the time....

Oh hell! What was he even doing here? He was out of his freaking mind.

He started to turn around when the door opened and she stood there, blinking. "Sid, what are you doing here?"

He'd intended to act all serious and dignified, but the minute he saw her, he couldn't keep a goofy smile off his face. "Hi, Lana. I, um, I stopped by to see how you were doing. I mean, you were pretty upset last time I saw you."

She returned his smile and actually reached out and took his hand and pulled him into the apartment. "How sweet. Won't you come in?"

He hesitated. "Um, if you were on your way out, I could leave..."

"I was only going down to check the mail. That can wait." She pulled him inside and shut the door behind them.

He stood in the small entrance hall and tried not to stare—at her or her home. She was beautiful, of course, her dark hair hanging loose around her shoulders. It was longer than he'd thought. "I like your hair like that," he blurted, then immediately regretted it. Gee, she was going to think he was just full of class.

She fingered one of her dark locks and looked pleased. "Do you? I usually wear it up at work, but here at home I like to leave it down."

"It looks nice. Soft."

Soft? What kind of thing was that to say to a woman? It's not as if hair could be hard. Well, maybe, but not *her* hair.

"Won't you come in and sit down." She led him into a living room that was decorated all in white, from a soft ivory shade to the flat white of milk. The sofa was covered in a white brocade. He was almost afraid to sit on it. What if he had grease on him from his motorcycle? He settled for sort of perching on the edge. It wasn't comfortable, but then, nothing would be as long as he was in the same room with *her*.

She sat down across from him, in a white leather chair. "How did you know where I live?" she asked.

He squirmed. One look into her gorgeous green eyes and the story he'd made up to tell her flew right out of his head. "I picked the lock on Mitch's office one night and looked the address up in his planner." He cringed, waiting for her disapproval.

But she continued to smile at him. "Mitch would pitch a fit if he knew." She leaned forward and put her hand on his knee. "But don't worry. I won't tell."

He about stopped breathing when she touched him. She must like him a little bit to do that. Her hand looked small and pale against his thigh. Only when he started feeling dizzy did he remember to inhale again. She smelled like vanilla. His favorite. Or at least it was now.

She took her hand away and leaned back. "Do you often go around picking locks?" She didn't sound as if she disapproved. In fact, she looked interested.

"Um...not often. Back in high school I got into a little trouble."

"Were you a *bad* boy, Sid?"

The way she said the word "bad" made him break out in a sweat. Like it was something she liked. A lot. "I guess I was."

She twirled a lock of hair around her finger, a Mona Lisa smile on her face that made his heart pound. "Oh, I think you still are. A very bad boy."

He sat up straighter. "Yeah, well, I guess I can be."

He risked a grin. "I can still pick a lock or bypass an alarm system when I need to."

"Then maybe you can help me."

His smile faltered. Was she plotting some crime? He glanced around the room again, at the rich upholstery, the gleaming brass lamps, the oil paintings on the wall that looked like they belonged in an art museum. She didn't look like she was hurting for money, but you never knew about some people.... "Uh, what do you want me to do?"

Instead of answering the question, she leaned back in the chair and folded her arms across her chest, her expression transformed to a pout. "Mitch thinks I'm repressed."

His spirits sank to somewhere around his ankles. Mitch again. He should have known she wouldn't be over a guy like that so soon. After all, the two of them were a perfect pair: both rich, beautiful, dignified and solemn.

"I'm not repressed." She frowned. "Well, maybe a little. But he didn't help any by treating me like some fragile little virgin. I mean, I know I haven't had much experience, but I can learn." She leaned toward him again her eyes pleading. "A woman can learn these things, can't she?"

He stared into her eyes. They were the most gorgeous shade of green. Like verdigris on copper. Or new aspen leaves reflected in a pond. Or—

"Sid, I'm asking you to help me. Will you do it?"

He blinked, forcing himself to pull away from those green depths. "Help you with what?"

She reached out and took his hand. Her fingers were cool, her skin soft as lambskin. "Will you help me to come out of my shell? I know there's so much more to love and…and to sex…I'm tired of missing out. Teach me how to be a wild woman, Sid.''

He knew he ought to say no. That she was only using him to win back Mitch, the man she really belonged with. But when she squeezed his hand and gazed at him with that pleading expression in her eyes, he couldn't bring himself to say no. He swallowed, trying to find his voice. ''All right,'' he croaked. ''I'll teach you. To be a wild woman.'' He just hoped one day Mitch would appreciate the sacrifice Sid was making for him.

10

MITCH WAS IN HIS OFFICE the next morning when Sid knocked on the door, then stuck his head in. "Um, Mitch, there's a couple of dudes here to see you."

Mitch didn't look up from the file box he was going through. "If it's salesmen, tell them we don't want any." He pulled out a file folder labeled Thanksgiving 1985 and opened it. Apparently Grif had kept every receipt, letter and report he'd ever written or received, each meticulously sorted and filed. Most of the stuff was meaningless paper, but every once in a while Mitch found something interesting. For instance, here was a receipt for fifty frozen turkeys. *Fifty.* What would you do with fifty turkeys?

"I don't think they're salesmen. They say you know them. Somebody named Archie and an oriental dude—Ping or Ling or—"

Mitch shoved the file folder back in the box. "It's Ping. Chef Ping. He's the chef for my new restaurant. And Archie Patterson is the architect." *What the hell were they doing here?*

He followed Sid out of the office and found Archie, impeccable as always in a gray Armani suit, nose to nose with Blowup Betty, while Chef Ping, wearing a blue and red track suit, examined a cock ring as if it might be a fascinating new kitchen tool.

Mitch rushed over to them. "Gentlemen, what brings

you here?'' He put his hand on Archie's shoulder and steered him toward the door. ''If you'd wanted to meet, we could have arranged to have lunch. In fact, why don't we go somewhere now? My treat.''

''It's only eleven o'clock.'' Archie stopped and frowned at him. ''I never eat before noon. It upsets my digestion.''

''We came to see this place.'' Ping laid aside the cock ring and smiled at him. ''I want to find the best place for my kitchen.''

Fine. He supposed the only thing to do was to humor them. ''I thought back in this corner.'' He gestured toward the far right-hand side of the store. ''That's where the plumbing is located.''

Ping waved his hand in dismissal. ''No matter where the plumbing is located. Must consider the best feng shui. The best location for my kitchen is here, in this area.'' He indicated a space now occupied by the costume racks. ''We''ll have eating areas over here.'' He marched across the room and gestured toward the bondage display. ''And the cash register goes here.'' He strode to the far left side of the building. ''This is a very good site for money.'' He nodded, then turned and collided with Jill.

She was dressed as Nurse Betty today, in a short white skirt, a blue and white striped pinafore that barely covered her breasts, white fishnet hose, spike heels and a scrap of a nurse's hat. As a prop, she carried an oversize syringe with a long rubber needle. The effect was both alarming and erotic. Ping's mouth gaped open, then he snapped it shut and bowed low. ''Am honored to meet you, beautiful lady.''

Mitch groaned. Ping spoke English better than many

native-born speakers, but he liked to use his pidgin English to catch people off guard. Or to charm women.

Jill certainly seemed charmed. She giggled as he bent over her hand. "Nice to meet you, too. What brings you to Just 4 Play?"

"My friend here—" He nodded to Mitch. "Is to open grand restaurant, where I am master chef. I create masterpieces of Chinese cuisine." He squeezed her hand. "You come. Eat free."

Archie sidled over to Mitch. "Nice place you have here," he said. "You sure you want to close it?"

"Yes." He looked around. Sid was helping a customer choose from an array of spiked dog collars. Two coeds were giggling over by the greeting cards and an older man contemplated a display of rubber garments with the solemnity usually reserved for major investment decisions. He would have expected solemn, fastidious Archie to be offended by the tackiness of the products if not their sexual nature. "What's so great about it?" Mitch asked.

"It's so…unusual." Archie picked up a pink feather duster and fluttered it back and forth. "So…fun."

There was that word again. The nastiest three-letter word he knew. "About the restaurant," Mitch prompted.

Archie reluctantly laid aside the feather. "Yes, the restaurant. As soon as Ping decides where the best 'ambiance' is for everything, I'll get to work on the plans."

Jill had led Ping over to the costume rack and was showing him a gladiator's breastplate and short skirt. The chef was nodding and grinning as if she'd just suggested they run away for a wild weekend fling, though the short, round chef didn't really seem Jill's type. "He'll look ridiculous in that getup," Mitch said.

"Yes, I agree, he's much more the Roman Emperor type. Say, a short toga…"

Mitch glared at Archie, then stalked over to the chef and Jill. "Ping, I thought you came here to discuss plans for the restaurant."

"Yes." He looked up from adjusting the breastplate over his track suit. "I think this young lady would make a perfect hostess, don't you?"

Apparently Jill had noticed the slipping accent. She winked at Mitch, then turned her hundred-watt smile on the lecherous chef. "Thanks, but I don't think the restaurant business is for me."

"Why not? Wonderful late hours. You meet so many interesting people." He leered at her chest. "Perhaps not so interesting as here."

"Chef Ping, why don't you come into my office and we can go over the floor plan." Mitch took Ping's arm. "You can show me again where you want to put the kitchen."

"Yes, yes. But first, I will take this." He held up the gladiator costume.

"Great. It comes with its own sword." Jill held up the plastic prop.

"Oh, no, I don't need that. I have my own sword." He waggled his eyebrows suggestively.

Mitch curled his fingers into fists. One more word and he'd be forced to strangle the chef. If the man wasn't such a brilliant cook, he would have done away with him sooner.

Jill led the way to the front counter, Ping trailing at her heels like a cocker spaniel pup. Along the way, he snatched up a bottle of Kama Sutra oil and another of Motion Lotion.

"Oh, I'll take some of that." Archie stepped forward

and claimed his own bottle of lubricant. "And this." He added the pink feather duster.

Mitch stifled a groan and stepped back. One problem with owning a business like Just 4 Play was that you learned way more about people that you really wanted to know.

"Uh, boss, can I speak to you a minute?"

Mitch hadn't even noticed Sid standing beside him. Another measure of how distracted he was. "Sure, Sid. What's up?"

A good question, since the store manager didn't look quite himself today. Mitch couldn't put his finger on what was wrong. Maybe it was the long-sleeved white shirt Sid wore that covered most of his tattoos. Or maybe the ordinary tennis shoes replacing his usual motorcycle boots, rendering him two inches shorter.

Mitch's gaze traveled upward. No, it was the hair. There was a definite blond stubble on either side of the Mohawk, which didn't look as bright as usual. "You're growing in your hair," he said.

Sid self-consciously ran his hand over the stubble. "Yeah. I guess I ought to shave it all clean and start over, but I haven't got around to it."

"Just looking for a change?"

"Uh, yeah." He sidled toward Mitch's office. "Can we talk a minute? In private?"

"Sure." They moved into the office and Mitch shut the door and took his place behind Grif's massive desk. It was emptier now than when he'd first taken over the business, though he'd kept Grif's bowling trophy and police cuffs in sight to remind him of the many sides of his uncle. "What can I do for you? Is something wrong?"

Sid turned a straight-backed chair around and straddled it. "I sort of need some advice."

"Definitely shave your head."

Sid stroked the rooster-comb center tuft of hair. "You think so?"

He nodded. "I do."

"Okay, but that's not what I came in here to talk about."

Mitch sat back, hands folded on his stomach. "So spill."

Sid glanced toward the door, then leaned forward, voice lowered. "I want some advice on women."

Mitch laughed. "I'm not exactly an expert in that area."

Sid frowned. "I'm seeing a new woman. A very classy lady. I thought you might know what she would like."

"What she would like?" He picked up the cuffs and began playing with them. Snapping and unsnapping them. "Do you mean what she would like for dinner, or to do on a date, or as a gift? I suppose that depends on the lady."

"No, I meant what she would like in bed."

Mitch choked. "What? Why would I know that?"

Sid looked more unhappy than ever. "You know more about posh women than I do."

Mitch tossed aside the cuffs. "Posh" women? Did he know anyone who fit that description? He shifted in his chair. "Wouldn't she like what all women like?" Whatever that was.

Sid shook his head. "Women are different. Some like things real active. Others want them loud. Some want you to get a little rough with them. Or they want to get a little rough with you."

Mitch contemplated this wonderful array of women. Clearly he'd been missing out. He leaned forward, elbows on the desk. "I don't mean to disillusion you, but I haven't had your experience in this arena." He cleared his throat. "Most of the women I've been with are pretty conventional."

Sid scooted his chair forward. "Meaning?"

"You know… Lights out. Clothes off. Missionary position." He shook his head. In the current setting, all that seemed so dull.

Sid nodded, his face serious. "Okay, I can do that. So they don't want anything special?"

"Come to think of it, Sid, I think anything special would be appreciated." Until he'd come to Just 4 Play, he hadn't realized how much variety existed in the sexual world. Maybe Jill was right and he could benefit from a little more risk-taking and adventure in the bedroom.

Speaking of Jill, she was still out there with Chef Lecher and his flirty architect. He shoved out of his chair. "I'd better get back to Ping and Archie."

Sid rose also. "Thanks, Mitch. This has been really helpful."

He didn't see how, but he nodded. "Good luck with your new girlfriend."

"Yeah, I'm gonna need it."

Back in the showroom, he found Jill perched on the stool behind the counter, listening as Ping related the plot of a movie. "Is most popular film in China," he said. "The hero is samurai who sleeps with one hundred women. All beautiful." He leaned forward, showing all his teeth. "Almost as beautiful as you."

Jill looked up and caught Mitch's eye. She looked

heavenward and sighed. A clear signal for him to rescue her.

He clamped his hand on Ping's shoulder. "Now that you've finished shopping, let's go into my office." He steered the chef toward the door. "I think it's time for Jill to go change clothes." If she insisted on dressing in costumes at work, he'd have to find her something more suitable. Like a nun's habit.

AS SOON AS THE DOOR to Mitch's office closed, Jill's smile faded. "I can't believe he's going to let those two turn this place into a restaurant," she said.

Sid looked up from a magazine he was paging through. "It could be worse, you know. He could be opening some chain franchise." He looked around. "One of those theme restaurants where all the waiters wear costumes and the food has cute names."

She straightened her pinafore. "Now there's an idea. We could open a sandwich shop at one end of the store and call it the bondage café. The counter staff and cooks could dress in whips and chains."

"Yeah. And if you complained about the food, a man in a G-string and mask would come out and whip you."

Jill giggled at the thought, but immediately sobered. Apparently their one scorching sexual encounter hadn't been enough to convince Mitch to change his mind about closing Just 4 Play. "Sid, you have to help me," she said. "What can we do to convince Mitch to keep this place open?"

Sid turned a page in the magazine and shrugged. "I don't know. Maybe he's right. Maybe this isn't the kind of place a gentleman should be associated with."

She stared at him. "A gentleman? Since when do you

give a flying fig about that?'' She leaned closer, scruti-
nizing him. "What's gotten into you anyway?''

He gave her a blank look. "Nothing's gotten into me.
I just think this is Mitch's business and he's entitled to
do whatever he wants with it.''

She snatched the magazine out of his hand and turned
it over to the front. "*Esquire*? Since when do you read
Esquire?'' She looked from Sid to the magazine and
back again. "And what's with the long-sleeved shirt and
the hair and…'' Her gaze dropped to the floor. "Tennis
shoes?'' She put her hand to his forehead. "Are you
feverish?''

He swatted her hand away. "I'm not feverish.'' He
grabbed the magazine and stuffed it under the counter,
his face flushed. "A man has a right to change his image, doesn't he?''

"Yeah, but why?''

He shrugged and looked away. "Maybe I think it's
time for a change.''

She sat back, stunned. Sid, of the tattoos and earrings
and outrageous hair was trying to be *ordinary?* Not even
his mother, to whom he was devoted in every other way,
had been able to convince him to tone down his image.
What had happened to him?

"It has to be a woman,'' she said.

His face grew redder. "Why would you say that?''

"Only an attempt to impress a woman would make a
man change everything about himself.''

He made a grunting noise and turned his back to her.
She shook her head. "Sid, it won't work.''

"You don't know what you're talking about.''

"It won't work because if you want someone to love
you, they have to love you for yourself. If they don't,
it's all a sham.''

"Maybe my real self is more conservative than you realize." He turned around again. "I wasn't born with pink hair and a dozen tattoos, you know."

She folded her arms across her chest. "Has this woman actually objected to your hair and tattoos?"

"Well...no. But she's very conservative herself. And I'm sure her family—"

"We're not talking about her family, Sid. What does *she* think of you?"

His mouth turned down and he shook his head. "I don't know. She says she wants to hang out with me, but...I don't know."

She slid off the stool and put her arm around him. "I'll let you in on a secret, but only if you promise not to tell any other men."

"What's that?"

She leaned closer and lowered her voice. "Women love bad boys."

He frowned. "What are you talking about?"

She grinned. "Women love guys who are rebels. Unconventional. Dangerous. Men with a wild side, whether it's hidden or right out there. We think they're exciting, and they also allow us to indulge in the fantasy of taming them."

He glanced at her. "So you want wild men who aren't really all that wild?"

"In a manner of speaking." She squeezed his shoulder. "My guess is that this conservative woman is really longing to ride off in the darkness with you on your motorcycle, to have all the adventures she could never have with the ordinary, conservative men she meets every day."

Sid made a face. "I don't know..."

"Trust me on this, Sid. Women...especially conser-

vative women…like wild men. Be yourself and this
woman will be thrilled.''

He scratched his ear. ''Maybe.'' He frowned at her.
''Does this mean that wild women like conservative
men?''

''I'm not sure it works quite that way, but it's an
interesting theory.''

''I was just thinking of you and Mitch.''

''Me and—'' She laughed. ''He does present a challenge, but that's as far as it goes.'' She glanced toward
his closed office door. ''Mitch and I are playing a game.
But that's all we're doing.''

Sid shook his head. ''Whatever you say. I don't think
you give the man enough credit. He's the type who takes
even games seriously.''

''Tell me something I don't know.'' She straightened
her pinafore. ''But I'm still calling the shots. That's all
that matters to me.''

''Maybe so.'' He shrugged. ''Or maybe he only wants
you to think that. Mitch might have you right where he
wants you and you don't even realize it yet.''

She glanced toward the office door. She would admit
Mitch had been keeping her hot and bothered lately, but
that was as much her doing as it was his. After all, one
stuffed-shirt businessman was no match for a wild
woman like her. Maybe it was time to turn up the heat
another notch.

11

THAT AFTERNOON, JILL LEFT a message on Mitch's voice mail, telling him she thought it was time for another "lesson." "Meet me at the shop after work," she said. "I have a surprise for you."

As soon as the store closed, she gathered up her "props" for the evening. Thank goodness for her employee discount. She lit candles around the office, then changed into a pale blue silk negligée. Last time she'd aimed for tough and sexy. Tonight she wanted Mitch to see a softer side of her.

While there was something to be said for spontaneity and sex, she had to admit planning a seduction and waiting for Mitch to arrive added a delicious edge to desire. As she walked around the room arranging items to set the stage, her body tingled with awareness. The silk caressed her skin and sent tremors of arousal through her. She hoped Mitch would be here soon. Had she ever anticipated the arrival of a lover so much?

The bells on the front door chimed, announcing his approach. Her pulse beat faster as she turned to greet him. The look on his face when he saw her made her throat tighten. He stopped, one hand on the office door, and his gaze swept over her like a long, languid caress. "You look beautiful," he said at last, softly shutting the door behind him. "Silk suits you."

"It's from our Bridal Nights collection." She held out

her arms to better model the short peignoir and matching panties. "Not everything we have here is sleazy."

"I never said that."

"No, but you thought it."

He was dressed more casually tonight, in a pale blue golf shirt, khaki shorts and leather sandals. She hugged him, slipping her hands under his shirt to caress his bare back. "I thought we'd try something a little different tonight," she said.

He shaped his hand to her hip. "Everything with you is different."

"I wanted to show you some more of the merchandise we carry." She helped him slip the shirt over his head, then led him over to the bed. "Why don't you sit right here, like this…." Before he could protest or resist, she snapped the fur cuffs to his wrists and fastened them behind his back. Then she propped pillows around him. "There. Are you comfortable?"

He arched one eyebrow. "Around you? Never." His voice was a low growl, his expression guaranteed to send a jolt of heat straight to her groin. He settled back against the pillows. "But this will do for now."

"Good. I promise I won't hurt you." She leaned over the desk and switched on the stereo. Soft music filled the room. "The CD is called 'Sensual Nature,'" she explained.

She sat back and looked at him. Though his expression was relaxed, his shoulders remained rigid, as though he was ready to burst from the cuffs at any moment. She smoothed her hand down his arm. "Relax. Just let yourself go with the flow. Part of the appeal of being tied up is the idea that you can really let yourself go because nothing that happens is your fault. It's a way for people to lose their inhibitions."

"What would you know about inhibitions?" But his tone was teasing.

"You might be surprised. Now sit back and be prepared to enjoy yourself."

"Are you going to blindfold me, too?"

"No. Tonight I want you to see everything and pay attention."

"Will there be a pop quiz later?"

"You never can tell." She unfastened the single pearl button at the neckline of the peignoir and let it slip from her shoulders. She was left wearing bikini underpants and a strand of pearls connected to her nipples by elastic loops. The pearls swayed with each movement, tugging gently at her nipples.

Mitch's eyes widened. "Doesn't that hurt?"

"No, it's very comfortable. It's from our body jewelry collection."

She gently massaged her breasts, smiling as he began to breathe faster. "Do you like to watch?"

He wet his lips. "I like to watch you."

"I like watching you watch me." She moistened her fingertips and rolled her nipples between thumb and forefinger, tugging them into stiff, aching points. Mitch licked his lips and swallowed, his jaw tight.

"I want to watch you, too." She rocked forward onto her knees and helped him out of his shorts. He wore blue bikini briefs beneath his shorts, the fabric stretched taut by his erection. She smiled. "What do you think? Should we let him out to play?"

He leaned toward her, as far as the cuffs would allow. "If you do, I promise I won't hurt you."

Laughing, she slipped the underwear down his hips, across his perfect cheeks and down his thighs. She took her time, letting her fingernails graze his skin, admiring the way his erection strained toward her. He was hot and heavy in her hand. She cradled him for a moment, letting the tension build between them.

"Is this my surprise, because I have to tell you, I was expecting more."

"Your smart comments are destroying the mood I'm trying to create here. What can I do to shut you up?"

He gaze flickered to her breasts. "I can think of a few things."

"Hmm. How about this?" She guided one breast to his mouth.

Needing no more encouragement, he began to lick and suckle, first one breast and then the other as she knelt in front of him. His tongue traced circles around each nipple, flicking at the thin elastic holding the pearls in place. Heat built within her with each caress of his mouth.

She felt on the verge of climaxing, and she'd barely started with her plans for the evening. She sat back again, moving out of his reach, and took a deep breath, collecting herself. The air conditioner came on, sending cool air across her damp nipples, and she bit back a moan.

She picked up a bottle she'd laid out on the table beside the daybed. "We have a number of different lubricants for sale," she said, surprised at the tremor in her voice. She squeezed a drop onto her finger then spread it on his erection. He was incredibly hot and hard, the skin over his balls stretched tight. He pulsed in her hand, silently communicating how much he wanted her.

She caressed and stroked him, bringing him to the edge. When he was trembling in her hands, she drew away. "You're torturing me," he rasped.

"I am." She smiled. "I have lots more planned for our evening."

She moved away from him again, and slipped off her panties, then sat at the end of the bed, legs apart so that he could see her. She applied another drop of lubricant, and touched herself. The lubricant was hardly necessary, she was so wet and ready for him.

He groaned, his body straining for her, his gaze raking over her like a heated touch. She stilled her trembling hand, pulling back, her gaze locked to his. The air between them seemed to hum with unfulfilled desire.

"Don't stop," he said in a rough whisper.

"I thought it might be fun to show you one of our vibrators." She selected a small red cylinder from the items on the table. "This one is called a Pocket Rocket." She twisted the barrel and the vibrator began to buzz. She held it against his leg. "It's actually great for massage."

"And I'll bet everybody who buys one uses it for that."

She laughed. "Well, some probably do."

"Show me what *you* use it for."

She cradled the vibrator in her hand and studied him through veiled lashes. Was she ready to reveal this much of herself to him? It was one thing to surrender to desire in his arms, quite another to let him watch. "Go on," he urged. "I want to see you come."

She rocked back on her heels, legs apart, the pearls tugging at her aching nipples. With her hands, she spread apart her folds and found the sensitive nub at the heart of her desire and held the vibrator alongside it. Fierce arousal jolted through her. Mitch stroked her leg with his foot, silently encouraging her. She forced her eyes open to look at him as wave after wave of sensation flooded her, and the tenderness in his expression sent her over the edge.

She closed her eyes, giving herself up to the sensations, shaking with her release, a keening cry rising above the music. When at last she shut off the vibe and lay back, he was still watching her, his eyes dark, demanding. "Do you know what you want, Mitch?"

"I want you. Now."

With shaking hands, she unrolled a condom and sheathed him, then slid over him and began to move, riding him. His hands still bound behind him, he arched against her, driving himself into her, each collision sending new shock waves through her, building her arousal once more.

She came quickly, catching her lip between her teeth and moaning. He joined her, his own moans deep echoes of her cries. As soon as she collapsed against him, she reached around and unfastened the cuffs. His arms came around to pull her tighter against him, rocking her as if he would never let her go.

They didn't talk, merely held each other. Words seemed inadequate after what had just happened. She lay with her head cradled against his shoulder, his arms still around her tightly. She felt as if they were still joined somehow, even after he had withdrawn himself from her.

The candles flickered, sending shadows dancing across the walls. The CD stopped playing and silence enveloped them. She thought he'd fallen asleep and closed her own eyes, but opened them again when he spoke. "I liked watching," he said.

"It's very erotic," she agreed.

"It is." He caressed her shoulder. "But it's not just the act, it's the idea that you would be so open. Sharing all your secrets."

She frowned. She hadn't meant it that way. "I have plenty of secrets left."

He turned and propped himself on his elbow, so that he was looking at her. "So I'm right. Underneath that fun-seeking exterior, you have things to hide, just like the rest of us."

She looked away. "I don't have anything to hide. But that doesn't mean I have to tell you everything."

"Of course you don't. But if you want to, I'm ready to listen."

Why did he have to do this to her? She sat up, pushing away from him. "You're getting too serious. You're supposed to be focusing on physical pleasure, not all this emotional stuff."

"I guess I can't separate the two."

"Well, that's your problem." She climbed over him, out of bed, and headed for the dressing room, where she'd stashed her clothes.

What was it with Mitch, anyway? she thought. *Why did he always have to read so much into things?* She tugged her jeans over her hips. Just because they had great, mind-blowing sex didn't mean they had any deep emotional connection. Sure, maybe they clicked on a deeper physical level, but he ought to be enjoying that, instead of analyzing it to death.

She found her bra and fastened it around her. Why did she waste her time with him? Was saving the store really worth being subjected to this…this analysis? Just because he made her feel like no man had ever made her feel didn't mean what they had was so special. She pulled her shirt over her head and shoved her feet into her shoes. There were lots of men out there and plenty of them would be interested in a good time with her.

But some small voice inside of her whispered that none of those other men would ever get to her the way Mitch had in the short time they'd been together.

JILL DIDN'T VISIT THE cemetery often. She avoided places like this, that made her feel so sad and lonely. But two days after she and Mitch made love, she found herself drawn to Rocky Mountain Perpetual Care. Not that it wasn't a beautiful place. The flat expanse of ground on the edge of town was bisected with low stone walls and clumps of pine and aspen. Visitors had a good view of the Flatirons in the distance, their gray and red rock faces reflecting the bright summer sun. Here and there, flowers bloomed in jars and vases beside the stones.

She knelt and shoved the bunch of supermarket daisies she'd brought into the vase at Jenny's grave. The cemetery was beautiful, but in a still, sterile way. Jill preferred livelier surroundings, places with noise and busyness to drown out the grief that tended to sneak up on her when she was alone and quiet like this.

She pulled up a grass runner that was encroaching on the brass plaque and brushed her hand across the engraving. Jennifer Sheldon Davenport 1970—2000. "Surprised to see me here, sis?" she said. "Maybe not, if you've been paying attention to what's going on in my life. Can you believe I'm letting a man mess with my head this way?"

She sat back and drew her knees up, wrapping her arms around them. When she was in college, she'd come home on weekends and pour out her boyfriend troubles to her sister. Jenny was married with her own problems then, but Jill had been too caught up in her little world to notice.

Jenny would smile and shake her head and say the same thing she'd probably say now if she were here: "Jilly, you had better start thinking with your head instead of your hormones or some man is going to knock you for a loop. You'll be saying 'I do' and 'I will' and you'll never know what hit you.''

Only later had Jill thought to ask her sister if that was what had happened to her. ''Do you wish you'd thought more before you married Greg?''

''I wish I'd waited a while.'' Jenny turned onto her side, trying to get comfortable in the hospital bed. Even with the morphine drip, everything hurt by then. ''Oh, Jilly, there was so much I wanted to do with my life. So many fun things I never got to try.''

Jill hadn't cried then, but she had wept oceans of tears later, mourning all the good times Jenny had missed. Her big sister had married at nineteen and spent the next ten years working to put her husband through medical school, then caring for his ailing mother. She had postponed having children, given up vacations and classes, put off learning to ski or to paint or any of the things she once talked about doing. Then in the space of a year, her husband had left her and she'd developed pancreatic cancer.

''I've been having enough fun for both of us,'' Jill said, pulling more grass from around the grave marker. ''But Mitch—he's a hard man to figure out. I mean, it's obvious we're total opposites as far as the way we think and feel about things. But get us in bed and suddenly we're in perfect synch. At least physically.''

She yanked at a stubborn weed. ''The whole point of this little seduction is to show him how much *fun* sex can be, but he always ends up taking things way too seriously. How am I supposed to convince him to keep the store open if he can't just relax and enjoy the moment instead of getting all philosophical on me?''

And that's the only reason you're interested in him? Because you want to save the store and keep your job?

She winced. She didn't believe in ghosts or people reaching out from beyond the grave, but she knew her sister well enough to know this was something Jenny would have said. Jenny was big on telling the truth and taking responsibility for your actions.

She brushed dirt away from the marker. "Okay, so maybe I have the hots for him, too. And you know me— I love a challenge. I'd love to help Ice Man thaw out a little."

A ground squirrel poked its head up from a nearby clump of grass and chattered at her. Jill laughed. "Don't mind me. I'm just sitting here talking to myself." She rose and brushed the dirt from her denim skirt. "I guess I have to figure my own way out of this one, huh, sis?" She smiled down at the brass marker. "I think if you were here, you'd tell me to go with the flow myself. I mean, it's not as if I'm not enjoying myself."

She turned and walked back toward her car, through the neat rows of markers, past the occasional more ornate memorial carved in stone. With only two weeks left until her deadline, she really needed to get busy. There must be some way to get Mitch to reveal his inner wild man—that part of him that had to appreciate the appeal of a store like Just 4 Play.

Maybe the store was the wrong place to act. To Mitch that was a place of business, where he was reluctant to shed his businessman's demeanor. "I need to get him away from the office," she mumbled. "But how? I could ask him out, but what if he says no? Maybe Meg—"

"Do you always talk to yourself like this?"

She jerked her head up and stared, wide-eyed, at Mitch Landry in the flesh. He was standing one row over, beside a large black tombstone. The sun behind him spotlighted his broad shoulders and glinted on the gold flecks in his hair. A breeze pushed back the sides of his coat, revealing a crisp white collarless shirt beneath. He looked like a model for a men's clothing catalog, or the kind of man who starred in her best fantasies—all lean muscle, fabulous hair and brooding good looks. *Oh man, do I have it bad,* she thought as she walked toward him.

12

MITCH WAS STARTLED TO LOOK up and see Jill moving between the rows of grave markers. She'd walked past without even seeing him before he finally found his voice and called out to her.

"Hi, Mitch," she said as she walked toward him. "Um, what brings you here?"

She was wearing some silky, summery top and a long jean skirt, slit up the side. She looked young and vibrant and every part of him wanted her in a way he couldn't remember ever wanting a woman. "I was about to ask you the same thing," he said, surprised at how calm he sounded.

She glanced behind her. "I was visiting someone."

Who? he wondered. *A relative? A former lover?* "So am I." He nodded to the stone. "What do you think?"

She stepped back and bent to read the inscription on the stone. "Griffeth Landry. 1945—2003. Businessman, sportsman, philanthropist. His generosity benefited many." She smiled up at Mitch. "Grif would have loved it."

He shoved his hands in his pockets and regarded the stone. The masons had done a good job with it, shaping a simple tablet, outlining the letters in gold leaf. The results were bold and dignified. A big statement for a big man. "I hope so. I wanted to do something...he did so much for everybody else, but never really made a big deal of it."

She nodded. "That was Grif. He said he liked to work behind the scenes."

Her voice held a note of fondness. Mitch envied her whatever memories made her smile that way. "Did he spend much time at the store?" he asked. "I mean, did you get to know him very well?"

"He spent quite a bit of time there." She laughed. "He liked to flirt. And he told bad jokes. He came across as a guy who really knew how to have fun."

"Unlike some people you're too polite to mention."

She looked away, biting her lip. "I didn't say anything."

"You didn't have to. I know what you think of me." He sighed. "And you're right."

She whirled to face him again. "I am?"

He nodded, feeling grim. "I know I'm not the most exciting guy to be around. I do tend to take things too seriously sometimes." He shrugged. "What can I say? I haven't had a lot of time for fun these past few years."

He started walking away. She caught up with him and slipped her arm through his. She was warm and smelled like jasmine. "Don't be so hard on yourself. You can always learn how to have fun."

He looked down at her. "You seem to be making every effort to teach me."

She squeezed his arm. "Don't tell me you haven't enjoyed our lessons."

"I never said I didn't enjoy them." Truth was, he'd enjoyed them entirely too much. When he was with Jill, he forgot about all his responsibilities and obligations. Every sense focused on the moment as the past receded and the future disappeared.

"Oh, it's obvious you enjoy certain aspects of our time together." She stopped and faced him, looking into his eyes, as if searching for something. "But I never get the impression you've really let yourself go. Abandoned yourself to the moment."

"Just let it all hang out. Have a good time with no strings attached, is that what you mean?"

"I didn't say no strings." She wagged her finger at him.

"Oh, yes. The store." He shook his head. "You won't change my mind about that."

"Because it isn't respectable?"

"That's part of it." And maybe because he felt out of his league there, like an alien on another planet. Better to go with a restaurant, something more conventional and familiar.

"Fun and respectable don't always go together." She smoothed his lapels. Her fingers were long and slender, the nails coated in pale pink.

"They do in my case."

She trailed one finger down the center of his chest, sending lightning bolts of sensation radiating outward. "I'm still determined to change your mind."

He captured her hands in his and looked around them. "This seems like a strange place to be having this conversation." He looked at her again. "I know it's none of my business, but what *were* you doing here?"

"Visiting my sister." On impulse, she tugged him back the way they'd come. "I'll show you."

He released her and she raced between the rows of graves. He followed at a slower pace, striding over the grass with heavy steps. He joined her beside the marker and read the inscription. "Older sister?" he asked.

She nodded. "Two years older."

"Were you a lot alike?" He tried to imagine a slightly older Jill. Surely there couldn't be two women like her in this world.

"We used to be. When she was in high school, she won a glee club award for 'Most Enthusiastic.' When she was in college, her freshman class voted her 'Girl Most Likely To.'"

"Most likely to what?"

She grinned. "You fill in the blank. Jenny would do almost anything."

"What happened?"

"She married young, spent a lot of years taking care of other people, being responsible and dependable and all those things." She looked at him, her eyes bleak. "She was thirty years old when she died of cancer. She never got to do all the things she used to talk about doing with her life."

"So you're determined not to make the same mistake?"

She shrugged and turned away, hugging herself. "Let's just say Jenny taught me an important lesson. 'Life's too short' isn't a cliché, it's the truth."

"So your philosophy is, if a person wants to do something, they should do it, and worry about the consequences later?"

"Not if it's robbing a bank or jumping off a cliff, but most things, yeah." She stretched her arms over her head. "People don't take enough chances in life."

She whirled to face him. "If you could do anything you wanted right now—anything—what would you do?"

He looked into her eyes, the color of a mountain lake, dancing with life and light. "If I could do anything, what would I do?" he murmured. He put his hands on her shoulder and drew her close. "This." Then he bent and kissed her, a soft meeting of their lips that deepened as he felt her melt against him.

She tasted of peppermint, warm and sweet and meant to be savored. Her lips were satin-soft, her tongue agile and teasing. He nipped the side of her mouth and she laughed, a sound that rose between them like champagne bubbles, light and celebratory. He pulled her closer and felt the hard points of her breasts against his chest, his erection straining at his fly. She ground against him, letting him know she wouldn't object if he tried to take things further.

Damn! Why did he get into these situations in public? Reluctantly, he released her. She stepped back, eyes glazed. But she was smiling. "What was that all about?"

He shrugged. "You could say I'm learning to act on impulse."

"I like your impulses." She wound her arms around his neck and pulled him close once more. "Why don't we try that again?"

Hands at her waist, he pushed her gently away. "I don't think so."

Her face clouded. "Why not?"

"For one thing, those two old women over there look likely to have a stroke any moment now if we keep this up."

She followed his gaze to a pair of matrons standing some distance away. The two women stared, openmouthed, brows furrowed in disapproval.

Jill smiled and waved. "It's all right," she called. "We're just rehearsing." She leaned closer to Mitch and whispered, "It's one play you won't want to miss."

Choking back laughter, he dragged her toward the

parking lot. "You are incorrigible," he scolded as he unlocked his car door.

"Guilty as charged. Who wants to be corrigible anyway?" She put her hand over his and stopped him from opening the car door. "So now what?"

He pretended not to know what she meant. "Now I'm going back to work."

"After that kiss?" She put her hands on her hips and scowled at him. "I can think of a few other activities that would be more appropriate. Most of which involve both of us getting naked.

He chuckled. "I assure you I'm tempted."

"So why not give in to temptation?" She tugged at his arm. "Didn't you say you were going to try to change your super serious ways?"

"I did. But I prefer to take things at my own pace."

"Neither of us is getting any younger here, Mitch. What's the big attraction of going slow?"

If she only knew how much he wanted to drag her into the car right now and get after it. He studied her face, looking for some clue as to her true motives here. "I already told you nothing you can do will change my mind."

"That's what you said. I'm not so sure I believe that." She reached up and undid the top button of his shirt. "That's enough for me to keep trying." She moved to the second button. "Or are you afraid I'll succeed?"

He put his hand over hers to stop her from going further. "Maybe you haven't noticed, but it's broad daylight out and we're in the parking lot of a cemetery."

"So?" She glanced around them. The two matrons were making their way across the parking lot. Jill smiled and waved and they hurried away. Then she looked back

at Mitch, her expression serious. "Tell me the truth—
do you want me, right now?"

He glanced down at the obvious bulge in the front of
his trousers. "I don't think there are any doubts about
that."

"Then what are you waiting for?" She walked around
the car and opened the passenger door.

"What are you doing?"

She smiled and slid into the passenger seat and faced
forward, ignoring him.

He got in the car. "What are you doing?" he asked
again.

"You said you wanted me now. I want you, too."
She reached over and squeezed his thigh, then slid her
hand over to cover his crotch. "I'm teaching you to be
more spontaneous."

"Jill, we can't—" But she was already unzipping his
pants, pulling down his underwear to caress him. He
uttered a noise between a gasp and a groan.

"I think we are." She dragged her fingers up the un-
derside of his penis, her fingernails lightly raking the
sensitive head.

He glanced around him, but the images he saw were
filtered by a haze of desire.

"Don't worry. No one will see us. Haven't you noticed how few people come to cemeteries in the middle
of the day in the middle of the week?" She kissed his
ear, her teeth nipping at his earlobe, sending an electric
shiver through him. "The car windows are tinted and
you're parked at the far end of the lot. There are plenty
of spaces closer, so no one is likely to park beside us."

"What if they do?"

"If they do, we'll simply explain we were comforting

each other in our grief.'' She opened her purse and took out a small gold-capped bottle.

''What's that?'' he asked.

''A little something to make things go smoother.'' She poured lotion from the bottle into her hand and the exotic aroma of jasmine and spices filled the car. *Her* scent.

She smoothed the lotion across her hand, then took hold of him once more. He jerked in surprise, but her hand on his thigh steadied him. Her caress was firm, but light, skillful. She traced the length of his shaft, then slipped farther down to cup his balls, squeezing gently. His breath caught, and again she kissed his ear. ''Do you like that?''

''Uh.'' It was the only sound he could utter, she had him so mesmerized, her fingers encircling him with a steady pressure. She began drawing circles around the base of the head, her tongue echoing the movement against his neck.

She was leaning over the stick shift, her upper body pressed alongside him. The thought passed through his mind that this probably wasn't very comfortable, but then that bit of common sense was banished by another surge of desire as she rapidly slid her hand up and down his straining erection.

He slipped his arm around her, enjoying the sensation of her breast soft against his side, her hair tickling his neck. She increased the pressure on his penis and he let out a long, low groan. Who would have thought an old-fashioned hand-job could have him on fire this way? He was like a teenager again, at the mercy of some girl he'd brought out in his car. Except Jill wasn't ''some girl.'' She was a woman capable of confusing and delighting him in the same breath.

''Relax,'' she whispered. ''Enjoy the moment.'' She

bent and sucked at his nipple through his shirt. He caught sight of himself in the rearview mirror, his eyes glazed, jaw slack. Anyone looking in the car at this moment would have no doubt what was going on.

He struggled to assume a composed expression, but Jill's insistent hand and teasing mouth made the effort futile. He was literally shaking, close to losing control. He put his hand on her back, thinking to tell her to stop now, he'd finish this himself, but then it was too late. He shuddered with release, pressed back against the seat, eyes closed. He didn't give a damn who saw him now, only please, don't stop.

He felt her draw away, and somehow got it together enough to dig his handkerchief from his pocket and hand it to her. After a moment, she returned it, and he cleaned himself off and zipped up his pants. Only then did he look at her. "That was pretty incredible."

She smiled. "See, the world didn't come to an end or anything. There are rewards for living in the moment."

He nodded. "I can see that." He shifted in his seat and leaned toward her, pressing her back against the seat with one hand. "Now it's your turn."

Her smile vanished. "That isn't necessary."

"But I insist." He let his gaze drift over her, from the sexy pout of her mouth, over her erect nipples, barely discernable against the fabric of her dress. His eyes came to rest on her crotch. "Take your underwear off."

"Mitch, really."

"Take them off." The words weren't a request, but an order. Her eyes widened and for half a second he thought she might slap him and storm out of the car, but instead, she stayed, and shimmied out of her underwear.

The pair of white silk bikinis she handed him was warm and slightly damp, scented with her musk. He felt himself growing hard again as he reached over and flipped up the front of her skirt to reveal the nest of light brown curls between her legs. "Let me see," he said, coaxing her thighs apart.

A sly smile on her face, she complied, playing the wanton. But her hands, curled into fists at her side, betrayed her uneasiness. She wanted to be the one to give orders, not to take them. He reached his hand between her legs. She was hot and wet. "So jerking me off turned you on," he said.

She nodded and ran her tongue along her lips. "Yeah."

"But maybe I can do better." He slid one finger into her and felt her tighten around him. He buried his thumb between her folds until he found the erect nub, the "magic button" that would start the fireworks. Her eyes fluttered closed and her lips parted. His erection twitched in response.

He tried to move closer, but the stick shift was in the way. He looked around them, wishing they were someplace less public. He had half a mind to start the car and drive to his apartment, where there was privacy and a bed and room to do this properly.

She squirmed beneath him, arching toward him, silently pleading for release. No, there was no time for relocating now. He wouldn't make her wait any longer.

He stroked her gently, then with more firmness. Fast, then slow, the scent of sex and jasmine and the sight of her writhing beneath him making him hard all over again. He watched her face as she lay back and surrendered herself to the experience, the moment, just as she was always preaching at him to do.

He felt the growing tension in her, saw her arch against his hand, her head thrown back. She moaned softly, a sound that rose in pitch, eery and erotic. As her body tensed with her final release, he pulled her close, burying his face in her neck, the tremors of her climax vibrating through him.

They sat for a long while, her head crushed against his shoulder, his hand still on her, until she gently moved out of his embrace. "For a man who was reluctant at first, you catch on quick."

"I always aim to please, ma'am."

She made a face. "Well, *sir,* you know what would please me most."

So they were back to that, were they? Did she never give up? "I'm not going to keep the store open," he said.

"Then I guess I'll have to keep trying to change your mind." Her eyes sparkled, as if she was in on some secret joke.

He shook his head. "What am I going to do with you?"

"I'd say you seem to be doing a good job of figuring that out." Her laughter floated back to him as she slipped out of the car. He watched her walk away and wondered at the elation rising in his own throat. He and Jill were playing an odd game here, one he was sure he would win. But who was to say if he let her win, he'd really be a loser?

13

IT WAS JILL'S TURN TO OPEN the store the next morning. She arrived feeling worse for wear after a restless night. Thoughts of Mitch kept her awake. When she'd finally fallen to sleep, she'd dreamed of Mitch, his sweat-slicked, naked body tied to her bed while she tortured him with her tongue.

She'd awakened horny and irritable. Men! Despite her best efforts, he'd once again ended up with the last word yesterday. Honestly, why did they have to make sex into this whole power struggle thing?

She'd fix him. On her way to work, she'd come up with a plan. Soon she'd have him so hot and bothered he'd be begging to come over to her place and let her show him how it's done. She smiled to herself as she went around the store, gathering up various items and attaching sticky notes to them. When Mitch found these ''gifts'' on his desk, he'd have a good idea of what she had in mind for him.

She was still chuckling to herself when Sid came in the back door. At least, she thought it was Sid. He'd shaved off the Mohawk and removed most of his jewelry except for a single, discreet diamond stud in his left ear. In place of his usual T-shirt and jeans or leather he wore an actual suit, charcoal-gray wool complete with pin-striped shirt and a red and navy tie. He carried a brief-case, which he placed under the counter.

He turned and caught Jill watching him. "What are you staring at?"

"Sid—what have you done?"

He smoothed his hand over his naked scalp and tugged at his tie. "How do you like my new look?"

"I...I don't know." She walked around him, marveling that he had put together such a completely white-bread conservative ensemble. He looked like he could run for office. And win. "It's so different."

"The clerk at Joseph A. Bank said it was the perfect suit for a young businessman on his way up."

"I'm sure it is, but..." She bit her lip. "I take it you're still seeing this woman—the conservative one?"

He sorted through the morning mail. "We've had dinner once. We're going out again tonight."

"So she hasn't seen the 'new you' yet?"

"No, it's a surprise." He looked up from the mail, his expression anxious. "Do you think she'll like it?"

"Sid, I think she probably liked you before. Didn't you listen to anything I said, about women liking bad boys?"

He shook his head. "She isn't like that."

"How do you know if you don't give her a chance to see the real you?"

His shoulders sagged. "She wants me to help her get her old boyfriend back. I'm trying to change her mind."

She fingered the edge of his suit coat. "Is this how her old boyfriend dresses?"

He nodded. "Except he's not bald." He touched his naked head again. "And he has money." His brow furrowed. "I haven't figured out how to overcome that yet."

"You shouldn't have to overcome anything," she said. "She should like you for yourself."

"Women say that, but I don't believe it."

She put her hands on her hips. "Are you saying we're liars?"

He dropped a pile of junk mail into the trash can beside the counter. "Let's just say you have a distorted view of reality."

"*I* certainly don't."

He laughed. "You're one of the worst. Look at you. From the minute you met Mitch, you've been ragging on him about having more fun, taking more risks. You're like every other woman I ever met. You meet a man and the first thing you do is try to remake him."

"Don't tell me you don't agree that Mitch needs to loosen up." She grabbed a cloth and began furiously polishing the glass of a display cabinet. "And don't forget, I'm doing this to save your job."

"I never asked for your help, did I? Maybe this is my chance to move on to something else."

"Something your new girlfriend would approve of?"

"Why not? Maybe that's a point in my favor. If women want to improve men, they should appreciate the cooperative ones."

"There's no such thing as a cooperative man." She grabbed up the bottle of glass cleaner and stormed off to the opposite side of the store. Of all the ridiculous, infuriating attitudes. You go out of your way to help a man, and he doesn't even appreciate it. As if she didn't have enough problems in her life right now, she had to deal with not one, but *two* impossible men.

WHEN MITCH WALKED IN the front door of Just 4 Play, he wondered if someone had turned the air-conditioning down too low. The air definitely held a chill, though he soon realized it had nothing to do with the thermostat.

"Here's your mail," Sid said, handing him a stack of envelopes.

Mitch tried to avoid staring at his manager's newly shaved head. To think he'd grown used to a pink Mohawk. "Has Archie Patterson called to say the new plans are ready yet?" he asked.

"He hasn't called since I've come in." Sid's voice was frosty. "Jill opened this morning. You could ask her."

Mitch looked at Jill, who was busying herself taking books off a shelf and putting them back in the exact same spot. She hadn't said a word when he walked in. Was she embarrassed about yesterday? "Jill, did Archie Patterson call this morning?"

She didn't look up. "No. Maybe he's forgotten all about your plans. Maybe *he* thinks you should keep this place the way it is."

"Maybe some people know how to embrace change and move on," Sid said. "*Some* people aren't stuck in the past."

Now what was that all about? He looked from Sid to Jill and started to say something, but she looked as if she'd gladly bite his head off. He turned to Sid. "Uh, nice suit."

Sid smoothed his lapels. "Do you think so? Thanks."

Shaking his head, Mitch retreated to his office. After a restless night, he'd hoped for a peaceful morning, but apparently he wasn't going to be so lucky.

Considering that the cause of his restlessness was out there now rearranging books and ignoring him, he supposed peace had been a little much to expect. He'd stayed up half the night alternately cursing and congratulating himself on letting her seduce him at the cemetery yesterday. No man in his right mind would have turned down an opportunity like that.

But that didn't mean Jill had any kind of hold over him. She couldn't manipulate him into doing what she wanted just because she knew how to manipulate him sexually.

But knowing that was cold comfort at three in the morning when he woke from episode six and counting from what might be the world's longest running wet dream. This particular version had involved a naked Jill wielding a cat-o'-nine-tails and a can of whipped topping. He got hard again thinking about it.

As soon as she'd left yesterday, he'd realized he still had her panties. He'd stuffed the scrap of white silk into his pocket and found his hand straying there for the rest of the afternoon. They were still there, keeping him balanced on the sharp edge of desire.

Yeah, a peaceful life, much less a peaceful morning, was really reaching for it.

He walked over to the desk and the first thing he noticed was the objects grouped in the center of the blotter. He picked up a bottle of green lotion. *Go the distance!* it proclaimed. *Increase your endurance.* A yellow sticky note on the front bore a message in Jill's handwriting. *You're going to need this.*

He examined a black satin blindfold. *What you don't see can drive you wild.*

Nipple nibblers. *Your bod or mine?*

He laughed. "Cute. Very cute. And definitely your bod." He could think of several ways to put all of this "merchandise" to good use.

He sat behind the desk and flipped through the mail. "Now this is interesting." He studied an envelope stamped with the Boulder Chamber of Commerce's seal.

He slit open one end and shook out a heavy embossed invitation.

The pleasure of your presence is requested at our Annual Awards Banquet. Now why would the Chamber of Commerce invite the owner of Just 4 Play to their banquet, when they'd previously turned down Uncle Grif's application? He tossed the invitation in the trash. If they wouldn't accept Grif, he didn't want anything to do with them.

An hour later, he was reviewing cost estimates for the remodeling work when the phone rang. "Mitch, it's Mort." As usual, Lana's dad sounded loud and chummy, more like a used car salesman than a banker. "Did you get your invitation to the Chamber Banquet yet?"

"It came this morning. But I'm not a member. Why do they want me at their banquet?" He picked up the blindfold and turned it end over end. The satin was cool and slick beneath his fingers. It might be fun to try this on Jill and...

"They want you there because I told them they want you there," Mort boomed.

Mitch laid aside the blindfold. "Do they know I'm the new owner of Just 4 Play?"

"They know you're the future owner of Ping's Peking Palace, the first five-star oriental restaurant in Boulder county."

"Except that the restaurant isn't open yet."

"It will be, boy. Archie Patterson came by this morning to show me the plans."

Mitch frowned. "I haven't even seen the plans yet. What's he doing showing them to you?"

"Oh, Archie and I go way back. Besides, he knows I'm the money man here."

"Sure." Mitch fought a sour feeling in his stomach.

"When you see Archie again, tell him the man whose name is going on this would appreciate seeing those plans sometime."

"Now don't you worry about a thing. This is going to be big. I have a sense about these things and I'm never wrong. A year from now, we could be talking about a whole chain of Ping's Peking Palaces throughout the southwest. In five years, we could go national."

Except that's not what Mitch wanted. He wanted one good restaurant that he could watch over and control. Already, he could feel that slipping away from him.

Mort must have taken his silence for agreement. "Good, I'll look forward to seeing you at the banquet."

"Uh, will Lana be there?" Not that it mattered, but he wanted to be prepared, so it wouldn't be awkward.

"No, I asked her to accompany me, but she has other plans that evening." He lowered his voice. "Just between you and me, she's seeing someone new. This time it might be serious."

Was Lana ever anything but serious? "Why do you say that?"

"I've never seen her like this. She's dressing differently. Acting differently. She even forgot our Tuesday night dinner date. She never misses that."

Mitch smiled at Mort's peeved tone. "That sounds serious, all right."

"I don't know what's going on. She's either ill or in love."

"I'm happy for her."

"You could have had her if you'd played your cards right. But I won't hold it against you. I like the way you think and I believe we've got a real future together. See you Saturday evening."

Just what he wanted, a future of loudmouthed Mort

Montgomery telling him what to do. He hung up the phone and tried to imagine Lana in love. The thought made him smile. Good for her. He was glad she was happy.

He fished the banquet invitation out of the trash and read it again. Mr. Mitchell Landry *and guest.* Who could he invite to go with him? He could go stag, but then there'd be that awkward empty chair at his table, and perhaps pointed remarks from Mort Montgomery about what a fool he was for letting Lana get away.

His gaze wandered to the collection of playthings on his desk. He smiled. Yes, he'd ask Jill. This would be the perfect chance for them to get to know each other better, away from the sex-charged atmosphere at work. He'd have a chance to explain all the reasons closing the store was the right thing to do for all of them.

WHEN SID ARRIVED AT LANA'S condo that evening, he was surprised to find her dressed in a miniskirt and silky blouse instead of her usual suit. His confusion must have registered on his face. "Don't you like it?" she asked.

"Yeah… Yes. It looks nice. Real nice." The blouse was a soft pink shade, almost the color of her skin. She'd left the top button undone, so he could see the deep valley between her breasts.

He waited for her to say something about his suit, but she didn't. Instead she stared at his head. "You shaved your head."

He smoothed his bald pate, still self-conscious about all that naked flesh. "Yeah, uh, I was getting a little tired of the Mohawk."

"Oh. Well, I like the bald look. I mean, it looks good on you." She shut and locked her door, then slipped her arm through his and walked with him to the curb.

"I thought we'd go to the Boulderado, if that's all right," he said.

"Oh." She looked disappointed. "I eat there all the time." She squeezed his arm. "Let's go someplace different."

"Okay. Like where?"

"There's this new Indian restaurant over by the mall. I hear you sit on the floor to eat."

A trendy place. He should have known she'd like something like that. "Sure. That's cool."

They reached his bike. He hadn't been too sure about the Harley, but it was the only transportation he had. "I hope you don't mind riding my bike. Or we could take your car...."

"No, the bike is great." She ran her hand along the leather seat. "I've always wanted to ride one."

He gave her a helmet, then strapped on his own. He'd had to get a smaller size when he shaved his head. She climbed on behind him and hugged him close. Her skirt rode up high on her thighs. He was aware of her breasts pressed against his back. She had nice breasts. Full and round. He shifted in his seat, hoping she wouldn't notice his arousal. She'd probably think he was some kind of pervert.

He started the bike and she squealed. He grinned as he guided the bike onto the street. He'd heard some women really got off on the bike's vibration between their legs. Lana snuggled closer, her arms tight around his ribs. Maybe she was scared she'd fall off.

He found the restaurant without too much trouble, a low-slung building decorated inside with lots of red and gold draperies, low mahogany tables and lots of floor pillows. The waitress led them to a table in a shallow alcove. Instead of sitting across from him, Lana scooted around the table to sit beside him. "Isn't this cozy?" she said.

"Yeah." He wished he had the nerve to put his arm around her, but he didn't want her to take things wrong. A sophisticated guy would no doubt take things slower.

They ordered wine and tandoori chicken. When the food arrived, Lana plucked a morsel of chicken from the skewer and offered it to him. "Tell me if it's any good."

Her fingers grazed his mouth as he accepted the chicken and her eyes seemed to sparkle with delight in the lamplight. Feeling bolder, he chose a piece of chicken to feed her. "What do you think?"

"Mmm." She suckled his fingertips and all the breath rushed out of him. His appetite for food fled, replaced by another, stronger appetite.

He looked away, not sure what to do. Did she have any idea how crazy she was making him?

"Why are you being so quiet?" she asked. "I thought you were going to teach me to be a wild woman."

Yeah, so she could get Mitch back. But Mitch didn't want her back. And Sid did. Want her, that is. "Uh, yeah." He picked at his food, not even seeing it. "So what do you want to know?"

She leaned close and licks her lips. "I want to know how to drive a man wild."

She was doing a pretty good job with him already. "Well, yeah. There are a lot of things you could do." For instance, just sitting there beside him eating dinner was doing a pretty good number on him.

She leaned closer still, her breast resting against his arm. "Kiss me, Sid. That's a good place to start, isn't it?"

He looked around at the other diners. Despite the alcove, their table felt exposed. "Uh, I don't think this is the place." He struggled up onto his knees, thankful for the long suit jacket to hide his obvious erection, and signaled for the check. "Why don't we go somewhere quieter?"

Outside once more, she clung to his arm as they walked to the bike. "Will you take me to the store?" she asked.

"The store? You mean like the grocery store?" They were out on a date and she wanted to go shopping?

"No, I mean the store where you work. Just 4 Play." She giggled. "What a name."

He stopped and looked at her, surprised. "But... you've already seen it." And from what he remembered, she hadn't liked the place much.

She made a face. "I was upset then. I didn't really look around." She stroked her hand down his arm. "I want you to give me a private tour."

14

THE STREETS AROUND Just 4 Play were quiet, most of the businesses closed and deserted. Sid steered the bike through the alley around back and parked beside the Dumpster. He let them in with his key, then reached into the alarm panel and unhooked a wire.

"What are you doing?" Lana whispered.

"Bypassing the alarm." He pulled her inside behind him and shut the door.

"Why not just turn it off?"

"It registers with the alarm company when it's turned off. I'd rather not have to explain what I'm doing here with you."

Small lamps on tables through the store allowed them to see most of the merchandise. He showed her the costumes first. That was about the tamest thing he could think of to start with. She admired the belly dancer's costume, then held out the ever-popular Nurse Betty. "I think the dancer is cute, but what's so sexy about a nurse?"

"Uh, well, guys get off on things that don't always make sense to women." Good thing he hadn't shown her the schoolgirl outfit. Or the baby doll pajamas. He shrugged. "Our brains are wired differently, I guess."

"That's why I'm here. To learn about things like that." She pulled out a carpenter's tool belt and held it against him. "You'd look nice in this."

"Really?" He'd never been much for costumes, himself, but if she liked it...

She'd already moved on to the lingerie. "How do you think I'd look in this?" She held up a red lace thong.

He swallowed hard. "I think you'd look good in anything, Lana."

"Oh, Sid, you're so sweet."

That's me. A regular patsy.

She took his hand and led him to a display of body jewelry. "Why aren't you wearing *your* jewelry tonight?" she asked.

He patted his eyebrow, which felt naked without its customary ring, not to mention the barbell he'd removed from his tongue, and half a dozen other studs and loops he'd left lying on the dresser. "I thought maybe it was a little much," he said. "That you didn't like that sort of thing."

She looked startled. "Where did you get an idea like that?"

He flushed. "Well, you know... You're kind of conservative and all..."

She frowned. "Do you think that's a bad thing?"

"No! Of course not. I just thought..." He swallowed hard. He didn't know what to think. Why hadn't he kept his mouth shut?

"It's okay. I guess to someone like you, I do seem like a real stick in the mud."

"Someone like me?"

"You know, someone...unconventional." She looked him up and down. "Someone...extraordinary. Not someone ordinary like me."

He started to reach for her, but hesitated. "Lana, I don't think you're ordinary at all."

She raised her chin. "I'm trying not to be. That's why

I had you bring me here.'' She studied the display again and selected a set of nipple rings. "How do these work?''

"Uh, you know, they uh, they clamp on to…on to your nipples.'' He was grateful for the darkness to hide his blush. Honestly, he usually had no problem talking about anything and everything to do with sex. He spent his days explaining the finer points of dildos and the best ways to heighten sexual arousal to total strangers and never even blinked. But with Lana, it was different…

She looked puzzled. "And that feels good?''

"Well, it makes them more sensitive.''

She handed them to him. "Maybe you could try them on me.''

"N…now?'' He glanced around them. "Here?''

"Don't you want to help me be a wild woman?'' She started unbuttoning her blouse. Underneath, she wore a lacy black bra that fastened in front.

He couldn't believe she was doing this. Maybe he'd fallen asleep and this was some wild dream. This was *Lana*. Miss High Society. And she was taking her clothes off. For *him*.

Her bra drifted to the floor beside her shirt. He forced himself to breathe deeply. *Just stay cool,* he reminded himself. *Don't let her think you can't handle this.*

Her breasts were just as he'd imagined, full and heavy, the nipples dark and thick. Her skin looked like ivory in the dim light. "Go ahead,'' she said. "Put them on.''

His hands trembled, so that he had to make several tries to attach the rings to her nipples. His fingers brushed against her and she let out a breathy gasp. He stifled a groan and wondered if he'd embarrass himself by coming in his pants. He finally got the rings on her and stepped back to try to regain his composure.

The chain that connected the rings hung down into her cleavage, tantalizing. She looked down at herself, then smiled at him. "You're right. It feels good...sexy."

It looked sexy as hell. He didn't know how much longer he could keep up this charade of pretending not to want her.

"Now you look overdressed." The next thing he knew, she was taking his jacket off. She started unbuttoning his shirt. He stood there like a statue, afraid to move. If he so much as touched her, he wouldn't be able to stop.

He sucked in his breath as her fingernails grazed his chest. "Lana, I really don't think..."

"That's much better." She undid the last button and pushed the shirt back onto his arms. Her eyes widened when she saw the rings in his own pierced nipples. "*Oooh*, we match." She hooked her pinky in one of the rings and tugged lightly. Just enough to send a jolt of electricity through him.

He clamped his hand over her wrist and gently pushed her away. "I wouldn't do that if I were you."

Her smile vanished. "Did I hurt you? I'm sorry. Let me kiss it and make it better."

The first swipe of her tongue over his sensitive nipple almost brought him to his knees. A low groan escaped him and he put his arms around her, thinking he ought to push her away, but unable to do anything but cling to her.

She laved first one nipple, then the other, her own naked breasts brushing against his stomach. His cock strained against his fly, painfully erect. He was so close to the edge now the slightest breath might set him off.

Finally she raised her head and smiled at him. "Is that better?"

He managed to nod and grunt something unintelligible. How long before he could get away from her, into the bathroom where he could give himself some relief?

But his torture wasn't over yet. As he watched, dazed, she unzipped her skirt and let it slide to the floor. She wore black lace bikini panties, and thigh-high stockings held in place by a garter belt.

Shut your mouth, Sid, he warned himself. *You're starting to drool.*

"Is this okay?" she asked, adjusting one of the stockings. "I used to think garter belts were for old ladies, but I understand men really like them."

"Uh, yeah." Men like him. Something about that few inches of naked skin above the top of the stocking....

He shook his head, trying to clear it.

"What's the matter, Sid? Don't you find me attractive?"

"Attractive?" Where did that squeaking in his voice come from? He cleared his throat and tried again. "Believe me, Lana, any man who saw you now wouldn't ever be able to think of another woman again."

The answer didn't erase her look of disappointment. "We're not talking about any man, Sid. We're talking about you." She took a step toward him.

He backed up. No sense going there again. "Of course I think you're attractive," he said. "You're gorgeous."

"Then why are you avoiding me?" She had him backed against the wall now. He closed his eyes and tried to think of something non-erotic. Algebra equations. Motorcycle maintenance.

"Look at me, Sid. Please."

He opened his eyes, and found himself lost in two of

the most beautiful green eyes he'd ever seen. "Why do you think I wanted to come here with you tonight?" she asked.

"Because…because you wanted to find a way to get Mitch back." The words cut him, like broken glass.

Her eyes widened. "Is that what you thought?"

"You said Mitch thought you were repressed. That you didn't want to be that way."

"So you agreed to help me so I could get Mitch back?"

He nodded. Right now, the whole idea sounded pretty stupid.

She reached for his hand and held it. "This doesn't have anything to do with Mitch." She placed his palm flat against her belly. It was warm and soft, and oh, so female. "I asked you to help me because I wanted to be with you." She guided his hand down, beneath the elastic of her panties, toward her heated center. "Feel how wet I am for you?" she whispered.

He slid his finger into her. She closed around him, hot and slick. With his other arm, he gathered her close, burying his face in her neck, breathing in the sweet scent of her. He couldn't believe how he was shaking. But she was shaking too, tremors moving through her as he stroked her with his finger, moving slowly back and forth, forcing himself not to hurry.

After what could have been a minute or twenty minutes, she gently pushed away, forcing him to withdraw his hand. Smiling, she reached for the zipper on his trousers. "Let me see you," she said.

He might possibly have set a new record for stripping down. Shoes, socks, belt and trousers went sailing across the room, until he was standing before her, naked except for his nipple rings and half a dozen tattoos.

She looked away, and he was pretty sure she blushed. "What should I do next?" she whispered.

Her shyness touched him. He gathered her close once more. "You don't have to do anything," he said. "Just follow my lead."

Scooping her into his arms, he carried her to Mitch's office, to Grif's daybed. He swept a stack of papers from the spread and deposited her there, then leaned over and switched on the desk lamp. Candlelight would be better, but that would come some other time. He hoped there would be many other times for them.

He hooked his thumb under her panties and slid them down her hips. She got the idea and helped him finish taking them off. She reached down to unsnap the garters, but he stopped her. "No, leave them. I like them like that. Sort of a frame." He smiled down on her, savoring the sight, then backed toward the door.

"Where are you going?" She sat up, alarmed.

"I'll be right back."

He grabbed a pack of ribbed condoms from the display by the front counter, then on impulse snagged a feather duster and dusting powder from a shelf. When he returned to the office, she was still sitting up, looking worried.

"Hey, you didn't think I'd leave, did you?" He sat beside her and laid the condoms and dust on the corner of the desk.

"What's that?" She looked at the feather duster.

"Something I thought you'd like." He flicked the tip of the feathers across her nipple and she gasped. He reached for the jar of dust. "Lie back now. Enjoy."

The dust shimmered in the lamplight, like powdered gold. He laid a trail across her breasts, down her torso, between her thighs, then followed with the duster, tickling, teasing. She gasped and writhed, her eyes dark pools, her lips parted.

He trailed the duster to her crotch, and parted the folds, revealing the swollen bud hidden there. As he stroked, she moaned and arched toward him. "Sid!" she cried, anxious.

"Shhh." He lowered his mouth to her breasts, suckling first one, then the other, the nipple rings clicking against his teeth. He substituted his finger for the feathers, rubbing, stroking...

He could sense her reaching, nearing the edge. He lowered his mouth and began to lave and suckle in earnest, tasting her juices as she cried out in release.

He fumbled with the condom packet, ripping the cellophane and throwing it to the floor. She sat up and helped him roll it on, though the first touch of her fingers almost sent him over the edge. For once, he was grateful for the slight dulling of sensation the condom provided, to help him last a little longer.

He knelt between her legs and entered her, groaning as he filled her. Slowly...so slowly...he began to move, long sure strokes, then faster, more forceful ones.

She wrapped her legs around him and dug her nails into his buttocks. He stroked her with his thumb, feeling her tighten around him as she neared a second climax. Closing his eyes, he increased his pace, giving himself up to the heat and pressure and driving sensations.

With a final powerful thrust, he cried her name as the shuddering climax tore through him.

He lay atop her, not wanting to crush her, but craving this closeness. She pulled the covers up over them and smoothed her hand down his arm, idly tracing the outline of his dragon tattoo. "Sid, do you think I'm too repressed?" she whispered.

He tried to choke back his laughter and ended up coughing. She sat up and watching his spasms, her brow furrowed. "What's so funny?"

"You." He reached down and tweaked her nipple ring. "You are definitely not repressed."

"Oh good." She smiled and reached for the feather duster. "I've been thinking…maybe now it's my turn to use this on you."

"SPILL, GIRLFRIEND. YOU ARE going to tell all before this car goes anywhere."

Jill frowned at her best friend, Cassie Walters. "What makes you think I have anything to tell? I just felt like going shopping."

Cassie tapped the steering wheel of her new Saab. "That's not what you said on the phone. You told me we had to make an emergency shopping trip, and that you needed me to help you pick out a killer outfit. What I want to know is why? Who is this outfit supposed to slay?"

Jill worried her lower lip between her teeth. Okay, so maybe she'd been a little panicked on the phone. When Mitch had asked her to be his date to the Chamber of Commerce banquet, she'd had a sudden picture of herself and Mitch, seated at a long table surrounded by Lana Montgomery look-alikes in designer gowns and real diamonds. "I have to find an outfit for a fancy dinner," she said.

"What kind of dinner? A wedding reception? A date with a playboy millionaire?"

"Um…a Chamber of Commerce banquet."

Cassie turned toward her. "The Boulder County Chamber of Commerce Awards Banquet this Saturday night?"

Jill nodded glumly. "Totally not my scene."

Cassie laughed. "Not exactly my scene either, but Guy and I will be there."

"You will?"

She nodded. "He's up for 'Young Entrepreneur of the Year.'"

"Congratulations. His store must be doing really well." Guy Walters owned a large outdoor equipment store in Boulder. He'd fallen for Cassie when she and Jill worked at his favorite coffee shop. He'd pursued her relentlessly until she admitted she was in love with him. The man who'd been Boulder's most eligible bachelor was now a besotted newlywed.

"Stores. He just opened another one at Flatirons Mall."

Make that newlywed millionaire. "That's great. Tell him I said so."

Cassie lowered her sunglasses and looked Jill in the eye. "You're changing the subject here. *Who* asked you to the Chamber banquet?"

"Oh…my boss." *My handsome, aggravating, too-sexy-for-his-own-good boss.*

Cassie made a face. "I thought your boss was some middle-aged playboy."

"Yeah, he was. But he died. This is his nephew, who inherited the store."

"Does this nephew have a name?"

"Mitch. Mitch Landry."

"Ah. Now we're getting somewhere. So tell me about Mitch."

She shrugged. "What's to tell?" *That I can't stop thinking about him? That every time he walks by my nipples salute? That he's obviously trying to drive me crazy?*

"Well...how old is he? What's he look like?"

"He's in his early thirties, I guess. He has brown hair and brown eyes, and he's tall. Of course, everybody's tall to me."

"Brown hair and brown eyes." Cassie shook her head. "That doesn't tell me anything. Is he George Clooney or Groucho Marx? Has he got a butt you'd follow anywhere or a face that would stop a truck? Does he get your motor running or make you run the other way?"

Jill started giggling. "Stop! Stop! Where do you come up with this stuff?"

Cassie had to wait for her own laughter to subside. "Sometimes I'm just inspired. Now come on, confess! Is Mitch Landry a hunk or not?"

Jill blotted her eyes with her fingers. "Definitely a hunk," she said. "And yeah...he gets my motor running all right."

"So have you slept with him yet?"

"Cassie!"

"Well, have you?"

She nodded. "We have." Although there hadn't been any sleeping involved at all.

"Then what's the problem?"

Wasn't that what she'd been trying to figure out? "Mitch and I are good in bed, but otherwise, we're total opposites. He's so conservative and serious." She shook her head. "Mostly I think he doesn't like it when I try to call the shots."

"So stop calling the shots."

She made a face. "Where's the fun in that? Besides, if I wait around on slowpoke Mitch, nothing will ever happen. The man's conscience and his overblown sense of responsibility keep getting in the way."

"So what you need is a dress that will make him forget all about responsibilities?"

"Yeah. But I can't look like a slut or anything. I don't want to embarrass him in front of all those business people."

Cassie started the car and put it in gear. "I'm sure we can find something suitable. By the time we're through, Mitch won't know what hit him."

They headed for Pearl Street and the stores along the pedestrian mall. Jill remembered the shopping expeditions they'd made when Cassie and Guy were first dating—when Jill first discovered Just 4 Play. Back then, Cassie had been the reluctant one, not wanting to get involved with Guy. But he'd persisted, and look how well things had worked out.

Now she was not only working as a massage therapist in Guy's store, she was ski racing in the winters. She'd gained the kind of confidence Jill had always hoped she'd find.

Not that Jill wanted that kind of success with Mitch. She wasn't looking for flowers and lace and happy ever after. Those things were fine for Cassie, but not for someone like her. That kind of life was too ordinary. Too boring.

They headed for the evening gown section of Jessica McClintock. As they flipped through the racks of gowns, Jill rejected one after the other. "Too dowdy."

"Too slutty."

"Makes me look fat."

They trooped to the next store and started over again. "This Mitch guy must be really special, huh?" Cassie said as she rifled through a rack of designer knockoffs. "Are you in love?"

Jill almost dropped the dress she was holding. "Of

course not. How ridiculous. What makes you think I'm in love?'' She shoved the silk sheath she'd been holding back onto the rack. ''I'm only doing this to try to keep my job.''

Cassie frowned. ''You have to sleep with him to keep your job?'' She leaned forward, her voice urgent. ''Jill, he sounds like he ought to be reported!''

''No, it's not like that. Mitch would never… It's just…'' How could she explain? In the cold light of day this whole scheme of hers sounded preposterous, even a little silly. ''Mitch wants to close the store and open a Chinese restaurant,'' she said.

''Oh, no!'' Cassie touched her fingers to her lips. ''But it's such a nice store. And doesn't it make money?''

''It makes tons of money, but that doesn't matter to Mitch.'' She pulled out a gold lamé one-shoulder gown and frowned at it. ''He thinks a restaurant would be more respectable.''

''I suppose it would be.'' Cassie went back to looking at dresses. ''But it wouldn't be nearly as much fun. I still don't see what this has to do with your relationship with him.''

Jill shoved the dress back onto the rack and pulled out a green velvet number. ''Mitch doesn't see the fun side of Just 4 Play. I think he thinks we just sell a bunch of tacky, sleazy stuff. I thought if I could actually show him some of the merchandise…in action, so to speak… he'd rethink shutting us down.''

''Uh-huh. Are you sure this is just about keeping your job?''

She avoided looking at her friend. ''What else would it be about?''

"I don't know. When you talk about Mitch, he sounds like a nice guy. Really decent."

She made a face. "I'd like it if he were a little more *indecent.*"

Cassie smiled. "You know what I mean. He sounds like the kind of man a woman could settle down with."

"I'm not interested in settling down. You know that."

"But why not? I mean, with the right man…"

Jill shook her head. "I don't want to look back in ten years and see all the things I didn't get to do because I tied myself down too young."

Cassie's smile faded. "This is about Jenny, isn't it?"

Jill looked away. "She told me not to make the same mistake she did."

"Jill, you're ten years older than Jenny was when she got married." Cassie's voice was soft, but every word was an arrow to a bull's-eye. "You don't have to worry about putting your life on hold the way she did. You've already done so many things she didn't get to do— you've finished your education, traveled, learned new things."

"Who says I'm ready to stop doing those things?"

"Making a commitment to another person doesn't mean you have to give up any of that. It can mean you have someone to share all those things with."

"Easy for you to say. You married an outdoor adventurer. Mitch is Mr. Conservative. Mr. Responsible." Not that she'd consider marrying him. The attraction she felt for him was purely physical. Nothing more.

"I'm only saying you ought to give Mitch a chance. Has he given you any reason to think he'd stifle you?"

"Only that he's conservative, responsible, worried about what people think…." And he had the ability to make her forget about everything and everyone when he was around. Is that what being in love did to people? Made them lose track of themselves?

Cassie laughed. "Okay. Okay. I get the idea. But it wouldn't hurt you to think about finding *someone* to settle down with. And Mitch seems like as good a candidate as any."

She rolled her eyes. "Don't do this to me, Cassie."

"Do what?"

"Try to 'convert' me. I swear, happily married people are as bad as ex-smokers or recovering alcoholics. They want everyone to see things their way."

Cassie smiled. "Okay, so maybe I am guilty of a little of that. But you're my best friend. I want you to be as happy as I am."

"I'm happy. And I'll be happier when Mitch finally admits that sex can be fun and a store devoted to sexual fun is a great idea."

"Okay. Do you think this dress will do the trick?"

Midnight-blue chiffon fell in tiny pleats from a banded collar, with a keyhole neckline that would show a lot of cleavage, without looking trashy. The soft fabric would drape every curve, and a slit up the side would give a glimpse of leg when she moved.

"Sexy, but classy." She nodded. "It has definite possibilities." With the right accessories, she'd give Mitch an evening he'd never forget.

15

MITCH COULDN'T BELIEVE he was actually *nervous* about
this date with Jill. First of all, it wasn't really a date. It
was a social obligation. A business function. A chance
for him to explain his reasoning about the store and
make her understand that, while he was definitely attracted to her, she wasn't going to change his mind about
what he should do with his future.

So why was he nervous? He glanced in the rearview
mirror and smoothed his hair. Maybe he should have
worn the gray silk tie instead of the navy...

Oh, hell. He sounded like an old woman. *Get out of
the car and get on with this,* he ordered himself.

Jill's apartment was in a converted house near the
university. A Bohemian kind of place where students,
professors, artists, musicians and various free spirits con-
gregated. A sign beneath the apartment number read No
Whining!

Mitch rang the bell and waited. The door across the
hall opened and a white-haired man in a pink paisley
shirt peered out. "If you're one of those evangelist fellows, you don't want to mess with Jill," he said. "The
last one quit the ministry after a half hour with her. Last
I heard, he was working as one of those Chippendale
dancers."

"Um, I'm not an evangelist." He straightened his

jacket and wondered again if he should have gone for the gray tie.

"She's pretty rough with salesmen, too. Keeps 'em talkin' for hours, never buys anything."

"It's all right, Professor Simon. Mitch is my date."

Relieved, Mitch turned to smile at her, but the expression faltered before it reached his lips. Dazed, he had an impression of soft curves draped in some sort of shimmery blue fabric. Her hair was up, revealing the long creamy column of her neck and the soft curve of her bare shoulders. She looked beautiful. Elegant. And sexy enough to make a man forget his own name.

"Date, huh?" Professor Simon grunted. "Not your usual type. Thought he was one of them evangelist fellows."

"Everything's fine, Professor. I promise." She put her hand on Mitch's arm. "Why don't you come inside while I get my wrap."

He followed her inside, eyes focusing on the subtle sway of her hips. The fabric of her dress shifted over her bottom with each step. He fought the urge to reach out and cup her backside. Would it feel as smooth and satiny as it looked?

"Don't mind Professor Simon. He takes a sort of fatherly interest in me—thinks he has to look out for me." She handed him a fringed silk shawl and turned her back to him.

He draped the shawl around her shoulders. From this vantage point, he was looking almost straight down on the oval cutout in the front of her dress, into the deep cleft between her breasts. The hard points of her nipples were just visible beneath the folds of fabric, teasing him with their nearness. He felt himself grow harder, and forced his gaze away.

"What happened with the evangelist?" he asked when she'd turned to face him again.

She laughed. "Oh, that. Well, he was really a very handsome young man. I told him good looks were as much a gift from God as a beautiful voice or a talent for teaching. And that since it was sinful to waste a talent, he really ought to be taking advantage of that great body of his instead of hiding it under an ill-fitting suit."

Mitch could imagine an innocent young man falling under the spell of Jill's unabashed sex appeal. The poor boy probably forgot all about religion as soon as she opened the door. "So he really became a Chippendale's dancer?"

"A very good one, from what I hear."

She locked the door behind them, then walked beside him to the car. The fabric of her dress rustled when she walked, making him think of the sound it would make sliding to the floor.

He opened the passenger door and she slid inside, the dress falling open at midthigh to reveal her smooth, lightly tanned skin. So she wasn't wearing panty hose. What else wasn't she wearing?

He reminded himself he had no intention of finding out as he walked around to the driver's side. The whole point of this evening was to convince her how wrong it would be for them to continue this pretense that anything she could do would change his mind.

"I found out some friends of mine will be attending the banquet tonight."

"Oh, who is that?"

"Cassie and Guy Walters. He owns Mountain Outfitters. He's up for an award."

"You'll have to be sure to introduce me."

"I will. You'll like them both." She smiled. "Actually you could say it's because of them that I got the job at Just 4 Play.''

''How is that?''

''I took Cassie shopping one day not long after she'd started seeing Guy. I'd been in a couple times before, but I guess that was the first day I really saw the possibilities of a place like that to help someone in a relationship. I went back a couple of times by myself to shop and one day I saw the Help Wanted sign in the window and knew that was the job for me.''

''What did you do before that?''

''I was a barrista in a coffee shop.'' She laughed. ''Don't look at me like that.''

Too late, he realized he had been frowning at her.

''I know exactly what you're thinking, and I've heard it before.'' She adjusted the shawl across her shoulders. ''Why is a woman with a college education content to work at so-called menial jobs?''

''I wouldn't have used the words 'menial' but you do seem overqualified for the work you've chosen.''

''That's just it—it's work I've *chosen*. I like working with the public. And I like working an unconventional schedule, and not being forced into some corporate mold.'' She tied the ends of the shawl in a knot under her breasts. ''This way, if I suddenly decide to take off on a six-month trip to the Amazon, it's easy for me to pick up and go.''

Had he ever been that free in his life? He shook his head. Never. He couldn't even imagine. ''What about your family, other obligations?''

''My mom and dad are in the Galápagos this year, studying turtles or something. Jenny was my only sibling. I don't even have a cat.''

"No commitments," he murmured. "Don't you get lonely sometimes?"

She turned slightly toward him, the dress falling open at the knees. "Why should I be lonely? I have friends all over the world."

But there was a difference between having friends and having someone special to share your life with, wasn't there?

"I'm glad Cassie and Guy will be there tonight. I was afraid I wouldn't know anyone and you'd know everyone."

"Actually I don't know very many people who will be here." Mort, of course. Maybe Archie. A few others, familiar to him from various small business seminars or open houses held in the area.

"But I thought these were your friends."

He shook his head. "No. Acquaintances. Not friends." Strange, a few weeks ago he wouldn't have made the distinction. He would have seen the people at tonight's banquet as important contacts, people who could help him get ahead. People he wanted to have as friends.

Now the harsh words in the Chamber of Commerce's rejection letter to Uncle Grif left a bitter taste in his mouth. He no longer saw those business and society people as so important.

Jill reached out and squeezed his arm. "I'm sure we'll have a wonderful time tonight," she said. "In fact, I'm making it my personal mission to see that you enjoy yourself. After all, who knows when we'll have a night like this again?"

"I CAN'T BELIEVE I LET YOU talk me into doing this again." Sid bypassed the alarm, then shut and locked the door behind him and Lana.

She smiled and squeezed his arm. "Don't tell me you didn't enjoy last time."

Heat spread up the back of his neck as he remembered the last time. "You know better than that. But what's wrong with my apartment?"

"You have a roommate, remember?"

"We could always ask him to leave. He'd be cool about it. Or what's wrong with your place?"

"My place is so boring." She smiled and looked around them. "It's a shame Mitch is going to shut this place down."

"You didn't think that the first time you were here."

"I guess I changed my mind." She gave him a smoldering look. "About a lot of things."

He reached for her, but she moved away. "I was thinking tonight we might try on a couple of the costumes."

Frowning, he followed her over to the costume rack. It's not that he didn't enjoy being here with Lana, or being anywhere with her, for that matter. But how much of their sudden relationship had to do with him, and how much with the shop?

She selected the French maid costume and held it against her. "How do you think I'd look in this?"

"You know I think you'd look great in anything. In fact, I think what you've got on right now is pretty hot." He moved closer and pulled her into his arms. What she had on was a conservative black suit with a tight, straight skirt, a long jacket and a starched white shirt underneath. Ever since he'd picked her up this evening, he'd been thinking about peeling off that prim and proper outer layer to reveal the wild woman hidden underneath.

"Mmm. I'm glad you're wearing your leathers tonight." She nuzzled against the lapel of his jacket. "I think they're very sexy."

"Uh-huh." He kissed the top of her head, inhaling the vanilla scent of her perfume. "I still think we ought to get out of here and go someplace more private. What if someone comes in and we get caught?"

"The store's closed, isn't it? And Mitch isn't likely to show up. He's at the Chamber of Commerce banquet."

Sid frowned. He was sure he hadn't mentioned Mitch's plans to Lana. "How do you know that?"

"My father told me." She began kissing his throat. "I think he wants me and Mitch to get back together."

Sid stiffened. "Have you told him about me?"

"No. It's none of his business." She grinned up at him. "You're my little secret. Or maybe I should say, my big secret."

She tried to cuddle closer, but he gently pushed her away. "Lana, don't you think you're going to have to tell your family about me if we keep seeing each other?"

"One day, sure. But not right now. I'm tired of them interfering in my life."

He frowned. "Are you sure you're not just ashamed of me?"

Her eyes widened. "No! Sid, why would you say that?"

He crossed his arms over his chest and looked at her. "I'm not stupid. I know I'm not exactly the kind of guy a woman takes home to Mr. and Mrs. Establishment."

"I'm a grown woman. If I want to date someone, I will. And it won't matter to me what my parents or anyone else thinks."

He shook his head. "I think you mean that, but I'm not so sure you can."

She put the costume back on the rack and came over to him. "Sid, what is this about?"

He studied the toes of his boots. "I think...I care a lot more about you than any woman in a long time. Maybe more than I should. I just want to know what I'm getting into here."

He was startled to hear a sound like laughter. When she looked up, she was smiling and shaking her head. "Poor Sid. Don't you know you can't be practical or plan ahead when it comes to matters of the heart?" She stood on tiptoe and slipped her arms around his neck. "I felt something special the first time I saw you. It wasn't logical or reasonable. It scared me, but I couldn't ignore it. I didn't dare."

"But was it me that made you feel that way, or...or the leather and jewelry and wild hair...and the fact that I work at a place like Just 4 Play?"

She looked into his eyes. "As crazy as it sounds, I really think it was you. Something in you stirred up something in me." She pulled his head down to hers and kissed him, a long, slow, sweet kiss that made his heart pound and his head spin.

When they parted again, he smoothed his hands down her back. "So, you think we could make it in spite of our differences?"

"I don't know anything for sure. Except that you worry too much." She smiled. "Let's take it one day at a time and see where things lead." She pressed close against him. "Now do you want to be the carpenter tonight, or my Roman slave?"

SHORTLY AFTER THEY ARRIVED at the banquet hall, Jill retreated to the ladies' room to touch up her makeup. Mostly she wanted a chance to collect herself. She would

need all her wits about her if this evening was going to
turn out the way she wanted it to.

Just when she thought she knew Mitch, he surprised
her again. Take tonight, for instance. She figured he'd
be raring to go out there and mix and mingle, to make
a good impression on all the movers and shakers in the
Boulder business world. Instead, he'd seemed nervous,
reluctant to even be here. As if he was afraid they
wouldn't like him.

Or maybe that he wouldn't like them.

She pulled out her lipstick and touched it up. Ravish-
ing Red. She'd read a study once that said that men
instinctively saw red lips as a sign of sexual arousal. As
if she wasn't already sending out half a dozen other un-
conscious signals. The truth was, she'd been hot and
bothered all afternoon, thinking about tonight.

She could tell by the way Mitch looked at her when
he thought she wasn't paying attention that he liked the
dress. That he liked her in it. Now if she could only
convince him that he'd like her more out of it.

The door swung open and Cassie walked in. "There
you are. I've been looking all over. What are you doing
hiding in here?"

"I'm not hiding. I needed to freshen up."

Cassie took a step back and let out a wolf whistle.
"You do look hot in that dress, girlfriend."

She smiled. "I feel hot. Did you see Mitch?"

"I did indeed. He's the one who told me you were in
here."

She watched Cassie's face in the mirror. "And, what
do you think?"

"I think you need your head examined if you let this
one get away."

She straightened and smoothed the dress over her

hips. "I think I'm using the right bait to reel him in tonight." She dropped the lipstick back into her purse. "Are you and Guy sitting at our table?"

"We weren't, but I switched place cards with some old man. I don't think he was too happy about it. Mitch seemed pleased, though."

"He probably took one look at you and forgot all about me." She shook her finger at her friend. "You'd better watch out, or I'll tell Guy."

"I'm sure Guy is worried." Cassie leaned toward the mirror and smoothed her hair. "I might as well be invisible, seated at a table with you and that dress. We'll be lucky if we're not mobbed by your many admirers."

"Better have some more wine. It's going to your head."

Still laughing together, the two friends joined Guy and Mitch at a table for six near the back of the room. The third couple introduced themselves as Barbara and Ben Berman. "Berman plumbing and hardware," Ben said, offering a card. "My specialty is low-flow toilets that really work."

"I guess that's pretty important." Jill managed to keep a straight face and slipped the card into her evening bag.

When she sat down next to him, Mitch leaned over to whisper in her ear. "Only three more hours of this. Aren't you glad you came?"

She choked off a giggle. "I'll do my best to keep you awake."

A troop of waiters dispensed salads to each table. Maggie Berman prodded hers with a fork. "What is this supposed to be?" she asked, holding up a dark green frill.

"It's arugula," Cassie said.

"Hmmph." Mrs. Berman dropped the offending morsel. "Looks like ditch weeds to me."

Halfway through this first course, Mr. Berman began a long story about installing plumbing at the state penitentiary. Jill slipped off her shoes and nudged Mitch's ankle with her toe.

His fork stilled halfway between his plate and his mouth. She watched him out of the corner of her eye, a faint smile on her lips. She began to stroke his calf, up and down, slowly. Sensuously.

He leaned over and whispered in her ear, "What do you think you're doing?"

"You looked a little uptight. I thought I'd help you relax."

"I don't need your help, thank you." He moved his chair over, just out of her reach.

Dinner arrived under a metal cover—chicken breast on a bed of rice, covered by a sunshine-yellow sauce, with a side of zucchini and carrots. "Hope you're hungry," Mitch said.

"Not for food." But she spoke only loud enough for him to hear.

She knew he had heard because he looked at her more closely. She picked up her fork and pretended great interest in her dinner.

Halfway through this second course, she noticed an older man at another table staring at them. "Mitch, who is that?" she asked, nodding toward the man.

He ducked his head, frowning. "That's Mort Montgomery. President of Guarantee National Bank."

"Is he related to Lana Montgomery?"

"He's her father."

She regarded the old man again. She supposed there was a faint resemblance around the nose and eyes, though Lana must get most of her good looks from her mother. "Is that why he keeps staring over here? Is he mad at you because you and Lana split up?"

"I don't think so. I think he's pissed off because he was supposed to be sitting here and Cassie switched the place cards."

She laughed. "Maybe you can speak to him later and apologize."

He shrugged. "I'm just as glad he's not sitting here. He gets on my nerves."

"Oh? Why is that?"

He glanced toward Mort, who had turned back around and was eating. Then he moved his chair closer to hers again. "He seems to think that because his bank is loaning me the money for the restaurant remodel, he can tell me what to do."

"One more reason not to remodel." She leaned back to allow the waiter to take her plate.

Mitch shook his head. "You never give up, do you?"

"Never." She met his gaze and held it. "I always get what I want...eventually."

"That's something we need to talk about—"

"Ladies and gentlemen. If I may have your attention, we'll get started with tonight's program."

The others at the table turned their chairs to face the dais at the front of the room. Waiters delivered dessert: chocolate-dipped strawberries.

Jill soon lost interest in the speakers and focused her attention on the strawberries, her absolute favorite dessert. They made the whole boring dinner worthwhile.

MITCH TRIED TO PAY attention to the banquet speaker, who was outlining plans for economic development for the coming year. Certainly this would have some bearing on Mitch's own success. He'd be wise to pay attention.

Except that Jill was sitting beside him, infinitely more interesting than the speaker. He glanced at her during a lull while the speaker shuffled through his notes and watched, mesmerized, as she selected a strawberry from the plate in front of her and began to lick off the chocolate coating.

Her tongue darted out to encircle the narrow end of the berry, then flattened to smooth over the sides. She worked quickly, daintily, finally sucking off the last bit of chocolate before popping the naked berry into her mouth.

He let out the breath he'd been holding and grabbed for his glass of water. "Mitch, are you okay?" She leaned toward him, concerned. Unfortunately this provided him with a stunning view of her cleavage. "I'm fine," he croaked, and drank more water.

"Here. Have a strawberry." She selected a berry from the dish and held it out to him. He tried to take it from her fingers, but she pressed it against his mouth. "Go ahead. Take a bite."

He bit, sweet juice spurting out and running down his mouth. She captured the drips with her fingers, and licked them off, sliding the full length of each finger into her mouth and withdrawing it slowly. "Good, isn't it?" she murmured.

Mitch looked longingly at his now empty water glass. Not that that had been doing much to cool him off anyway.

"Here. Finish your berry." She held the half-eaten fruit to his mouth again and he accepted it. But along with the berry, he captured the tips of her fingers. She giggled as his tongue brushed against her and her eyes darkened with arousal.

The speaker finished and announced the time had come to hand out awards. The Bermans declared that they were leaving. Mr. Berman solemnly shook hands all around and passed out more business cards.

Jill scooted her chair closer to Mitch, until her thigh was almost touching his under the table. "I want to see the podium when Guy goes up to get his award," she explained.

He nodded, aware of the warm length of her so close to him. She reached past him for creamer for her coffee and her breast brushed his arm. He was pretty sure she wasn't wearing a bra.

Guy was announced as Young Entrepreneur of the Year. He went up to accept the award, taking Cassie with him and leaving them alone.

Jill reached over and began stroking his thigh, her finger tracing the seam of his pants up the outside, then around to the inside. Up…up.

He grabbed her hand before she reached his crotch. Already his erection strained against his zipper. No telling what would happen if she touched him there.

She smiled, and obligingly moved their now-entwined hands away, this time to her own thigh, guiding him along the path of her slit skirt, up, up, to her hip, to her waist. Her skin was cool and silky against his fingertips.

She leaned over to whisper in his ear, "I'm not wearing any underwear."

He swallowed. "I noticed."

"Panty lines would ruin this dress, don't you think?"

He tried to pull away, but she held him fast, this time bringing his hand down, around her thigh to her crotch.

She was warm and wet and naked. Very naked. Shaved. The image this conjured raised his temperature another notch.

"Jill, you've got to stop this!" he hissed.

She looked at him with a challenge in her eyes. "Why?"

"Because it's crazy!" She was driving him crazy. If she kept this up, he'd be tempted to dive under the table with her, business community be damned.

She smiled. "You exaggerate. But to my way of thinking, even one reason why it's a good idea is enough to make it worthwhile."

He looked her in the eye and lowered his voice. "I don't intend for anything…physical to happen tonight. I invited you here so that we could talk and get to know each other better without sex getting in the way."

She released his hand and rearranged her shawl over her arms. "I know you're not really against sex, Mitch. You're just afraid to let yourself go. Afraid of what might happen if you put your own thoughts and feelings and desires first for a change."

Her words startled him. Was she right? Was all his talk of propriety and common sense merely a smoke screen to hide his fear? But what was he afraid of?

He looked around them, at the tables full of bored businessmen and women in their fancy clothes. Once upon a time his goal in life had been to impress people like them. To make them accept him into their ranks. To earn their respect for himself and Meg.

But now he realized that respect was worthless. Whatever they said to his face, it wouldn't change how they felt about him in their hearts. He would always be "that Landry boy" from the wrong side of town. Grif Landry's nephew who inherited the sex toy shop. For years after his restaurant opened, the old guard would probably still refer to it as "the Chinese place where the sex shop used to be."

He glanced at Jill. She was sipping her coffee and listening to Guy thank half a dozen people who had helped him to win this award. She looked like royalty, sitting there. Above them all. Maybe because she didn't care what anyone thought of her. He envied her that courage. Had her sister taught her that, or did she come by it naturally?

He shoved back his chair and stood. She looked up at him. "Where are you going?"

"I need to get out of here. Get some fresh air."

"All right." She stood and gathered up her purse."

"No, you stay." He lowered his voice, aware of the censorious looks from those around them. "Stay with Cassie and Guy."

"No, I'm coming with you."

16

SHE STOPPED HIM IN THE HALL outside the ladies' room. "Do you mind waiting while I go in here?"

He cocked one eyebrow. "Afraid I'll run away?"

"You might try." She trailed her finger along his lapel. "But I'd catch you."

He chuckled and shook his head. "I'll wait for you."

He leaned against the wall and thought about Jill. When had a woman ever made him laugh so much? Or made him want her so much? What was really happening between them? She said she didn't want commitments and he couldn't afford to give her any.

But she was lying. What woman—what person—didn't want a lasting connection to another person? Without that connection there was always a void to fill. Look at his mother. Though there had been subtle signs of her illness for years, it wasn't until after his father's death that she became unable to cope. She'd lost her connection to the man she loved, and eventually to the world.

Not everyone reacted so drastically, but still, it proved how much people needed to belong. He needed it. Jill needed it. They'd both find it one day, with someone else.

The thought hurt deep in his chest. Jill had shown him so much passion and given herself so generously, but knowing it couldn't last made him feel empty inside. If only his life weren't so complicated right now...

"Mitch! I've been looking all over for you. We need to talk."

He looked up and saw Mort Montgomery striding toward him.

He straightened, forcing a smile he didn't feel. "Mort. How are the awards going?"

"Long as usual." Mort pulled out a handkerchief and blew his nose. "Why some people think they have to thank everyone from their mother to the janitor, I'll never know." He shoved the handkerchief back in his pocket. "Listen, we were supposed to sit together tonight and then some woman had the nerve to change the seating cards. Not a friend of yours, I hope?"

He looked down at his shoes and made a noncommittal noise.

"She was probably a friend of that plumber, Berman," Mort continued. "Annoying man. Very lower-class. I can't believe they let someone like that in, but apparently someone on the board owed him a favor."

Mitch glanced toward the ladies' room door. What was taking Jill so long?

"I've been thinking about the grand opening for Ping's Peking Palace," Mort continued. "What would you think of hiring Chinese acrobats from the circus to perform in the center of the restaurant? We could bill it as a real cultural activity. It would get us a lot of attention."

Mitch shoved his hands into his pants pockets. "I haven't thought much about the opening yet. Remodeling hasn't even started."

"You've got to think ahead, boy. The key to success is making a grand statement. Don't settle for what the other guys are doing. I'm also thinking Chinese dancers. Pretty girls. You know what they say, sex sells.'' He elbowed Mitch sharply in the ribs. ''And you'd know about that, wouldn't you?''

''Look, Mort, I appreciate your…your enthusiasm. But I want a more…a more *dignified* image for the restaurant. Something elegant. Not circus acrobats and exotic dancers.''

''No, no, no. If people want elegant, they'll go eat French food. Or steak. With Chinese food, they want fun. Entertainment. Eighty choices on the menu, chopsticks, food they can't recognize or pronounce.'' Mort tapped his chest. ''You leave it to me. I know about these things.''

''And I know what I want in my restaurant.'' He straightened and folded his arms across his chest. ''I didn't ask for your input, Mort, and I don't want it.''

''Well.'' Mort took a step back. ''Are you forgetting where the money is coming from to pay for this pipe dream of yours?''

''It's coming from the bank. A legitimate business loan.''

''I got you that loan. They wouldn't have looked twice at somebody with no real background, no family name, no Ivy League education. I did it as a favor to Lana. I can see now she was smart in dumping you.''

''Goodbye, Mort.'' Jill or no Jill, he had to leave. If he stood here one minute longer, he was going to say something, or do something he knew he'd regret.

At that moment, she emerged from the ladies' room, her eyes glowing with some private mirth. She nodded to Mort, who stared at her, mouth opened, then slipped her arm into the crook of Mitch's elbow. ''Come on, darling," she said. "Let's leave this boring place with all these boring people."

She waited until they were in the parking lot before she burst out laughing. He joined her, tension draining from him. "I'll bet he's still standing back there with his mouth hanging open," Mitch said. He squeezed her hands. "You showed up at exactly the right time. I was on the verge of decking him."

"I was standing in the foyer, listening, trying to decide if I should interrupt or not." She made a face. "He's not a very nice person, is he?"

He shook his head and unlocked the car door. "I think he saw me as a puppet he could manipulate. And I guess for a while at least, I let him get away with it." He frowned and looked back toward the banquet hall. "I thought he and others like him could get me to where I wanted to be, so it didn't matter if I didn't particularly like them or their methods."

She came around the car and took his arm. "Let's not go yet," she said. "You wanted fresh air. Let's go for a walk."

"All right." A walk might be just what he needed. Fresh air and a chance to put some physical distance between himself and Jill. If he stayed with her in close quarters much longer, no telling what he might do.

THE PARK WAS ONE OF MANY such green spaces dotted throughout the city. A shaded cinder path wound alongside Boulder Creek, interspersed with marble benches and picnic tables. They passed a ball field, the vapor lights casting a pink glow over the empty base paths and pitcher's mound. They came to a bridge over a waterfall and crossed over to a small island.

The night air was cool, but not uncomfortably so. Jill

drew her shawl more tightly about her shoulders and reached for Mitch's hand. He hadn't said a word since they'd left the parking lot. She knew his mind was still back at the banquet, perhaps rehearsing things he wished he'd said. Or things he wished he hadn't said.

"What will happen now?" she asked. "Will you lose the money for the restaurant?"

He shook his head. "It's a legitimate loan and it's been approved. I don't think they can pull it."

She heard the doubt in his voice.

"It's going to be a struggle to do things the way I want now. Mort's going to be after me every step of the way."

"But it will be worth it to have things the way you want," she said.

He glanced at her. "I'm surprised you're not telling me to give up on the restaurant."

They came to a bench by the side of the path. By silent agreement, they sat down. "You already know what I think," she said. "I'm just trying to be agreeable."

He laughed. "When were you ever agreeable?"

"Oh, I can be." She slid her arm around his neck and kissed him. Tenderly. A kiss meant to comfort as much as to arouse.

He responded, his arms encircling her, his mouth opening to taste her more fully. She slid into his lap, her breasts flattened against his chest, the sensitive tips aching with need. His erection strained between them. "You want me, Mitch. Why not admit it?"

"I never said I didn't want you." He looked at her, his eyes dark, and so serious. "But where exactly are we going with this…relationship?"

"Why do we have to go anywhere? We're two people

interested in pleasing each other and having a good time.''

"I'm not sure looking at it that way is such a good idea.''

"I think it's a very good idea." She tried to kiss him again, but he pushed her away.

"No, Jill. I mean it. There's no sense continuing what we both know won't lead to anything.''

Why does it have to lead to anything? She stood. All right. If he was going to be stubborn about it, she had a plan B. "You're right," she said. "Why should we do this to ourselves?'' She handed him her purse. "Would you hold this a minute?''

He accepted the purse and she reached down and slipped off one shoe.

"What are you doing?'' he asked.

She handed him the shoe, then the other. "I don't intend to be frustrated one minute longer." Then she started walking down the path, toward a grove of trees in the center of the island. "Catch me if you can, Mitch,'' she called over her shoulder. "I promise I'll make it worth your while.''

MITCH STARED AFTER HER, still cradling her shoes and purse. Was she going off the deep end? Crazy even?

He thought of his mother's first breakdown after his father's death. She'd taken off all her clothes and run screaming into the street. A terrified Mitch, only seventeen at the time, had run after her. It had taken him and two paramedics to subdue her.

But no, there was nothing manic about Jill's behavior. In fact, she was almost too casual. Deliberate.

He followed her down the path. A dozen yards farther

on, he came upon the shawl, in a heap in the middle of the path.

He picked it up. Some distance ahead in the darkness, he thought he heard her laugh. He set off again, faster now. He almost wasn't surprised when he spotted the dress, a dark blue puddle on the gravel. He added it to his collection and hurried on.

The path disappeared into the trees. When he emerged on the other side, he found her, seated on a marble bench in front of a cluster of bushes. She was naked except for a single strand of pearls between her breasts.

His steps slowed, then stopped.

The moon shown like a spotlight on her ivory skin, shadowing the valley between her full breasts, highlighting the dusky nipples. His gaze dropped and he saw that he'd been right before—she was shaved completely naked, her every secret exposed.

She stood and started toward him, the pearls swaying gently. He dropped the armful of clothing and stood still, waiting.

When she reached him, he gathered her into his arms. "Mitch, your heart is pounding."

"You frightened me, running away like that." He buried his nose in her hair, savoring her sweetness, fighting for composure. "I thought…" He shook his head. "It doesn't matter what I thought." He raised his head and smiled down at her. "You won't stop at anything to get what you want, will you?"

"Only because I want you."

What man could hear those words and not be undone? She loosened the knot on his tie and he helped her remove it, and the rest of his clothes, until he was standing naked before her.

She stroked his erection, sending a tremor through

him. Some part of him whispered that he could still stop her, but he was through lying to himself. "I want you, too," he whispered, and kissed the tender skin beneath her jaw.

She led him to the bench and pushed him down, then she straddled him. She was wet, and hot, and smelled of jasmine and sex. "What is that perfume you always wear?" he asked.

"Oriental Love Potion."

He fingered the pearls. "Do we sell it at the store?"

"Oh, yes. And lots of other wonderful things." She shifted in his lap, each movement bringing them closer together, closer to the edge.

She bent her head and began to kiss his nipples, first one, then the other, her tongue licking and teasing, first sucking, then bathing them with her hot breath. He tried to move away, to slow things down a little, but she clamped her thighs tightly around him, trapping him.

The pearls hung down, tickling him, and her hair, coming loose from its pins, trailed across his neck. He closed his eyes, telling himself he would sit back and enjoy. Everything would be fine.

A faint noise in the stillness startled him. He opened his eyes again and straightened. "Do you think it's safe here? Maybe we ought to go back to my car, to my apartment."

"It's a public place. Someone could come along any minute." She smiled at him. "That adds to the excitement, don't you think?"

"Then we'd better hurry." He smiled weakly. "I don't know how much more excitement I can stand."

She shifted, so that she was sitting sideways in his lap. "First, I want to show you something useful. Do you know what the G-spot is?"

"I've heard of it. I thought it was a myth."

She smiled. "Oh, no. It's very real. If you stimulate a woman's G-spot, you can give her the most incredible orgasm."

She leaned back, then took his fingers and guided them inside her. "It's a concentration of nerve endings two to three inches inside, toward the front. Stroke it gently."

He knew he'd found the right spot when she gasped. "Y…yes. That's it. *Ohhhhh.*"

He bent and suckled her nipples, raising his head from time to time to watch her. A warm flush spread up from her breasts. Her lips were swollen, parted, her eyes closed. She trembled and he sensed she was very close to her release. A wave of incredible tenderness swept over him. He loved that he could make her feel this way.

The crunch of gravel sent his whole body on alert. Then voices drifted to them, just on the other side of the path.

He grabbed Jill by the shoulders and shook her. "Someone's here," he hissed.

She looked at him, dazed. He shoved her toward the bushes behind them, then hurried to gather up their clothes and dove in after her.

On his knees, he peered through the bushes and watched a couple take their place on the bench. Jill knelt beside him. "My shoes!" she whispered.

She pointed toward one end of the bench. Her shoes lay there on their sides. "Maybe they won't see them," he said.

"Maybe not."

The couple began to kiss, the man's hand sliding under the woman's shirt to cup her breast. Mitch felt his cock jerk in response. Jill eased him back. "We might

as well make ourselves comfortable," she said. Her
tongue grazed the edge of his earlobe, sending a shiver
through him that had nothing to do with the cold.

He lay down on the shawl and she nestled alongside
him. It wasn't as close as he wanted to be to her, but it
was as close as they could get.

On the bench, the woman began unbuttoning the
man's shirt. "I feel like a voyeur," he whispered.

"Then close your eyes and don't look." She kissed
each eyelid shut, then skirted his mouth and began kissing her way down his throat, to his chest.

"What are you doing?"

He tried to stop her, but she shook him off. "I'm
distracting you."

She kissed his nipples, then trailed a path to his navel,
across his stomach, down to his cock. She licked the
head, teasing it, then smoothed her tongue along the
shaft. He thought of the strawberry, so expertly denuded
by her tongue. He clamped his teeth together, strangling
a groan. On the other side of the bushes, the woman
giggled, then her laughter became a low sigh.

Jill leaned away from him, reaching for her purse.

"What are you doing?"

"I brought some condoms." She pulled out a packet
and tore it open with her teeth. The condom looked like
a bright red balloon.

"It's red."

"Part of our Neon Nights collection." She began un-
rolling it over him.

"That looks ridiculous."

She giggled. "Yes, well, the male anatomy certainly
proves the creator had a sense of humor."

He bit his tongue to keep from laughing out loud. He
couldn't remember ever laughing during sex. Sex was

serious business. But not to Jill. With her it was…dare he say it? Fun.

His laughter faded as she slid over him. She tightened around him, then withdrew. Her strokes were long and sure, building in intensity. He closed his eyes and surrendered to the sensations. He brought his hands up to caress her buttocks, her breasts. The pearls swung between them, swaying with their rhythm.

Jill rode him hard, never letting up. He dug his heels into the ground, and groaned as spiraling waves of release washed over him. He told himself to stay in control, to wait for her, but he'd been to the edge already too many times tonight. As he finally went over, in his mind he screamed her name, though in reality it emerged a whisper. "Jill." He drew her close, savoring the sensation of her body beside his. "You are amazing," he gasped after a while.

He felt her smile against his chest. "I could say the same about you."

"Are Romeo and Juliet still out there?"

She raised up on one elbow to look out. "Still there. Looks like they could be there a while."

He closed his eyes. "Then I guess we're stuck here for a while."

"Then we might as well make good use of the time." She slid down his body once more, her skin warm and satiny against him.

He opened his eyes wide when he felt her tongue on him once more. "What do you think you're doing?" he growled.

Her laughter was muffled. "What does it feel like I'm doing?"

"No, Jill, I don't think—" But his body obviously had a different opinion. When he raised up on his elbows to look at her, he realized he was hard all over again. "I don't believe this," he said, looking down at himself.

She smiled and reached for her purse. "I have another condom."

"Another red one?"

"Green this time."

"Great. I'll look like an alien."

"I've always wanted to make love to an alien."

"You'll have to settle for me."

"Even better."

"Wait." He stopped her as she started to unroll the green condom. "Come up here for a minute." He patted the ground beside him.

She lay beside him with her head on his shoulder. He smoothed his hand along her shoulder, down the dip of her waist, across the curve of her hip. He wanted to fix this moment in his mind, this sensation of being so close to her.

They kissed, the long slow caress of lovers who have all the time in the world. The frantic urgency of their earlier lovemaking was gone, replaced by this sweet languor. He traced the bow of her mouth with his tongue, then trailed a path down her throat, pausing to feel her pulse throbbing against his mouth in a rhythm that matched his own heartbeat.

Behind him, he could hear the other couple, the rustling of their clothing, the low muffled moans that spoke of their own lovemaking. The sounds fueled his own desire. "Lie back," he urged Jill, pressing his palm against her stomach. "Let me enjoy all of you."

She lay back, eyes open, watching him. He stroked her breasts, first with his fingers, then with his tongue. He started slowly, intending only to tease a little, but her response urged him for more. As he licked and suckled, she squirmed beneath him, and bit her knuckle to keep from crying out. He'd never known a woman who was so incredibly responsive, or one so aware of her own body.

He moved down, trailing his tongue across her belly, to the juncture of her thighs. She was smooth and soft, totally naked, the sensation kicking his arousal up another notch. He traced his tongue along her sex, tasting the saltiness of their previous coupling.

He flicked his tongue across her, smiling at the way she arched toward him, offering herself. Then he began to lave her in earnest, caressing the tender flesh, his head turned to watch her reaction.

She was beautiful, in this as in everything else. Head back, eyes closed, hair in a wild tangle around her shoulders, she gave herself up to the moment, her body poised, anticipating ecstasy. He slid two fingers into her, wanting to feel the moment she came.

She let out a muffled cry as her climax rocked through her. He buried his face against her thigh, his arms around her, holding her as she shook. Then she was tugging at his hair, her voice a harsh whisper. "Hurry," she said. "I want you in me."

He fumbled with the condom, cursing the person who had designed the packaging. Finally he ripped the plastic with his teeth and rolled on the bright green bit of latex. "I do look like an alien," he muttered.

"No. The Jolly Green Giant." Jill's eyes sparkled with laughter and more than a little appreciation for his green-clad member.

"Fee, fie, foe, fum. Look out, Jilly, here I come."

She was laughing when he slid into her wet heat, but her laughter soon changed to low cries as they moved in rhythm. He reached down to stroke her, coaxing her to move with him to another climax.

Again, he kept his eyes open, watching her. He could never get enough of watching her. He'd never known a woman who was so open, so willing to share of herself, to let him really see her in these moments of lovemaking. Jill didn't hide behind soft lights and dark rooms, or turn her face away from him. She was willing for him to see everything as passion overtook her.

His vision blurred as his climax surged through him, stealing breath and thought. Jill followed him, arching beneath him, her fingers digging into his back.

They lay together afterward, their bodies entwined, unmoving, unspeaking. Her uninhibitedness moved him. He didn't delude himself that he was the first. She'd made no secret of her experience with men. And he had had his share of women. But none like Jill. None so reckless and open. None who made him feel more of a man, more of a person, apart from family situation or business prowess or social standing. When Jill looked at him, he felt she really saw *him*. She had stripped him naked physically and emotionally. Being with her filled him with elation and scared him to death.

17

JILL WOKE THE NEXT MORNING, wondering if the previous night had been a dream. Had Mr. Conservative Mitch Landry really made her scream like that? Had they really gone through not two, but *three* condoms, including the Super Stud, which she'd only brought to show him the wide variety the store had to offer?

She closed her eyes and fell back on her pillow again. And had he really been so sweet and tender afterwards, helping her dress and then later, kissing her so sweetly at her door, refusing her suggestion that he come inside and never leave?

She felt like crying, just remembering. He had been such a *gentleman.* Sweet and caring as if…as if he really loved her.

She sat up again, heart pounding. What was happening to her? Of course Mitch Landry wasn't in love with her. In lust…but not in love. And why was she making such a big deal out of it? It wasn't as if she hadn't had great sex before. She smiled. Maybe not that great. With Mitch, it was always…different. Less about her own pleasure and more about pleasing him. He was always so busy worrying about other people—his sister, Grif, even her and Sid. She'd wanted to give him some moments solely for himself.

But then he always turned the tables and did so much for *her.* She glanced at her bedside clock. Less than eight hours since she'd seen him last and already she missed him. Not only the sex, but *him*. She missed his great smile, and the way he talked so formally when he was nervous, the way his mouth said he didn't approve of something she was doing, while his eyes told her he did.

She buried her face in her hands. "What have I gotten myself into now?" She was *not* going to fall in love with Mitch Landry. The idea of spending the rest of her life tied to one man was ridiculous. Especially a man like Mitch, who could be so infuriating.

She threw back the covers and headed for the bathroom. "Some women are the marrying type, but I'm not one of them," she said. "I don't mind hanging out with Mitch for a while, but he has got to understand that I'm not interested in anything permanent."

She stripped off her nightgown and turned on the shower. As she reached for a clean towel, she caught a glimpse of herself in the mirror, a dreamy expression in her eyes, her lips still swollen from Mitch's kisses. *Liar* the image said to her. She closed her eyes and stifled a sob. *Oh, girl, you have messed things up this time. What are you going to do?*

"JILL, WHAT AM I GOING TO do about you…about *us?*" Mitch was confident no one could hear him in the empty store. Just 4 Play was closed on Sundays and he'd come here with the excuse that he needed to work.

Really, he'd come here because it was the closest he could get to being near Jill without actually going to her apartment. He didn't dare do that. If he went there, he'd have to stay. And then he'd never want to leave.

But coming here hadn't been such a great idea, either. Everywhere he looked, something reminded him of her, or of their wild lovemaking here, at the cemetery and last night in the park. The belly dancer's costume she'd worn the day they met shimmered on a mannequin in the front window. The Neon Nights condoms were on a special sale rack by the front counter.

He stopped in the "notions and lotions" department and searched the shelves, then pulled down a bottle of Oriental Love Potion body oil. Closing his eyes, he inhaled deeply the jasmine-and-sex scent that was Jill.

"Get a grip, Mitch," he said out loud, and shoved the bottle of oil back onto the shelf. Last night especially had been awesome—the stuff of fantasy. But that was the whole point. Passion like that couldn't last in the practical, everyday world. Jill had said as much herself when she'd made it plain she wasn't interested in long-term commitment.

Even if it were possible for them to stay together— and that was a big *if*—he wasn't in any position to offer a woman permanence. If and when the restaurant got off the ground, he couldn't guarantee it would be a success. And he still had Meg's medical school tuition to pay for. It might be years before he could afford to get married and settle down.

He shook his head. No, he might as well stop thinking about Jill and get to work. The future depended on work, and it was something he was good at. Something he could control, unlike his mixed-up feelings for Jill.

He collected the Saturday mail from the basket under the counter and went into his office. Uncle Grif's smiley-faced daybed cover was crooked again, some of the smiles twisted into grimaces. He thought of the times he had lain there with Jill. She was a woman who could make even smiley faces seem erotic.

He pushed the thought away and tried to focus on work. He sat at his desk and opened the first envelope, the monthly bill from the security company. He supposed he'd have to let them know about the upcoming remodeling. They'd probably want to move some of the security sensors, or set them differently.

He scanned the bill, then turned to the attached report. It was a record of things like false alarms, number of times the system had reset itself, power outages and things like that. Mostly it was rows of zeroes. Which made the five in the column labeled "silent intruder" stand out. On five different evenings in the past two weeks, a "silent intruder" was recorded.

He picked up the phone and dialed the alarm company. "This is Mitch Landry at Just 4 Play. I'm looking at my monthly report and don't understand what a 'silent intruder' is."

"A silent intruder is when the motion sensors detect movement, but the alarm itself never goes off."

"You mean, the alarm is disarmed."

"No, it's still armed, but the movement detected never triggers an actual alarm."

He glanced up at the light box in the far corner of the room. Every room had a similar sensor, which glowed red with the alarm was armed, and green during the day when the alarm was shut off. "What would cause a silent intruder warning?"

"Have you noticed anything missing, sir? Any merchandise or money?"

He wasn't sure. He'd have to ask Sid, but the manager certainly hadn't said anything about any thefts or losses. "I don't think there's anything missing."

"Then it's either a malfunction or an animal."

"An animal?"

"A mouse. Or a squirrel. Sometimes they get into places looking for food. But they're not large enough to set off the alarm. If I were you, I'd put out a few traps, see what shows up.''

He hung up the phone, still puzzled. He hadn't noticed any signs of mice or marauding squirrels. And would an animal only show up a couple of times a week?

He made a mental note to ask Sid, and picked up the next envelope. A note on official county stationery informed him that his permits for Ping's Peking Palace had been approved. He could start work right away.

He laid the letter aside on the blotter and waited for the feeling of accomplishment or excitement or anticipation that should follow such good news. Instead a sense of disappointment filled him. The dream he'd held for so long didn't really seem like his anymore.

Archie still hadn't dropped by with the new plans, though he'd been quick enough to share them with Mort Montgomery. Mort was likely pissed at him and would spend the next few months, or years, making his life hell, interfering at every turn, as if the restaurant was his own.

He'd apply for Chamber membership and they'd probably accept him, and then talk about him behind his back the way they did the plumber, Ben Berman.

And Jill would leave, and take a job somewhere else, or take that trip to the Amazon she'd talked about. He'd have stuck to his guns and proven his point, but he'd have nothing to show for it.

He pressed the heels of his hands to his eyes and grimaced. Jill again. It all came back to her. Ever since they'd first made love, she'd turned his life upside down, and now he couldn't imagine not having her in his life forever, no matter how impossible that was.

And it *was* impossible. He couldn't be in love with Jill. It made no sense. It would never work. If he kept telling himself that, maybe he'd even come to believe it.

MONDAY MORNING WHEN SHE came into work, Jill decided Sid looked as awful as she felt. His hair was growing back in little spikes all over his head, and he had circles under his eyes a zombie would be proud of. When she had to ask him three times to hand her the price gun so she could finish marking down a group of clearance items, she couldn't hide her irritation.

"You know, you shouldn't party so hardy when you have to come to work the next morning," she said. "You're just about useless."

He gave her a vacant stare. "What? Did you say something?"

"Actually I've been talking for the last ten minutes and you haven't heard a word I've said."

"I'm sorry. I'm a little distracted, I guess."

"More than a little." She shoved aside the items to be priced and leaned on the counter across from him. "What's up?"

He sighed, and plucked at the ring in his right ear. At least he was wearing his jewelry again. Without it, he'd looked naked. "I think I'm in love."

"Uh-huh. Haven't I heard this before?"

"No, I mean *really* in love. As in forsaking all others and all that."

She studied him more closely. It was true she'd never seen Sid this...*moony*...before. "Who's the lucky woman?" she asked. "Anyone I know?"

"It's the one I told you about."

"The classy lady?"

He nodded. "I found out she doesn't want her old boyfriend at all. She wants *me*."

She grinned and shoved his shoulder. "Didn't I tell you? I'd say she sounds like a pretty smart lady."

He sighed again. "Yeah."

"So why don't you look happier?"

"Jill, what am I going to do? This woman is rich and beautiful and sexy and she wants *me*."

"I still don't see the problem."

"It's just..."

They fell silent as Mitch came in. "Good morning," he said, pausing by the counter.

My, didn't he look chipper? And good enough to eat. She kept her expression neutral. "Good morning, Mitch."

"Morning," Sid said glumly.

Mitch looked at the two of them. "Is something wrong?"

"Sid's upset because he's in love with a rich, beautiful woman who is also crazy about him."

Mitch frowned. "And why is this upsetting?"

Sid glared at her. "I've been trying to explain to Jill that me and...and this woman...are from such different backgrounds, I don't see how it can ever work out between us."

Mitch nodded. "I can see how that could be a problem." He tugged at the knot of his tie. "But maybe your differences are precisely what draw you together. Maybe this woman has spent years dating men just like her and she's bored."

Why did he look at her when he said that? None of the men she'd dated had bored her. Though none of them had excited her the way Mitch did, either. "Maybe Sid is exactly the kind of man she's been looking for for years," she said. She met Mitch's gaze and held it. And maybe it didn't matter what you thought you wanted or what you ought to have—when the chemistry was right, you couldn't help yourself.

The thought scared her, but she forced herself to face

it. She didn't know what was happening between her and Mitch, why he made her feel the way he did, but she wasn't going to run away from it. And she wasn't going to let him run away, either.

"I guess I'll just hope for the best and see what happens." Sid slid off the stool and stretched. "Did you have a good weekend, Mitch?" He glanced at Jill. "I forgot to ask you, how did the Chamber of Commerce banquet turn out?"

"Oh, it was fine." He pulled a packet of condoms off the display, examined it and put it back. "Yes. It was, uh, very nice."

Very nice? One of the most mind-blowing experiences of her life and all he could say was very nice?

She glared at him, but he didn't seem to notice. Why wouldn't he look at her? Was he embarrassed? Or worse, did he regret what had happened between them? *Why* were men so hard to figure out?

"Sid, have we ever had a problem with mice?" Mitch asked.

Mice? She blinked. What did mice have to do with anything?

Sid shook his head. "No, I don't think so. Why?"

"Oh, just curious." He started away from them, then turned back. "Do we have a video camera?"

"Uh, yeah. I think there's one in the closet in Grif's— I mean your office."

He nodded. "Thanks."

She stared after him, anger building, as he walked into his office and shut the door.

"So the banquet went okay?" Sid asked.

"I thought so. Now I'm not so sure." She shoved the price gun at him. "Will you finish marking these? I have something I have to do."

When she stepped into Mitch's office, he was halfway in the closet. "Mitch, what's going on?" she asked.

He emerged from the closet, a video camera in his hand. "The security alarm's been showing an intruder some nights. The security company thinks it might be a mouse or some other small animal. So I thought I'd set up a camera to see if I can find out what it is."

"I'm not talking about that. I'm talking about us." She moved over to stand in front of him. "I mean, what's going on with us?"

"You mean besides fantastic sex?" His mouth twitched, as if he was trying not to smile.

How could she stay angry when he looked at her that way? "So you admit it was fantastic?"

He nodded. "I've got scratches on my back to prove it."

She couldn't hold back the laughter anymore. "What have you done with the serious man who used to work in this office?"

"A better question might be what have *you* done with him?" He set aside the camera and gathered her into his arms. "And what am I going to do with you?"

"You could start by kissing me."

He did so, a long slow kiss that led to his hand cupping her breast. "You know, there's this nice daybed right here."

She pulled back. "I'll admit it's tempting, but it wouldn't be very nice to leave Sid with all the work."

He gave a mock sigh. "I suppose you're right. And I have to call the architect. I need to talk to him before Mort Montgomery does."

The elation she'd been feeling vanished. "You mean, you're still going through with the remodel?"

He looked puzzled. "Why wouldn't I?"

"I thought after the other night, what you said about Mort, and the Chamber of Commerce people…after what happened between us…"

He frowned. "You didn't really think I'd change my plans just because of what happened in the park, did you?"

"Yes, I did. I thought I'd finally made you see how good sex could be…how the products we sell here are fun and…and even helpful—I thought you'd feel differently about the store."

He took a step back. "When I was making love to you last night, I wasn't thinking about the store, or about merchandise, or any of those things. I didn't realize to you it was just a form of propaganda."

"Mitch, that's not what I meant—"

He turned away. "I think you'd better leave now. The sooner I can get started on the remodeling, the better for all of us."

She stared at his back, fury growing within her. "I thought that night I was finally getting through to you—making you see that you could live life on your own terms instead of selling out to somebody else's vision of what you ought to do and be."

He whirled back around. "No, what you were really doing was trying to make me fit into *your* vision of what I ought to do and be. You want a man you can fit into your mold and that man isn't me."

She stepped back, stunned by this outburst. "That… that's not what I meant at all," she stammered. But was it? Had she been trying to make Mitch into a different type of man to justify her attraction to him?

"Just…go," he said.

"It could have been so good between us," she whispered. ''If you'd have taken the moment for what it was, and not tried to read more into it.''

He stood still, his head bowed, not answering. After a moment, she turned and fled, swallowing tears. She'd been right all along. She and Mitch had no future together. They looked at life too differently.

Then why did it hurt so badly to lose him, if she'd never really had him in the first place?

18

MITCH WAITED UNTIL JILL and Sid were gone for the night before he took the video camera out and set it up. He'd spent the day talking to the architect and the construction superintendent, discussing permits and blueprints, reviewing estimates and data sheets. He'd filled every moment with facts and figures, details and numbers, not giving himself a moment to think about Jill and what had happened between them.

But now, alone in the darkened store, the hurt came rushing back. Hurt that he'd been naive enough to believe she really felt something for him, instead of realizing she'd been using him, playing with him to get what she wanted.

She'd warned him, hadn't she, that she was out for fun? "You always take things too seriously," she'd said, and she'd been right.

Fine. That's the kind of man he was. Life was full of serious matters. Obligations. Responsibilities. Maybe Jill couldn't see that, but he knew. And now that she was out of his life, he'd get back to those responsibilities. Forget emotion and passion.

Right now, he concentrated on setting up the video camera. He'd purchased a simple motion detector that would start the tape running when triggered. Of course, if it was something as small as a mouse, he might not get lucky enough to spot it. But if it was something bigger…

He opened the back of the camera to insert a blank tape and was surprised to see a tape already in it. He popped it out and read the hand-written label. "Bachelorette Party." Had somebody been making their own naughty video? Sid…or even Jill?

He walked over to the TV cabinet and inserted the tape into the VCR. While it rewound, he found the remote control and turned on the TV. This was either going to be very interesting…or very dull. But it wasn't as if he had anything better to do tonight.

Jill's face appeared on the screen, her hair done up in two little-girl pigtails. As the camera moved back, he could see she was wearing baby-doll pajamas and fuzzy pink slippers. She had a bottle of champagne in one hand, a pint of ice cream in the other. "Welcome to Cassie Carmichael's bachelorette party," she said.

Cheers went up from the half a dozen other women in the room. They were dressed similarly, in pajamas and slippers, more ice cream, bottles of wine and boxes of chocolate scattered around them. "As you can see, we have everything we need for a great party." Jill gestured at the various refreshments. "And we're ready to give Cassie a last blast with her gal-pals before she becomes an old married woman."

More laughter and applause. "Everybody knows all the best parties involve presents," Jill continued to narrate as the camera focused on a large pile of gaily wrapped packages. "So we've gotten together to present Cassie with a few things we know she'll be needing in her married life."

The camera shifted to Cassie as she tore into the first of her gifts. Hoots of laughter greeted the unveiling of a voluminous flannel nightgown and one of the largest pairs of panties Mitch had ever seen. "Those are for the nights when you don't want him near you," a woman in red, footed pajamas said.

"And for the *other* nights—" A black woman in an oversize football jersey handed over a silver gift bag. Mitch recognized Just 4 Play's logo on the bag.

Cassie pulled out a leopard-print bustier and thong and made a face. "They don't look very comfortable."

"Honey, you won't be wearing them that long," someone said.

Jill stepped forward and took the lingerie. "Allow me to demonstrate." She mugged for the camera. "When choosing sexy lingerie, you want to give it the drop test." She released the leopard-print ensemble and watched the pieces drift to the floor. "You want to know how good they look lying on the floor, because that's where they'll be spending most of their time."

Gales of laughter greeted this announcement and Jill curtsied for the camera.

The next box revealed an extra-large bottle of aspirin and a positively giant purple vibrator. "For times when he's too much…or not enough!"

Other gifts included body paints, penis-shaped soap, an assortment of colorful condoms and a blindfold and feather duster "to keep him in line."

Mitch found himself chuckling along with the women. They were having such a good time, and Jill was directing it all. "All right, all right," she said, clapping her hands to get their attention. "Now it's time for party games. And the first one is…True Confessions!"

"Uh-oh, what kind of game is this?"

"Do we really have to tell the truth?"

"I'm only going to tell false confessions. They're much more interesting."

Jill sat on the floor amid a pile of pillows. "The idea is for each of us to tell our favorite sexual fantasy," she said. "I'm talking your deepest, darkest desire. The thing that gets you excited just thinking about it."

"All right, but then I'm going to need to borrow that vibrator, Cassie."

"No. It's all mine." Cassie grabbed the toy the women had already dubbed "the purple monster."

"No fair! You already have Guy Walters. He ought to be stud enough to keep you busy."

Jill shushed them. "All right everybody. Who wants to go first?"

The black woman—Mitch finally figured out her name was Geneva—stuck up her hand. "I'll do it. And it's not gonna surprise any of y'all to know that my fantasy involves food."

A new wave of laughter. Geneva sat back and closed her eyes, a smile on her face. "All right. Here goes. My fantasy involves being blindfolded while some *handsome* man has his way with me."

"If you're blindfolded, how do you know he's handsome?" Jill asked, giggling.

"I just know he is. Now this is my fantasy. You hush."

"All right, all right. Go on."

"Okay. So this *handsome* man—did I mention he smells really good too? Anyway, he puts this blindfold on me that's made out of this soft, satiny stuff, and he takes off all my clothes…real slow. Then he takes a feather and starts stroking me with it. Tickling, then just barely trailing across my nipples." She covered her breasts with her hands. "Then he has something soft and furry, like rabbit fur, and he's doing the same thing, stroking me with it, all over. And all the time he's doing this, he's telling me how beautiful I am, and how hot he's getting just watching me.

"Then he takes a piece of ice and starts doing the same thing, trailing it all across my body, until he gets to right down between my legs, and I can feel it all melting there."

The other women were silent, focused on Geneva as she described her fantasy. Mitch could feel the tension between them, and his own growing arousal.

"Already, I'm so turned on I can't hardly stand it," Geneva continued. "But instead of doing anything about it, this man goes away and leaves me alone."

"The bastard!" someone said.

Geneva chuckled. "No, because he comes back. Now, he starts feeding me things." Her smile broadened. "Good things."

"Like what?"

"Like plump, ripe strawberries. And a peach that's so juicy the juice runs down my chin and drips onto my breasts and he has to lick the juice off. And rich, dark chocolate, with raspberry liqueur in it, that spurts out when you bite into it."

"I'm getting hungry just listening to this fantasy," Cassie said. "Somebody pass me that box of choco-lates."

"He brings champagne and gives me a sip, then drib-bles it down my body, across my breasts and my stom-ach, across my thighs and between my thighs. It's cold and the bubbles tickle, and then his mouth is on me, very hot."

"Speaking of hot..." One of the women fanned herself.

"By this time it feels like every nerve in my body is on fire for this man. I'm aching for him, begging for release. He kisses me, and says he has something else for me to taste. Then I feel his weight shift and something touches my lips, and I realize it's him."

"Ohhhh."

"Now there's something you won't find in your refrigerator."

"At least, I hope not!"

Geneva's laugh was low and throaty. "At first, I take just the head in my mouth. I run my tongue around it and I hear him moan. And I know he wants me as much as I want him. So I go a little deeper. But he's really big, so I can't get him all."

"Of course he's really big."

"This *is* a fantasy."

"After a little bit, I can tell he's really close to coming, so I push him down, and he enters me. We start moving together, in this perfect rhythm. He knows just what to do to take me to the edge, then back off, so that each time, I climb a little higher. And he holds himself back, until finally, I can't stand it anymore, and I just…shatter around him. And then he comes too and it's…it's incredible." She sighed, and opened her eyes. "And that's my fantasy. And as soon as I find that handsome man, I intend to make it come true."

Jill fanned herself with a magazine. "Whoo, Geneva. Can I borrow that fantasy some time?"

Geneva curled her legs beneath her. "Now I want to hear *your* fantasy."

"Yeah, you started this." Cassie nudged her. "What's your true confession?"

Jill laughed. "After Geneva's 'gourmet' experience, mine is going to seem pretty silly."

"Does it involve midgets or circus clowns?" a woman asked.

"No."

"Then it can't be that silly."

"All right. Here goes, then. My fantasy is to be kidnapped by a marauding pirate."

"A pirate? As in a wooden leg and eye patch?"

She giggled. "No! As in a gorgeous man in tights and jack boots, and one of those flowing shirts unbuttoned to his navel. With a sword and everything."

"He'd better have a sword or this fantasy's going to be awfully disappointing!"

Jill shook her head. "In my fantasy, this swashbuckling pirate comes to my bedroom one night and kidnaps me and takes me back to his ship, where he makes me his prisoner."

"I've always heard rape fantasies were popular, but they've never done much for me," one woman said.

Jill turned to her. "Oh, no, he doesn't rape me. In fact, he's a perfect gentleman."

"Where's the fun in that?"

Jill smiled. "His goal is to *win* me. After all, I'm an innocent virgin."

More loud laughter. Jill assumed an expression of mock offense. "I said this was a fantasy. Anyway, my pirate is determined to teach me the joys of sex. So, for the first day, he only talks to me. He tells me how beautiful I am, and how he's going to make me feel even more beautiful.

"The second day, he brings me a new silk gown that is so soft and almost transparent. It's cut low over the tops of my breasts, but just sort of flows over the rest of my body. And he rubs perfumed oil on my wrists and my neck and between my breasts.

"The third day, he kisses me. On the cheek and on the throat and finally on the lips. He teases me with his tongue, mimicking what he's going to do to me later."

"You have to watch those tongues," someone commented.

"On the fourth day, he finally touches me. He strokes my back and my bottom and fondles my breasts. He teases my nipples with his fingers until they tingle and ache. He caresses my thighs but never goes any further."

"This man has some self-control. I'll say that."

"The fifth day, he kisses my breasts, and licks my nipples, sucking and teasing until I'm practically screaming with need. I'm hot and aching and begging him to give me relief, but he tells me I'm not ready yet."

"Now that's cruel!" someone protested.

"The sixth day, he comes to me naked. I can see how much he wants me. How much he needs me. He strips the dress off of me and begins kissing me again—my mouth and then my breasts. But this time, he holds me closer, letting me feel his body against mine. He trails kisses down my stomach, down to my crotch, to where I'm aching for him.

"I want him so badly I think I'll come right away, but he doesn't let me. 'Not yet' he whispers. Then he kneels between my legs and enters me. I'm so ready for him and he fills me completely. He starts moving in and out, and at the same time, he's stroking me with his thumb. We're moving together and waves of sensation rock through me. And when I finally come it's like a jolt of current through me. And then he climaxes right after me. And it's the most awesome experience."

"I wouldn't care if a guy *did* have a wooden leg if he could do that for me," Geneva said. "Whoo, girl, that was *hot*. Too bad there aren't any real pirates anymore.''

"Yeah." Jill sighed, a dreamy expression on her face. "Too bad."

Mitch leaned forward and switched off the tape. He was shaken, moved beyond arousal to a kind of empathy. Who would have thought a take-charge woman like Jill craved being swept away like that? Beneath her no-nonsense exterior was someone vulnerable and…and romantic.

So why then did she insist on taking the lead in sex? Was she afraid of what would happen if a man came along who *could* sweep her away?

He put the videotape in his desk drawer and sat staring into the darkness. Maybe all of Jill's talk of no commitments and keeping things casual was a lie. He knew damn well *he* felt something special when he was with her. Was it so far-fetched to believe she'd felt it, too?

He got up and finished setting up the camera. He didn't know why Jill was afraid, but he knew one thing about fear: the more you tried to ignore it, the stronger it became. Maybe he and Jill needed to look their fears in the eye and shrink them to a manageable size. Together, they could figure out where to go from there.

19

ORDINARILY, JILL WAS NOT the sort of person who minded being alone. Sure, she enjoyed going out with friends and having a good time, but she could get just as much satisfaction at home alone curled up with a good book or a movie.

But tonight, nothing satisfied her. Every book she picked up was boring; everything on television seemed silly. She paced her apartment, irritated at everything she saw. Damn Mitch Landry! *He'd* done this to her. He'd taken something wonderful and fun and made it complicated. All his talk of responsibility and duty and…and commitment had worn off on her.

She caught sight of her reflection in the darkened kitchen window and shook her head at her woeful expression. "The next thing you know, I'll be mooning over babies or…or buying *sensible* shoes!" Who would have thought Jill Sheldon—the original "Wild Woman" —would sink so low?

The doorbell rang and she went to answer it, hoping it was a psychic pizza deliverer bringing her a free pizza, or a salesman she could torture.

Her stomach did a somersault when she looked out the peephole and saw it was Mitch. He had a big bunch of flowers and a shopping bag. With trembling fingers she unfastened the locks. "Mitch! Hi." Honestly, why was she so happy to see him? She tried to frown. "I thought we didn't have anything to say to each other,'' she said.

He walked past her into the apartment, and turned and handed her the flowers. "I'm man enough to admit I was wrong. I want to make it up to you." He reached into the shopping bag and pulled out a bottle of champagne and a deluxe assortment of chocolates.

She accepted these gifts, fighting a smile. "You really know your way to a woman's heart."

He followed her into the kitchen. "Why don't I open the champagne while you find some glasses," he said.

"All right." She avoided looking at him while she hunted in the cupboards for two champagne flutes and a vase for the flowers. What exactly was going on here? Was Mitch really willing to agree to a relationship on her terms?

He poured the champagne and held up his glass. "To us."

She stared at the bubbles gathering on the rim of her glass. "Um, what about us?"

"I guess that's what I'm here to figure out." He leaned back against the counter. "I'm hoping you'll cooperate with me in a little experiment."

"Experiment?" The skin along her arms tingled. Something about the look in his eye...

"Oh, I think it's something you'll like." He loosened his tie.

She set aside her glass and moved closer. "Then maybe I'll cooperate."

"Good." He whipped off the tie and pulled her closer in a long, slow kiss.

Now this was more like it. If they could concentrate on their physical attraction...

Something tightened around her wrists. She realized

it was the tie. Laughing, she tried to pull away, but Mitch drew her back to him. "It's okay," he said. "Trust me."

He picked up the shopping bag and tucked the champagne bottle under one arm. "Which is your bedroom?"

"First door on the left." She nodded in the right direction.

He headed toward the bedroom, pulling her along behind him. A nervous giggle bubbled in her throat, along with a slow smoldering heat that started between her legs and curled through the rest of her body. What was Mitch going to do?

In the bedroom, he set the shopping bag and champagne on the bed, then went around lighting candles, until the room was bathed in a soft, golden glow. He folded back the duvet on the bed, then turned to her. "I'm going to undress you."

He seemed to be asking permission, so she nodded. After all, he'd seen her naked before. And it was what she wanted too, though she'd prefer to undress herself.

That was impossible with her hands tied behind her, however, so she stood still while he unbuttoned her blouse and peeled it back across her shoulders.

He worked slowly, deliberately exposing her a bit at a time. His breath was warm across her stomach as he bent to unsnap her jeans, and goose bumps rose on her flesh as he moved away and the cooler air of the room rushed over her.

He steadied her and helped her step out of her jeans and then she stood there, clad in bra and panties, her blouse wrapped around her wrists. He smiled and snapped the waistband of her panties. "Cute."

She looked down at the white cotton underpants decorated with little pink hearts. "If I'd known you were coming, I'd have worn something more erotic."

"I happen to think pink hearts are very erotic." He unfastened one wrist, then slid the blouse off of her, followed by the bra. He tossed the clothing aside, then bound her again. She thought of protesting, but didn't, telling herself she could do this. She could trust him.

He gathered her breasts in his hands, holding them. Her nipples rose against his palms, demanding attention, but he only squeezed her gently and moved away.

He untied one wrist and helped her into bed, then raised her hands over her head and bound them loosely to the bedpost. "Comfy?" he asked.

"I'm not *un*comfortable." At least not physically. What was he going to do? She wasn't worried he'd hurt her, but she didn't like not knowing what was going on. Not being in charge...

He moved to the side of the bed and began undressing. She turned her head to watch. He removed his clothes slowly, but she didn't have a sense that he was putting on a show for her, only that he was not a man in a hurry. Which was too bad, because she was already feeling impatient for something...anything...to happen.

He turned to face her, candlelight flickering on his bronzed skin, sharply etching every muscle and plane. She couldn't deny this man stirred her in a way no other had.

He sat on the edge of the bed. "I've been thinking more about what you said, about the products we sell being fun and even useful. So I thought it would be a good idea for me to get better acquainted with some of them."

She smiled. "That's what I've been saying all along."

"See, I *have* been listening." He picked up the shopping bag. "So I did a little shopping this evening." He pulled out a satin blindfold.

"Is that for you?" she asked.

"No, it's for you." He leaned over her, lifting her head from the pillow and fastening the blindfold. It was soft, completely obscuring her vision. She shivered and licked her lips. "I'm not sure I like this."

"Oh, you'll like it. I promise." She heard the rustling of the bag. "Another thing I found was this." Something tickled her jaw.

She smiled. "It's a feather."

"A Fantasy Feather Duster, to be exact." He trailed it along her throat, around her breasts. She gasped when it touched her sensitive nipples.

"How does that feel?" he asked.

"It…it tickles a little." She giggled as he brushed the feather across her abdomen. "But it also feels…nice." The feather trailed across her thighs, down her legs, to her feet. Back up again, to pause over her sex, barely touching her.

She arched toward it, craving more, but it retreated.

She sagged against the bed again, but a new sensation claimed her attention. Something soft and furry cuddled against her neck. "That's not an animal, is it?" she asked, alarmed.

He laughed. "No. It's actually those fur-lined handcuffs you 'demonstrated' to me a couple of weeks ago." He dragged the fur across her breasts. "I remembered how soft the fur felt."

"Yes. It is soft." And very erotic. Blindfolded, it seemed every other sense was on alert. The slightest touch set her to tingling. As he stroked her with the fur, she felt every movement keenly. She imagined she felt his gaze on her, too, watching her. The thought excited her even more.

The bag rustled again and suddenly the scent of strawberries surrounded her. "I found this at the store, too." His finger brushed her lips and she tasted strawberries. "Strawberry Nipple Nibblers."

"I see you really do know the stock." He kissed her and the heat of his mouth made her lips tingle.

Then he massaged some of the cream into her nipples and they began to tingle also. He kissed her breasts, first one and then the other, and took the nipples into his mouth. "Tastes good," he mumbled.

The cream made her more sensitive than ever. As he flicked his tongue across her, then suckled harder, she writhed beneath him, her impatience building.

He smoothed his hand across her belly, then slid lower until he was parting her folds to find her pearled center. He stroked her gently, and she felt a corresponding tingle. "Mitch!" she cried.

He licked her, gently at first, then with more pressure. She told herself to relax, to surrender to the pleasant urgency, but she was too on edge. She didn't like feeling trapped this way, or not being able to see…or…oh sweet mercy, she'd never felt so out of control before, hurtling toward climax without having any say in the matter.

When she was sure she couldn't hold out any longer, he raised his head, leaving her trembling. He laid his hand on her thigh, soothing her. "It's all right," he said, his voice ragged. "We're only getting started."

More rustling, then the smell of peaches. "Taste this." She obediently opened her mouth and he fed her a bite of peach. The fruit tasted sweet, the flesh velvety against her tongue. Juice ran down her chin and he hastened to lick it up. She smiled. "That's good," she said. "Let me have some more."

He fed her another bite, only this time, it was strawberry, the seeds crunching between her teeth. "I remem-

ber watching you eat strawberries at dinner the other
night,'' he said. ''I never got a hard-on watching somebody eat before.''

''Untie me and I'll show you more.'' She hoped he
didn't hear the pleading in her voice.

He chuckled. ''Oh, no. I'm not ready to untie you yet.
Tonight, I'm in charge.''

The words sent a shiver through her.

He fed her more strawberries, and chocolate filled
with sweet caramel. Something about all this was
vaguely familiar, but she didn't have time to figure it
out. Every moment, new sensations swept over her.

She heard the clink of a glass, and he stretched alongside her, his body warm, his arousal prodding her in the
hip. ''Do you trust me?'' he asked.

''No.'' She didn't trust anyone.

He covered her breast with his hand, thumbing her
nipple, sending jolts of sensation through her. ''Come
on now. Do you trust me? You know I won't hurt you.''

''I know you won't hurt me.'' She was sure of that.
But she didn't like lying here so passive, only receiving
and not giving.

''All right then. Tell me what you feel.''

Something cool and liquid trickled across her chest,
pooling in the valley between her breast. She smelled
the tang of wine, then felt Mitch lapping at her. ''Champagne.''

He trickled some of the wine between her lips, then
across her breasts. He chased each drop with his tongue,
capturing it all before it could dampen the sheets. He
moved down, filling her navel, tracing a path to her
heated center, where he licked up every drop, and stayed
to bring her to the edge once more.

She arched toward him, moaning with need. ''You're

very close, aren't you?'' he murmured. ''Almost there. I promise, it'll be good.''

His fingers slipped inside her, stroking. ''What was that about the G-spot? Was it right…here?''

''Mitch! Oh…oh!'' She bucked beneath him as he stroked faster. He began licking her again, banishing her last bit of control. Light and heat filled her, and she screamed his name.

He lay alongside her, holding her as aftershocks raced through her. Then he undid the blindfold and looked down on her, his face so serious. ''Are you all right?''

She wasn't sure she'd ever be the same again. She smiled weakly. ''That was incredible.''

He smoothed his hand up her arms. ''See? It can be good, even if you aren't calling the shots.''

She nodded. ''I guess it can be with you.''

He reached for the binding at her wrists. ''Do you want me to untie you?''

She started to answer yes, but something in his eyes asked her to trust him still. She swallowed her fear and shook her head. ''No, it's all right. I…I trust you.''

He crushed her to him, his kiss fierce. His hands still on her, caressing, he knelt between her knees and entered her. Desire swelled anew within her, and she closed her eyes and gave herself up to the wonderful friction of his thrusts.

She arched toward him and he slipped his hands under her buttocks, holding her up off the bed as he drove deeply into her, each stroke stronger and faster. She felt herself climbing again to that wonderful height. But this time, she wasn't afraid. She gladly surrendered control and fell freely, even as she felt the power of his own release.

Afterward, they lay together, not speaking. Her arms

freed, she wrapped them around him, and savored his solid warmth. The candles burned low, and some of them went out. "What are you thinking?" he murmured, long after she thought he'd fallen asleep.

"I'm thinking this changes things," she said. "Though I'm not sure how."

He rolled over to face her, and cradled her head in the hollow of his shoulder. "I wanted you to see the possibilities," he murmured. And then he did fall asleep, leaving her to stare into the darkness, wondering if this was what it meant to be in love, to be so unsure of herself, and yet so certain that she couldn't be happier than she was at this moment.

20

WHEN JILL WOKE THE NEXT morning, Mitch was gone. She frowned at the note he'd left on the dresser. *I had to go in to work early to see about something. See you later. Mitch.*

No "Last night was the most awesome night of my life," no "I could hardly bear to leave you," no "I love you."

She winced. Where had *that* come from? Neither one of them had said anything about love. Neither one of them expected it. She crumpled the note and tossed it in the trash, then got dressed. Everywhere she looked, something reminded her of last night—the empty champagne bottle in the wastebasket beside the bed, the half-eaten box of chocolates on the nightstand, his tie draped around the bedpost.

She unwound the tie from the post and brought it to her nose, inhaling the faint scent of Aramis. She'd keep this, as a memento of last night. A kind of trophy. Smiling, she went to the dresser and knotted the tie around the collar of the sleeveless blue chambray shirt she wore. When Mitch saw it, would he remember too?

Unfortunately a troop of tourists descended on the store to giggle and gawk fifteen minutes after they opened and Jill didn't have a chance to even say "Good morning" to Mitch. Between defending the store's merchandise to one outraged woman "Yes, ma'am, marriage counselors have actually recommended our store to their clients,'' and explaining the benefits of various types of vibrators to a pink-faced middle-aged couple, she scarcely had time to think for the first hour or so.

When she did finally bump into Mitch, literally, as she stepped back from straightening the costume display, all she could manage to do was blush and stammer. "Good morning, Jill," he said, his hand warm on her shoulder as he steadied her. "I see you found my tie."

She smoothed the end of the tie. "Oh, uh, yes."

He looked over her head, at the rest of the store. "Looks like we had a real rush in here this morning."

"We did. Some tourists from Nebraska heard about the place and walked over to see it. I think our fame is spreading." *And how could you even think of closing the place down now?*

"I know." He moved away from her. "Construction is due to start next week."

"So you really are going to go through with closing the doors?"

He looked away. "I don't know. I…I need more time to think."

He didn't have much time, but she guessed he didn't need her pointing that out to him. Still, his answer disappointed her. She turned away from him, and began sorting through the thinning ranks of costumes.

"I'd better get back to work," he said, and walked away.

Why hadn't he said anything about last night—about *them?* For that matter, why hadn't she had the courage to speak up?

Was it because, outside of the bedroom, it was harder to see how to make things work in real life? Jill thought Mitch should keep the store open, but more importantly, she thought he should quit letting responsibility and the opinions of others rule his life. If he couldn't unbend, just a little, how would they ever compromise on anything else?

So what if he opened a restaurant? That didn't matter so much anymore, though she'd miss the fun she'd had working here. But if Mitch opened a restaurant and joined the Chamber of Commerce and got caught up in making a success of himself, would he expect her to tone down her wild ways? To attend boring business functions and make small talk to people she didn't like or respect? To become the perfect social accessory?

The frightening thing was, she could almost see herself doing those things, literally killing off part of herself, if it meant staying with Mitch. She stared at the beaded top of the belly dancer's costume she'd worn so long ago and blinked back tears. Better to give up Mitch now, and get the hurting out of the way, than to wake up ten years from now, as miserable as Jenny had been.

She'd gotten along fine all this time, hadn't she, assuring herself that she didn't need a commitment to anyone else to be happy. The difference was, before she'd believed the words. Now she knew part of her would always love Mitch. She'd given a part of herself to him she could never get back.

MITCH COULDN'T BELIEVE he'd been such a dolt, mumbling all that nonsense about not knowing whether he wanted to keep the store open or not. What the hell did any of that matter compared to what he felt for Jill?

But the moment he'd seen that tie around her neck, he'd been transported back to last night. In his mind's eye, he'd seen her lying on her bed, so beautiful and vulnerable, surrendering everything to him. The memory had left him speechless, able only to mutter inanities.

Later, he'd find a way to make it up to her. To really talk about what the future might hold for them. He didn't know if she felt as strongly about him as he did her, but he had hope. They'd probably both have to compromise some to make things work, but he thought they had a good shot.

In the meantime, he'd called the security company and learned that the alarm system had registered another silent intruder last night. Time to see if the video camera had captured anything.

He had taken the camera off the tripod and brought it into his office when he arrived that morning. Now he slipped the tape out of it and turned on the VCR, thinking again of the tape in his desk drawer of Jill and her friends. He'd have to watch the rest of that one later. No telling what other fantasies the women had confessed to.

While the tape rewound, he leaned back in the desk chair and looked around the office, at the dark paneling and dented filing cabinets, the faded posters and make-shift entertainment unit. When they remodeled for the restaurant, he'd have his office made over as well. Despite the pleasant associations the daybed held for him, he was thinking of replacing it with a couch. A very comfortable couch, with plenty of room to stretch out on.

He'd keep the chair, though. It was comfortable and masculine, and it reminded him of Uncle Grif. He felt a twinge of guilt at the thought. No doubt Grif had wanted him to keep Just 4 Play going. He didn't have any children to leave the business to, so he'd passed it on to Mitch.

At first, Mitch had looked on the inheritance as a

windfall. The capital he needed to open the restaurant. He hadn't felt any emotional obligation to Grif because, after all, he'd hardly known the man.

But that had changed the last few weeks. Spending so much time here in this room where Grif had practically lived, going through his files, learning things about his uncle he'd never guessed, Mitch had begun to feel close to the older man. He'd seen the kind of man Grif was, and the kind he wasn't.

Grif wasn't the kind of man who bowed to public opinion. He did what he thought was right and the rest of the world be damned. It was a hard line to take sometimes, requiring the sacrifice of prestige and position and maybe even money. But he'd taken it. Mitch admired that in his uncle, though he didn't know if he could be that strong himself.

He'd bought the tombstone as a gesture of respect, but he wished he could do something to show the world he'd come to love his uncle.

The tape from last night began playing, showing the darkened interior of the store. Then he heard a sound like voices whispering. Something moved in the corner of the picture.

He leaned forward, trying to make out what it was. The object disappeared, then appeared on the screen again. It was a person. No, two people. Two naked people. He hit the pause button and stared at the screen in disbelief, then began laughing out loud. His world was full of surprises so far, and this had to be the biggest one of all.

BY LUNCHTIME, JILL HAD decided that the only thing to do was to talk to Mitch and let him off the hook. She'd tell him she understood all the reasons they could never make it as a couple: their backgrounds were so different, they wanted different things in life and all that. She'd have to call upon all her limited acting ability to pull it off, but it would be for the best.

But when she knocked on Mitch's office door, no one answered, though she knew he was in there. She knocked again, then tried the knob. It was unlocked, so she peeked inside.

Mitch was sitting at the desk, turned toward the TV, bent double with laughter. When he turned and looked at her, he actually had tears running down his face!

"What is it? What's so funny?" She glanced at the television screen. At first it looked like one of the X-rated videos they sold, with a couple going at it like rabbits. That surprised her a little. Sure, guys liked that sort of thing more than women did, but why would he be watching this in the middle of the day? Especially after last night?

"Um, maybe I'd better come back another time." She started backing toward the door, but Mitch motioned her toward him again.

"No, no. You won't believe this." He paused the tape and motioned at the screen with the remote. "This is the tape I made last night of the 'silent intruder.'"

She leaned closer and peered at the screen, then her eyes widened. "Oh my gosh, it's…it's Sid." She'd recognize that dragon tattoo across his back anywhere, even if the tush wasn't familiar. She put her hand over her mouth and giggled. "Who's that with him?"

Mitch rewound the tape until the woman's face was visible. Jill gasped. "That's Lana Montgomery!" She squealed and collapsed into a chair. "Oh, this is too funny."

Mitch shut off the tape and ejected it from the player.

"Lana and Sid." He chuckled. "I wouldn't believe it if I hadn't seen it with my own eyes." He tapped the tape against his leg. "Just goes to show you never really know people."

"Do you mean you didn't think Sid could go out with a woman like Lana?"

"I mean the Lana I knew didn't have an uninhibited bone in her body. I guess sometimes, it just takes the right person to reveal that side of someone." He looked thoughtful. "Or the right place."

"What are you going to do? I mean about Sid and Lana? You aren't going to fire him, are you?" Though what difference did that make if he was going to close the store anyway? she thought sadly.

"I'm not going to fire him." He stood and slipped the tape into his jacket. "I do think I'll let him know I have this, though, and suggest he and Lana take 'play-time' somewhere else."

On his way out of his office, he stopped and looked back at her. "I wanted you to be the first to know. I've decided not to close the store. If this place can turn uptight Lana into a passionate temptress, it must be performing a needed service."

"So seeing that tape changed your mind when I couldn't?"

He shook his head. "No, you had something to do with it, too. And Grif."

"Grif?" She looked puzzled.

"I think this wasn't just a business for him—it was kind of a statement. 'This is what I'm about, so take it or leave it.'" He shrugged. "I figure he did fine without being a darling of society and I can do the same. I guess being around this place has taught me there's all different kinds of respect and some of them are more worth having than others.''

After he was gone, Jill stayed in the office a while longer, trying to muster up the joy she knew she should be feeling at Mitch's announcement. He wasn't going to close the store. She and Sid would still have jobs. She could still come here every day and have fun disguised as work.

But she could only manage a feeling of mild relief. And a bit of pride that Mitch had found it within himself to do the right thing.

But overwhelming any happiness she should have felt was a great sadness. Mitch had reached a decision about the store, but he hadn't answered the one question she most wanted answered: What was he going to do about her—about *them?*

21

MITCH SPENT THE REST of the day on the phone, canceling contractors and breaking the news to everyone who needed to know that Ping's Peking Palace wouldn't be opening anytime soon. At least not at this location.

Chef Ping took the news philosophically. "Oh well, I think I can find someone else to build the restaurant. And I liked your store. I will come and see you there sometime."

Mort Montgomery was less pleasant. "You're making a big mistake," he said bluntly. "No respectable person in this town will have anything to do with you as long as you're in charge of that smut shop."

"It's not a smut shop, Mort. As for all those 'respectable' people, my uncle got along fine without them and he was a better man than they'll ever be."

"Which shows how little you know." Mort made a *tsking* sound. "I hate to see it, I tell you. We could have made that restaurant a huge success."

"No, *we* couldn't have. Goodbye, Mort. And good luck."

It was after six when he made the last call, to Archie, the architect. Mitch was tired, but content. He figured Uncle Grif would be pleased, and Jill, too, though she hadn't said much when he'd told her the news.

Things still felt awkward between them. He wasn't quite sure how to smooth them out, but he knew he had to try. But when he finally emerged from his office, he discovered she'd gone home early.

"Did she say why she had to leave?" he asked.

Sid shook his head. "Just said she had things to do."

He thought about going to her apartment. But he still didn't know what he'd say to her. Now that they'd be seeing each other on a regular basis at work, did she want to keep things as they were between them, or did she expect something more from him? And was he ready to give more?

He ended up staying at the store until closing, waiting on customers even, something he hadn't done before. He found he enjoyed the work. He recommended Oriental Love Potion to a college girl who was looking for something exotic. When a young man selected a package of Neon Nights condoms, Mitch was able to assure him that they really did glow in the dark.

He browsed the shelves, discovering merchandise he didn't know they carried. For instance, they had a whole section of games, including a box of plastic bubbles, each containing a suggestion, ranging from sweetly romantic to nicely naughty. The directions called for the couple to add the bubbles to a bath and take turns drawing the bubbles and acting on the suggestions. Wouldn't that be a fun one to try with Jill....

"Excuse me, I'm looking for a salesclerk who was in here a couple of weeks ago. A cute little blonde?"

Mitch turned and found a balding, middle-aged man. Slightly behind him stood a pleasant-faced, middle-aged woman. "You must mean Jill. I'm afraid she's off tonight."

"Oh." Clearly disappointed, the man turned to his wife. "She was so nice. I wanted you to meet her."

"Can I help you with something?" Mitch asked.

"I don't know." The man tugged at his collar. "I was really hoping to speak to Jill."

"Are you the manager?" The woman spoke.

Mitch glanced toward Sid, who was on the other side of the store, showing vibrators to a pair of young women. "No. I'm the owner."

"Even better." The woman stepped forward. "I want you to know your store probably saved our marriage."

"Oh?" Mitch remembered the man now. The one who'd been ogling Jill while she massaged his hand. "How is that?"

The woman looked at her husband. "Larry here is a good man, but after twenty years, he'd forgotten all about romance. The things he got at your store—the books and lingerie and candles and such—they helped both of us remember what's it like to take a little time and effort for love and sex."

Mitch smiled. "I'm glad we could help."

"So we're thinking that now we're ready to, uh, branch out." The man was pink-faced. "You know, try some new things." He looked around. "I was really hoping Jill could suggest something."

"But I'm sure you have some good ideas, too." The woman smiled at Mitch. "What would you suggest for a couple of old married folks looking to spice things up?"

Mitch swallowed. Did he dare admit he wasn't exactly an expert in this arena? "Um, I'm not sure exactly what you'd like," he stammered.

"Well, what do you like?" The woman's grin widened. "We don't want anything too wild, but we're willing to try something different."

His eyes scanned the shelves, hoping for inspiration, then his gaze landed on the bubble bath game. That wasn't too wild, was it? He grabbed the package off the shelf. "Here's something fun and...and romantic." He handed it to the woman. "You take turns selecting bubbles and acting on the suggestions."

She popped open one of the bubbles and read from the plastic strip inside. "Give partner a back rub." She glanced at her husband. "What do you think?"

He nodded. "It's a good start."

"All right." The woman turned back to Mitch. "We'll take it."

He rang up their purchase and wrapped it in the store's signature pink and gold tissue paper. "You will tell Jill we stopped by, won't you?" the man asked.

"Oh, yes, I'll tell her." Mitch handed over their purchase. "Have fun."

The woman laughed. "Oh, I'm sure we will!"

He chuckled to himself. Fun. A three-letter word he'd once despised. But Jill had been right all along; Just 4 Play was fun, and fun was a good thing. Now if he could only convince her he'd learned that lessen.

After the last customer, he returned to his office. Sid stopped by on his way out. "Thanks for being cool about that tape and all," he said. "I swear I didn't know the alarm would still register after I bypassed it."

"It's okay, Sid. Just don't do it again okay?"

"Okay." Sid lingered in the doorway, shifting from one foot to the other.

"Was there something else?" Mitch asked.

"I was wondering if I could have the tape. You know, for Lana. I think she'd get a kick out of it."

Mitch was careful not to smile as he took the tape out of the drawer and handed it over.

"So uh, you're okay with me and Lana?" Sid asked. "I mean, you two were split up and all...."

"I'm okay with it. In fact, I can't think of a more perfect couple."

"Good." Sid looked relieved. "Glad that's clear. Guess I'll be going."

"You go on. I'll lock up."

After Sid left, Mitch was restless, not wanting to go home to his lonely apartment. He could call Meg, but she was probably busy with schoolwork, or out with friends. He looked around the office, noticing once more how depressing the place looked. Restaurant or no, he intended to remodel this office.

He might as well finish clearing it out now. He'd tackle the one job he'd been putting off—that walk-in closet that held everything from the video camera to an old set of Grif's golf clubs.

He went to the storeroom and got a box. Everything to go to a storage facility could go in there; everything else was destined for the trash.

Tax records—in the storage box. Receipts for the 1996 Coors Classic golf tournament—toss.

After half an hour he was beginning to wonder if his uncle ever threw anything away. He found receipts for practically everything the man had ever bought, years' worth of old magazines and mail-order catalogs, manuals for computers and other office equipment that had been out of date for ages.

A box on the top shelf held a sad-looking black toupee. Mitch set this aside for a third category—things to be donated.

At the very back of the closet, he came upon a shoebox, filled to the brim with letters, packets of eight to ten envelopes each, bound together with thick rubber bands. Nobody he knew wrote letters anymore, so these had to be old.

He picked up one of the rubber-banded packets and looked at the loopy, old-fashioned handwriting. The envelopes were blue, made of the thin paper people used to use for airmail. The letters bore military postmarks. Of course. These would have been letters Grif received when he was serving in Vietnam.

The rest of the closet's contents forgotten, he carried the box over to the leather chair. He undid the first packet and opened the first letter. It was written in a soft, feminine hand.

Dear Grif,

You've only been gone one day and already I miss you. I thought you might like to know what I am doing with myself while you are away, so I intend to write every week. That way, we can keep in touch and maybe I won't miss you so much.

This afternoon my friend Connie and I went to the movies and saw *Cleopatra*. I think Richard Burton is the grooviest, though Connie likes Paul Newman best. Afterward, we walked down to Gold's Department Store and looked at the store windows. They had the cutest miniskirt for sale there. Mom and Daddy won't like it, but I'm going to buy it as soon as I save enough of my allowance.

Mitch chuckled to himself. The letter continued in this vein, a perfect picture of a week in the life of teenage girl, circa 1962. It ended with the word Love, in big, loopy letters, and a girlish signature: Tracy.

He stopped and stared into space. Tracy was his mother's name. What a strange coincidence.

He read the next letter, and the next. Two years' worth of correspondence. The woman who wrote the letters grew up on the page, her concerns changing from the latest fashions and music, through graduation, to a secretarial job.

By this time, Mitch knew he was reading his mother's words. She had worked as a secretary before she married his father, and the people she mentioned in her letters—her mother and father, her younger sister Sue and her grandparents in Grand Junction—were all familiar to him.

He was fascinated by this glimpse of her, as a young girl, before any possibility of himself or Meg had entered her mind. He stared at the handwriting on the page and tried to imagine her, seated at a little desk in her room, or at the kitchen table in his grandparents' house, writing these words to a young man half a world away.

But why was she writing to Grif? What had he thought, receiving them? He had obviously valued them enough to keep them, but why?

He continued to read, unable to tear himself away. The tone of the letters grew more serious as he moved deeper into the box. Tracy's feelings matured along with her, from flirting friendship, to romantic love. Mitch had a funny feeling in his stomach as he read them. This didn't fit with the reality he knew. What was going on?

The last two letters were bound by themselves with a brown shoestring instead of a rubber band. The few pages were yellowed, the writing smeared in places, as if they'd been much handled.

He opened the first of the letters and brought it closer to the desk lamp, puzzling out the faded writing.

Dearest Grif,
I can still call you Dearest, can't I? You will always be dearest to me. I don't understand why you tell

me not to wait for you. This war won't last forever
and I know you'll be coming home. Don't you
think it would be good to have a wife waiting for
you, so you can start life fresh?

I know you say you have your mother and your
brother to look after, but I don't mind. I'll help you.
And it isn't as if Dickie is a baby. Why, he and I
are the same age and he already has a good job
downtown. I see him almost every day when I go
to the café for lunch.

And I know you say you'll need to find a job
and establish yourself when you come home, but I
know you'll be able to find something. And I can
keep working until we've saved enough money for
a little house. Things aren't that expensive here and
I'm sure we'll manage.

Anyway, I don't think any of that matters. I love
you and you love me and we ought not think that
kind of love comes along every day. I'm sure it
doesn't. So please say you'll change your mind.
Write and tell me you still want to be with me and
I will be the happiest girl alive.

Mitch laid aside the letter, trying to absorb its contents. So his mother had been in love with Grif. But he
had told her not to wait. That he had too many responsibilities to think of getting married at that time.

A shiver swept through him as he looked at the second
letter, unopened on the blotter before him. Though he
knew what had happened, he had to find out for sure.

Dear Grif,
I waited a long time to hear from you again after
my last letter. I know you received it because my

friend April Sanders's brother Alan is in your unit and he said the day you got that letter you went out and got drunk and ended up in the stockade for three days.

Then Dickie came and said you'd given him a message to give me—to stop writing you and to forget about you. I cried, and Dickie was very sweet to try and comfort me. He came by the next day and the next to see how I was doing, and after a while, he asked me out.

Since I couldn't have you, I figured your brother would have to do. And I found out he is really a good man, maybe better than you, because he wasn't afraid to tell me he loved me.

Anyway, you told me not to wait, so I didn't. The next time you see me, I will be Mrs. Richard Landry. So you see, I did what you said. All except one thing. You told me to forget about you, and I could never do that. I'll never forget you, Grif. And I'm hoping that somehow, you'll never forget me, either.

Mitch's eyes stung, and a knot rose in his throat too big to swallow. Now he knew why Uncle Grif hadn't come around much all those years. Why his mother clung so fiercely to his father, as if afraid he might abandon her as well.

And maybe he knew why Grif had left everything to him. Because his uncle knew they were alike, and he hoped he could keep Mitch from making the same mistakes he had.

He put the letters back in the box, and carefully replaced the lid, his heart pounding. He only hoped it wasn't too late for him to do what he should have done all along. To hell with responsibility and waiting until the time was right. He loved Jill and he had to tell her.

I love you and you love me and we ought not think that kind of love comes along every day. I'm sure it doesn't, his mother had written. "I think you were right, Mom," he said as he headed for the door. He only hoped Jill would listen.

WHEN JILL COULDN'T FAKE being cheerful anymore, she went home and threw herself a private pity party. She put on her flannel pajamas and went through half a box of tissues and a whole pint of mocha fudge ripple. It didn't exactly make her feel better, but she couldn't feel much worse. She didn't have much practice falling in and out of love, but from what she could tell, it was a pretty miserable business.

She was thinking of opening up another pint of ice cream when someone knocked on the door. She shuffled to the peephole and stood on tiptoe to look out, but the hallway was empty. Curious, she unlocked the door, and opened it, keeping the chain in place.

Mitch stepped out of the shadows. "Stand and deliver, *mademoiselle.*"

She covered her mouth with her hand, too startled to speak. He was wearing the pirate's costume from Just 4 Play. The one she'd ordered and built her favorite fantasy around. The tall leather jackboots clung to his thighs, which were sheathed in close-fitting tights. He wore a full poet's shirt, open to the waist and belted with a wide leather belt. A scabbard hung at his side, and he brandished a silver sword. "Unlock the door, maiden, and allow me to enter," he declaimed.

"Oh, Mitch." She sighed, and fumbled with the chain.

The door across the hall flew open and Professor Simon, dressed in a paisley smoking jacket, looked out. "What do you think you're doing, young man?" he demanded.

Mitch flushed. "I'm uh…I'm—"

"We're practicing for a play, Professor." Jill tugged on Mitch's sleeve, urging him inside.

The professor peered closer. "Oh, it's you again." He looked Mitch up and down. "You look a great deal different today. Not nearly as stuffy."

"It's a costume, Professor," Jill said. "We're uh, we're doing a revival of the *Pirates of Penzance.*"

"Gilbert and Sullivan, eh? One of my favorites! *Oh, I am the model of a modern major general…*"

The professor was still singing when Jill dragged Mitch inside and shut the door. "What are you doing in that costume?" she asked.

He struck a pose, sword raised. "I've come to ravage you, my dear."

"But…why?"

He raised one eyebrow. "I need a reason?"

She sat on the sofa and pulled him down beside her. "At any other time, I might have said no, but now, I think you *do* need a reason, Mitch. Are we still playing games here?"

He sheathed the sword and sank down beside her. "No, this is no game." He took her hand. "I know you think I'm too serious sometimes, but the truth is, I am seriously in love with you. And I know I'm taking a risk here…but I hope you're in love with me, too."

There she went, puddling up again. She wasn't even sure she could get the words out, but she knew she had to. "I am, Mitch. I never thought it would happen to me, but I think I've fallen in love with you." She threw her arms around him and hugged him tightly, never wanting to let him go again.

Finally he drew back and looked down on her. "What is this—tears?" He brushed his thumb along her cheek.

"Only because I'm so happy."

He shook his head. "If you're crying, it's going to make it tough for me to ravage you."

"Then let me see if I can make it a little easier." She threw her arms around him again and kissed him for all she was worth, all the passion and love she felt focused on their lips.

After a moment, he pushed away again and grinned at her. "I think on the first day, we're only supposed to talk. On the second day, I can touch you. Or is that the third day?"

Her eyes widened. "How did you know…?"

"I found the tape from Cassie's bachelorette party— the one with the true confessions."

"That's why the whole thing the other night—with the fruit and everything—was so familiar! That was Geneva's fantasy."

He nodded. "But you said you'd like it for your fantasy, too."

"But this…" She fingered the sleeve of the pirate's costume. "This is really my fantasy."

He swept her into his arms and marched toward the bedroom. "Is it all right with you if we dispense with the first few days and go straight to day five?"

"Absolutely." She lay back in his arms. "Ravage me, *monsieur.*"

"I intend to ravage you now, and for years to come. In fact, my goal from now on is to fulfill all your fantasies." He deposited her on the bed and began unbuckling the sword belt.

She grinned up at him. "Now that sounds like a deal I can live with." Happiness bubbled up in her like champagne. "I never knew a relationship could be so much fun."

"Then you must have been in the wrong relationships." The sword landed on the floor, followed shortly by the shirt.

"I think I've found the right one now." She sat up and began removing her own clothes. "And I don't intend to let you get away. Even if it takes fur-lined handcuffs and a whip to keep you with me."

He tossed one of his boots aside and waggled his eyebrows. "Is that a promise?"

"Oh, it's a promise, my mad pirate. Now come here. I want to show you something...."

Epilogue

"SHOULD THE SEXUAL TRIVIA books be displayed with the games or with the other books?" Jill asked as she and Sid unpacked the latest shipment of merchandise one Wednesday afternoon.

"With the books, I guess. The games section is pretty full." Sid was looking like his old self these days, his Mohawk completely grown in and dyed lemon-yellow, his various rings, studs and barbells back in their appropriate places. The only real difference in his appearance was the new tattoo on his left bicep—a heart inscribed with the word "Lana."

Jill set aside the carton of books to be shelved later and opened a box of bath toys. She took out a vibrating bath sponge and grinned. Mitch would probably like this. She'd have to suggest they try it out soon.

In the three months they'd been together, Mitch and Jill had experimented with just about every other product Just 4 Play offered. For someone who'd started out uptight, Mitch was proving to be an amazingly fun and inventive lover. Oh, he still had his conservative, conventional side, but she'd come to believe that wasn't all bad. There was something to be said for a man you could count on. Jill knew Mitch was the kind of man she could depend on for the long haul. Maybe even forever. A thought that would have frightened her a mere few months ago.

She opened another box and smiled as she unfolded layers of purple and blue translucent scarves. "Seduce him with the dance of the seven veils," she read from the cardboard tag attached to the hem. Beneath the veils she found a sequin-studded bikini. "*Oooh,* this is nice," she said, lifting the ensemble out of the box.

"It's gorgeous." Tami, who had recently gone from part-time to full-time hours, came over to admire the outfit. "You should try it on."

"I think I will." Jill headed for the dressing room. On the way, she passed Lana, who had stopped by to bring Sid lunch. "Love the new outfit," she said, admiring the leather pants and jacket ensemble.

Lana smoothed her hand down the supple leather jacket. "It's my conservative, yet sexy look." She laughed. "A big change from the suits I used to wear, but I like it."

"I like it a lot." Sid came up behind her and enveloped her in a hug. "Thanks for the lunch, sweetie."

"You're welcome, tiger."

Jill hurried into the dressing room, stifling her laughter. Did she and Mitch get that silly over one another? Maybe so. She had to admit, the man really got to her.

She slipped out of her jeans and sweater and into the sequined bikini and multiple veils. The peekaboo effect of the filmy veils over the glittering sequins was sexy and fun. In other words, perfect for her. She couldn't wait to see what Mitch thought.

As if on cue, the man himself walked into the store as she exited the dressing room. From halfway across the room, he found her, zeroing in like a laser on target. As his gaze swept over her, a smile tugged at the corners of his mouth. He nodded, silently telegraphing his approval.

"Mitch, we need to order more of the Motion Lotion and the Love Beads," Tami said. "We're almost out."

"Everything's selling like crazy since you put the ad in the college paper," Sid said. "We may need to think about hiring another full-time person."

"Sounds good to me, Sid. You know I trust your judgment."

Jill made her way to him, walking with an exaggerated sway of her hips, enjoying watching desire build in his eyes. When she reached him, she stood on tiptoe and kissed his cheek. "How are things at your real estate office?"

"Boring as usual, compared to this place."

"You should move everything into the office here."

"I would, but I'm afraid I'd be too distracted." He smoothed his hand along her bottom. "Is this new?"

"Just came in today."

He nodded. "I like it."

"I thought you might." She followed him into his office, where he took off his suit jacket and hung it on the back of his chair.

"I had an interesting conversation with Chef Ping this morning," he said.

"Oh." She sat on the corner of his desk, the veils falling back to reveal her bare thigh.

Mitch glanced at her, then away, and tugged at the collar of his shirt. "Yes. He's opening his own restaurant on Pearl Street and wanted to know if I'd be interested in backing him."

"And are you interested?"

"Yeah. I think I am. It's a good opportunity for him, and it would be a good investment for me. It never hurts to plan for the future."

She smiled. That was Mitch. Always thinking ahead.

Something she never did if she could help it. Except lately, she'd been thinking more about her future with him....

He moved past her, to the front of the desk, and began sorting through his mail. "I saw Lana out front."

"She stopped by to bring Sid his lunch."

"They seem to be doing really well together. Do you think they'll get married?"

"I don't know. Sid wants it, but Lana says that's too conventional. She's enjoying being a bad girl, living with him." She shrugged. "Some people aren't interested in marriage."

"Uh-huh." He set aside the mail and drummed his fingers on the desktop, staring down at it as if trying to come to a decision. Why was he acting so strangely?

She put her hand on his shoulder. "Mitch, are you okay? You look a little pale."

He shook his head, then reached into his pocket. "I've been thinking a lot about us."

She smiled. "Good things, I hope."

"Yeah. Good things." He glanced at her. "I mean, things are going well, aren't they?"

She nodded. "Yes, things are going very well." Better than she'd ever dreamed.

"And the business is doing well." He looked around the office, which he had yet to redecorate, beyond replacing the daybed with a luxurious leather sofa. A very comfortable sofa, as she could attest. "Meg starts med school next year and I was thinking it might be time..."

His voice trailed off and he pulled a small velvet box from his pocket. Jill's heart rose somewhere in the vicinity of her throat and she scarcely heard his next words. "I know one time you said you weren't interested in being tied down to any one person, but I'm hoping maybe the last few months have changed your mind.''

Heart pounding, she took the box and opened it. A perfect diamond solitaire glinted back at her, like a miniature sun, full of light. ''It's beautiful,'' she breathed.

Mitch shifted from one foot to the other, shoved his hands into his pockets, then pulled them back out. ''If you don't like it, we could change it for something else. Or...''

''No.'' She put her hand over his mouth to silence him. ''I like it.'' She fit the ring on the third finger of her left hand and admired the glow. A girl could get used to this.

She looked up and found him watching her, a frightened, questioning, hopeful look in his eyes. She smiled and wrapped her arms around him. ''I love you, Mitch.''

All the tension went out of him and he sagged against her, holding her tightly. ''Are you saying you'll marry me?''

She drew back far enough to look him in the eyes. ''I don't recall hearing a proposal.''

''Will you marry me?''

She tilted her head to one side, considering. ''I'm not sure I heard you right. After all, this moment only comes once in a girl's life. She likes to know it was done right.''

Mitch frowned at her a moment, then understanding dawned. He stepped back and lowered himself to one knee. ''Jill. Darling.'' He took her hand. ''Will you do me the honor of being my wife?''

She grinned at him. ''I can't believe I'm saying this, but yes. I will marry you, Mitch. Darling.''

He stood and lifted her off the desk, whirling her around before crushing her to him and stealing her breath with a kiss. A long, deep, toe-curling kiss that promised many more of the same in the years ahead. When he finally released her, she was dizzy and giddy with happiness. Who would have thought being in love...real love...would feel so good? "I'll marry you. As long as it doesn't have to be conventional," she said. "I can't really see myself with white lace and roses."

"What did you have in mind? The Elvis Chapel in Las Vegas?"

She trailed one finger down his chest. "I was thinking maybe...the Amazon."

He laughed. "I'll go anywhere. As long as it's with you." He pulled her close once more and began kissing her neck, while his hands explored the naked flesh beneath the veils. "I like this costume. Will you wear it tonight?"

"Only if you'll wear your pirate costume."

He nipped at the edge of her bra top. "Your wish is my command."

She laughed. "And that's just the way I like it."

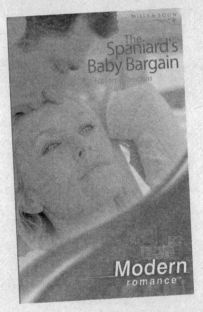

SILHOUETTE®

Desire 2 in 1

Passionate, dramatic love stories

BEAUTY AND
THE BABY
Marie Ferrarella

SOCIAL GRACES
Dixie Browning

MILLS & BOON

**Volume 5
on sale from
5th November
2004**

Lynne
Graham

International Playboys

*Mistress and
Mother*

MILLS & BOON

**Volume 6
on sale from
3rd December
2004**

Lynne
Graham

International Playboys

*The Winter
Bride*

M390

Susan Andersen

hot

"Bright, smart, sexy,
thoroughly entertaining."
—Jayne Ann Krentz

& bothered

Published 15th October 2004

New York Times bestselling author

Carly Phillips

Simply Sinful

*Sometimes temptation
is impossible
to resist...*

Published 19th November 2004